Praise for Sycorax's Daughters

"*Sycorax's Daughters introduces us to* ...*new legion of gothic writers. Their stories drip with history and blood leaving us with searing images and a chill emanating from shadows gathered in the corner. This anthology is historic in its recognition of women of color writers in a genre that usually doesn't know what to do with us.*"

Jewelle Gomez, author, *The Gilda Stories*

"*The daughters of Africa always have been beset by horrors on these shores. This groundbreaking anthology of stories and poems courageously explores and deconstructs horror tropes of monsters, spirits, curses and death through the experiences of African-American women shaped our shared history. My love for horror began with my mother, the late civil rights activist Patricia Stephens Due, who taught me that art could be a healing way to confront and give coherence to our more dangerous passages in life. That is the essence of this volume. Contributors to Sycorax's Daughters range from established authors like Sherée Rene Thomas to newcomers, all of them writing with passion and power to delight, inform and intrigue you—oh yes, and to haunt you, body and soul.*"

Tananarive Due, American Book Award winner, British Fantasy Award winner, author of *Ghost Summer* and *My Soul to Keep*.

"*Sycorax is the mother of Caliban in Shakespeare's The Tempest, but she's never seen in the play. Despite this erasure, Sycorax's presence permeates the story: the powerful witch who was banished while pregnant; through whom Caliban claims the island belongs to him; whose memory is used by Prospero to keep Ariel in line. These male characters speak for her in The Tempest, but in this anthology, Sycorax is given a voice.*

But this anthology is more than interpretations of the legacy of a silenced African woman - it's deeply informed by a history of real life horrors. From the forward by Walidah Imarisha:

"for Black people and other people of color, the history of slavery, genocide, white supremacy, and colonialism is the only true horror story, and it is one we continue to live every day..."

As always, some stories work better than others for me, and every reader will have their own favourites. But every story is an insight, and it's given me a new list of writers to look out for."

Narrelle M. Harris, author, *Showtime*

Sycorax's Daughters

Sycorax's Daughters

Copyright © 2017

Edited by: Kinitra Brooks, PhD

Linda D. Addison

Susana Morris, PhD

Cover art copyright © 2017 by Jim Callahan (@jimcallahanart)

Author Copyrights and Permissions listed at rear of the book

Additional Cover Design by Rebecca Sims

Additional editing assistance by: Wei Ming Dariotis, PhD.

Published and printed in the United States of America.

First Edition

Library of Congress Catalog Card Number 2016947578

ISBN 13: 978-1-941958-44-5/eBook: ISBN 978-1-941958-45-2/Kindle: ISBN: 978-1-941958-51-3

Printed in the United States of America.

For more information, contact queries@cedargrovebooks.com

www.cedargrovebooks.com

Sycorax's Daughters

Edited by
Kinitra D. Brooks,
Linda D. Addison,
and
Susana M. Morris

Cedar Grove Publishing
San Francisco, California

Dedications

Kinitra D. Brooks:

To Isabella and Gregory, may this be the first of many times you will see your names celebrated in print!

And to my lovely co-editors, Linda D. Addison and Susana M. Morris, for going along with all of my hare-brained ideas. You ladies continue to see me through and I thank you.

Linda D. Addison:

To Kinitra D. Brooks for conceiving/co-editing this book & co-editor Susana M. Morris for adding precious time to the shaping & all sisters who live/ survive/create/nurture Light in the shadows of a hungry universe.

Susana M. Morris:

To my wonderful co-editors, Kinitra and Linda, who make work a pleasure.

To the brilliant authors featured in the collection who make me want to sleep with the lights on.

Acknowledgements

Boundless gratitude to:

John Jennings for bringing publisher Rochon Perry (Cedar Grove Publishing) to us.

Rochon Perry of Cedar Grove Publishing for her belief and enthusiasm for our project.

Walidah Imarisha for taking time from her schedule to write an extraordinary Forward.

To all the authors that contributed to the volume. Thank you for sharing your extraordinary work with the world.

To all the little black girls who love zombies and monsters and were disappointed when Kendra, the black slayer, died after only two episodes.

To my Husband, who remains my anchor. To my Mother, for encouraging my love of reading and my Father, for encouraging my love of horror. And to my Sisters who always help me keep it together to face another day.

—Kinitra

Contents

Foreword
by Walidah Imarisha

I first met *Sycorax's Daughters* co-editor Kinitra Brooks at a conference called AstroBlackness II in March, 2015 that impacted deeply how I think about horror, oppression and Blackness. Organized by the Black sci fi visionaries John Jennings and Adilifu Nama, it was the second conference of its kind, and the theme was "The surreal, the speculative, and the spooky."

The conference was just a few months after the non indictment verdict against Darren Wilson, the white police officer who murdered 18-year-old Michael Brown, a young unarmed Black man. Between Brown's murder and the time of the conference, countless more Black people had been gunned down by police across this nation, and we see that catastrophe has not slowed. Neither has the outrage, organizing, and resistance led by Black youth under the banner #BlackLivesMatter.

As part of his testimony to the grand jury who found he should not be indicted for Michael Brown's murder, Wilson said, "…[Brown] looked up at me and had the most intense aggressive face. The only way I can describe it, *it looks like a demon,* that's how angry he looked" (emphasis added). Much of our conversations at Astroblackness II centered around three main ways horror relates to Blackness in America: the ways Black people are portrayed as the ultimate evil to justify historically and currently our exploitation, containment, and murders; the fact that for Black people and other people of color, the history of slavery, genocide, white supremacy, and colonialism is the only true horror story, and it is one we continue to live every day; and the fact that resistance of the oppressed to these structures has always been seen as the most frightful abomination that could be birthed.

Through these lenses, we see that horror as a genre often explores how we deal with those pasts that are not past, those corpses that refuse to lay quietly in their unmarked graves, those creatures born of pain, abandoned, who refused to die. In horror, we see the present through the eyes of the past. *Sycorax's Daughters* allows us to explore our own connection to history, as individuals and as a society. Horror, as these stories intone, is collective trauma compressed into one tangible form that can reach out and touch you. Ghosts are the past that is not past.

I appreciated greatly Kinitra's work at the Astroblackness conference, as it focused on the pressing intersections of both race and gender, highlighting the ways Black women are present or absent (or both) in most mainstream horror narratives, and what messages that sends about society, about Black communities, about Black women themselves. I am so thankful she and the other co- editors Linda Addison and Susan Morris have continued this work not just as analysis, but as a visionary space where Black women explore horror on their own terms.

Sycorax's Daughters fundamentally shifts the ways horror stories are told even when using familiar tropes like sirens, zombies, ghosts. Through nuanced story-telling that eschews cheap fright, the reader explores the textured reality of terror, the human in the horror. This collection allows us to challenge the notion this nation holds that Blackness, and therefore Black people, are the ultimate horror. By engaging Black women as both the authors of these stories as well as the majority of main protagonists, we finally hear the so-called "demons" speak.

These writers seamlessly weave together threads of race and gender into a beautiful tapestry upon which lay these haunting stories, challenging how one of the mainstays of our society is the cautionary tale of the monstrously feminine and the ways women with agency become the worst evil. In these stories Black people's, especially Black women's, liberation torment white society in a cold sweat. We see that America's nightmares are not just raced; they are gendered.

In many of these stories, the Black women in them would be categorized as the monstrous, but the narratives exist through their eyes. These tales breath humanity back into the masks of horror society have stitched onto our faces. Even living in lands of evil, mutilated by leviathans, most of these characters never become monsters themselves - even when they take life - and perhaps even more importantly, they never become victims. And through this centering of Black women, our understanding of what the real horror is transforms as well.

The backdrops of these fiendish tales are landscapes of gentrification, white supremacists, brutal cops, and the ultimate horror story, slavery.

Next to these, devils and vampires are almost banal.

These tales are also rooted in resistance, in cultural, social, and political histories and conditions, like the early 1980s South Bronx as hip hop is birthed. They happen next to books by Black anti- colonial leader Amilcar Cabral, to a soundtrack of unruly jazz, in the midst of protests against police brutality.

This collection blends poetry with these horror short stories in a way that challenges our understanding of the monstrous, because every one of the poems is about the reality of Black women's lives. here is nothing magical, fantastical, or otherworldly about these poems, which are Frankensteined together from the daily wickedness Black women endure. From a blues poem about police violence to one about sexual violence, placed next to these supernatural tales, we see the real everyday terror as the most horrific of them all.

Sycorax's Daughters also shows the different relationship Black people have to the supernatural created of sorrow. While the larger white society lives in terror of liberated Blackness, of the "demons" unleashed coming after them, we know many of our spirits haunt us out of love, out of a desire for all that was unfairly stolen from them. And we need them, because sometimes all we have is our ghosts. As hip hop emcee Khingz said, "I'm happiest when I'm haunted/It means I'm not forgotten."

Even when the stories hurt, we know it is not intentional. We know this because Toni Morrison wrote in her haunting story *Beloved,* "Anything dead coming back to life hurts." Blackness is massacred in the streets every day, and every night we perform the alchemic necromancy to bring it back from the dead. And we pay the horrific price.

Reading this collection, I breathed in these stories and the monstrous resurrection they carried inside them. They have stayed with me, haunting me, some of them hurting me. And I do not want them to leave, because they bear witness to the ways we live with the past that is not past every moment of the day.

We Black people cannot outrun our demons. Nor should we ever want to. We will embrace them as our lost Beloveds, and listen to the songs they sing to bring us through the darkness.

—Walidah Imarisha
Co-editor of *Octavia's Brood: Science Fiction Stories From Social Justice Movements*

Introduction
by Kinitra D. Brooks

Sycorax's Daughters:
We've Always Been Here

We named this collection *Sycorax's Daughters* because we insist that Black women have always been horror creators. Each author featured is a descendant of Sycorax, the deceased African sorceress in Shakespeare's *The Tempest* (1611). Sycorax and her daughters reflect the culture critic bell hooks' concept of the absent presence of Black women in popular culture. As Shakespeare ironically, and perhaps unwittingly, develops her, Sycorax refuses to be excluded from the play's spectacle. Her absence in silenced erasure is subverted by Shakespeare's depiction of her presence as an idea that produces fear and suspicion in the play's (white male) major characters. Sycorax's daughters are directly influencing the trajectory of horror fiction by forcing the genre beyond its centralizationof whiteness and maleness—even as they are deprived of the mainstream access to self-articulation.

Black women have always been here, creating horror and subverting its problematic obsessions with Negrophobia and Gynophobia. Take, for instance, Zora Neale Hurston's folktale collection *Every Tongue Got to Confess*, which is derived from interviews with former slaves in the early 20th Century and highlights Black women's long-established interest in horror. The literature of the rich communal oral folk culture and tales passed down through generations demonstrate that horror discourse is an established tradition in Black communities. Yet despite growing evidence, including contemporary authors such as Jewelle Gomez, Tananarive Due, and LA Banks, Black women remain an absent presence in horror literature.

It is here where Sycorax's Daughters intervenes. For there is radical potential in shifting the center of horror. Sycorax's Daughters centers Black women horror characterizations and creators in response to the male-centered discourse that dominates contemporary Black horror fiction and parallels the defaulted whiteness of contemporary women's horror fiction. Sycorax Daughters spotlights the gaps being outright ignored in the horror genre by offering racially gendered horror fiction that exemplifies the work of Black women horror creators and their growing influence in the genre. In this way our project fills the lacunae by privileging Black women's visions of self in horror over their previous problematic characterizations as constructed by others. Sycorax has ensured that her daughters are provided the opportunity to speak for themselves.

I implore you to listen to their voices as you read the following works. And pay particular attention to the unique horror epistemologies in their texts that interweave the ancient dictates of the African ancestors with the futuristic exploration of folkloric values.

Tree of the Forest Seven Bells Turns the World Round Midnight
by Sheree Renée Thomas

Thistle stepped over an upturned root that twisted from the dark, wet earth.

"Your mama live near the river?" "Naw."

"Your mama live in a tree?" "Nope."

"Then what we doing?"

"Mama the river and the tree." She moved with deliberate grace, each footfall a code that unlocked another hidden key. Wilder should have known. Every other word out of her mouth was some strange, cryptic poetry. She was more siren than sage, more whistle than song. In the few months they'd been hanging, he had gotten used to her "magic woman" guise. Bohemian bruja, wide-hipped hoodoo. Unlike the other women Wilder tried to lay with, Thistle felt sincere. At least she was original. Most other relationships Wilder had had, all ended the way he felt now, lost. With the others he would soon lose interest — or they would, tossing him back on the street, the fascination over before it had begun. Then he'd be off, duffel bag in hand, looking for cover. To Wilder, everyone worked so hard to be just like the next. What was the challenge in that?

Thistle stood with her back to him, all curve and joy, a plum-skinned promise of delight. He tried to follow her, but his feet wouldn't move. With each step forward he kept stumbling backward, as if his body wanted, *needed* to withdraw every footstep, to retrace their path under that lone glimmering star. His car was locked and parked way down the road that flanked high above the river. If he hadn't been with Thistle, he never would have seen the trail.

"What I'm trying to understand is why we got to come see her in the pitch damn night?" He held himself steady, grabbed hold of a tender birch tree. All he saw was branches and limbs and more wobbly trees. Bark fell away from his hands in flakes, fluttered to the damp ground like layers of skin. "I'm cool with meeting your family, but why can't we go to Piccadilly or the China Inn? Don't your mama like buffet? That's what *normal* folks do."

Thistle turned her head, hesitated. Even in the deepening darkness, Wilder could see her eyes narrow into slits, her full lips poked out like she might offer a kiss. "When have you known me to be normal?"

Laughter shook the leaves of a mayhaw. Fireflies flitted a warning message in the faded light. Wilder didn't see. His eyes were in the future, back to the cool thin sheets in the rented room. The air was hot and humid, thick enough to slash a knife through. The sky was full, twilight now turning away from dusk. A super moon and that strange twinkling star Thistle swore was a planet. Which one did she say? *Venus.* Or was it Jupiter? Wilder used to know stuff like that, back when he thought it was important. Astronomy, astrology, tarot cards, and divination, none of it foretold anything close to what Wilder had come to know, his hard truth. Ghostly light shone through the waist-high grass, and the blossoming weeds cast shadows across Thistle's face, her arm outstretched to him like a luscious vine. This he believed in, this he could follow — the curved finger of flesh. An open palm, his favorite invitation.

"It's just a little further."

"I hope she got something to drink."

Thistle giggled, moved through the path, a silent wind. Wilder had made her a jacket with spikes on the shoulders and bright, colorful Ankara print for a lining. He hadn't sewn anything new until she'd tumbled into his life like a weed. In the black, weathered upcycled leather and the scraps from an old African caftan, she looked like the punk queen he imagined her to be. He had woven the jacket for her, his first gift, when she initially refused to go out with him. "I'm not fit for human consumption," is what she'd said. "Try harder," is what he heard. Wilder was persistent. He'd followed her, held signs at every protest, passed flyers out with other activists at the Riverwalk, harangued downtown hipsters who would bulldoze century trees for their new LEED condos.

Finally, at a Mid-South Peace & Justice Center ice cream social, she relented. The jacket she donned like a crown. And she had worn it every day, her second skin she called it, even in the 105° heat.

But Thistle never sweated. A fact that startled Wilder, made him lie awake some nights and wonder, that, and her spooky, stony sleep. Gulping it down every chance she could get, Thistle drank water like a catfish, slept like an old dead log.
But each time he saw her, a wildfire in his arms, remarkably awake, or asleep, corpse-like by his side, he grew more fascinated.

Wilder had met her at a friend's lecture at Rhodes on the music of John Coltrane, sacred geometry, and physics. Melvin discussed how Coltrane had composed "A Love Supreme" using African fractals and indigenous design, the same design found in ancient West African compounds, in passed-down rites of passage and patterns of braided hair, in the wooden sculptures of the Mende, in pine cones, and even in drops of water. Melvin was a philosopher, the baddest bassist in the world — *Time Out New York* had declared it, and Wilder knew from personal experience that to be true. Only one other bassist gave him a run, and she wasn't a bassist at all. She was a goddess; she was music itself, not even a fair comparison.

Wilder had been planning to give Melvin the full Memphis roots midnight tour when he spied Thistle, fluttering in the periphery of the concert hall. Her back was pressed against the yellow papered wall, arms folded, as if she was too good to squeeze her hips into the plush student seating. Her eyes were closed, head nodding, as if she was hearing some other music beneath Melvin's words.

Later Wilder would learn she was rarely still - except, frighteningly so, in her sleep. Awake, she flitted through the world, an emerald-throated hummingbird. Even now she stooped to caress a crooked row of foxgloves. Her bangles stacked high up her arm like brass armor, glinted in the night. "Look how they bow their heads." She stroked the purple blossoms as if they were pets. "They're always the first ones asleep." She rose and darted ahead, a bejeweled black dragonfly.

Barefoot, Thistle used to collect ferns and moss and polished river stones, dark mushrooms and wild weeds for the birdcages and terrariums she hung throughout the city. She said her found art was a public indictment, a statement from the elders. Wilder never asked who the elders were. He simply chalked it off as more of Thistle's spirit speak.

So when she grabbed fistfuls of earth and held them before her nose, as if to breathe a prayer, Wilder only shrugged. "You should take off your shoes," she said and kicked off her boots, the tongues lolling as if they were hot and tired, full of thirst.

"Here? I'm not doing that." Thistle tied her shoestrings together and flung the pair over her left shoulder. The strings got caught in the patch of spikes. She shrugged, the leather jacket arched across her back like a pair of wings. "The earth is cool and damp here," she said and held out her hand. "Come on, every step is like a kiss." Wilder shook his head, no. She threw her head back and danced, her toes sinking into the moist grass. "Best massage ever."

Wilder paused. "I can think of better."

A sudden burst of wind carried Thistle's laughter through the air, lifted it above his head, lingered in his ear. The breeze felt cool, inviting. He sighed and unlaced one shoe.

"Got me messed up," he muttered and kicked off the other.

He stuffed his socks in his back pocket, strung his shoes over his shoulder, and dug his toes in. The grass smelled sweet and wet, felt like heaven on his soles and heels. Within the circle of trees, he went beyond thought, beyond feeling. As his feet sank into the earth, he felt himself yielding to a soft green breath, a sensation he hadn't felt since childhood. He stood there, eyes closed, remembered what it felt like to run barefoot without worry, without fear. A deep presence filled the space around him, within him. Wilder glanced up, saw in moonlight the silvery threads of a webbed work of art, dangling from an elm. And like his lover, the spider was nowhere to be seen.

"Thistle?"

Only the familiar whoosh of the river replied. All he heard was the waves of the water, sloshing somewhere ahead, down below, and the sound of his own voice whispering in the waist-high grass and weeds. Slowly his eyes adjusted to the dark and the silver. The light was strange, as if waking inside a dream. Wilder followed the crush of green, where Thistle's hips had slashed through the ferny veil. Her footprints led him inward, deeper into the night where he didn't want to go. He walked in slow, plodding steps at first, searching for Thistle's trail, but each time he moved, he felt the air move behind him, only to turn and find no one there. Uneasy, Wilder moved faster, twisting through the rambling path, fighting the woods. He ducked beneath branches, cursing as he worked to untangle them from his hair. Instead of thinning out, the trees grew thicker all around. Wilder didn't like it here, the way the ground sucked at his feet, gentle at first, but more insistent with each step, as if the land was hungry.

He stopped. *That* was how she looked — hungry.

Those nights when he would wake, the room suddenly filled with the weight of a presence that made him turn over only to find Thistle lying flat on her back, hands at her side, still and cold, eyes flung wide open, mouth parted...

"How does it feel?" he had asked once, when the sun had risen and she moved, thankfully, once again part of the living.

"Like I woke up dead." Wilder remembered frowning until she kissed him. "It's like my mind is awake but this body is not..." Thistle often spoke of herself as if she was not part of herself, as if every day was an out of body experience and Wilder was her witness.

"Like you're trapped?" he'd asked.

"No, like I'm finally free." Her arms were wrapped around his throat, his head resting in her hands. She was curled beneath him, their legs entwined, her breath like peppermint and lemongrass, sweet herbal spice.

"But your eyes are wide open and you look…you look…"
"What?" She stared as if to dare him.

Wilder had searched for another word to describe what he could not say. *Dangerous* is how she looked, *feral,* but what he whispered then was "terrified."

Thistle raised one brow, rubbed her knee. "Sleep paralysis, common enough. I've had it all my life. It's like the body is paralyzed and your mind is still awake. REM atonia, when your brain awakens and your eyes start to open. You become alert, conscious." Sitting cross-legged on the rumpled sheets, she gulped noisily from a glass of water, then pressed a cool fingertip at Wilder's temple. "But then you realize you can't move, you can't speak, and you feel a weight pressing down on you, on your chest, and you feel like you can't breathe, you can't…"

"That's fucked up."

Her tongue darted out, licked the tip of his nose. "It's merely a question of transitions. The brain and the body, the spirit and the mind, move all the time, between state to state. Sometimes you are just caught in between."

"If I had to sleep like you, I think I'd just skip sleep." "I don't sleep. I wait."

But she didn't wait. She'd left him, creeped out alone in the damned woods. And she didn't sleep. She didn't sweat. And when she did sleep, she looked wide awake. Dead. Thirsty. Hungry.

The last few weeks she had given up her normal diet of vegetables, fresh fruit, and nuts. "What happened to the kale?" She had only shrugged. Wilder was relieved. It was as if his whole body was starving and all he needed was to nibble on one bit of bacon for release. He hated pretending, acting as if he was into all that vegan stuff. He had done worse for less. Hunger was something he'd gotten used to, a dull ache until he did some odd jobs or found a steady gig, or another cool-sheeted bed to lie in. With Thistle's new appetite, Wilder ate heartily, satisfied. He collected every meat recipe he could remember, and watched as Thistle sat eating strip after strip of barely cooked meat, mostly seafood, from the river that she caught herself, and piles of fresh water mussels with garlic and butter and white wine sauce.

Thistle was in a good mood these days, almost giddy, and she slept, if you could call it that, less and less. Wilder had started to think that this was one time it would be alright, until she had insisted it was time for her mother to meet him.

Wilder stooped to scrape a pebble from between his toes and rose, wiping a streak of mud against his thigh. When he brushed his hair out of his eyes, he saw a circle of stones. Wilder frowned. It was as if the trees had hidden them. One minute there was a wall of green, the next, a circle of stone. They rested upon each other like giant children holding hands in a ring. The wind picked up here, the air cooler. It carried the rustle of leaves and the rush of waters, the sound of the reeds clattering in the breeze, as if each were an open throat, rising to speak. Wilder wrinkled his nose. The wind carried a strange scent, something that made him wipe his face with his sleeve. Wilder had lost Thistle's trail. Instead he felt as if he'd stumbled upon an ancient conversation, the rocks and the grass, the river and the moss arguing about shadow and light. Wilder didn't like the sound, the sounds. They buzzed in his ears like static, a cloud of gnats. The hair on his arms felt prickly. He wanted to put his shoes back on, drive as fast as he could all the way home, but he realized he had dropped them somewhere back in the thickening bush. *Out here wrassling weeds.* And where had she brought him?

Wilder felt as if someone had told him to drive to the end of the world, to drive and drive and when he got there, keep driving on.

Ferns and foliage had sprung up where he didn't recall seeing them before. The great stones seemed to rise higher, pressed all around him like a great crushing wall. The air felt old, godless. Why did Thistle leave him, alone in the dark in the middle of night, and who would choose to live in such a place?

He felt the slow shifting of eyes he could not see, then a sound like a bell, Thistle laughing, her voice high and clear. She was waiting for him, beside a tree just beyond the tallest rock, the one shaped like a raised elbow and a fist. A large web, the shape of a shield, sparkled in the moonlight, inches from his face. Wilder recoiled, waved his hand.

"It's bad luck to kill a spider," Thistle said, and she ducked beneath the web and pulled him close. Her voice was a murmured apology in his ear, as her nails scraped his jaw, razed the skin. Her ringed fingers ripped away at his collar, exposed his throat. Thistle tore off his shirt, kicked it into the ground that was covered in a thin layer of rising mist. She rolled up his tank, scraped at his back and neck, her tongue deep in his throat, stumbling through the tangled branches and moss-covered stones until he fell limp, into a bed of leaves, shoulders stooped, arms hanging at his sides. Tiny hot scratches scraped along the softness of his belly, down the length of his arms; a cut stung on his chin. Thistle nipped, nibbled at his nose.

As odd as she was, Wilder loved being with Thistle. He felt himself expand in her presence. Her strangeness and stories awakened in him a vague awareness of his own. It wasn't that he didn't care about the land or "her sisters," the damn weeds and the river, or whatever Thistle was always so amped up about. It's just that he saw the state of the world as out of his hands — something decided by others more predatory, more resourced than he. For Wilder, fighting was a losing proposition. Someday the meek would inherit the earth, but not in real time, so why spend what little time you've got, stressed? Wilder didn't want to make a difference; he wanted fucking change. When that didn't happen when he thought it should, he gave up.

A long time ago Wilder had had skin in the game. He'd put his neck out there, like Thistle, believing, marching, singing, guitar playing, airbrushing, phone banking, door knocking, and leafleting, only to have it crushed by the world, again and again. There had been some successes, but the failures were more than he could bear.

The night Thistle finally came to him, he had marched with her and the others against the Stiles Water Treatment plant. Stiles was vile. It dumped partially treated sewage wastewater into the river, claiming rapid dilution by the Mississippi's vast flow and hiding under the cover that the river was used mostly for industry and commercial traffic. Thistle and the other activists knew that state law required all Tennessee waters to be fishable and swimmable. The only folks who fished and swam in the river bottoms were too dumb to know better or desperate or both. Or Thistle. Thistle painted a beautiful, huge canvas mural that had to be carried by twenty hands, calling for disinfection and respect for her "mother," the river. Wilder joined the protest only because he wanted to be near her. He wanted to show that he was willing to go wherever she was, that he was down with the cause, her cause, even if it didn't make much sense.

When he dropped out of school, Wilder had spent years on the streets lonely and hungry, and denying both while searching for truth in flesh. He couldn't find his tribe, but wherever he wandered, music was his solace. Wilder never stayed in one place long, never loved one heart long. He had learned to survive, to protect the soft parts of himself. But the world had eaten his spirit up and spat him out, left him pulp and gristle at Thistle's feet.

"It's not enough that I'm barefoot and getting eaten up by bugs, but now we've got to play hide and seek in the dark?" Thistle bowed her head, smiled. Wilder held her close, lifted her chin.

Damp pine needles pricked his back. "You know we could have done that back at the house."

"Mama's not back at your house." "Where the hell is Mama?"

Thistle pulled away and rose, turning her back to him. He stood up, wiping matted leaves off his legs. "What's wrong?" She didn't answer but offered her hand, her palm cool and damp. Wordless, she led him through an opening in the stone door he had not seen, her hand still clasped in his. As they walked, waves of coolness trickled between his toes, tickled Wilder's soles. He looked down, stared at the flat surface of the water. It stared back up at him, a dark mirror. A dense, blue fog clung to the trunks of the trees.

Behind him, the old stones groaned. Up above, the stars revealed themselves one by one in the veil of night.

"This way. She's here."

Together, they waded through the river mud and muck. Thistle held his hand in a tight, possessive grip, squeezing his fingers with her silver rings, as if he might flee. She walked with her back to the darkness, her eyes willing him forward toward a tunnel of trees ahead. Her feet moved expertly, as if she had walked the unseen path a hundred times before.

"Slow down, Thistle, you're going too fast. You're going to fall."

"Hasn't happened yet." The hair bristled on the nape of his neck. How many times had she walked this path before?

Thistle's steps through the stream had become quick and light, silkfire dancing through the night. She moved as if possessed, as if each step were a key she played in a song for the earth. Wilder's footsteps were heavy and unsure. His breath grew ragged. Sweat trickled down his chest and back, made his skin stick to his tank top, made him wipe his shoulder with his chin.

They passed a stand of young saplings. Thistle paused to stroke their stalks tenderly, whispered as if telling them secrets. The wind rustled in a red maple's leaves. She tilted her head, as if to listen. Wilder sighed, swatted a mosquito that looked big as his hand. "Please, can we go now? I don't want to be out here all night, Thistle. I'm getting eaten alive here."

She stopped. He could hear distant voices, perhaps from a barge floating by. A muffled grumbling sound rumbled through the air, like the echo of trucks speeding across the I-55 bridge. Wilder frowned. The old bridge was too far away for that. "Let's hurry, then. You're more than ready," Thistle said.

"Look, we could be home by now, eating. I know you're hungry.

You're always hungry these days. I mean, why are we here? Is this even necessary right —"

"I wanted to show you where I came from," Thistle interrupted. "Who I came from, why I am."

Wilder shuddered. His feet were cold. The drying sweat had chilled on his skin, but despite his discomfort, he accepted her answer. It was what he'd wanted to hear. For months she had been secretive, silent. If he hadn't seen her student ID, he never would have known that she had been working on her master's in bryology. Her thesis was on the role of moss in rejuvenating human scarred land, healing poisoned waters. "Ecological succession" is what she'd called it. "Every hour the Mississippi River Delta is disappearing; one football field of wetlands vanishes at a time. Your levees have strangled it, your channels and canals have allowed saltwater and waste to poison it. Whole ecosystems are drowning in muck."

"You think moss and algae and shit can save it?" he'd asked. She'd nodded. "I do." Wilder had snorted. Thistle had sat back, watched him in silence. Maybe that was when it had changed. Her sleeping patterns, her eating, everything, even the way she looked at him, held him when they made love, before she drifted off into her pen-eyed sleep.

Thistle claimed she already had a lifetime of degrees in environmental forestry and the science of trees, but moss was a new interest for her. The change in scale, she'd said, the smaller focus, enriched her life, changed her view.

"You have to expand your vision and make your spirit very small. I'm so used to being —"

"Being what?" he'd asked. She'd slipped the photo card back into her satchel. Her face was ashen, her lips a thin, grim line.

"Being rooted in everything."

Now she looked amused, almost giddy. She moved in an intoxicated sway, as if she was dancing to a furious music. "Remember when you asked me about the others, the ones before you?"

"Yeah, and you said to leave the past the past." She smiled. "Don't you want to know?"

"No, I don't." Wilder's eyes darted, like the fireflies that fluttered past them. He was starting to imagine movement in the dark. A rustle by that tree, a whispered hiss underneath a bush. He grew more unsettled the longer she stared at him, humming and swaying. "I know everything I need to know about you — don't need to know anymore — and besides, I've already met your mother. See," he said and stomped his feet in the rising water that grew colder, "the river. And here —" He leaned against a gnarled, narrow blackgum, so twisted it almost looked bent. "The tree. Pleased to meet you, Mama. Now can we go?"

Thistle shook her head. "If you core these trees, you'll find that some of them are over 150 years old. Or older, like that one there. So now you've met Loridant. He was one of my favorites."

Wilder frowned. "Favorite what?"

"They say he disappeared after he led an expedition here, when the Chickasaw tended this land, but I see you have found him."

Wilder jerked away from the alligator bark, sucked in air, steadied his voice. "Come on, where is she? I see you're not going to end this game until I meet her, so let's go."

He marched ahead of Thistle, snatching at branches that leaned in his face, swatting at the high grass, cursing the weeds that created a wall around him. *Why did he let her toss his good shirt?* His white tank top wasn't much defense against the scratches and the bug bites. It glowed in the dark, making him look like a ghost slipping through the trees. The air was more fragrant here, dark and sweet, cloying. He could hear Thistle giggling behind him. She was practically singing now.

"There better be some Fireball when I get there."

Wilder would have kept marching and cussing if he hadn't fallen into the marsh.

"What the — Thistle? Thistle!"

It was as if the land had given up and the river had taken over. Wilder found himself knee-high in a black bowl of muddy, sludge-like water, but it wasn't the water that worried him. The moonlight reflected an image so uncanny that it made the inside of Wilder's scalp itch.

Straight ahead, in the center of the circle was a huge cypress tree. Its great dark, tall plumes stabbed against the sky. Its trunk or trunks rose from the water in a huge entwined knot, covered in green fungus. It appeared to combine at least two other trees. Huge tangled roots rose in and out of the water, like knobby knees, a great serpent's nest. The limbs were massive and coiled in the air like mighty arms. The bark around its base was smooth, save for a series of fire scars, as if someone had tried to burn it, many times over. Standing in the shadow of this giant, Wilder felt as close to God or the Devil as he had ever felt.

Thistle stopped just short of the water. Her face calm, her eyes shining in the light.

"Mama."

The ground shook, rippled beneath them, and the triple tree seemed to bow in answer. *This shouldn't be here.* Wilder knew nothing like that grew in the area. Maybe a couple hours away in Mississippi, where the cypress trees in Humphreys County were some of the largest in the world, 97 feet around, 118 feet tall, the South's own sequoias, or maybe down in Texas and Louisiana, but not down in the delta in the mouth of the river in West Tennessee.

As if hearing his thoughts, the tree's great limbs bent forward, but Wilder did not feel any wind or breeze. Instead, the water around him began to warm and bubble. Water lilies with huge poppies bobbed and floated in the bubbling water. Wilder tried to back out, his voice lost in the rumbling of the strange tree, but something twisted around his ankles, held him in place. He screamed, fearing it was a snake, and reached into the water. Instead of scales, his fingers felt wet vines and scalelike leaves. He tried to rip the heavy vines off, his fingers digging into them. He yanked one and tossed it. It landed in the muddy pool with a splash, heavy as a walking stick. Wilder felt the air whirling behind him. He turned to see the triple tree's branches twisting like angry snakes.

Wilder turned to run, but his legs were caught again in a nest of vines. They dug into his flesh, stung and burned him like fire ants. "Thistle, help me. Why are you just standing there?"

She stared past him, at the great knotted tree, at the swirling waters; then her eyes rested on him.

"You could say," she said, "in my way, I *am* helping you. This is one of the oldest, most sacred spots. Right now, you are in the intersection of the river and the tree. You are in the delta of civilizations, a place most dear to me, the place where I was born. Where I am seen."

Wilder flailed his arms in the water, legs rooted. "Listen, baby, I see you and you are so beautiful to me — I just need you to help me right now. See if you can help pull me up. I'm tangled in these weird vines. Some kind of bad storm is coming, and I think that old tree is about to fall down."

Wilder didn't like how she was looking. She was facing him, but her water-eddy eyes seemed to peer through him, focusing on something else. Wilder felt more wind at his back. The air filled with the rustling of leaves and needles, the sound of a hundred cicadas, a humming buzzing sound that rattled his ears, jarred his teeth.

Thistle closed her eyes and nodded her head. She opened them, a peaceful smile on her face as she crouched before him. "I like to believe in balance, in the natural order of things. I take from life, and I like to think that I'm giving life as well." She reached above him. Wilder gripped her arm.

"Thistle, please," he hissed. He leaned forward and stroked her cheek, his muddy fingers caressing her hair. "I don't know what's happening, but I need you —"

"You don't see me," she said. "Even now. You never did." Thistle jerked out of his grip. A clump of black hair fell away in Wilder's hand. He stared, his breath shallow.

"Thistle, what's wrong?" he whispered. He held the hair for a moment, then let it drop into the water. It floated like a feather.

"Are you sick? Why didn't you tell me? Is that why you wanted me to meet your mother? How long have you known?"

His mind was racing, panic spreading. If she had cancer, he thought he could deal. *Maybe.* He wanted to hold her, but he

17

couldn't get out of the water. He was pulling with all his strength, and the vines that held him barely budged. *Why did he have to find out like this?*

"You're going to have to try, baby, to pull me, or go for help. I can't stay out here, not like this."

Thistle's eyes were on the hair that still floated on the skin of water. Her hands flew to her scalp.

"Damn," she said. She held her hands up. Her nails were gone. She slipped her silver rings off and tossed them into the water next to Wilder. They sank with tiny little bubbles. The nail on her index finger dangled by a thread of cuticle. No blood, just dry, flaking skin. The air hummed again, a whispering sound like many rushing waters. "I know, Mama," she whispered. "I know."

"Thistle, stop it." Sickness and anger rose to his throat. "Your nails are falling off. You're falling apart, and you're talking crazy!" He swallowed, covered his mouth with a muddy fist, lowered his voice. "What kind of cancer do you have?" She frowned at him, stared. Wilder shook his head, tried to make sense of Thistle's decay. *How could she hurt like that and not bleed?* "You wouldn't accept chemo, no matter what the doctors said, so that means you've been trying to fight it naturally this whole time?" He closed his eyes. "That's why you've been eating all that weird shit?" *But her hair, her hair fell out in his hand.*

He shook his head, confused. "Baby, I'm so sorry. Why didn't you tell me?"

Wilder jerked and strained in the mud, trying to walk. He clawed at the sediment and silt, his legs struggling underwater. For a moment he felt the vines loosen from his knees then creep up his legs again, holding him still. The vines pricked and stung him more, held him tighter. Everywhere they touched him, his skin felt itchy and scaly, as if sunburned. His legs began to feel heavy, leaden.

He tried to reach for Thistle, but her eyes looked different. They caught the silver light, giving her face an eerie amber glow.

Her skin was ashen, her cheeks hollow.

Thistle stared in the space above his head, as if she hadn't heard anything he'd said. Wilder looked up to see one of the knotted tree's long thick branches hovering above him. He froze. Thistle picked seven bell-like yellow blossoms from the limb and held them in her open palms. An invitation.

Wilder shook his head no, but Thistle kissed him, her mouth filled with tiny razor-like teeth. He tried to pull back, but he felt sleepy. Her tongue was sweet, like honey and mead, and she held him as she always did and whispered to him, the songs that only she could sing, with words that only she remembered the meaning to. His eyes grew bleary, and he heard more than he ever had — the croak of the plump, brown toad beneath an unfurled leaf, the jewel beetle scuttling across algae-covered bark, and the wind in the leaves, the many hundred leaves rustling above his head and a chorus of crickets.

Thistle smelled of maple syrup and buttermilk, of wet grass and rain-soaked walking sticks, of a wet stone covered by moss and babbling brook. Her eyes were too round, too full of silver and purple-golden light. Her skin was riven by deep whorls and lines, as if it had been carved with a knife.

When Thistle fed him the seven bells, Wilder's mouth was still full with the taste of sweet nectar, but then the blossoms stung the inside of his jaw, and the tip of his tongue went numb. He stared at her, struggled to keep his thoughts clear, to make his lips and teeth form words. Only shallow gasps escaped, a jaw harp deflated, out of tune. Recognition clouded his eyes. Wilder's heart was brittle, ready to break.

As the poison flowed through him, he felt the hum of a strange touch; fallen roots blossomed in electric earth. He was being lifted, carried backward through the waters.

"Don't struggle," Thistle called to him. "Mama just wants to meet you."

As the vines covered him, the limbs pulling him closer to the great tree's bosom, Wilder felt pieces of himself, like pieces of dusk, fall apart and be gathered in the bark and dirt. Thistle was naked. Now he could see her — a body no longer woman but willowy tree. Her bright round forehead shone in the moonlight. Her skin was tattooed with the whorls and swirling textures found on old-growth trees. Snails and mussels clung to her legs. Flowering vines and green moss wrapped around her thighs. Wilder thought he saw blue mountains, perhaps galaxies flowing in her ancient hair that now fell away in clumps like riverweed and algae at her feet.

If he could move he would have reached for her. He would have tasted her with his fingertips and tongue, but she was out of reach. He wanted to cringe, to creep away. He wanted to lean into his lover's palms. He couldn't do either, so Wilder no longer tried to move.

His eyes asked the question his lips could not.

"People are the cancer," she said as she flicked an emerald beetle from her shoulder and followed him into the muddy pit. "Not all of them, of course, but enough of the wrong ones to

wreck the balance. The movement needs people with heart," she
said. "Spirits committed to systemic solutions, long-game change,"
she said. "But that's not you, is it, Wilder? At least not yet."

Wilder felt his breath grow short. Where each began, a tickling
fire flowed through his blood. Seven thousand songs surged from
stones as Thistle walked over to him. In the ghostly light she still
looked almost human, beautiful. Wilder's ears hummed. Alarm,
desire, and fear echoed in his temples, a competing heartbeat.

She embraced him, smelled like the strange, yellow blossoms.

Thistle caressed his throat with a sandpaper tongue; the skin
peeled off in gentle flakes like wet dark bark. "I told you Mama
would love, love you…" Her voice was airy, a solemn fractal,
whispery as the wind. Wilder craned his neck to reach for her.

The fragrant pheromones released from the tree dulled his
pain, mixed it with his hunger. Even in the face of his dwindling
energy, the memory of life fading fast, desire welled inside him;
however, Thistle had completely transformed. She was no longer
recognizable, and he was no longer sure how he could love her, but
he did.

———

He remained still as a rock in a river of sound as Thistle and
her Mama pulled apart the disparate shreds of who he used to be.
In their presence, his thoughts felt noisy, cluttered. He tried to clear
his throat to speak, but he could not feel it or his mouth. A gurgle
and a rush of air escaped the hole where his throat and esophagus
used to be. If he were a pipe, she could have played him. Wilder the
bone harp, the baddest instrument in the world.

Thistle gently ran her fingers across his chest, then ripped his tank off. His eyes widened. "Don't worry, Wilder," she said, her lips and sawteeth stained blood red, his back sinking into the smooth base of the knotted tree. Mama licked him, and he sensed another part of himself slide away. A spine of bones exposed to the night's air, he thought he could hear pieces of the old flesh drop into the waters, remnants of his former selves sink into the muck, but he was no longer certain if he still had ears.

"The Tupelo, Black Gum tree has a strong heartwood," Thistle said. "It's one of the oldest native trees here, like the oaks, and the poplars, but, of course, not as old as Mama. And you've probably guessed, Mama is not from around here. She came with the river. But Wilder, you'll have plenty of time to contemplate the true meaning of change. Mama will keep you company. She'll sing you the old songs and tell you her stories. She'll keep you safe with the others until —"

Brambles curved around his chin. Thorns pierced his flesh while he tasted her final honeysuckled kiss. His thoughts disappeared in the rising mist. Wilder's mind rang with a new truth. He would die here. Perhaps he would be reborn. To spring from the earth, a fresh green shoot, dark roots twisting deep beneath the river's belly. A sapling tree, straining for the scent of rain, reaching for change. Wilder felt as if he had traveled through a dream, as if he woke beneath a river and there was no way back through the forest except to become clear water, a spring to fill and heal himself. His eyes wide awake, his body unable to move, his fear vanished into the dark center of things. As Wilder watched over Thistle's shoulder, her tiny teeth sinking into his cheek, he saw where she had dropped the first gift he had made for her, into the bubbling earth. Muddy watery fingers reached in languid waves to snatch the jacket up. The world afar,

the last spike floated
in dark womb-water, shimmered

a sinking star.

The Lonely, Salty Sea
by A. J. Locke

My lover and I,
we stand on a cliff
overlooking the sea,
watching the days ignite
and the birth of nights.
Then one day, said he to me;
you have set fire to my soul my dear,
did you know?
In your eyes there shine things
much brighter than stars,
and these are things I know,
because stars are too far off to be sure.
My love for you
is more vast than the sea,
because even the ocean has an end,
but not you and I my dear,
what we are is infinite.
And now I must tell you a secret,
said my lover to me;
sometimes I dream
of being buried with you at sea.

We sink to depths unfathomed,
with our arms around tight,
and our hearts beating their last,
and though it is but a dream,
will you dance this dance with me?
I smiled at him,
this captor of my heart,
and took his hand,
while the breeze of day
turned into the wind of night,
and said I,
dreams are best when realized.
Then with his hand in mine,
we danced, I and he,
towards the cliff's edge,
and the lonely, salty sea.

Scales
by Cherene Sherrard

Ilhas perdidas
no meio do mar,
  esquecidas
num canto do Mundo
em que as ondas embalam,
  maltratam,
abraçam...
— "Arquipélago," *Jorge Barbosa*

It felt good to vomit in the morning. The taste of everything acidic and rotten leaving her in one, sometimes two, voluptuous heaves. Afterwards, Vriel swished lukewarm water around her mouth. The faint metallic tang of the filter dislodged the bitter taste of bile. It left her euphoric until David asked:

"Maybe you're pregnant?"

There, just beneath his casual tone, she could hear the hopeful lilt he tried to suppress. Furious, she smiled wider.

"I suppose there's a .5% chance, right?" She kept it light, but he pressed her.

"You wouldn't do anything without talking to me first?"

"You're going to be late," she said, cracking one of the eggs.

She slowly plucked away the shell until she heard him shut the door, and tried to picture her anger pooling from her heels and evaporating upward towards the skylight.

When she returned to her room she noticed her fountain pen, carelessly left on the bed, had leaked a jagged blue squiggle across the crumpled beige duvet. Next to it, a silk swathed notebook — a birthday gift from David — lay open. She must have been writing when she fell asleep last night. Drawing the book into her lap, she reviewed her midnight meditations: *On gloomy days, drowning seems kinder than resisting the call. It begins with a tug on your big toe, a subtle pull that spreads to the entire foot, but is still bearable: mosquito's sting, a shoe pebble. Then, abruptly, it's gone. Only to reappear days or weeks later as a blockage in your ear: a whirring, ringing hum. You yawn, tilt your head, and turn the volume up on the television, but it just gets louder. Then all at once it's in your belly. Food loses its warmth leaving acidic tides cooled by sweet, icy drinks — the only thing you can stomach. The pain has the dull torment of a toothache, but just when you want to yank it, make it sharp and focused, it rises in the lower abdomen, clustering around the hips and the groin. To hear Cassia tell it, it's the feeling you have just before an orgasm, or a deep swell, but ultimately there is no climax. As you near fulfillment, anticipating its crash into rock and sand, it abates in soft foam.*

The indulgent lyricism of her own writing put her to sleep. Some hours later, she woke to the tinkle of wind chimes. She smelled Cassia before her eyes adjusted to the bright sunlight pushing itself into the gloom of her bedroom. Cassia's still damp hair reminded Vriel of wet coral, and the bergamot oil she used to dress it put in her mind of an unripe orange. The music came from her sister's silver bangles.

"Tiger's eye," Cassia said, her voice mimicking their mother's affectionate echo. She could almost feel the shade of her mother's hand tilt her chin slightly upward in wonder at the color of her irises, ordinary in every other family she knew.

Vriel pulled her chin away from her sister's probing fingers. "I won't die, Cassia."

Her sister's presence always had a surprising effect on her. Sometimes, she made her agitated and annoyed. Other times, her presence was soothing.

"You might wish you had," Cassia said. "*He* wants you to see a doctor."

Cassia was squatting in front of David's aquarium. It was a huge modern design constructed from an innovative material that eliminated glare, creating the impression that an invisible wall protected the fish from the outside air. She knelt behind the tank, and peered at Vriel through the glass, her magnified image out of place among the neon submarine and simulated kelp. Two multicolored angelfish and one lumbering Oscar swam towards her palm, sucking at her through the glass. She returned the Oscar's kiss, leaving a moist, pink stamp.

The tank had been empty when Vriel first moved in with David. They chose the fish together. Though his selections invariably died, hers thrived.

"How do you know so much about fish?" he said, as they flushed the latest casualty: an expensive Yellow Damselfish.

"My father was an Ichthyologist," she said. "I never know when to believe you."

"Don't worry," she said. "I never lie."

It became a kind of game for him to try to catch her in a contradiction. To break one of the casual oaths she frequently swore. They appeared to have no relationship to each other, either in their severity or trivialness, but each was uttered with an observed solemnity, as if her speaking and his hearing had a binding affect. She knew that he kept score in a notebook identical to the one he had gifted to her. V's do's and don'ts it read in blue ink followed by: I don't eat red meat, I'll never get a driver's license, I refuse to see a doctor, I never watch animated films and I don't swim. So far the tally was Vriel five, David zero.

Cassia used a tissue to wipe her kiss from the glass, but the imprint lingered. Through its waxy stain, Vriel recalled her sister beckoning and sucking at the fish in the murky, salty waters of the marina, not far from their mother's condo in Venice. Unperturbed by density or depth, clarity or tide, Cassia swam. As soon as she was wily enough to venture out on her toddling legs, she made for the ocean. Vriel was from the first afraid of sea water; the clutching rhythm of the waves, the lurking monsters hidden by the sand clouds and above all, the tingling arms of the seaweed blooming around the legs of the boardwalk.

Once, as she played jacks on the edge of the pier, a favorite piece fell between the planks. She leaned over to watch as the sparkling red X plunged ten feet into the deep. Instead of the jack, she saw something else that startled her. Treading water effortlessly in a vortex of fish, was Cassia, flanked by silver backed trout, mammoth sea bass, and tiny minnows flipping their shining narrow sides like coins in a wishing well; her hair indistinguishable from the enormous kelp growing all around her.

Vriel was both fascinated and envious. She wanted to tell her mother. She wished she was a fisherman with a huge net to catch her sister and all those cloying, cold-blooded courtesans. Cassia was like the pied piper, her every breath a song indiscernible to human ears.

She did tell on her sister, but her mother only smiled and lay a finger over Vriel's lips. That look in her mother's eyes was neither anger, nor fear, nor curiosity, but pride. And it was never directed at her.

Cassia launched herself upon the bed, jolting Vriel out of the past. She rubbed her head against Vriel's shoulder. A low vibration passed between them, a purring.

"You feel better already don't you?" Cassia said, "Well enough to eat something? You've lost too much weight."

Vriel hated to admit it, but she felt the first surge of hunger in days.

Cassia's eyes betrayed a tolerant pity. Beneath it, Vriel could perceive an elusive contentment that she craved. Cassia moved away and the cold crept back up her spine. Cassia snatched up and began to read the latest entry in her journal.

"Surprise, David: what should be beautiful and mysterious is not. You have questions I'm sure. After all, Disney has retold tales of sea maidens, tail-burdened princesses in love with worthy land-loving gentlemen. It's all bullshit. There *was* a kernel of truth in the old stories. The little mermaid's sacrifice was rewarded with betrayal and death, in Irish lore stealing a selkie's skin chains her to a domestic life, the rusalka weeps for her murdered loves. A litany to women with no will of their own, flung about by the — this is too rich — by the whims of salt water?"

Cassia tossed the book back on the bed where Vriel watched the pages flutter as it landed at her feet.

"I had no idea you were such a poet," Cassia said with obvious contempt. "Are you out of your mind? Did you actually plan for him to read this?"

"I'm not like you," Vriel said. "You aren't dependent on others the way I am, I get tired of lying. You breathe on your own, but I'll never fit in there."

"Nor here," Cassia said softly, "At least you won't be sick."
"Maybe not physically."

"If you found a partner like yourself..."

"Who is like me Cassia? You certainly aren't. Besides, I don't see you settling down. David and I have a real life together."

David was the kind of man her father must have been: open, trusting, protective, and deaf to the unseen world. What attracted Vriel to him was that he assumed people were who they pretended to be.

They had met in an organic market. She was sorting through the kale for the freshest bundle. His common approach, "How do you cook *that*?" made her smile.

She took in his stylish glass frames, neatly creased dockers, sandals, and faded tee shirt. On his left arm, he cradled a basket filled with packaged foods. There was no reason for him to be in produce.

Half way through dessert on their first date, he said: "What... nationality are you?"

Vriel smiled. It had taken him longer than she expected to ask, but she still played dumb.

"What do you mean?" "You look so..."

"Exotic, foreign, anomalous…" She completed his sentence, thinking, *you should see my sister.* An abundance of brown hair, the exact color of *Laminaria agardhii* in sunlit water, accented Cassia's warm yellow skin. Despite the long thin braids she never cut, despite her swimming coach's insistence that they would slow her time, Cassia was never suspected for being other than what she was. Unless, Vriel amended, she got wet.

Vriel weighed what answer to give him. She knew what he saw. The cropped dark hair luminous as an oil slick, the sloping curve of her eyes that clashed with her sharply angled cheekbones, her full bottom lip, and last, her skin, a dark olive reminiscent of sodden army fatigues. She gave the easiest answer that usually foreclosed further inquiry: *My mother was Black.*

He nodded; it was what he'd already guessed.

Later, she would tell him what little she knew of ancestry. That her mother was from a barren archipelago off the West African coast called Cape Verde, no doubt as a joke by some Portuguese explorer. That she and Cassia were born in New Bedford in 1973, days after their parents fled the chaos resulting in the wake of Amílcar Cabral's assassination. That her father went back for a research trip and never returned. She would not tell him her real name.

Making love to David was like kneading dough: pleasurable, meditative, and monotonous. His skin was too soft, too pliable, against her thin, bony frame. *In the dark, I can't tell the difference between your arms and legs,* he whispered. Mostly, she found sex a bizarre exercise. As he lay on top, his hair tickling her chin, she wondered what it would be like with one of *them.* Cassia made oblique references once or twice, but Vriel hadn't engaged her, and was now sorry, because she had so many questions. Greek lore was full of men procreating with Naiads, but where are their genitalia, for instance? Sex triggered these thoughts, which inevitably depressed her. The tears startled David.

"What is it? Did I hurt you?"

In a hurry to assure him, she said, "Everything I know about myself is a myth."

She came to regret the slip. Her distance and obtuseness only encouraged him. Still, she was relatively happy until he raised the stakes of their relationship. It shouldn't have surprised her; he had been slowly walking the line over the last seven months. First offering her a drawer in his dresser, and then stocking the kitchen with vitamin water and nutrition bars as he converted his apartment into their apartment. It was a rare man who proposed without taking the time to be sure of the answer. He hadn't come to that yet, but she could feel him steering slowly in that direction.

David returned from work in time to catch her at the door.

Relief and irritability fought in the lines of his forehead. She almost laughed as he struggled to swallow his question, *can I come?* He looked like a faithful beagle unhappy to be left behind.

She kissed him on his brow, scarcely touching her lips to the fine hair on his forehead. He backed away awkwardly, off-balance.

"Sorry," she murmured, "It's this carpet."

Cassia drove Vriel to her favorite sushi bar. As the car pulled up into the strip mall parking lot she turned to her sister and said, "It's not real, you know. He seems the glamour, not you."

"I don't do that. Not since I was little," Vriel said.

Not since Curtis Hawthorne, Vriel thought.

Cassia looked sharply at her sister, who recoiled. Guessing the direction of her thoughts, she said, "I know you don't do it intentionally. It's always around you. Like a residue."

"Like soap scum," Vriel muttered.

Remembering Curtis' mother's disbelieving hysteria, *how could a child of eight drown in two feet of water with a hundred people within earshot*, pitched her backwards to 1983. They were a mob of third graders, holding hands two by two. Vriel and Cassia had been split up, as was always done with siblings. *At least they're easy to tell apart*, joked one of the camp counselors, superior in their adolescence. Vriel's group was called the Tortoi, and they were identified by lime green t-shirts with a huge turtle on the front. Cassia wore ice-blue, bleached almost white from repeated washings, emblazoned with a purple Octopus. A natural leader, she encouraged feats of defiance among her classmates. While the turtles were always the most pliable group of children, counselors drew straws to determine who would be responsible for Cassia's tentacled compadres.

That day, they were visiting Marineland. When the groups were together, Vriel kept watch for Cassia's mischief but the exhibits appeared to have wondered her into compliance. She stared in amazement at the shark encounter, hands flat on the glass, nose pushed wide. She leaned far over the rail to touch a sea lion's cold, slimy nose, and refused to pluck a starfish, averting her eyes as child after child pried them off the coral in the tide-pool.

It began with a dare. Curtis Hawthorne challenged Vriel to stroke the back of a stingray. When she refused, he called her scaredy-cat and sissy. Mortified, because Curtis was the camp's heartthrob, Vriel dared him back. He marched to the tide-pool courageously reaching out until their guide announced they were going to the arena to see the killer whales, causing all of the children to file out eager to see the famous Tamu. Bereft of an audience, Curtis shrugged. Uncharacteristically, she caught his wrist. *Wait, I dared you.*

He squirmed away, laughing.

He stuck his tongue out at her as she fumed. Cassia was nowhere in sight. Why were the others so eager to see her cowed but they did not doubt Curtis' courage? Vriel was quiet during the show; she didn't clap or cheer when the black and white behemoth sprayed the first four rows with water. Instead, she glared at Curtis while humming one of her mother's songs to herself. *Sib u odja c' ma um dia. Di mi bout a bem squice. Midjor bou cham more. Sem sufri es 'gonia.* The melody calmed her, even though it was not a lullaby.

She repeated that snippet in her head, mouthing the shapes with her tongue, emitting no audible phrase, just a low symphonic shudder.

As the show came to the close, Curtis was no longer watching the whale and her daredevil trainer; his eyes were stuck on Vriel. And she, lulled inward by her song, seemed oblivious to him. He could not turn away. She was singing a lovely song, a coaxing song. It was like passing a note, just for him, under their teacher's nose. He couldn't help but read it, even if it meant the principal's office, because the note, the song — pointed out the irresistible beauty of the rays, their long sword-like tales, the sweeping reach of their fins beneath the surface, their smooth, pale underbellies. He wanted to swim with the rays, he was hungry for their company. They would welcome him.

When it was time to leave, the counselor gathered their charges, counting pigtails and braids, flattops, and crewcuts. One of the "sharks" was missing. Who was it? Curtis? Later, a woman was screaming and Cassia was looking at Vriel with something like awe.

Cassia passionately defended a sullen Vriel as their mother calmly listened to what happened and assured Vriel that it was not her fault. For the first time, as she warned her to be more careful in the future, Vriel saw something new in her mother's eyes: a strange admiration. There was wonder in her voice as she kissed the top of her daughter's shaking head and said, "Who would have thought it? A siren that can't swim."

"Vriel," Cassia said.

The waiter paused at their table, pen poised. "I've already ordered the chef's combo." Vriel looked at the untouched menu.

"Um...I'll have two hamachi, two toro, and one tamago..." she said.

Suddenly ravenous, she contemplated the Emperor's boat, but restrained herself.

"...and a seaweed salad."

They sat in silence. Cassia sipped her miso, catching the tofu on her tongue, flicking the seaweed from between her teeth, while Vriel prodded her salad. Small bites slowly restored her until she felt like her usual defiant self.

"Our mother had to make such a choice," Vriel said.

"She chose *wrong*. Too selfish to care what would become of us."

"We wouldn't be here if she hadn't."

"At least she came to a decision, and stuck to it. You refuse to choose, and that's the tragedy, what's making you ill."

"I don't see the point in fighting. I let it take me; I ride it out. It passes," Vriel said

"Eventually, you won't even feel the call. It will be like a phantom limb and then and there will be nothing I can do for you."

"Alleluia. Do you remember when Mom took us to see *Splash*? That scene where Daryl Hannah fills a tub with warm water and Morton's to soak her tail? I was once that desperate," Vriel said.

Cassia gave her a peculiar look, as if she wasn't sure whether to laugh or slap her.

"What happened?" Cassia said.

Vriel looked away. The grains had irritated the webbing between her toes and no amount of Visine could get the redness out of her eyes.

The waiter returned with their sushi. "Can I get you anything else? More tea?"

They nodded. The sushi glowed like a cache of jewels on rice. Vriel quickly cleaned her plate and ogled Cassia's untouched spider rolls. Her sister slid her plate across the table, and Vriel finished what was left, including the fresh, nearly transparent slices of ginger.

The waiter brought two bowls of green tea ice cream, blushing. "Dessert is on me," he said.

Cassia paid the bill and handed the receipt, on which "call me" was scrawled beside a phone number, to Vriel.

Her one advantage over Cassia was that she could have nearly any man she wanted. All she had to do was form a melody in her mind and they flowed towards her as easily as the fish that hailed Cassia every time she dipped her toes in wild water. These easy conquests ultimately bored her with their selfless devotion, their perplexed love. Intelligent, capable achievers lost their drive, inspired only by the prospect of pleasing her. She feared to see that abject yearning in David's eyes; she couldn't justify another restraining order or another Karlton. He had overdosed on sleeping pills shortly after their break up. Out of courtesy, she braved the cold stares of his parents at the hospital. The sight of him -- pale, despondent, hooked up to an IV— was devastating. Still, he clung to her hand and begged. Then, only last week, nearly a year later, she ran into a friend of his at the Coffee Bean catty- corner from her apartment.

"Hey."

She quickly ordered her drink, pretended to study the menu.

But the voice caught up and held the door to the shop open. "Aren't you that bitch Karl used to fuck with?"

His face was a snarl. She held her breath as customers in the shop steeled themselves for a scene.

"Vriel, right?"

She froze. Taking her silence for assent, he let the door fall shut, and stood in front of her as she waited for her coffee. Barely lowering his voice he said, "You know his mother had to put another 72-hour hold on him just last month? He lost his job, apartment, everything."

She reluctantly met his eyes. He seemed to be searching her face for something. She could feel the recrimination, the disbelief coming off him, in waves.

She was nothing special, what had she done?

"Hey dude," the barista said, sitting her latte on the counter, "Chill, ok?"

The spark inside her flared to life and the anger in his face slowly drained away.

"Can I talk to you?" he said, bewildered by his own sudden shift.   She took her drink and fled.

"Let's go for a drive," Cassia said. It was not a suggestion.

They got on the freeway at Lincoln and headed West on the 10 until it turned into the Pacific Coast Highway. The little beach towns abutting the hills of the Palisades, the crowds drinking pineapple daiquiris at Gladstone's, faded away as they drove into the sherbet-colored sunset. Vriel had to shade her eyes against the glare. The road narrowed to a one-lane highway as the traffic thinned. She knew where Cassia was taking her. Every year at the same time, their mother drove them to a secluded lagoon far up the coast, past Zuma and the other beaches famous for their titanic waves, to a cove where the inshore waters were calm, deserted, lucid, and pestilence free. No traces of bonfires or teenage litter in the sand. The first time they went, Vriel and Cassia were thirteen. That's when their mother had told them. Cassia, it was clear, seemed to already know. In Vriel's adolescent opinion, it was another strike against their mother.

Shading her eyes from the sun, their mother seemed to be waiting for something.

"When I was a girl in St. Antao," she said, "we would ride the ancient sea turtles into the coves at *Ponto do Sol*, dodging the jagged roots of the sheer cliffs. We capsized the boats of the fishermen in the shallows and stole their beautiful pipes."

They drank in her words. These were the crumbs they used to piece together their mother's rarely spoken of childhood. The wistful recollecting stopped.

"One can't really hear what I'm telling you. It's better to see for yourself," their mother said.

Vriel hesitated to join her mother and sister in the tide-pool, which was shielded by a half circle of rocks from the sloughing currents.

Vriel waded in. Cassia promptly took her hand, while their mother vanished. Vriel looked to Cassia, who as always, only evinced calm disinterest. Only her own fear kept the Vriel's raw envy contained. Cassia sank beneath the water, submerging Vriel, who managed to gulp one deep breath before she went under.

What she saw, because she forgot to close her eyes, astonished her.

The salt did not burn and she could see

as clearly as she if she was wearing goggles through waters that possessed a luminescence so brilliant, it appeared as if someone was shining a huge flood light from the depths. Then, still holding 45 seconds of air in her fully extended cheeks, she finally saw what her mother was.

Her brown skin was altered, by what Vriel at first believed to be a trick of wave and light. Then, she realized it was her mother that was the source of the underwater luminosity. The upper part of her torso took on the reflective gloss of a golden oyster shell, while the lower part of her body appeared to be swathed with ropes of black-green-purple opalescence. Her legs were moving in swift undulation so that they appeared conjoined. In horror, Vriel parted her lips and the rest of her air rushed out. The last thing she saw was Cassia pulling her close.

When she awoke, she was alone on the beach, her cheek pressed to a pillow of sand. Their Toyota was still parked in the lot, but her mother and sister were nowhere to be found. She brushed the sand off her dry swimsuit and wondered how long she'd been asleep. Unsure of what else to do, she unlocked the car door and waited.

Some hours later, when they finally returned from wherever they had gone, Cassia had changed. She became reclusive and oddly protective of Vriel, as if she felt a kind of pity for her sister because she couldn't participate in something Cassia and her mother shared. Their secretiveness motivated Vriel to improve her swimming skills. Coached by her sister, she learned to dive and swim with efficiency, if lacking in speed and grace. But, however proficient she became, she knew that when they were together, Cassia restrained herself from plunging further into the deep.

After a time, she abandoned the lessons altogether, against her mother's warnings that her body craved the nutrients contained within the salt water.

Some years later, after a long fight with a rare cancer, their mother died. Before they moved into a cheaper apartment in Venice, they ransacked the condo, finding little of note to remember her by: a watercolor of a dormant volcano crowned with pine tress signed Y. Viera, aged five; a large opal ring set in a clunky silver setting; and several indigo and white *panos* that Cassia now used to wrap her hair. There were a few letters from their father: each one commencing, "My Beloved Ysabel" but revealing nothing beyond the usual lovers' pledges.

After their mother's death, they unceremoniously dumped their mother's ashes in the cove. Cassia frequently pressured Vriel to return there, but Vriel refused saying, "I don't believe in riddles and myths made up by a woman overcome with grief and loneliness."

"How can you say that?"

Cassia believed that Vriel would not be different in their mother's world. But Vriel always refused to go. If she never went, she never had to find out if her mother's race — what could she call them that didn't sound like something out of Hans Christian Andersen?

— would reject her or perceive some flaw. And she despised Cassia, hated her for not having to choose, for being accepted in both worlds and choosing the harder passage.

Then there was David, searching among the kale, who loved her before she had a chance to think about whether or not it was a good idea, and Cassia thought Vriel should give that up for her fantasy. When she was little, she felt disturbed by a Twilight Zone episode about a woman who wanders into a department store.

Directed to an upstairs floor, she slowly realizes that she is not a real woman, but a mannequin who has overstayed her vacation in the outside world. Her reluctance to remember is understandable, but selfish, since only one mannequin can go out at a time.

Whenever Cassia came back into her life, she couldn't help feeling as if Rod Sterling had sent her sister to bring her back to a prison from which she had escaped.

It was right after the conversation at the bakery that Vriel began to get sick. They had just finished their coffee when David gestured towards the glass display case, which was full of elaborate, inexplicably-named pastries like Napoleon or *baba au rhum*.

"I'm always suspicious when there's no day-old section," said David, "Can they really sell all this in a day?"

"Ask what they do with them," Vriel said.

"Miss," he said to the cashier, "what happens to the leftovers?"

"We throw them away."

"That's such a waste," Vriel said, a bit too loudly.

David blushed. The manager, a middle-aged Vietnamese woman with a light French lilt to her English came to the rescue.

"We donate," she said. "A truck takes them to a homeless shelter."

Vriel pictured rows of men and women in dark, worn overcoats crowded around a bench, stuffing their faces with lemon bars and marzipan. They were skeptical, but they dutifully deposited their dishes in the bins beside the trash can. As David held the door, she looked back. The manager was speaking quietly to the cashier. Flies trapped beneath the glass roamed from dessert to dessert like bees in heat. How had she not noticed that before? The croissant heaved in her stomach.

Later, while she remembered every trivial word that transpired, she could not recall when exactly they had broken faith with the other.

Vriel slumped in the passenger seat of her sister's marine Eclipse. She hadn't realized they had stopped.

"Do you want to get out?" Cassia said.

Vriel shook her head, cracked the window just an inch, enough to catch a whiff of the saltine breeze. She recalled a Coleridge couplet from her last year of college — *Water, water, everywhere, nor any drop to drink* — when she took an English elective entitled "Mutinies and Shipwrecks." They read *Moby Dick, Robinson Crusoe, The Odyssey,* and watched *The Bounty* starring Mel Gibson as Fletcher Christian. In these books, mariners died of thirst and exposure, contemplated man's insignificance in the face of nature's mad harmony, and futilely struggled to master that most unfaithful of mistresses, the sea. Occasionally these sailors sought solace in the ginger circles of native women's arms, adorning themselves with flora and fauna and local ink. In her favorite short story, the narrator discovers too late, due to his own blinding prejudice, that he has been a deluded participant in an elaborate ruse, and that the peculiar ship is in the midst of a slave uprising. At that moment of clarity, the narrator tells the reader "the scales dropped from his eyes." When she read that sentence she thought it perfectly captured how she felt the instant she saw her mother in the cove, just before she lost consciousness.

"What was that?" Cassia said.

"Oh," Vriel was startled; she hadn't realized that she had spoken the rhyme aloud. "Just something I picked up."

Cassia seemed to have something else on her mind.

"You know," she said, "on the island of *Brava* they worship us.

There's an entire festival where they cast boats filled with offerings onto the sea. And the water in the harbor is like warm scented tea. I wish you could experience that."

Cassia tossed the keys up on the dashboard and then reached in the backseat to grab her knapsack. The darkness of the new moon cast no shadows about the unlit abandoned parking lot.

But Vriel, who could always see like a cat in the dark, admired the curved outline of her sister's torso as she pulled her shirt over her head. Cassia wriggled out of her jeans, letting the seat back to give her more room to maneuver. At last, divested of her clothes, she unwound her batik headwrap, allowing her long braids to loop over her bare shoulders, white cowries scattered in her hair like dim stars.

Cassia was not one to give second chances. She did not ask Vriel if she was certain, if she had a last minute change of heart. She did not tell her that she had prepared a second bag and stuffed it in the trunk, next to the spare tire. She simply looked at her sister for a moment, keeping her eyes free of pleading and then said quietly, firmly, "Keep the car."

Cassia pressed something into her hand and Vriel turned away from the whoosh of air from the door opening, the knapsack sailing past her ear. She didn't watch Cassia fade into the dark. She imagined the pressure of bare feet denting the sand, waves breaking against ankles, the spray splashing upward, outward, then crashing over sand without a trace.

Only then did she open her hand. Resting on the pillow of her palm was her red jack. Vriel climbed over the stick shift into the driver's seat and turned the key. The headlights illuminated the yellow parking lines, the bits of green glass, the trash can and a no parking from 2am to 4am sign. As the car pulled slowly away, she remembered Cassia pulling her into the cold water, taunting, "What do you mean it's cold?" falling backwards into the tide, unafraid of the undertow.

Notes:

The lines from the epigraph from Jorge Barbosa's poem "Arcquipélago" translate: Islands lost/in the midst of the sea/ forgotten/in an angle of the World/where the waves cradle/ abuse/embrace…

The lines: *Sib u odja c' ma um dia. Di mi bout a bem squice. Midjor bou cham more. Sem sufri es 'gonia* are lyrics from Maria de Barros' song *Triste Gonia.* By Joao Santos/Djedjinho. Translated: If you think that one day you may forget me better let me die without having to suffer this agony.

Letty
by Regina N. Bradley

Folks say you start to see things when you laying there dying. I wasn't ready to see because I didn't expect to die that day. I worked in the saw mill as a dust sweeper because I refused to crawl on my hands and knees to scrub and clean for white folks. "You being uppity for a Negro girl," my sister scoffed. She didn't scrub floors but she cooked in white folks' kitchens. Same damn difference to me. That job at the sawmill paid better than any white person's dirty house. When I was hired, the manager said I had a strong back.

I swept the bottom floor to avoid mishaps. At night I swept the dust into the holding gate. This time, I didn't see the gate that held the sawdust swing open but I heard it snap. Even though flecks of sawdust danced 'round my eyes and lay gently on my lashes, they lay heavy on my body and chest. How can something so nothing feel so heavy? I close my eyes. They're burning. Shadows and sawdust. Shadows and sawdust.

When I open my eyes one shadow gets big. Real big. My head bobs like I been drinking hooch. The good hooch. The kind made with corn left in the fields too long and is a little too ripe and in the dark jar to save its flavor. People say the good hooch let you see the devil and if you share it, it can save you from death or hand you on to him. My head snaps up and down. The big shadow turns brown.

Then black. Brown. Then back black. I squint to focus. I see a head and shoulders. The sound of swishing comes from somewhere I can't see. Wood flecks stay in the air and silent.

The figure lets out a raspy voice. It sounds irritated. "Stuck, huh?"

"Just taking a break from sweeping is all." It laughs. "How you get in here?"

"Key." "Whose key?"

"Mine." The swishing turns to rustling that sounds like leaves scooped up dancing in the wind. The shadow thing comes close to my face. I'm queasy. It smells sweet and sour like old eggs. I squint again and see two wrinkly brown titties on the saw dust pile in front of me. Realize it's a woman. She got old woman titties but a young looking face. The shadow woman looks comfortable and stares me straight in the face. She got eyes that burn like hot coals. She don't blink. The three plaits in her hair twitch in place. The two by her ears look undone. I see she got wings. They look like old crow feathers. Her features run from my view because they hide behind a piece of iron that sits right down the middle of her face and across her nose and cheeks. Her face shiny like molasses. Got a shackle around her neck and three pokes sticking out. They're connected to a patch over her mouth with little holes. She thumps one of the pokes. "Like my neck jewelry?" she asks.

She don't move her gaze from me. "Know why I'm here, Gris?"

"Reckon it ain't to keep me company?"

The monster woman chuckles and breathes heavy. I see littlespecks scurry from behind the holes in her mask. They're bright red fire ants.

They run all over her mask and back underneath it. She hisses through her teeth as if they hurting her.

"You ain't my type. Half-dead and lame."

"Who dying?" I tense what I can feel of my shoulders. I ain't ready to die.

"Oh you dyin', swine," she says. She stretches her wings for effect. A bunch of black crow feathers shake to the floor and disappear.

"So you...you death?" "Whelp."

"But I thought — " sawdust finds its way into my nose and my throat. "But you a woman," I hack.

"Yep."

"But you a woman and got working man in the field stank." "I'll whoop you like a working man too."

"Please, Miss Death." "Letty."

"Please, Miss Letty. I ain't ready to go with you." "This ain't about what you want, Gris."

She grab my throat and lean in. Fire ants scurry from her face, down her arm towards the hand on my neck. Her hands were white and cracked.

"P-p-please, Miss Letty."

"Ain't no Miss required when you say my name." The fire ants lift their legs and feelers and stay scurrying towards me.

"Please, Miss Letty."

She loosens her grip and stands straight up. The fire ants retreat back to her face mask. She moan low as they move back under the mask and shakes her head like a dog with something in its ear.

A lone fire ant falls on my cheek and stings me. I blink hard. It stings me again. I look at Letty. She tall. Queenly even.

She ruffles her wing feathers and cocks her head to the side. Listening. I don't hear nothing.

Letty look past me out the mill window. Then she turn back to me.

"Look like someone wanna talk to you first," Letty say. She pushes her hands deep into her hips like she's disappointed. "Praise God."

"Naw, God ain't do this," she say. Her face shines and looks slippery. It's so slick I can't tell if she crying or sweating.

"Who saved me then?" "You'll see soon enough."

"Why your face shine like that? Looks sticky."

She raises her hands from her hips to her face mask. She tries to move it but her face mask look like its stuck on her skin.

"Cause it is sticky." "Honey?"

"Yes?" Letty makes a sucking noise through her mask. "No, I mean honey? Molasses?"

"Nan one. It's sap."

She frightful but even when I blink I see her plain as day. "What happen, Miss Letty?"

A fire ant pushes itself through a hole in the top of mask like an overseer. It stays put. I hear wailing. I don't know if it's Letty or the mask. Her ant overseer trembles but don't move.

Miss Letty's eyes burn a hole in my skull. She stares before she say anything.

"I was a cook once," she finally says.

"Where bout?" "Cypress Lake."

Cypress Lake was a bit down the road in Albany. The Cheathams owned that plantation. Cruel place. Many a nigger tried to run from there. Many a nigger never made it back alive.

"Damn good at it, too. Didn't feel like a slave in the kitchen," Letty say. "Didn't feel trapped in there. Felt the kitchen be mine."

"Why you a cook?"

"Cause I couldn't work the fields," Letty snaps. She shakes her head like a dog again. "Couldn't get the cotton fast enough. Too many seeds. Couldn't get 'em out good enough. They burrow too deep in the cotton head. Too much picking the head falls apart.

They ain't want that. Sometimes I dig so deep my fingers bleed. Got bright red blood on the cotton. Worst lashin' of my life." Letty's voice trail off.

"So they move me in the kitchen."

I nodded best I could. My daddy worked cotton.

"Missus Cheatham put me in the kitchen cause she thought I weren't much to look at but could work hard. 'You a dark little pickaninny,' she say. Truth is she thought Mr. Cheatham would leave me be. He known to mingle in bed with his slave women. But she thought I was young enough and ugly enough to miss his eye."

If she was ugly before, she didn't look much different. Letty's eyes glared red. "Mr. Cheatham come round soon enough. Touch my plaits one day. Grab my slip and yank it the next day. Sneak his hand on my thigh and try to move it up on the inside the next. Told me to giggle. Said it made him feel nice." Sounds like Letty sneeze and hiss. Fire ants scurry out from under the mask. She don't wail this time. She yell. She angry. Her wings flap strong one time.

Wind hit my face smelling like sweet old eggs. I want to throw up. "Missus Cheatham see Mr. Cheatham coming round the kitchen more often. She flat out ask me 'Letty, you taking a shine to my husband?' I can't look her in the face because I was taught to avoid eye contact to show respect. I dig my toe into the floor. Not cause I was likin' Mr. Cheatham but cause I didn't know how to tell her I didn't. Missus pull my hair and yank my head back. Her green eyes catch mine and stomp down hard. 'Mr. Cheatham is a great man! Great and much better'n the like of you, Nigger Bitch!'

She slap me with her free hand. What she said stung worse than the slap. More poison behind it."

Miss Letty look me in the face to search for understanding. I ran across a few southern white women like Missus Cheatham. The ones that think they ass don't stank and that God was their personal body guard. I ached for Miss Letty and for the other Black women who dealt with Missus Cheathams on a daily basis.

Miss Letty kept talking.

"Missus come and sit in the kitchen or the parlor by the kitchen every day for hours. She wanted to see. She would stare. Her eyes be like daggers. Sometimes she come in and slap me or beat me on my back for good measure. 'How could my husband want a thing like you?' she snarled at me. 'I should put you back in the field with the dirt.' Every day she sit and complain. Sit and complain.

"But I got tired of her hittin' me and callin' me dirt. I might've been a Nigger Bitch, Gris, but I weren't a stupid Nigger Bitch."

I cough up a dry sawdust coated chuckle.

"I was tired of Mr. Cheatham and Missus. So I make a plan. My very own plan. Every Saturday I make fresh biscuits with peach jam. Missus loved them hot biscuits and jam. Jimson, another slave from nearby Pine Blossom plantation, make the jam fresh during peach season. Jimson come to the back door of the kitchen and wink every time I answer it. Somethin' tried to grow between us. Tried hard. Shole did."

For a second, Letty's eyes wash out from burning coals to a woman who felt love's gaze. A woman that was trying to figure something out. But as soon as she let loose the thought of Jimson, the fire roared back to the coals in her eyes.

"Jimson ain't know I mixed a huge dose of white mulberry sap into the jam each Saturday. Tree grew right next to my quarters. Before I got up to start the house chores I went and tapped the sap to mix in with the jam. Every Saturday. Hot biscuits and peach and mulberry sap jam."

Letty nodded to herself. "Sometimes when I serve Missus Mr. Cheatham sitting in the parlor with her. I never look in his direction. But when I go to put his plate in front of him he sneak his hand under the table and squeeze my thigh. Squeeze hard and let go. Like he pumping a cow teat for milk. Then I sit in the kitchen and wait. Hear the scraping of spoons against the jar and the clink of forks across plates that I washed and prepared. Every Saturday."

"Shole 'nough, Missus start to act strange. Start to see things.

People in the corner of her room. Clocks running across the parlor floor. One time she claw Mr. Cheatham face bad because she saw bugs crawling around his face and neck. But she still ate those fresh biscuits and jam."

Letty lets out a careful sigh past the fire ants scurrying behind her mask. "Then Missus say she start seeing Coffey. Coffey was her chamber maid. Coffey bout twelve or thirteen with middle brown skin, a little puff of black hair, and sad brown eyes. The sun never shined on her eyes the right way. Sweet as pie and anxious to please Missus. Brush Missus hair. Empty out her pot. Warm up her bed in the winter. But Missus treat Coffey mighty bad.

She never got it right. She brush too hard. Say Coffey didn't warm up all the bed. But Coffey just curtsey and work. Missus beat her with the end handle of a whip cause Missus felt throwing the whip weren't ladylike. After Coffey's beatings she was a pitiful sight and Missus couldn't stand it so she threw her into her bedroom closet. Sometime she stay in there for days. We'd sneak her bread ends and sips of water when we could."

Letty pats her chest. "One night Coffey heart just give out. She curled up in Missus bed like she was trying to warm it. Missus come in and think she just fall asleep on her bed. She yell and scream at Coffey. Coffey don't move. She hits her in the head with the whip handle. Coffey still don't move. She hits Coffey on her back. Missus think Coffey in a deep sleep. She stomps barefoot to the top of the stairs and yells for me to get August. August is Coffey's brother.

Gruff, quiet, and mean looking. August come to Missus bedroom and see his sister curled in a ball like a roly poly. He try to eat his own moan. He pull his throat tight to stop from hollerin' out.

August puts one hand under her head and the other around her waist to lift her up. Missus snarl, hiss, and scream.

'Just yank her out. Yank her out! Damn you, August! Get her out my bed!"

August move slow. Tender. Missus hit him on his back with the whip handle. Tears fall. He still move slow and tender.

"Move quicker than that! If you don't move I'll lash you from here to Sunday!" Missus tiny white hands ball up and hit August on his back. He still moves slow and tender.

After Coffey die Missus move to another room.

But Coffey move with her. Coffey makin' herself known

because Missus' eating white mulberry sap. She stand at the end of Missus' bed. She stare and wait. Missus peek over her covers and look Coffey in her face.

"Why are you here, you pickaninny? Why? You're dead. Dead!" Coffey don't move. She stare. Missus wails.

"If you must stay, go on back into the closet. The closet! The godforsaken closet!" Coffey don't move. She stare.

Mulberry sap got Missus brain full. She starting to see Coffey everywhere. Mr. Cheatham grow worried.

"The closet! Oh Jim! I can't stand looking at her! Don't you see? Can't you see the pickaninny? She's right there staring!"

Mr. Cheatham sigh and look towards the closet. He don't see nothing. "There is nothing there, my dearest Amanda. No one's there, indeed."

"But she needs to be in the closet!"

Missus collapse back on her bed. She tired of seeing Coffey.

Mr. Cheatham sighs from deep in his chest and opens the window to let in a breeze.

"Maybe the smell of magnolias on the breeze will bring her around," Mr. Cheatham say to no one in particular.

Missus continues to whimper about the closet. Coffey stands at the end of the bed and stares.

"Should I bring her biscuits and peach jam, suh?" I ask. "She would like that. We will eat here."

I go to fetch the biscuits. I put another heap of mulberry sap in the jam. I think of Jimson winking at me and smile. Something was trying to grow between us. Force itself out and grow. "Letty, those biscuits!" Mr. Cheatham hollers.

I scurry up the stairs and serve Mr. Cheatham and Missus. Mr.

Cheatham stares at my hands. I look down and see the sap starting to cake over white. I brush my hands across the front of my dress.

"Why are your hands so sticky and white?" Mr. Cheatham stands up and looks down on me. I cringe.

"Spilled a bit of dough and flour to make the biscuits. Just forgot to wipe 'em clean, suh."

Mr. Cheatham look at my hands. He reaches out a finger to touch the top of my left hand. It presses down and the sap covers his finger tip.

"What's this?" He puts the fingertip to his nose. His eyes widen. Mr. Cheatham grabs my wrists and shakes me.

"What the hell is this?"

"Jam. It's jam, Mr. Cheatham suh."

"This ain't no damn jam. What did you do? What the hell did you do?"

He throws me to the floor. I curl into a ball like Coffey. Missus screams.

"You worthless nigger!" he yells. "Letty," I say.

He grabs my plaits and drags me down the stairs. He hits me with each fist as he shoves me down the stair and drags me outside.

Mr. Cheatham tells Peter to fetch him a knife from the kitchen. "The closet!" Missus yells from inside the house.

Mr. Cheatham cuts my plaits. He cut the braids by my ears like he cutting with a saw. He ties me to the Oleander tree and rips my dress. He doesn't lash me. He beat me with his own hands. Each blow I see white. Bright white. Could've been the sun but I feel it was God watchin me die. The blows to my face take away shapes. I only see colors and smell something sour. I wonder if the sour smell means my blood turning cold. I hear dirt moving.

Somebody lifts me and put me down deep into a hole. "Not the head," Mr. Cheatham say.

I smell Dirt. Oleander. Blood. Magnolia.

I hear Mr. Cheatham walk away. Then he come back.

Something wet hit my left cheek. Mr. Cheatham kicks dirt in my face. I can only move my neck. Then something thick and itchy hits the top of my head and covers my face. He put this mask on my face. I can't breathe nothin' but sticky and dirt. Sticky and dirt.

"Kick the nest!" Mr. Cheatham hollered. Letty gasps and stands up to shake out her dress. More fire ants fall from the creases of her crumpled dress and face mask.

"Jesus!" I holler.

"Naw, Gris, it ain't him," Letty say. She reaches her hand out to me. There ain't no skin.

"This ain't as bad as fire ants. You ready to come with me? You further along than I was when I was dying."

A Real Friend Will Let You Break
by A. J. Locke

Beneath this tidal wave of misery
there is some semblance of a face.
But your eyes are sunken and hollow,
and your cheeks are floppy bowels of flesh.
I can squish my fingers around in them
but that does not make you smile.

I suppose you've gone and
planted yourself to this spot.
Thrust your roots into desert ground
and suck on intangible things when you thirst.
But your throat is still parched, is it not?

You are a viciously empty shell.
So perhaps I will poke you until you shatter,
and leave the pieces for that miserable wave
to lick clean in salty contempt,
or perhaps choke and drown.
That way, whatever it is,
you can finally forget.

Ma Laja
by Tracey Baptiste

As soon as she put her foot in the shoe, she feel like Cinderella.

Oh! It feel good. But there was still the matter of the other one. She lean against the wall, and push the hoof in gingerly, afraid for the shoe, and she own hoof. But there. It fit. Just like the other one. Now she stand in front the mirror and watch sheself. Is the first time she could ever lif ' up she skirt and look at two foot. So many years she had to hide. How many is that now? So many she stop counting. She take a little walk in front of the mirror to see how the shoes fit. She smile. No more: one foot down, drag the cow heel. Now she was walking regular like other women. Who would know what she was? Even though these days, people didn't look so hard at you. They was always in them phones watching the world pass by with they hand in front they face. Not that it didn't have plenty maco spreading gossip around, but even the maco them was busy with they own thing and spending less time in other people business. It was the TV that started it. As soon as that box come in everybody house, people stop looking out they windows.

That make Ma Laja happy. She didn't need anybody watching she. Staying in the shadows by the edge of the road was how she survived all this time. Now the road them paved, and all them fellas driving on it fast.

As she stand there admiring the new shoes, the warm blood spread almost to she foot.

"Lord, no!" Ma Laja cried. "Not mih new shoes!"

She quick-stepped out of the way of the spreading pool, and toward the door of the shoe store. She took one more look back, at the boxes of shoes that other customers had tried on during the day, the shut blinds that meant the store was closing up, the manager's blood soaking up the carpet, his eyes staring blankly at the ceiling fan that rotated slowly, whoop, whoop, whoop over their heads, and her own self in the mirror, so pretty, the manager couldn't resist letting she try on that one pair of shoes even though the CLOSED sign was already out.

She thought, "Is a good thing it wasn't a woman, eh?"

Ma Laja liked to stick to the rules. These days though, some of them rules had to be adjusted, wiggled a little to allow she to live in peace.

She step outside the store and close the door behind her. The dark was welcoming. It fall around she shoulders like a cape. Ma Laja decide to walk around town a bit to test out how the new shoes would work. She didn't have to go far. It was generating plenty of looks already, even people in they fast, fast motorcars slow down to get a better look. Nobody had shoes like these. They was unique.

One guy leaning out he car say, "Mmm! Doux doux! You lookin' good, Mama. Whey you get them crazy shoes from?"

"Psst! Sweet thing! You going to a party or what in them fancy shoes?" A young boy call out as she pass him and his group of friends.

A couple of women walk by. They watch she foot, and then

watch straight ahead again, pretending not to see. But it was hard to ignore a pair of shoes that look like two cow feet. After she pass them, she could feel they eyes on the back of she, staring.

Ma Laja smile and draw sheself up to she full height. She never feel so good in all she born days. When was it she was born? She couldn't remember exactly, eh? In her earliest memory she look exactly the same way she look right now. Well, she used to change up the hairstyle and the clothes to go with the fashion, but her face never change. Sometimes she would see people that she know from years and years gone, and they faces was always different. First the cheeks them lose they roundness. Then the color slowly leech out. Then the skin get loose around they bones. Always changing. But not Ma Laja. She never change.

She turn down a narrow alley behind the row of stores, and follow it back to the river. Not too many people know 'bout that little road. No lady in she right mind would walk down it. Town was dark, but there it was darker, no street lights, nobody to hear if you call out for help. Dangerous for a woman. The heels of the new shoes click on the stones in the middle of the street as she walk, and it sound like music. Make she start to swing she hips.

"You ent 'fraid something happen to you on a desolate road like this?"

Ma Laja turn around and see a tall, dark-skin man watching she.

Something in his fingers curled smoke up into the air. She knew that scent.

"You got another one of them?" Ma Laja asked. She walked toward the man. He look surprise. Didn't expect she to be friendly. Probably expected she to try and run off.

"No, but you can share this one." He hold the cigarette out and smiled like a cat who corner a mouse. But he didn't know who he was dealing with. He shoulda run. But now, it was too late for he.

SHOESTORE MURDER MAN MISSING
MEN RUNNING OFF
EPIDEMIC, the newspapers say.

People was getting nervous. Nobody could understand what was happening. Every day a new headline. Every night a new man gone. The nights them was getting real quiet. There was only light reaching into the streets through shut doors like shards of fear. But plenty of brave ones was out and about still. It was nice for Ma Laja. It had been so long she didn't have such fun.

An evening, she scuff up the new shoes by the corner of St. James and Boulevard. As she lean down to rub off the dirt, a car pull up and a man ask she if she lost and want a ride somewhere.

She suck she teeth, steups. But it was a nice looking man, eh. In a suit. With a gold ring on he finger. The woman sitting next to he have she face swell up and she arms cross over she chest. But no gold ring.

Ma say, "Yeah. I looking for something."

From the front seat, the woman was saying "I really need to get home," and "That's probably your wife buzzing the phone." Ma Laja nearly abandon the whole endeavor, when the man say, "Leah, you're right. No need for both of us to get home late. I'll drop you at the bus and see you in the morning."

He drive them a little ways and stop at a corner, and didn't look at the woman until she get out the car. Then Ma Laja come around to the front.

"Is nowhere I going, you know," she said.

He say, "Those are interesting shoes."

The next day, it was LADY KILLER crowding up the front page and everybody eye bugging out they head as they read it.

Evening again and she walk to a street vendor for some coconut water. The machete ring against the husk as the vendor chop open the top and hand to she. It all went down in one gulp, some of the coconut water run down her bare neck and past the bony hill of her clavicle to the soft skin beneath.

"The flesh sweet," he say.

She nod and hand the coconut over. He hack it in two and slice off a little husk for she to scoop out the white jelly inside. She ate another one, and another as the light over the savannah dim and you could almost hear the sounds of doors shutting, locks clicking, bones trembling. The street lamps was on, buildings was shuttered again.

"Everybody gone," she said. "Why you ent packing up?" "You still here."

"I done, man."

"Nah," he say. "You ent done yet." She notice he glance down at she shoes.

The machete surprise she for sure. Is a long time she didn't see she own blood, and she forget how much hurt could hurt.

"I know who you are," the man say, swiping again with the blade. "They looking for you, you know." He jogged out of her reach and threw one of the older coconuts at her head. "If you think is me you go ketch—"

She reach him and they wrestle a bit behind the cart, in a veil of shadow between two street lights.

When it was all over she suck she teeth steups and roll she eyes.

She never did like mess eh. And even in the dim light she could see was lots to clean up. Worse still, the shoes them have blood and dirt stains and coconut jelly clinging to the fabric. She try to wash them off in a nearby standpipe, but it didn't work. The sole pull away, and the leather warp. It wasn't easy to walk in them after that either.

She look back toward the coconut cart and the man lying beneath. The shoes them leave a trail of blood to the standpipe.

The shoes, she thought. For days they meant she had feast and freedom. Now they was looking for she. And they was looking for the shoes. Ma Laja run through town toward the old cemetery. The rain-dampened ground was soft like flesh, making an unsteady path. And the whole time the shoes—on top of everything else—was getting more and more muddy. They was only a few days old. They shouldn't already be so beat up. It was the principle of the thing that made she vex. Vex enough that she was looking at she feet when she bounce up the young man near the cemetery fence.

Their bodies and bones and breath knock together all in one before they stagger apart. He was running from something in the graveyard, she running to it. Both of them look through the high wrought iron fence into the dark slopes of the burial ground, its stones reaching like bony finger tips to the moon.

He smelled like fresh dirt, and was holding something in his hand that shine in the little light left from the street lamps and windows. He wipe he hand on he pants and swallow.

"Good evening," he say.

Ma Laja nod. She try to go pass him.

"You eh see me, you hear?" He look through the fence again.

"If they find me, I go find you, you hear?" He look she up and down and stop at the shoes. He step back.

"I saw those shoes in the paper," he say. "The police say they were stolen from a shop where a man was killed."

Ma Laja step forward. "Well we is both thief then." He shake he head. Then he take off. Or he try.

A crack in the ground cut up she hand a little bit when she grab he and pull he down to the sidewalk. They was intertwined like insects, rolling off the sidewalk and into the road. He body was soft, which was a surprise, and smaller too under all them clothes. She manage to get she hand around he delicate little neck, but before she could snap it, the man whimper in a way that make she hand go slack. Then the man elbow she in the face, and pull heself to he feet. Ma Laja recover quick and get up too. They look at each other for a moment, panting, then the man take off again. She coulda let him go. She didn't need him. She already eat for the day. But he done see what she was and anyway, it wasn't greed exactly to have a few meals in a stretch. There was plenty of starving years when people was driving motorcar and nobody walking anyplace. It was stockpiling she was thinking of. Besides, he was a thief. Who would miss he?

She reach out she hoof and catch him at the ankle. He tumble face front into the hard sidewalk and come up bloody. She try to get she hand round he neck again but the man block she arm and break away. The indentation of she fingers still red around he neck like a fading tattoo. The man press up to one knee. Ma Laja slammed one hand against he head and into the shiny black metal fence. Blood run down it, glistening in the moonlight, looking like a mistake in the ironwork.

An icy grip take hold of Ma Laja from inside. Like the man had reach in she to pull something out. The feeling spread out through she body stabbing everything it pass, hardening all her insides, making it brittle, making even memories break away until some that was far beneath get unlock. She remember a girl. She remember a time before she was what she was. I think is Phylisia they used to call me, she realize. While the things that had hide her first memories was still getting scrape away, she saw the moon like a glass of ice water glistening down, and she think, Well it done now.

The sound of running feet came out of the cemetery a moment later. Two officers took a look over both people lying in the road and began to do CPR. A third walk over more slowly, he shoes ticking on the sidewalk like a clock.

"What we have here?" he asked.

"Two women," one of the officers said.

Ma Laja sigh. Her last breath. A woman? And then she smile. "Well is no wonder," she try to say. But she was dead a'ready. And them words stick in she throat as the last of the cold overcome she.

"Look at the shoes on this one," an officer said. "Think she's who we've been looking for?"

"I thought she was only attacking men. Why a woman now?"

"This one doesn't really look like a woman."

There was a pause. Then, "Interesting." Another pause. "Both dead?"

"Cinderella is," an officer said. "Not this one," the other say.

Ma Laja pause, hovering over all of them as she see the woman coming back. She try to reach she. Try to warn she. Try to tell she, "Is better you die. Just let the world go." But the woman eyelids flutter. "No," Ma Laja was trying to tell she. "Don't wake up!

You don't understand what it will mean."

"Look at this," another officer said. "It's a picture of herself.

She was carrying a picture of herself, but, it can't be. The date written on the back is nearly eighty years ago."

"Maybe a great-grandmother?" one say. "Family heirloom."
"Right."

"Wrong," Ma Laja tried to say. "Is me that was. Is me when another La Diabless come and take mih life. And then what happen to mih? Is the same thing that go happen to you if you don't dead this minute."

The officers revive the other woman. Ma Laja couldn't stay to warn she. Couldn't warn she if she tried anyhow.

Then the officer look more closely at the woman and say, "Do you see this? On her left leg? The hair looks like...it looks like fur."

The woman eye open. She took a breath. The first in she new life. And she knew exactly what she had become.

Red Scorpion
by Deborah Elizabeth Whaley

Red Scorpion shines
in its orange-red coat
but when the sun hits its shell
it looks as blonde as the desert sand
its shell grays and cracks with age
but don't be fooled
it is as deadly
and dangerous
as ever

It is cunning by nature
nocturnal
as it claws its way through the elements
ogling and immobilizing
its colorful, honorable prey

You see:

Red Scorpions are a smart species
the most clever among all the arachnids
it fights when it feels cornered
or when it feels threatened
even if for no reason
at all

It will hit you with its poisonous sting
killing you in the dead of night
and when no one is looking
it disappears into the desert sand
never to be seen again
and this is all a part
of its beautiful plan

Born Again
by RaShell R. Smith-Spears

Jane felt the young man's adrenaline running through him like rapids in a river. She inhaled deeply, never tiring of the smell of fear in humans. Sweetly pungent, it ran through his blood and out of his skin in fat drops of sweat and tears. The night's darkness had swallowed Jane, the man, and every glimmer of light and sound when suddenly the quick-fire snare of BBD's *Poison* dotted the air. *Never trust a big butt and a smile.* Two stark yellow beams chased the music and struck Jane's face. Grinning at the appropriateness of the song, she used the fleeing light to bear her fangs and stir more terror in the man's body. She laughed to watch the fear stretch his eyes and mouth, even his nostrils, into a grotesque portrait of dying humanity. She sniffed. Priceless. He had wet himself.

"Shall I get on with it?"

He shook his head, slinging tears and snot.

She laughed again and slowly, like a cat, licked the side of his face. Then, without warning, she lunged for his throat.

His skin tasted salty. His blood, however, was like sweet nectar. Young, fresh, untainted. Mmm . . . virgins were rare these days. She had considered seducing him, giving him a hint of pleasure before she killed him, but decided she didn't feel like it. Why should she do anything for him?

Besides, she had been more than sexually satisfied earlier in the evening by a very fine brother whose girlfriend was in the next room, completely oblivious to Jane's presence. She snuck in his window while he napped, fucked him, and mesmerized him to believe he was dreaming. She laughed at how she was really taking vampire clichés to the limit: seductive, mesmerizing, frightening, evil.

Licking her lips while simultaneously dropping this man's lifeless body, she sighed. With the high of the chase over, she crashed into the monotony of it all. After 142 years, it was the same thing, night after night. The humans were always the same; the game never changed. She lured them, they gave her chase, she overcame them, she drank from them, and they died or lived, forgetting her.

Jane patted her glossy black, finger-waved hair. She knew the style brought out her strong cheekbones, her darkly intense eyes, and her bold nose. Feeling seductively invincible, she stepped over the body into a puddle of water. It splashed onto the hem of the black leather pants that matched her red leather bustier. It was all cliché.

Coming out of the alley, she remembered the excitement when she was first turned: the intoxicating rush of p ower, the undeniable sexiness of her movement, the regenerative sense of purpose and belonging, the invigorating ability to right wrongs. She had been a slave and killing her master in a vampire-led slave revolt, she had taken control of her own life. She couldn't have dreamed the years that followed. She enjoyed turning women to empower them during the suffrage movement of the early 1900s. She had found pleasure in helping black farmers retrieve stolen land during the 1940s. But there was so much injustice. As soon as one field of hatred and oppression was burned, another crop came into harvest. It never ended and Jane grew tired. Soon, the people became casualties to the causes and Jane lost sight of them.

For now, Jane's physical appetites were fully satisfied, so she sauntered down the street toward her apartment. She passed darkened stores and closed office buildings, but came to an abrupt stop. Although the lights on it were out, Jane was a little surprised to recognize the car she passed as the one that had provided the headlights during her dinner. The man inside the Impala smelled unappetizing; his blood reeked of alcohol and his skin stank like sweaty feet. The hair on the back of her neck rose, however, as she wondered why he was sitting in the car, alone, with no lights on.

Was he stalking *her*? What an interesting twist that would be. She continued to walk past the car without slowing down. His car door unlocked, the click loud in her ear. It was just as loud as the rubbing of metal against metal as his car door handle moved, allowing him to open the door.

I'm gonna kill her!

Had he uttered it or just thought it? Jane stopped walking, preparing to turn and strike. The heavy door creaked open. She felt the familiar push against her gums as her fangs dropped. His feet thudded against the gravelly street like an anvil. Jane's fists clinched. She waited, listening to him walk away from the car.

"What is wrong with you, you skank?" the man yelled.

Jane spun around fast with her arm swinging. She wobbled off balance. She heard flesh hitting flesh and smiled to think she got him, even off-centered. She righted herself in time to realize she had not hit him and the man was not talking to her. He hadn't even seen her. He was yelling at another woman, one who was splayed out on the street next to a brown paper sack, broken pieces of clear glass and two limes rolled next to Jane. The woman was whimpering.

"Jackie, I told you to make it quick. And I don't even drink Seagram's. You are good for absolutely nothing!"

"I'm sorry," the woman sobbed from behind her hands.

"I have half a mind to leave you on the street. Make you walk home."

"No, no, Carlo, please don't do that."

"Get your fat ass in this car!" He reached down and yanked the woman up. He squeezed her arm and pushed her toward the car.

Jane retracted her fangs, but ran to them. "Let her go! You're hurting her."

"She can take it." He laughed. "Wait, who the hell are you?"

Leave. The woman's unspoken shout vibrated in Jane's head. She realized this was the first thing she heard from the woman's thoughts. Without really trying, she had been hearing the man's jumbled drunken thoughts the entire time, but the woman's thoughts were a void. Until she told Jane to leave.

"We don't know you. Get on out of here before somebody gets hurt." He sneered at her.

"Please, Miss, just leave. We don't want any trouble. I'm okay," the woman whimpered.

"You heard her! Now get out of here, you big-faced freak!" Jane could feel her gums tearing.

"Carlo, no! Please, Miss. He won't hurt me. Just leave," the woman begged.

"I will fuck you up!" Carlo threatened, but it wasn't clear to whom he was talking.

Jane didn't care. She grabbed him by the collar and lifted him three inches off the ground. Now staring at him eye-to-eye, she was about to bear her fangs when she felt the woman grab her by the elbow.

"Please, please, stop. Don't hurt him. He doesn't mean it. He's drunk."

Jane looked back at the woman, tears staining her smooth, round walnut-colored face. Her hazel eyes shimmered with fear and sadness. She looked at Carlo whose dark eyes also contained fear. Jane was aroused by it, wanted it to go on, but the woman's whimpering voice nagged at her. She dropped Carlo on his butt and kicked him.

"You're crazy! Both of you skanks are crazy! Get out of here.

I don't want nothing to do with neither one of you!" He was scooting back on the street toward his car door.

The two women watched as he stumbled into the car and drove off in reverse.

"Where are you going?" Jane called after the woman who had started walking away. "Do you need some help? Do you want to go to a shelter?" Jane started to follow her. She wasn't sure why she cared.

The woman stopped and looked at Jane incredulously.

"No. And I don't need your help. I just need to call Carlo and beg him to come back. Thanks to you."

"What? I just stopped him from beating your ass. You could be a little grateful."

"I didn't need your help. If you hadn't jumped in, Carlo would have put me in the car, then made me drive because he thinks I hate it, and everyone would have gotten home safely.

Now, somebody might get hurt." She started walking again, each step an angry stomp.

Anger, regret and disbelief swirled in Jane's head. It was easier to look out for her safety and her pleasure alone.

"But you probably don't care if somebody gets hurt. Your kind never does."

"My kind?" Jane asked.

"Yeah. I know what you are. I saw it in your eyes when you grabbed Carlo. You get off on people's pain and fear."

Jane shook her head, confused and hardly able to deny the pleasure his pain and fear brought her. "I . . . no. . . well, he deserved it."

"You don't know anything about what he deserves. And the man in the alley? He deserved it, too?"

"How do you know about the man in the alley?" She raised her eyebrow, intrigued.

"I saw you. When we drove by."

Jane stopped and pulled on the woman's shoulder to stop her from walking. There was no longer any fear in her face. Jane tried to hear her thoughts, but all she could sense were brief feelings of anger and sadness.

"And you're not afraid of me?"

"Being with Carlo has taught me that there are many things in this world to fear. You are not one of them."

"But I could kill you."

"I've lived through many deaths. I'm not afraid of the one you would bring. Now, please, if you want to help me, leave. I'm going to call Carlo and I don't want you to be here when he comes back." They had stopped in front of a pay phone. She pulled a few quarters out of her jeans pocket and stared at Jane expectantly before turning toward the phone.

"Okay. I'll leave — if you're sure?" Jane was confused by this woman.

"I'm sure."

Jane left. Normally, she dismissed women who insisted on being abused by their husbands and boyfriends. She had little patience for women who walked in weakness, and kept company with victimization when they clearly did not have to. But this one didn't seem weak. Although she took shit from him, she clearly wasn't afraid of Carlo and even though she knew what Jane was— had seen her feeding even—she had absolutely no fear of Jane.

And then, Jane could hear her voice so clearly in her mind, yet it was obviously only when she wanted to be heard. How could a simple human do that? Something was different about her, yet so familiar. Who was this woman?

Two weeks later, Jane could not stop thinking about the woman. She searched for her, but when each dawn chased her home frustrated, she gave up. Jane was surprised when two nights later, Jackie was pacing near her apartment building.

"How long have you been like this? A vampire?" Jackie's tone held no judgment, only curiosity.

"Lifetimes."

"Don't you feel . . . I mean, it's wrong. The evil you do. . . ." She wavered between confidence and uncertainty. "God loves you. He does, but your lifestyle displeases Him."

At first, Jane pulled up, prepared to do battle, but sensing the woman's hesitation, simply said, "Evil? Walk with me and I'll tell you about evil."

Jackie nodded. The two women walked together as Jane talked about her life in the 1800s.

"The things you must have seen. I can't even imagine . . . ." "You don't want to imagine. Some things should not be seen or imagined."

They walked in silence for a moment, passing trees and houses, eventually cars and stone retail buildings.

Jane decided to pull at the thread that had been bothering her. "I don't know why you are so attached to that bastard, Carlo. He's not worth it."

"I have my reasons." "Whatever. Let's go in here."

They stood in front of a small diner, a squat building with a dark green awning. Inside, the lights were low and the patrons were few.

"You're hungry for roast beef and potatoes?" Jackie smirked.

"No, but I thought you might be." Jane sneered.

They walked to a table in the back and sat quietly until they ordered and received cups of coffee.

Jackie broke the silence by finally asking Jane's name. After Jane's muttered response, the uncomfortable silence waved between them until Jane asked, "So, are you going to tell me your reasons?"

"No." Jackie stirred the coffee with a spoon, the clink of the metal hitting the cup's porcelain loud against their ears.

Jane grew frustrated and angry. Her cold skin pricked with stinging hot needles. She took deep breaths to stop her eyes from glowing gold.

"I was not a pathetic puppy," Jackie growled back. Her body looked as if it were about to lunge across the table at Jane. Then, just as suddenly, she fell back, deflated and defeated. "I . . . I need to know something."

"What?

"How do you live like this?"

"I don't need to be judged by you. I'm sorry I ever met you." Jane stood up, her eyes now glowing. Soon her fangs would drop.

She brushed Jackie's shoulder as she walked by her. Without warning, Jackie reached out and grabbed her wrist. She loosened it when Jane stopped walking, but she didn't let go.

"Wait. I wasn't judging you. I need to know because . . . I am . . . like . . . you." She whispered every word.

"I knew it." Jane stomped in place. "There would be times when . . . but you were just so . . . I. Knew. It." Like a flood, revelation rushed through her. The thing she had recognized in Jackie was that thing she saw in herself.

"Keep your voice down."

"These people aren't paying attention to us. But I knew it." "Sit down. Please?"

Jane sat down, her wide grin revealing the hint of fang that had dropped in the rush of anger-turned-excitement. Vindication tingled her skin. "When did it happen?"

"When did it happen for you?"

"Fine. Quid pro quo?"

Jackie nodded.

Without embellishment, Jane told her the story of her turn and the nights leading up to the slave rebellion. She watched Jackie's usually unreadable face lettered with admiration, horror, fear, and pleasure.

"But how could you kill another human being like that?"

Jane tilted her head, tamping down the anger always beneath the surface whenever *Master* Perry floated to the top of her thoughts.

"When I was about 15, I met a boy named Ennis. He lived on another plantation, but he was hired out to Master Perry's place. He had the most infectious laugh, and I fell in love with him the moment I heard it." She paused and smiled. Thinking of Ennis in those first days always made her feel human again. "After a while, we wanted to get married. His master was allowing him to use some of the money he earned to buy his freedom. He was going to work on buying my freedom, too.

"When I asked Perry for permission to marry him, well someone must have told him our plan because he refused us. Said he wouldn't have some half-free issue nigger putting ideas in his gals' heads about freedom. I was a hot head. I got angry and mumbled that he couldn't stop us from being married in God's eyes. Perry didn't want to hear nothing about God's eyes or any of his slaves thinking God would do anything for us that *he* didn't want to do. So, he smiled — it was an evil smile that ran down my body like a salamander — and he told me I could go, but I wouldn't be getting married. I left, glad that I didn't get punished for my insubordination, but worried. I couldn't read letters then, but I could read that man like a newspaper. He wasn't finished with me.

"A week went by. Ennis and I married in the spirit if not in the law. Of course, it was all very quiet on a Sunday. Old Hez, the preacherman, stopped preaching early and the few of us who knew walked down to the river. I wore my ma's wooden bracelet. Ennis, Ennis was beautiful." Jane stopped talking as she pictured the boy she had loved. His face came to her now as clearly as it had when they shared their first kiss as man and wife. She could see his narrow brown eyes that disappeared in a twinkle of blackness when he spread his full lips into a smile or into that beautiful laugh. She saw his strong, wide nose and his solid jawline. She could even see his brown skin, the color of wheat blowing free in a field. She almost reached out to touch it, but drew back when she remembered that many generations and just as many hurts separated them.

"It was a nice ceremony." She nodded, acknowledging Jackie's presence. "That night was the first time we ever made love. My ma and sister stayed with Old Hez's sister so we could have some privacy. I was nervous and he was nervous, but it was good. Sweet. And just as we drifted off to sleep, *he* bust through the door!"

"Who?" Jackie's face froze in suspenseful horror.

The left side of Jane's lips curled up revealing her extended fang. "Perry. He found out what we did and came down to let us know his word was the law. He glared down at me like he was trying to burn me with his eyes. I was naked, we both were, and Ennis tried to cover me with his body. That seemed to make Perry even madder. It happened faster than I could stop it. He grabbed Ennis by the neck, punched him in the face and threw him to the side of the cabin. Then he jumped at me, knocked me flat on my back, yanked down his trousers and . . . ." With closed eyes and tears coursing down her ebony cheeks, Jane continued through clamped teeth, "And rammed his thing inside of me. It hurt like hell, but not nearly as much as the dread I felt when I saw Ennis come to, stand up and try to pull him off of me. I was strong; I could handle it. I would have taken it all night if I could have stopped what happened next."

"What? What happened next?" Tears freely overflowed the rims of Jackie's eyes. She had reached across the table for Jane's hand when Jane started crying, and now she was caressing it with her thumb.

With more anger than sorrow, Jane looked beyond Jackie into the void of the past and told her, "Perry knocked Ennis back down. He got back up and they fought. I really think Ennis was trying to kill Perry. I was so scared. He was gonna get himself killed. There was no way he could win this. If he did kill Perry, they would find him and probably torture him before they killed him. And if he lost the fight, Perry would still have no mercy on him. But I loved Ennis, and I was desperate to help him. I lunged for Perry—I was going to pull him off of my husband, but he knocked me down hard against the ground. It stunned me. I couldn't move; I couldn't think straight. When I came out of it, I saw Perry grab Ennis around the neck, choking him and forcing him to his knees. In the struggle, he pulled out a knife and jabbed it into Ennis's back. He pushed Ennis down onto his stomach and then . . . and then . . . he, he took his manhood. It was like he had knocked me against my head again. I couldn't move. I couldn't scream. I couldn't even turn away. All I could do was cry. I couldn't see Ennis's face, but I feared I would never hear that beautiful laugh again. Perry showed me *his* face, though. While he was rutting against my man's backside like a pig, he turned to me and smiled, making me feel slimy and unclean. After he finished, he stood up, kicked Ennis between his legs and spat on me. He didn't even bother to close his trousers, just let his tiny pink dick hang out like a first prize ribbon. He looked at me and said, "You all belong to me. You don't get married if I say you don't." And then he left. I still loved Ennis, but he could never look me in the eye after that. I didn't think any less of him, but I guess he did. I mean, how do you come back from that?" Jane shook her head, still looking into the void of the past.

Jackie had taken Jane's hand and placed its palm sympathetically against her cheek.

Suddenly, Jane's focus shot back to the present. "So, you ask me how could I kill him, another human being? I just remembered that evil smile and realized he wasn't a human being."

The two women stared at each other, neither saying a word. The muted noise of people having dinner and unfettered conversation behind them seemed out of place in the world of hurt they were suddenly inhabiting.

The air was too thick, Jackie's gaze too sharp. The walls shrank toward Jane. She needed to get out into the open arms of the night. She jumped up and ran out, almost knocking over an empty table. She groaned aloud as she felt Jackie's presence immediately beside her. She couldn't believe she allowed that much emotion erupt in front of a woman who barely even revealed she was a vampire.

"What's wrong? What are you doing?" Jackie asked.

Jane refused to look at her, knowing her eyes held an oppressive weight of sympathy.

"I'm going home." She started walking, at a normal pace at first, but then she ran, almost flying. She tried to speed away from the memories of loving and the ghosts of ancient hurts that weren't dead after all.

"Stop!" Jackie grabbed her hand and brought her to a halt in front of her apartment.

Jane sighed and walked slowly into her apartment. Jackie was right behind her.

"I can't pretend to understand the horror you lived through."

Jackie's gentle voice caressed Jane's spirit. "I have judged you without knowing your story and that was wrong. I'm sorry. Can you forgive me?" She bit her bottom lip.

Jane was suddenly empty, but she knew feeding would not replenish her. She needed something else, something holding a grudge against Jackie would not replenish. She opened her arms to embrace her. Jackie fell into them with relief.

As the two stood quietly holding each other, it began so slowly they hardly knew it was happening. Like the quiet, but instinctive way that day slips into night, with the horizon softly kissing the bottom of the sun, Jane pulled Jackie closer to her body. Standing nine inches above Jackie's five feet, she had to bend to touch her lips. It was a hesitant kiss, unlike Jane completely, who was used to taking whatever she wanted. This time she wanted to give if Jackie would let her. Jackie did.

Jane entwined her fingers in Jackie's raven hair. Each feather-soft strand ran across her skin whispering secrets of Jackie's longing as well as Jane's own. Jane smiled against Jackie's caramel flesh, pulling it lightly with her front teeth, careful not to score it with her fangs. She wanted to push Jackie to her breaking point without taking her over the edge too fast; when Jackie did go over, she wanted to fall right with her.

But she could feel Jackie's hesitation. Jackie wanted this; they both knew it. She wanted it so badly she trembled. Jane wanted her to know it was okay to let go, to allow herself to be overcome with the pleasure of this moment.

With a slight nudge, she pushed Jackie down onto the couch. Removing Jackie's clothes and appreciating her nude torso, Jane intuitively knew that this was a creature that had been neglected for too long. She could tell by the tremble of her lips with each kiss Jane blew across her neck; the quiet moans that rumbled low in her body with the slightest touch; and the fevered way her hands shook when she reached up to caress Jane's face. She needed to know she was appreciated, wanted; Jane wanted to show her.

The more Jane kissed her, the more she hungered for her. They had moved past want; Jane needed to feel every inch of Jackie against her tongue, inside of her mouth. Without a second thought, she pulled the ebony orbs of Jackie's breasts into her mouth and suckled them.

Jane nipped the skin on the inside of Jackie's breast and licked the dark red blood that trickled down like a stream of raindrops. As she sucked and healed the wound, inhaling Jackie's cotton soft scent, she ran her hand down her torso, igniting warming spots of pleasure that she quickly cooled with kisses. Her hand, hot with its own need, popped the button of Jackie's loose black pants and slid into them.

Jane stood up and yanked down Jackie's pants, revealing the natural womanhood that pulsed with Jackie's need. Jane inhaled, grateful for heightened senses. The smell of Jackie's desire was intense, mesmerizing. Jane was immediately under its spell and could not have turned from it if she wanted to. She dropped to her knees and smothered her face and her will with Jackie's wetness.

The more she felt the tender flesh against her wet tongue, the wetter she felt herself become. The louder Jackie's moans grew, the more her own ache throbbed. She had never felt her arousal grow without ever being touched and simply because she was arousing someone else. She was connected to Jackie, her pleasure becoming Jane's own pleasure. Wave after wave of pleasure slammed against the dam of their resistance, threatening to overrun the wall or break it all together. Jackie's eyes were closed, her back arching as she hastened their carnal rapture with each thrust of her hips. Grabbing her fleshy buttocks, Jane squeezed them and pulled Jackie forward deeper into her mouth. They both were rocking. It was time. They were going over the wall with the tide of the pleasure and they could not stop it. It was building. It was strong. It was good. It was so good.

Oh God! It was a unified thought.

Jane plunged her fangs into Jackie's thigh and a tributary of blood rushed out to meet the thick river that flowed between Jackie's legs. Jane didn't stop licking until Jackie, who lay quietly shivering, was only wet from her tongue.

Jane stood up and pulled Jackie off the couch onto the floor into the cover of her arms and the two slept in sated bliss.

A sliver of moonlight fell through the parted curtains, waking Jane just as Jackie jumped off the floor in one fluid motion.

Jackie screamed.

"What the hell?" Jane sat up.

"Hell! I am going to Hell! Oh, my God! What have I done? Jackie snatched her pants from the floor and yanked them on.

"What are you talking about?"

"I let you seduce me. It's just like before. What is wrong with me?" She searched briefly for her bra that lay across the back of the couch. She jerked it on.

"What is wrong with you? What are you talking about, before?" Jackie shook her head wildly. "Oh, God." She snatched her blouse from under Jane and pulled it together.

Some of the buttons had popped off so it only closed at the top and at the bottom. She kept pulling the middle closed although there were no buttons.

Jane stood up and grabbed Jackie by her arms.

"Calm down, Jackie. There was nothing wrong in what we just did. Actually, it was the most beautiful experience I've had with anyone in a while." She tried to touch Jackie's cheek.

Disgust crept across Jackie's frantic face and curled her lip. The tip of a fang showed.

"You would think there was nothing wrong with it. But have you forgotten that I am married? And not gay?"

"Gay? That's so beyond what we are, isn't it? What we just shared was —"

"Wrong. I got to get out of here." "Jackie, wait."

She did not wait, however. Before Jane could stop her, Jackie was gone.

"Quid pro quo," Jane said the next night as she stood on the threshold of Jackie's doorstep.

"What are you doing here?" It was a stage whisper. Jackie pulled her cardigan tighter around her as her furtive glance seemed to take in everybody out on the street at dusk: there were a man rinsing his car, a group of young guys who smelled of marijuana, smoked and in bags, and a patrol car with officers watching the young guys.

"Why are you whispering? I just saw Carlo leave."

"What are you doing here?" Jackie asked at a normal volume. "Quid pro quo. You owe me a story." Jane pushed her way into the house, pushing Jackie aside with her body.

"And an explanation of what that was last night."

"I just had to go. That wasn't me."

"Really?" Jane grinned slyly. "You can do body possessions, too?"

"You know what I mean." She lowered her voice. "I'm not gay."

"Jackie." Jane sat in the oversized black leather arm chair that she assumed was Carlo's favorite seat. It smelled so strongly of him, she could taste alcohol and ass on the back of her tongue. "You don't know who you are."

Jackie stood in front of her, looking nervous as if she wanted her to get out of the chair. "I know I'm a child of God. I know I'm Carlo's wife."

"You don't know who you are. You walk around pretending not to be a vampire, ordering coffee and carrying a purse. What are you carrying a purse for? Do you need your Mentos to cover the smell of blood on your breath?"

"How dare you!"

Sliding to the edge of the chair, but refusing to get up, Jane went on. "Jackie, baby, you can only go out at night. You can read people's thoughts. You. Drink. Blood. If that's not a vampire, I don't know what is. And you say you're not gay, that I seduced you? No, baby, for the first time in a long time, I did not have to use my power of seduction. And if you hadn't told me with your thoughts — *with your thoughts* — your body was speaking loud and clear. You wanted me just as much as I wanted you. "

Jackie's eyes glowed a hot amber and baring her fangs, she hissed.

"That's right, sister, let the vampire out. But I'm not the one you want to turn it on; use that on your bastard of a husband."

Jackie's face collapsed. Her fangs retreated and her eyes became a dark hazel.

Jane's voice was tender when she spoke. "I don't understand. You have the power to stop him. Why do you let him hurt you?"

Plopping down on the matching couch in front of Jane, Jackie looked defeated.

"Quid pro quo," Jackie murmured. "I grew up in a very strict Baptist household in South Carolina. No boys, no R & B music, no make-up. My parents raised me to love the Lord and hate evil. Which I did. I do. But we all have our weaknesses. When I first met Carlo, I was sixteen and he was twenty-five. He was so handsome and smart and righteous. He was a member of the Black Panthers, you know." Pride glowed in Jackie's amber eyes. "He was strong and dangerous. I knew I wasn't supposed to be with him, but I couldn't help it. He was just so fine and proud. I had never met anyone like him. Well, one night I snuck out of the house to be with him and we . . . well, we sinned." She hung her head, her last words coming out as a whisper.

"What? Did you rob someone? Kill somebody?" Jane asked. "No. We had sex."

"What? Sex? God gave you those genitals, didn't He?"

"To be used in marriage. But I'm not going to argue with you. I know what he and I did — I did — and I know that God punished me for it."

"How?"

"I got pregnant." She stopped and rubbed her hand over her soft belly. "Carlo was just as scared as I was. He had a job, but we couldn't afford a baby. Plus, there was no way I was telling my parents. So, I did the worst thing I could ever do. I killed my own child."

Jane wasn't shocked by Jackie's admission although Jackie

88

seemed to expect it. She seemed to be looking for disapproval and judgment. Confusion played across Jackie's face in soft lines and arrested her words so that she stumbled them out.

"It was the worst thing I have ever done. And it is the cross I bear. After the uh. . . after I did it, my parents found out about me and Carlo. They threw me out. Carlo and I got married, and we really were happy. It was a blessing that we did not deserve. Since we didn't, I was determined to do everything right. I wanted to be the perfect wife. His clothes were always washed; his dinner was always ready when he got home; his house was always clean; I never complained when he wanted to go out with his friends. But when the time was right, the only thing I couldn't do was have his baby. We tried for two years, but it never happened again. The doctors told me that the man who performed my uh, who took my baby, messed me up and too much scar tissue had formed for me to ever get pregnant again." Jackie started to cry. "At first, Carlo was sympathetic and understanding. But after he watched more and more of his friends have sons to carry on their names, he started drinking. And coming home later. And hitting me.

"I missed us so much. I wanted to feel happy and special like I did in the beginning. I guess that's why I even listened to that man in the first place."

"What man?" Jane asked.

"The one that I . . . had drinks with." Her voice dropped to a whisper at the end.

"What's shameful about having drinks?" Jane grew annoyed by Jackie's religiosity and prudishness. Carlo was an ass; she deserved to enjoy life and if that meant having drinks with someone who didn't see her as a punching bag, so be it.

"I ran into him on my way home from the store one night. He was charming. I was intrigued by his accent — Jamaican. And he was fine. He talked me into meeting him again the next night. We met for two weeks, when he suggested we have drinks. I was so thrilled to be wanted again, to be seen, I didn't even notice that I was the only one drinking. Afterward, I knew what would happen. Carlo hadn't touched me like a woman in months, and he was always drunk anyway. This man had the softest hands. His lips moved like flower petals against my neck. I barely even felt his teeth puncture my skin."

"You mean?"

"Yes, the only other time that I willingly sinned against God, committing adultery in my marriage, I became this, this evil monster." Tears flowed freely down Jackie's face, shimmering like crystals against a background of silken tan. Her amber eyes glowed even brighter from the unshed drops.

Jane hesitated but finally reached out and pulled her into an embrace. They sat quietly in each other's arms, Jackie's whispered sobs the only sound in the room.

I'm sorry. It was barely even a thought, more of a feeling. She felt it with each gentle shake of Jackie's shoulders. This was not an easy life and to have to live it alone, with such regret and self-hatred made it even harder. She perhaps would not have chosen this life for Jackie — she wasn't sure Jackie could handle it — but had she been granted the choice herself, in spite of the loneliness and the fear of others, for the power to do what she did, to avenge the wrongs done to her and to Ennis, she would choose this life every time. But this woman, this scared, confused and exasperating woman, would never have chosen this life. As she soothingly stroked Jackie's shuddering back, Jane felt something turning inside of her; it pulled at her and tethered her to the woman she was touching. It was unsettling in its newness.

"You're not a monster," Jane cooed.

"I'm evil." She shook her head on Jane's shoulder. "I'm evil."

"You're not evil." Jane was emphatic. "We are what we are,

but it is not evil. I have lived a long time, and I've seen real evil, remember? People who hate because others do not fit within their idea of normal are evil. People who would hunt and hurt those who are different are evil. People who subjugate those they perceive to be weaker, in the name of their perversion of righteousness, they are evil. You look nothing like evil."

Jackie sat up and looked hard at Jane, her eyes searching. She wanted something, needed something, but Jane still could not read her mind. Giving up, Jane grabbed Jackie's chin between her manicured hands and pulled her hard to her own face. Although the moment was tender, the kiss was anything but. It was needy, full, and passionate. And, Jane noticed, it was returned.

"What the fu—"

Carlo stood in the open doorway. His face alternated between outrage, confusion, and curiosity.

"Carlo!" Jackie jerked out of Jane's embrace.

Advancing toward them with his arm poised to strike, Carlo yelled. "You're just a sneaky little whore."

"Hit her, and I will kill you." Jane jumped up in front of Jackie. "I should have knocked your big ass down when I first met you. And you," he turned back to Jackie, "if I knew you liked girls, I would have killed you a long time ago."

"Jackie, I'm sorry but I'm gonna have to put this man out of my misery." Jane's fangs were about to drop.

"No! Carlo is my husband. I'll deal with this." She walked over toward him.

"Deal with it?" Carlo laughed. "What the hell are you gonna do?"

"Let's talk this out, Carlo." Jackie was placating, and it annoyed Jane. She placed a hand on his arm. "It's not what you think."

"My wife is kissing another woman. What else could it be?" Jackie started to cry. "I'm sorry," she whimpered.

"Stop all that blubbering. The sight of you makes me sick." He shook her hand off and sneered at her, then Jane.

Everything was quiet, except for the sound of Jackie's sobs. They wore on Jane's nerves. How could this woman cry because of this idiot when she had the power to make him cry? He was the one who should be prostrate on the floor, begging for mercy and forgiveness. Annoyance and rage made her hands shake. She glared at Carlo, feeling the anger pool inside of her. Before she could stop it, her fangs ripped through her gums and she hissed.

"What the hell!" Carlo yelled and whipped a Glock 19 from his back waistband. He aimed at Jane and fired three times. One hit her in the shoulder, one broke a window and the other lodged in the wall next to the window.

Slowed by the sudden pain of the bullet, but enraged by his attempt to kill her, Jane lunged at Carlo, aiming for his jugular.

"No!" Jackie rammed into Jane and knocked her down. "I said I would deal with it."

Just as a stunned Carlo aimed again at Jane on the ground, Jackie struck forward like a cobra and sunk her teeth deep into the light brown flesh of Carlo's neck, instantly painting it garnet red.

His eyes bulged and his body convulsed as in a sweet agony, then it went limp and fell to the ground. Jackie, blood smearing the lower half of her face, stood frozen over his body.

"Jackie? Jackie, are you all right?" Jane jumped up from the ground.

"I've never killed anyone before." Her voice was distant, disconnected.

"You had no choice. He was going to kill us both." "I can't believe it."

Running footsteps scraping rocks and asphalt sounded outside. "We've got to get out of here, Jackie. The police heard the shot.

They're coming in."

"He was my husband for seventeen years."

"We've got to go, Jackie. Jail is no place for a vampire who will live for an eternity."

"Now he's just — gone."

"Go, Jackie. Go out the back. I'll stay and clean up."

Jackie stared at Jane, and for the first time, seemed to understand.

"I'll meet you at the café."

Jackie nodded and with one last look at Carlo's body, seemed to fly through the house and out the back.

It was a sloppy bite — the holes were torn, jagged, and still bleeding because she hadn't sealed the wound — but it was her first time. However, all they needed was something suspicious like a bite wound to bring unneeded scrutiny Jackie's way. Jane wasn't sure if anyone had seen her enter the house, although it was likely, but they certainly knew Jackie was at home.

She would be blamed for this, scrutinized, and torn apart.

The police, the media, the public—they were all vultures, predators ready to siphon a person's soul. Jackie, in her naivety, was neither prepared for nor deserving of that.

Jane picked up a pillow and placed it over the bite wound. She then picked up Carlo's gun and aimed in that direction. It was with great satisfaction that she blew two holes in the side of his neck and shoulder. She smiled, having scratched an itch that had bothered her for some time now.

Just as she wiped her prints off the gun, she heard footsteps stop in the door.

"Drop the gun and hold your hands up. Step away from the body," a gruff voice barked. It belonged to a slightly built black man in blue.

Jane looked up, the scent of alcohol swirling in Carlo's rapidly flowing blood intoxicating her just a little. It made her somewhat reckless as she thought of her options. She could rush the policeman and kill him, but maybe still be caught by his partner who was moving around to the back door left open by a long gone Jackie. She could mesmerize them both and just leave, but with Carlo dead and Jackie missing, that still put the focus back on Jackie. She could surrender and let the chips fall where they may.

She had lived her life, longer than she cared to and Jackie was just starting to live, had just gotten free of her enslaver. Jane could handle this, longed for it, she was surprised to realize. Invigoration cascaded through her like rushing tides and she felt that old hunger again: something, someone to fight for. She was a survivor, but she was a fighter, too, she thought as she slowly bent down and placed the gun on the floor. Nothing cliché about that.

94

Thirsty For Love
by Vocab

A vampire can't come inside until he is invited. So you are saying, I can't blame you, Lost Boy. You crossed over the threshold, and stole blood from the nape of my neck. Pecked hollowing holes and kept sucking me dry to the bitter end. I couldn't even call you boyfriend. You never did like titles, preferring ambiguous charades. Had me concealed in a coffin, hiding from sun rays, and the clarity that comes with luminous light. We could only be seen together in the cloak of night. I still fight to slay the demons you leave behind. Bats sway suspended, lining my cave of a soul. I have no crucifix or garlic, so, feeble minded, I fold. Hold tight to my holy water, though, hoping to cleanse the places you defiled. If only I had seen your ferocious fangs the first time you smiled. I mean, I was always taught to beware of wolves dressed like sheep. So on full moons, I would count silver bullets to fall asleep. I guess in our case, denial is the counterpart of deception. I should have recognized the clues and drew the connection; between the blood at the scene, and the stake you vehemently drove through my heart. Ironically, you also played the part of Van Helsing as if my bounty was a vendetta… inventing new weapons so that I could be slain. Then you departed as quickly as you came. But I would rather call you, Count Dracula, Baby, then call you by your real name. I am so shamed by the fang marks impetuously imprinted in my skin. Still, the seducing scent of sanguineous attraction is a curse that draws me back in. I now thirst for blood, from the primal hunting games, you taught me so well. I am doomed to roam the earth alone, but it feels like a torrid and tortured hell. So I am a shell of skin...where a woman used to be. My tale will be immortalized for centuries to come, but will you remember me?! Yes, I pale from my lack of iron coupled with emotional anemia. I despise my deficiency!! It's you who drew true blood and tasted the essence of who I used to be. The moon is calling. I need to drink. My body is weak from craving crimson in imminent urgency. These feelings curdle inside of me. My desire is bloody, Baby, bittersweet. I am a vampire, and I need to drink. It seems I am just as lost as the boy who found me, and left me starving, thirsty for love.

How to Speak to the Bogeyman
by Carole McDonnell

On the 17th of August, as he sat in his study eating vegetable soup with his girlfriend, Kayvon got a frightening call from his friend Michael.

Michael, of course, should not be calling. And Kayvon would've thought the call some kind of prank if he had not recognized his friend's voice. His friend's terrified voice. For Michael was indeed terrified, his voice so full of fear that Kayvon's first instinct was to attempt to comfort him. If he could get a word in edgewise. But although Michael was whispering, begging, pleading for help — words streaming out of his mouth a mile a minute — his desperation wasn't allowing Kayvon to speak.

"Kayvon!" he begged in a desperate whisper. "Kayvon! I know you can get me outta here. I know you can get me outta here."

He was almost crying. But people did not cry where Michael was. Could not cry.

"Michael?" Kayvon dropped his soup bowl onto his pillow. It was the first and only time fear would make Kayvon drop anything from his hands. His hands trembled, as did his voice as he repeated Michael's name. "Michael?" he asked again, his voice a whisper. All this prompted his girlfriend Sheilah to frown and to prepare to go into bitch mode. She had been experimenting on that recipe all day.

"Kayvon Jackson!" Sheilah shouted. "I just washed that pillow today. For heaven's sakes! Don't you know how to hold a bowl?"

"Kayvon! I got away." There was elation in Michael's voice, the kind of desperate elation that anticipated triumph…if help could arrive in time. "I managed to escape them. The one who was guarding me turned his back for a while. And the others weren't paying any attention to me. So, I managed to get away. They're slicing up Jiman and gutting him, Kayvon! Slicing him up! Oh, my God! Oh, my God! But I got away. You gotta tell me how to get out of here."

"Kayvon!" Sheilah shouted again.

But when Kayvon glanced up at her, the look of terror on his face, made her stop in mid-rant. Sheilah stared into her husband's ashen face, realizing perhaps this was not the time to discuss not appreciating her cooking. "What's the matter?" she asked, matching her tone to his horrified one. "Someone die? Michael? Someone in an accident?"

"It's Michael," Kayvon managed to say, his voice a questioning incredulous whisper.

"Michael who?" Sheilah sat beside him on the bed, wringing her hands.

"Tell me how to get out of here, Kayvon!" Michael shouted again.

Kayvon had known Michael since they were kids. Michael had gone down the wrong path. Drugging. Whoring. Pimping. But compared to the other guys on the block, he wasn't — hadn't — been so bad. Funny thing was, although they had stopped hanging out together, Michael had worshiped Kayvon and always came to him whenever he was in trouble. But this wasn't the kind of trouble anyone could get Michael out of. Michael was dead after all. Kayvon had been to his funeral the day before.

"It's Michael," Kayvon told Sheilah. "My friend who died?" Sheilah arced an eyebrow, looked at Kayvon as if he was nuts.

She rolled her eyes. "Seriously! The..."

But again she stopped in mid-rant. Kayvon looked dead serious. "He's calling you from beyond the grave?" she asked. "I've heard of. . .but what's he saying?"

"He. . ." Kayvon began.

But just then a blood-curdling scream came out of Michael's mouth.

"They're here! They found me! Kayvon! No! No! You can't drag me back! Get away from me! Don't touch me! Don't touch me! You can't. Nooo! Kayvon!"

And then the connection closed. Like that.

Kayvon sat like a stone beside his soup-strewn pillow. What had just happened? Sweat poured down his face and down his armpits along his stiff suddenly-numbed fingers and hands. He was silent and for about ten minutes, he could not think. He could only feel sorrow and pity and grief for a friend who had been desperate for help, who had called out to him, and whom he had not been able to help. He burst into tears.

Sheilah sat beside him in worried silence. After a long heart-breaking sob from Kayvon, she said, "That was really Michael?"

Kayvon nodded.

"He called from the other side?" Kayvon nodded.

His wife didn't immediately answer. Then at last she said, "I've heard about this kinda stuff. That sometimes people who have just died will call folks over the telephone. Was that it? Hey, maybe it's possible. Is that why you're shaking like that? Or did he call to give you some warning? Oh, no! Oh, my God, is one of our family members gonna die?"

She was getting herself worked up, as she always did whenever she anticipated disaster. "I think Michael called me from hell," Kayvon said.

"Hell?" Sheilah said. And a new kind of worried look came on her face. "Why do you think it was hell?"

Kayvon buried his face into his hands and shook his head repeatedly. "Oh, my God! Oh, my God! Oh, my God! This just can't be true! Is there. . . really a hell?"

All night he could not sleep. He cried and prayed to Jesus, although he had not prayed since he was in his teens. He wept for Michael that night as he had not wept for him at his funeral. He kept seeing Michael being dragged away to his own gutting or torturing for eternity. He could not get the horrible images out of his mind.

Terror is like that. Worry for our fellow man, especially if that friend is in a desperate state, is like that. So throughout the night, Kayvon's mind worked on the situation. Michael had called. Michael had been in some kind of torture. Michael had called his only "good" friend for help and Kayvon had not been able to help.

But how had Michael called him? Surely, there was no telephone in hell.

But perhaps. . . *Perhaps Michael so desperately wanted to call, and even in hell he'd created a means of communication.* Was it possible that even in hell people had desire and the ability to create? Even if it was only the desire to be free from torture. Torture. What kind of torture?

Perhaps the kind of torture that demons dream up. Demons had nothing else to do with their time, and they had more power than their fellow prisoners. Of course, torture was the demons' only joy. Slicing up and gutting Jiman. Oh, my God! Jiman had died six years before. Jiman hadn't been so bad either.

By the time morning arrived, he was awash with guilt and feelings of uselessness. Why had he not thought of telling his friend to call on Jesus? Perhaps death wasn't Michael's last chance to get to heaven. Why had Kayvon's mind been so clouded with the finality of hell that he couldn't think of a way out for his friend? He should've asked. Even just asking. After all, why had God allowed the communication if nothing resulted from it?

So, along with the feelings of uselessness was the matter of communication and portals. He rose from his bed pondering portals. Portals between here and there, then and now, past and present and future, spiritual and physical — and the fences that kept them closed off from each other.

Now there is always an outworking of spiritual encounters. When one's eye is open to some revelation of spiritual reality — especially if it happens in a particularly dramatic or painful manner — there is an aftermath. For Kayvon, it was an obsession with portals.

The obsession began subtly. First, he began to find it impossible to look into mirrors. This was understandable enough. What are mirrors if not reflections and images of the world behind him, a kind of unseen past? Then the notion of the unseen past subsumed into the idea that the mirror itself was a portal. The particulars of how that came about was not something Kayvon could readily understand but he began to understand that mirrors, being a different kind of seeing—could reflect not only the past behind him but unseen things that perhaps lingered at his side.

So he began to fear he would look into a mirror and see ghosts – particularly ghosts of doomed souls — standing behind him as he took his morning shave.

After that came the fear of closets. He began to understand that the telephone was a symbolic element that could bring about true communication and connection between the two realms. If one reckoned phones as portals, then wasn't it logical that a spirit could use any cupboard or closet door to enter his home. All this was truer than the natural facts of the physical realm; they were a higher truth revealed from a higher realm. The tangible facts of daily experience gave way to mightier, more spiritual, more divine facts.

He began to worry about the closets in his children's rooms.

Was it not possible that demons could enter into their rooms through those closets? But what could Kayvon do about that? The house needed closets. Sheilah was a shopping fiend. But as easily as the fear came, its soothing counterpart came. Did not the Bible say God's word was powerful and faith was "the substance of things hoped for"? And was not the substance an action? The substantiating of things hoped for? How could he substantiate a fence on that portal? How could he close it? By simply believing he had power to close it. By simply telling his children how to close portals.

So when his daughter, Violet, had a vision of demons under her bed and the boogeyman coming in through her closet, he told her she had the power to substantiate a fence against it. He armed her with Psalms 91 and other psalms of protection and the closet fear closed in on itself, conquered.

It goes without saying that minor mirrors were also considered by Kayvon's spiritual imagination: television, computers, radios were also portals. Through these portals came spirits. False or true. But more likely to be false. For God's word alone held truth. Was not Christ The Way? The One Way? The True Door? The perfect portal? Were not these spiritual promises nothing more or less than spiritual facts? Facts to which the lesser facts of demons and wrongly-opened portals would have to yield?

Over time, he even developed the skill of seeing the portals people carried around inside them and could perceive with his spiritual sense the emotional, spiritual, and physical portals in human bodies. Thus, he became well-known in the little churches of his region as an exorcist and as a man highly-skilled in removing ghosts, demons, and other unwanted spiritual phenomena from people, animals, places, and things. And because of his experience with Michael, he managed to keep his soul pure because he had no desire to end up in hell. Nor did he wish anyone else to end up in that terrifying place. And this is perhaps why Kayvon was so passionate in his battles against demons: he always remembered his friend's post-death telephone call.

So, instead of keeping his knowledge to himself, he gave countless seminars to churches and paranormal societies on the efficacy of Christ's blood and name in casting out spirits. These seminars were invariably entitled "How to Speak to the Boogeyman." And often, after studying under Kayvon's tutelage, many would return to him rejoicing about their freedom from the bondage and terror of evil spirits. It must be said that there were a few who attended Kayvon's seminars who were not successful against demons, sprites, ghosts, and poltergeists. Invariably, they were people who either refused to give up a cherished object (for instance, a piece of Mummy cloth bought in Egypt, an Hawaiian or Mexican artifact or some other item whose preciousness they valued more than their very lives) or those who simply refused to use the name of Jesus Christ to expel the demon. For although there are exorcists in many lands, those shamans, priests, and witch- doctors are accustomed to pleading and bribing spirits or even sending the spirits into the bodies and houses of their enemies.

Some, it is true, trusted only in the power of human authority to cast out unfleshed beings. But even they often failed because they either would not accept the lordship of Jesus Christ over all things or they could not quite believe in the power of the great gospel.

Around this time, a child named Ethan Chen was brought to Kayvon's attention. The little boy had been silent and sullen for quite sometime, and seemed unwilling to tell his parents his fear. At last, the child was taken to a psychologist, an Iranian-American by the name of Saladin. Something in the kindly eyes of the therapist made the child take courage and tell the adult all of his fears. This is how the child explained the situation. He would lay in his bedroom, his head covered under the Mickey Mouse blankets, hoping she would not come. But she always did. At least two nights a week. She, it turned out, was a headless female torso who would materialize in his room. Ethan's bedroom door would clamp shut under his shaking hands. His fingers would go clammy and inside his Spiderman slippers, his little hammer-toed feet would grow

cold. He would shout and plead and beg the looming specter
to not hurt him, to just leave, leave, please, please! She would call
to him, laughing. And that was damn strange because she had no
mouth, at least no physical one his little kid eyes could see. When
she spoke, her voice grated, like fingernails against a blackboard,
and it sounded muffled as if it came from behind some thick
invisible wall. Which Ethan figured was understandable because,
after all, she had no mouth. And, as providence would have it, it
turned out the psychologist believed in spiritual matters. Djinns, evil
spirits, ghosts, and all such matters. But he, as a Moslem, would not,
could not, in anyway invoke the name of Jesus as Lord.

Saladin, therefore, passed the matter to Kayvon, for they had
met at a conference on the paranormal earlier that year.

Dr. Saladin ventured to bring the entire family together to battle
the entity. But when he and Ethan tried to explain all this to the
child's mother, it was all to no avail. Ethan tried to explain how the
room would go cold when the spirit entered. And he followed his
mother around when bedtime came, telling her repeatedly that a
naked female spirit without a head lived in the walls and came to
visit him at nights and could his mother please sleep in his room
with him, or maybe could he sleep in hers, especially since now his
daddy had run off. He told his mother, "when she comes into the
room, the room smells like dead people."

His mother stroked his bowl-cut hair and responded, "Son,
how do you know how dead people smell?"

He answered, "I just know."

His mother, who was a nominal Korean Christian who had
fled all things supernatural as a reaction from her family's history

of shamans, merely responded, "That psychotherapist is feeding your fear by allowing your imagination to run away with you. I'm glad you feel free to tell us all your fears, but my son, none of this is real." She told the psychotherapist that if he didn't desist in nurturing the child's fear, she would have his license revoked. Thus, the psychotherapist was removed from the case but not before he had given the child Kayvon's telephone number. The child, at first, did not call Kayvon because they had not been properly introduced. So the torment continued.

One day, the child's mother asked if he wanted to switch rooms with his sister, Ruth. Such a question only showed how much she disbelieved him. He thought of Ruthie alone in that room and what the spirit would do to her. He decided he didn't want Ruthie to be hurt. "I'll stay in my room," he said. He said this although he was sure the spirit would kill him but he was prepared to fight her. He fought her a long while. Needless to say, he figured it best to not even mention that the spirit tried to force sex on him.

At some point, although his mother had balked at the idea of bringing the entire extended family together, Ethan told his Uncle Li all about his peculiar problem. His uncle who believed in such matters, said it was a demon, and that such things were common.

This uncle therefore tried to persuade Ethan's mother to take him to a Shinto priest. But Uncle Li was also a drunk and Ethan's mother thought her brother was a man whose mind was filled with grandiose ideas born from drink. She blamed the uncle for filling Ethan's head with superstitious old stories and added that he was probably the one who had planted the thought in Ethan's mind in the first place. Uncle Li attempted to battle the spirit by himself, using candles, talismans, and charms he had bought from Chinatown. But, as often happens when one dabbles into spiritual matters that are too large and complicated, Uncle Li only infuriated the spirit. A week after his imperfect attempt at exorcism, Uncle Li died. Suddenly and strangely. He also left a note among his sparse belongings telling his sister that he knew the spirit was going to kill him. Although Ethan had been pondering telling his grandmother about the spirit, he decided against it because he loved his grandmother and did not want her to suffer a similar fate.

Ethan got to reading the Bible and visiting the local shrines whenever the family went to the city to Chinatown. He took to buying Catholic candles at the supermarket and burning them on rocks in the woods near their upstate New York home. He'd buy talismans from a friend of his who knew shamans in the city. He stopped complaining about the spirit. His mother noticed his new-found peace and said it was good he was well again, and that he could study the spirituality of other cultures if he didn't go overboard. His older brother, Arnold, said he was just a silly kid turning to religion because his dad had deserted the family for his sleazy co-worker and because he watched too many news programs.

Ethan listened to them, tried to mull over their words, and sort through what was happening in his room at nights. He read about generational curses. He read about haunted houses. He read about psychosis, mental illness, and depression. But nothing helped and after a while it just seemed to him that neither Buddha nor the Christian God were strong enough to help him. He began to believe the entire thing was his karma. Yet, he kept wondering why such a bad thing, such a weird thing, should happen to him.

And all that time the Beloved, as the spirit called herself, kept attempting to seduce him. At night she would appear suddenly in his room and tell him laughingly to lift the covers, to not be afraid of him, that she was there to protect him and love him. The silky smoothness of her ice-cold breasts, the rawness of the moist place between her legs (even though she smelled like garbage and a dead dog he once found in the woods) — they seduced. After a while, he gave in to her. What joy she brought him! What shame too!

Terrified at first at the sudden venture into sexuality, he grew to like the wild force of her sex, grew to love her. But she was headless, mouthless, lifeless.

He was no more than eight years when the visitation began, about ten when he began to give in to her. That was about the time he began to realize that goodness was all a crock. Or at least that goodness had little power. Heck, his dad wouldn't have dumped his mom if the world so was good and if God had any control.

But still, he did feel that he was a bit abnormal. He knew that love between a spirit and a human could never be permanent. One day, he told the Beloved so.

She answered him, "One day, you will touch my human flesh, hear my human voice, and enjoy my human body."

"How will I know you?" he asked. After all, the Beloved had no head.

"You will find me," she answered. "Seek me. Love many women. Seek and you will find me."

And that's what he did. He dated many women, of all colors, but none of them thrilled his body as much as the Beloved did. There was always something lacking. He told this to the Beloved when she visited him. "I searched," he pleaded, "and none of these women give me the pleasure that you do. Their bodies aren't as cold as yours. They don't look like you. They don't smell like death."

"You will have to search for me in other places," she said. "Climb windows, enter locked houses. Find me. I will live in one of those women. Find me, and pleasure me."

And that's what he began doing. He was eighteen when he raped the first girl. But even then, the pleasure was nothing compared to what the Beloved gave him. He didn't like to see the girl lying there under him, crying. The Beloved told him that guilt prevented him from enjoying himself, that he should cast guilt aside. The Beloved had spoken the truth. After the fifth rape, he began to allow pleasure to flow into his body. The pleasure helped to push the guilt away. When he pushed himself into the women, he felt the Beloved's joy working inside him.

About this time, he found a slip of paper on which a telephone number was written. Not knowing to whom the number belonged, he called it.

"Hello?" he said, awkwardly. "Who is this? I found the number in my bag."

"Ah, you found my number?" Kayvon asked. "I did!" Ethan stuttered. "But who are you?" "Who are you?" Kayvon asked.

"I'm Ethan."

Kayvon thought for a moment. He had a gut feeling, and he always trusted his gut. "Are you, perhaps, being tormented by a demon?" Kayvon asked.

Ethan was amazed. Someone had just read his mind. Perhaps there was a God. Perhaps something was more powerful than good after all. "I am! I am!" he said, delighted.

"And do you want me to rid you of it?" Kayvon asked.

Ethan thought for several seconds. The exhilaration he always felt when the spirit lay with him. The future she promised…he could not give it up. No, no, he could not. So he said to Kayvon,

"No, it's okay. I'm okay."

Kayvon was disappointed, but added, "Shall I tell you how to get rid of the Bogeyman anyway?"

Was the Beloved the Boogeyman? Ethan thought. But surely not. The Beloved was a bringer of joy and power. She made him feel special. From what Ethan had heard of the Boogeyman, the Boogeyman only terrified little kids.

"I used to be afraid of it," Ethan said. "But not anymore. I don't need to know."

Kayvon's ultra-aware gut suddenly began acting up. The flesh of his skin went all goose-pimply. He pondered commanding the spirit to leave this reticent boy immediately. But then checked himself. If the spirit left the boy, and the boy remained empty of any knowledge of God, wouldn't the spirit return with seven more worst?

"Just let me visit you," Kayvon pleaded. "We can. . ." But as he spoke, the boy quickly hung up.

All that night Kayvon was plagued with nightmares. His sleep was riddled with visions of headless women and of souls suddenly snatched from life and worst, most of them, being tossed into hell. "How awful, how awful," he woke up screaming. Grief and weeping assailed him! For it was one thing for someone evil to roam the earth. But how much worse for a decent but unsaved person to be suddenly murdered, suddenly slain, then thrown into hell without hope of salvation from tormenting demons. That encounter with Ethan was one of the only losses in Kayvon's many battles against evil portals.

Now, sitting on his bed in Attica, Ethan no longer felt or even understood the terror that used to make his little boy body tremble.

He did not like being in jail though. The Beloved had been faithful throughout all his ten years of murdering and raping. She always protected him. Even when he murdered those two little four year old girls in the park. The Beloved had told him to, and he understood the expedience of it. There was little about the Beloved's commands that he never understood. She was always right. Hadn't she told him to decapitate several of the women he had raped? To make them in her image? Hadn't he done that? And those women's bodies had never been found. If only he had listened and had avoided the woman in the mall, the woman who turned out to be the mother of his son. If he had done as the Beloved had ordered, he would not have ended up in jail.

He lay in his cell remembering his trial and thinking. How strange it had been to hear the court officers, the prosecutors, and the cops call him a rapist! Surely a rapist wouldn't kneel between the legs of a woman to pleasure her! How could the judge not understand that he was searching for his truest love? Detective Ramsey had even called him a sick puppy. Stupid woman! When he got released, he wouldn't immediately kill her though. That was just the kind of thing the cops would expect of him. He'd bide his time. Besides there were more important things to do. He still had to find his son. The Beloved wanted that. And he had to find the Beloved also. The true physical living representation of the Beloved who had loved him all those years when he was a boy. The Beloved with a head, a mouth, human flesh. He would search for her again. As long as it took ... and he would find her.

As for Kayvon, when the trial was depicted on the true crime channel, he had been one of the few viewers who believed Ethan's testimony of a demonic Beloved who came through his closet. The others thought it was some silly made-up insanity defense. But Kayvon knew better. Kayvon continued to save many souls from demons throughout most of his life. And often, as he saw an entity fleeing back through whatever portal it came, he would think, "Perhaps, perhaps, God will use what I've done as Michael's own redeeming work. Maybe I will see Michael in heaven one day. Who knows? Maybe he's there already."

Sweet Jesus in the Corner
by Tenea D. Johnson

Names
stick in her craw.
As she tries to digest
the regret of years living what life no one else wanted:
scrubbing, struggling, scrabbling work
until there was nothing good but
two blissful mornings spent picking flowers,
when no remembered that they needed her to do
what they were capable of & on that last day, in the corner of
her room
Sweet Jesus saying it's time to let that go, dandelion, & off she
floats: seed, precious weed.

The Monster
by Crystal Connor

With every breath she took she inhaled fire. Both of her feet were swollen, cut, and bleeding; pain exploded from her feet to her jaw with each step. Her hands, arms, and face were scratched and cut. The pain in her side was so intense, she might as well have been pierced by the Spear of Destiny. The trees blocked out the light of the moon; it was so dark she couldn't see the tips of her fingers on her outstretched arms. She'd just returned home from the war and was in excellent physical condition; otherwise, she would have been caught two miles ago. She kept running. She ran faster.

#

After only four days of what was supposed to be a two-week visit, Maleka Davidson was leaving Alabama. Maleka hated this place. She was disgusted by the opulence of poverty. The stifling heat reduced her to the sin of sloth. Her head hurt from trying to decipher these coded Southern sayings. Just last night, she figured out that the word Bard meant borrowed, Southern translation for the state of Georgia was Jawjuh, and that she was from the Nawth as in, and I quote,

"Ya' people from up Nawth sure do talk funny."

It was almost as if she needed an English-to-Southern-United-States dictionary.

Maleka was tired of eating fried food and drinking either grape or red Kool-Aid made with three cups of sugar, despite the directions clearly stating that only one cup was needed. She was especially terrified of all the large and strange bugs that could star in their own horror movies. Maleka took a break from packing; even the slightest of physical activities made her sweat profusely. She lay on the bed and smiled about the conversation she had had with her uncle this morning at breakfast, revolving around the apparently sacred origins of grits.

"Maleka, y'all eat grits up Nawth?" Bryannah asked.

"Of course we do," Maleka explained to her 12-year-old cousin. "There are quite a few farms within driving distance of Seattle that grow corn, but that ..." Bryannah looked puzzled and Uncle Emmit angrily interjected before Maleka could continue.

"Ain't nothing as good as grits can be made from corn!

Dontcha read yo' bible?" "My bible?"

"Exodus 16:15. What poured down upon hims chirren when they was roamin' roun' in dem woods was grits. It says so right in da Bible, '*It's the food the LORD has given you to eat.*'

"So the manna that God rained on the Israelites on Mount Sinai was really grits?" Maleka asked slowly.

"Ain't is what I said?"

Why not? Maleka had spent the last year fighting in the streets of a foreign country because someone had misinterpreted the holy writings of an ancient text, so why should it be any different right here at home?

Using her toast as a spoon, Maleka took another bite of the buttery, salted grits and smiled. It was no wonder her uncle had mistaken them for ambrosia. Uncle Emmit went on to explain that after the miracle on Mount Sinai, there was no mention of grits for another 1,000 years.

Experts, he explained, found evidence that grits were only used during secret religious ceremonies – and were kept away from the public due to their rarity.

The next mention of grits, he continued, "Was found in all dem ashes over there in Pompell in a famous woman's diary."

"Do you mean the ruins of Pompeii? What famous woman?" Maleka inquired.

"Herculaneum Jemimaneus." "Who?"

"Girl, you just as slow as molasses running downhill in January. Aunt Jemima." Laughter erupted from the breakfast table.

And if it wasn't Uncle Emmit's wild stories that re-invented history, it was her auntie Tammy's constant complaint of how nothing made sense.

"Look at this damn blue bird sitting his ass upon that Goddamned tree branch! Look at him; that's a damn shame. It just don't make no damn sense!" No one offered that birds were supposed to be in trees; everyone just chuckled and shook their heads, and Maleka did the same.

Maleka was going to miss them but she just couldn't stay in the South. She was mortified that her extended family members, and their neighbors and friends seemed to perpetuate the negative stereotypes of blacks in the South. In her family's defense, the whites down here didn't seem much better. With their UFOs, swamp monsters, unfounded fear of the government, pickup trucks, and Confederate battle flags, Maleka couldn't help but hear that banjo song from the movie Deliverance every time she listened to them talk.

The woman who lived across the street from her grandmother's house always dragged a broom behind her wherever she left the house, even if it was only to check the mail. When Maleka asked her great-grand-aunt why she did that, she was told, "Cuz she dohn wants deze fixuhs tuh git her foot track." Maleka knew what fixuhs were before she had a chance to unpack. Fixuhs were evil spirits, and apparently, they were everywhere. The first night Maleka stayed in her grandmother's house, she noticed a broom upside down by her bedroom door. When she took the broom into the kitchen to put it away, pandemonium broke out.

Her cousin Maybell explained that the broom was placed outside her door to protect her from the hags, and this protection was necessary because she had seen a hag with her own two eyes. Maleka thought if she drank as much as her cousin did, she would probably see things too. Not only were there hags but also there were signs, omens, dreams, mojo rings, witches, wearing a dime around your ankle, charms, talismans, myths and swamp monsters. Maleka's sleep was unrestful, and during the day, she was jumpy and on edge.

"You all packed and ready to go?"

Maleka jumped nearly five feet off the bed at the sound of Leticia's voice, and her cousin laughed until tears rained down her beautiful ebony face.

"Girl," Leticia said as soon as she caught her breath. "You is just as nervous as a long-tailed cat in a room full o' rocking chairs."

"I must have dozed off; I didn't hear you come in," Maleka said through her smile. "Yeah, I'm almost done."

Leticia sat on the bed next to Maleka and pushed herself back until she was resting against the wall. Maleka did the same.

"You really can't stay no longer?"

"Ticia, it's so hot down here, I can barely think. Hey, why don't you come up to Seattle? Once I get home and settled, I can buy you a plane ticket. You can stay as long as you like. I think you'll like it. It's really pretty, there's lots of water, and its cool."

"Girl, I ain't never been on no airplane before."

Maleka could hear the fear in her cousin's voice. The two were the same age, 28, but her cousin had never traveled outside of her county.

"So? There's a first time for everything. You can catch the Greyhound … I know! What about Amtrak? That'll be cool … to ride the train across the country; I can even get you your own private cabin!"

"I don't know."

"Well, just think about it. OK?" "I will."

Both girls looked toward the door as their grandmother walked through it. Fat Mike was behind her, carrying a large Styrofoam cooler that looked heavy, even for him. Her grandmother had packed a feast that would have fed an army for a month.

The cooler was filled with fried-pork-chop sandwiches with mayo and hot sauce, buttermilk fried chicken, scuppernongs, Maypops, onion-and-tomato sandwiches, potato salad and macaroni salad, cracklings and half a dozen banana moon pies.

"Grandma, this is too much food. I'll be home in just a few days."

Maleka really wasn't protesting, because her grandmother had packed all of her favorite food, even if it was more than she could eat in just a few days.

Fat Mike went to load her car, and her grandmother sat on the edge of the rickety bed and touched Maleka's face before she started talking.

"Now don't you go wandering too far off de road, don't let darkness catch ya' and stay out dem woods at all cost. If you hear a chain rattlin' on de tree, you best be movin' along, cuz it might be a plat-eye."

Great, Maleka thought. *Just what I need, another Southern monster.* She had no idea what a plat-eye was, and she wasn't going to ask. She didn't want to know. All she wanted was to be back in the Great Pacific Northwest where all she had to worry about was good old-fashion ghosts, Bigfoot, and the occasional serial killer.

Her grandmother handed Maleka a small burlap sack tied closed with a piece of twine. "Keep this witchya at all times, no matter what happens."

Maleka took the little bag with trembling hands. She didn't want to take this with her; she didn't even want to touch it. This was what she wanted to get away from in the first place. Maleka dropped the amulet of protection into her handbag and gave her grandmother a big hug and kissed her goodbye.

#

On a winding road that seemed to stretch on forever, Maleka saw a filling station that hadn't been updated in the last 100 years.

She even heard the cheerful "ding-ding" as she pulled up to the pump. The breeze in the wake of a passing semi felt good against her sticky skin. She was grateful for the cooler temperatures chasing the submerging rays of the sunset.

Maleka bought two bags of ice, a six-pack of Coke, oil, and a road map. She had GPS on her cell phone, but no signal in almost three hours. She also bought 45 dollars' worth of gas and some candy. The old man smiled at her as she dumped the stuff in front of him to ring up. Maleka returned his smile while looking away from his blue running eyes, wrinkled skin and broken teeth. As Maleka was rummaging through her purse for cash, because Visa wasn't really everywhere that she wanted to be, the charm her grandmother gave her tumbled out on to the vintage countertop.

Maleka had made it halfway back to her car before the old attendant came chasing out behind her.

"Hey, girl, wait a minute, you done left yo charm."

Maleka turned to the sound of his voice and almost ran from the man who was holding the small bag her grandmother had given her. When he extended it for her to take, she flinched away from it.

"Oh. Thank you, sir, but I don't think I need it."

The man looked at Maleka with a flash of anger and it was clear that he was personally offended by her fear of it.

"Your peoples gave this to you for good reason. You need it for protection. I reckon you a long way from home, so I suggest that you take this with you."

Maleka took a step away from the man and shook her head. "I don't think it's a good idea to mess with stuff you don't understand," she said.

"Girl, you don't have to believe but you can't afford not to listen." The man warned as he walked up to her and dropped the charm into one of her bags.

Maleka slowly turned around and walked away from him,

so shaken up she almost forgot to pump her gas. She drained her cooler, crammed in the six cans of Coke, and replaced the melted ice. She added oil to her car, opened the map, charted her course, and cursed the non-existent signal on her phone. As Maleka was placing the trash into the plastic bags, her attention was once again drawn to the charm resting at the bottom. She tossed all the trash on top of it, balled up the bags, and threw them away. As she sped away, she noticed the old man watching her leave from the window.

Maleka had been driving in the dark for almost two hours.

When she learned to drive, the freeway scared her the most, but her stepfather took her on her first night drive and she was calm and confident.

When they drove at night, there was really no need for his instructions, so he just let her drive. The night lessons were Maleka's favorite time with her stepfather. He didn't warn her about the dangers of boys, drugs and alcohol, he did not bitch at her for not doing her chores or getting just a C on her math test, or quiz her about military terminology. It was just she and Dad spending a few hours at night driving under a blanket of stars. Maleka always enjoyed driving at night; she appreciated the solitude and welcomed the memories.

She could have shot herself for tilting her head all the way back to drink the last of the Coke. She looked back at the road in time to see a deer bolt out in front of her car and freeze a few feet ahead of her. Despite everything she had been taught, Maleka slammed on the brakes and yanked her wheel heavily to the right. Her car slid off the pavement and lost traction in the gravel.

She tried to right herself but overcorrected, sending the vehicle over the yellow line. As she fought the car to avoid oncoming traffic on the two-lane stretch of road, the car returned to the correct lane before leaving the road, going into a ditch, and slamming into a tree.

"Goddamn it!"

Maleka put the car in park but left the engine running, afraid that if she turned it off, she wouldn't be able to restart it. The front of the car was damaged, but not badly enough to deploy the airbags. She rubbed her head, unhooked her seat belt, and snatched her cell phone off the floor in front of the seat next to her.

No service.

"Fuck!" Maleka threw the phone back on the floor with such force that it bounced up and landed on the passenger seat. She pounded on the steering wheel and looked into the rearview mirror.

The deer was still standing in the middle of the road. It turned its head to look behind them before returning its gaze to the car. The deer raised its head to the sky, and Maleka watched the antlers of the large animal retract back into its head.

That's not what you saw; you hit your head pretty hard, and your vision is blurry. That isn't what you just saw.

Maleka watched the deer stand on its hind legs and take the form of a man.

He started to walk slowly toward the car.

Don't let darkness catch ya and stay out dem woods at all cost.

Maleka moved the rear view mirror so that she could watch the man approaching as she reached beneath the seat for her gun. Without taking her eyes off of him in the rearview mirror, Maleka put her car in reverse and then back in drive and back again until she gently rocked her car out of the ditch. Only when she got the car back on the road did she take her eyes off the man.

She pulled away slowly, but as she picked up speed, the front bumper, which was being dragged beneath the car, punctured a tire. The car began to wobble before it took a nose dive to the right, the tire so damaged that she was driving on the rim. She drove another 200 feet before the car died completely.

She was on a slight decline, so she let the car coast down a bit, then steered the car off to the side of the road when she felt it losing momentum.

"FUCK!"

A quick glance in both the side and rearview mirrors did not reveal the man's whereabouts, but she knew he was still coming.

Maleka took a deep breath and let her training take over. Her mother taught her how to shoot a Smith & Wesson model 29.44 Magnum, and her Uncle Sam had given her a badge marked "expert."

The Wonder Nine Maleka held in her hands was Smith & Wesson's M&P, with a 17-round capacity, and a velocity 100 feet per second above what was advertised. Maleka had no doubt of the weapon's capability, but she couldn't shake the feeling she needed something more.

Keep this witchya at all times no matter what happens.

"Fuck."

She pulled the lever on her seat until the headrest was lying on the back seat, turned around, and pressed her back into the steering wheel, and waited for the man, deer, or whatever the hell it was that caused this accident.

Maleka reached over, opened the glove box, retrieving the four extra high-capacity magazines. She grabbed the phone off the passenger seat and shoved the clips and phone into the back pockets of her blue jeans. It wasn't long after that she saw the top of the man's head crest the hill.

"Guard me, O Lord, from the hands of the wicked; protect me from the violent ..." Maleka's prayer was interrupted by movement on the edges of her peripheral vision. She was hesitant to take her eyes off of the approaching man, but whatever was on the other side of the road was closer to her than he was.

Blurs of black and gray shapes became sharp lines, defined images ... more deer, methodically taking the shape of men.

Don't panic.

"Deliver me from those who work evil; from the bloodthirsty, save me."

As if adding an exclamation point to her prayer, she pulled the trigger, killing a beast whose metamorphosis was nearly complete.

The rear window imploded. In the rain of broken glass and shadows Maleka fired six more rounds in rapid succession, crawled to the passenger side of her car, and ran into the deep, tangled abyss of the Alabama wilderness.

Don't let darkness catch ya', and stay out dem woods at all cost.

#

The tree-lined paved road was lit by stars, but Maleka was plunged into absolute darkness once she entered the forest. Afternearly tripping and breaking her ankle, Maleka kicked off her flip-flops and immediately gained speed. It was a double- edged sword, as her tender spa-pampered feet quickly yielded to the unforgiving rough terrain of sharp rocks, jagged twigs, and tangled, knotted tree roots that carpeted the floor of the wilderness.

As she ran, she unbuckled her belt and threaded her gun through it so that she wouldn't lose it. She refastened the belt loose; the gun beat against her thigh as she ran, but she wanted to be able to maneuver her weapon freely when she needed to.

Instinctively, she stopped running. Maleka slowly, blindly, extended her hand out in front of her, and before her arm was fully outstretched, her fingertips brushed against the rough bark of a large tree. Maleka stepped closer, put her cheek against the tree, and then extended her arms outward as if to give the tree a hug.

With her arms fully extended, the tips of her stretched and exploring fingers still felt bark on both sides.

Maleka kept her right hand on the tree and used her left hand as a feeler to detect any other large objects in front of her, until the large timber that blocked her path was behind her.

Her fear heightened her sense of awareness, and her deprivation of sight sharpened her ability to hear, Maleka found it easier to just close her eyes rather than peer into the darkness. She controlled her breathing and concentrated on the muted sounds of the forest.

The terrain underfoot became soft. Instead of rocks, pinecones, and fallen branches, Maleka felt leaves, moss, and mud. She stood still, cocked her head, and listened. The absence of sound alarmed her, but she continued to walk, slowly at first, then faster until she was once again running at full tilt.

The ground was soft and soundless, but as she picked up speed, she heard branches snapping behind her to the left. Hoping to achieve the same level of strength, speed, and victory as the Greek

Goddess Nike, Maleka ran. And ran, and ran. And slammed into a low-hanging branch.

There was a flash of bright light around the edges of her vision, her feet swung out from under her, and she landed on her back. Her lower back just above her tailbone exploded in pain as it came into contact with a fallen log, and as her head bounced off the ground, Maleka bit her tongue. Running headlong into a thick branch had caused worse injuries than the car accident.

Maleka swallowed blood and listened to the sounds of the forest. Nothing. She performed a quick mental diagnostic of her body and categorized her injuries. She told herself she was fine and slowly sat up. Without warning, it started raining, not the light misty drizzle that she was accustomed to in Seattle, but a hard and heavy downpour of torrential rain of biblical proportions.

"Are you fucking kidding me?" Maleka screamed up to the heavens. "Is this your idea of a joke? Well I don't think it's funny! Didn't you hear me calling you for help?"

Maleka was standing, though she did not remember the physical act of standing up. Her hands were balled into tight fists, and she defiantly stared into the night sky and blinked away the rain.

"Give me a fucking break, answer my prayer, do something! I'm not asking you to part the sea, I need a little help. Is that asking for too much? Are you there?"

God did not answer her. She couldn't hear anything over the rain. She still couldn't see, so despite nearly having been decapitated, Maleka started running. She counted her steps as she ran. There were 2,112 military steps in one mile with a 30-inch step. Maleka's running stride was 70 inches, so she knew she had run nearly two miles since plowing into that tree.

The soft mud that had padded Maleka's footfalls was now an enemy combatant. Encouraged by the rain, the mud became thick and hostile, her feet were buried to her ankles with each step, she had to use force to wrangle her foot free, and before she knew it, she was calf deep in mud.

"This is fucking bullshit."

Maleka took a deep breath, turned around, and slowly made her way out of the deep mud. A bolt of lightning arched across the sky. In the flash of light, Maleka saw she was in a small valley. It took her almost a full minute to register what she had seen on the valley ridge.

Her pursuers had morphed themselves into one of the most feared and formidable canines on both the face of the planet.

The wolf.

Maleka now had to run from a pack of wild dogs that had the ability to run at speeds of at least 40 miles per hour and sustain those speeds for several miles at a time.

Though there was nothing remotely humorous in Maleka's situation, she started laughing.

#

Maleka bolted away from the descending predators. It took her ninety steps to reach the slight incline that marked the valley wall. Digging in with hands, forearms, knees, and feet, she scrambled up the hill. When she reached flat land, she stood up and ran. Maleka counted sixty steps before she tripped over an exposed tree root.

She reached out with her hands to break her fall, but she kept falling.

Maleka slammed to the ground on her shoulder and began to tumble, roll, and slide. Once again laughing, she received a mouthful of dirt, leaves, and, to her utter horror, a bug. She hated watching the damsel in distress trip and fall in horror movies, and yet here she was falling for the second time.

Did she see lights? Maleka slid to a stop on her face, stood up, and ran. The lights shone through the window of the cabin like a beacon promising a safe haven from this storm.

She could hear the footsteps of the dogs behind her. She thought she heard them running past her as well, and knew that they were racing ahead to cut her off and surround her.

With every breath she took, she inhaled fire. Both of her feet were swollen, cut, and bleeding. Pain exploded from her feet to her jaw with each step she took. Her hands, arms, and face were scratched and cut. The pain in her side was so intense, she might as well have been pierced by the Spear of Destiny. The trees blocked out the light of the moon. It was so dark she couldn't even see the tips of her fingers. She'd just returned home from the war and was in excellent physical condition; otherwise, she would have been caught two miles ago. She ran faster.

She was so close that the warm light glowing in the window offered enough light to see the edges of her surroundings, but she didn't look at what was moving within the shadows. She jumped over the four steps of the cabin's patio and slammed her shoulder into the door, expecting resistance, but with one turn of the knob, the door opened.

The rug slid under her feet and she almost fell ... again. As Maleka regained her balance, the only thing she saw was a pair of denim-blue eyes. It took three seconds for her vision to pan out, allowing the panoramic view of the inside of the cabin to come into focus.

The man was shirtless and tattooed. On his broad and chiseled chest was an eagle in flight, and clutched within its mighty talons was a large swastika. The man was sitting in a chair, his foot on the edge of the table, and his chair was tipped back on the two hind legs. Covering the wall he was leaning against was a large Confederate battle flag – an image that, for the majority of Black people living in the United States, is a symbol of racism. His hair might have been red or blond, but his head was shaved. He wasn't alone. Another man stood by the window, and yet another sat on a small sofa directly in front of the man she had first seen.

Maleka spun around, slammed the door closed, and engaged the deadbolt. Once the door was closed, she saw a large chair. It was as heavy, and she used all her strength to drag it to the door and position the chair under the door handle. Maleka stumbled a few steps back and turned to face the men she had locked herself inside with.

For almost five minutes, no one spoke.

She pressed her hand to the pain in her side and took a closer look at the guy by the window. He wasn't standing, as she first thought; he was sitting on top of some type of cabinet. He had a huge sucker in his mouth, and she could smell the cherry scent of the candy. He had the same denim colored eyes as the one leaning back in his chair. He wasn't completely bald, because his red hair had grown out a little. It reminded Maleka of a peach. The thought of such a juicy fruit only served to underscore the dryness of her parched throat. As if reading her mind, he tightened the cap on his bottle of water and tossed it to Maleka. She drank it down greedily. Cool water ran down the sides of her mouth as she drank until she started coughing.

Both of the man's arms from shoulder to wrist were covered in colorful, incredibly detailed tattoos, but what stood out the most were the flags. On the inside of his upper right arm, near his chest, was a tattoo of a red flag with a black swastika in the center. On the left was the American flag. The man sitting on the couch wore a Dewalt wife-beater and a ball cap that read, *The South shall rise again*. It was clear that the one leaning back in his chair and the one in the window were related, possibly brothers.

The cabin was just one big square room, the kitchen was along the wall to her left.

A large brick fireplace sat in the center of the widest wall, and there a door off to the side that Maleka guessed to be a bathroom. There were three sleeping bags rolled up in the corner along with a slew of hunting rifles.

On the wall above the couch hung pictures of Hitler standing in a moving Jeep, bikini-clad blond women displaying tools, and redheads posing with cars. There was also a poster of the University of Alabama football team running on the field. Maleka was surprised to see that poster hanging so proudly, as most of the players in the poster were black.

Finally, the guy in the window swirled his candy to one side of his mouth and asked, "So what the fuck are you running from to make you think you're safer in here with us than out there with a gun strapped to your belt?"

"A pack of wolves," Maleka answered.

"No ma'am, you might wanna try that again. We ain't got no wolves down here." The candy man explained.

"I know, but they weren't wolves at first." Maleka's thoughts were jumbled and confused.

"See, she told me to keep it with me, then I didn't think I needed it, so I threw it away," she said.

"You threw what away?"

"I really didn't think it would do any good; it's just a stupid superstition."

He slowly took the candy out of his mouth and asked again, "You threw what away?"

"The man at the gas station tried to give it back to me, but I didn't take it."

"HEY!" he shouted. "Do you hear me fucking talking to you?

I'm not going to ask you again. What did you throw away?"
"The charm," she said.

"The charm?" he echoed. "What charm, what was it for?"

Maleka noticed how his eyes lowered to the gold cross she was wearing around her neck as he asked the question.

"It was to protect me from the monster."

The man leaning in the chair slowly lowered it back to all four legs, and the one on the couch took off his ball cap and ran his hand through his thick blond hair. As his blond locks unraveled to fall against his sculpted shoulders, Maleka knew without a doubt that this man was a direct descendant of Thor.

"Travis, she's high. She's probably from California, and they say they got some good-ass weed out there."

The three of them shared a laugh as Travis put the candy back in his mouth and leaned against the window.

"I'm not high, and I'm not from California," Maleka hissed.

Travis shrugged his shoulders. "That might be so, girl, but you ain't from around here. You say you ain't high, but you done spooked yourself so bad you ain't thinking straight, and you ain't making no damn sense, so I can't tell either way." "I scared myself?" Maleka was furious.

"What you was running from is most likely coyotes."

"I know the fucking difference between a wolf and a coyote," she started, but the man in the chair interrupted her.

"Really, Big City? Because you said they weren't wolves at first, so what were they then, dingos?"

More laughter. "Fuck you!" she said.

"Fuck you too, you stupid fucking nigger cunt bitch! There ain't no fucking wolves down here.

The only dogs we have out there in our woods are the coyote and maybe … maybe a pack of strays. You was running through the woods at night. It's dark out there, and the woods has a way of playing tricks with your senses. You was just seeing things."

"Caleb's right," Travis explained. "You fucking people are all the same; you come down South and act like it's a trip to the fucking zoo. Y'all come down here so that you can laugh at us ignorant, po' white trash, redneck hillbillies, and point at the dumbass country niggers."

"Y'all watch movies like Deliverance and think we're just a bunch of inbreeds sitting down here making moonshine, playing banjos, eating fried chicken and spitting out watermelon seeds. Then the next thing you know, y'all is running through the woods in the middle of the night, shooting at shadows and running from dogs."

More laughter. Maleka started to say something, but stopped.

She turned her head toward the door. The others heard it too. Scratching. The door shook gently. Something heavy landed on the roof, and the ceiling creaked in protest under the weight of whatever was walking across it. Everyone looked up at once.

The door shook again, forcefully this time. Travis tracked the footsteps on the roof with his head, leaning farther and farther back until he was looking directly above him. There was a long deep howl lasting almost ten seconds before the others in the pack answered the call.

Everyone started moving at once. Maleka unhooked her gun from her belt and reached into her pockets for the extra clips.

Without taking his eyes off the ceiling, Travis stood, slowly turned around, and closed the interior shutters.

Caleb grabbed the hunting rifles leaning against the fireplace. The man sitting on the couch ran past Maleka to close the shutters in the kitchen in the nick of time. The glass in the kitchen window shattered, but the shutter was not breached.

"Ryan," Caleb called and tossed a rifle to the man who now stood behind Maleka. The silence that followed was deafening. With the enveloping hush, everyone looked at Maleka, who was looking at Caleb with a look that said I told you so.

Travis ran from the window to loom over her. "You fucking threw the Goddamn charm away? You just fucking threw it away?"

Travis was a foot taller than Maleka, and as he screamed down at her, she realized the candy he had had in his mouth was not cherry flavored but, in fact, strawberry.

Neither his size nor his proximity intimidated Maleka, since both were to her advantage.

Maleka had mentally established that the inside of the cabin was her zone of security, and she knew where everything was.

"Travis," Caleb warned.

"If you knew it was to keep you safe, why did you fucking throw it away?" Travis said.

She knew how many steps it would take to reach Caleb, understood that he would have to be the next one neutralized, because under no circumstances was she going back outside into unfamiliar terrain while it was dark.

Caleb called his brother again, "Travis."

"Y'all think y'all so much better than us, so sophisticated and educated," Travis said.

Maleka's breathing slowed. She was unprepared to deal with deer that changed into people and then into wolves, but fighting men was what she had been trained to do, and she had seventeen confirmed kills under her belt this year alone.

Maleka slowly slid one foot in front of the other, but kept her hands at her sides, assuming a basic battle stance. Close-quarters combat was Maleka's specialty. Because of her stealth, speed, agility, and ferocity in hand-to-hand combat, comrades in her unit started calling her "the black mamba."

Caleb walked to his brother's side and gently pulled Travis away from Maleka and protectively stood between them.

"What the fuck were you doing out in the woods at night for anyway?" Travis demanded over Caleb's shoulder.

"They crashed my car."

"Of course they fucking crashed your car! Dumbass." Travis was furious and pacing back and forth.

"I don't understand why you're so upset, Travis," Maleka

taunted. "You said I was shooting at shadows and running from dogs. Maybe we should open the door and give them some doggie treats and scratch their heads."

"Travis. There are four of us in here and enough guns for three each. We just have to maintain our zone of security until morning, and then we'll be able to offer adequate cover to reach the truck. The nearest town will be our extraction point," Maleka explained.

Travis and Caleb looked at each other in astonishment, and Maleka fought feelings of frustration.

"Extraction point?" Travis echoed. "Are you in the Army?" Something else jumped onto the roof. The door bulged in violentlyas if kicked, but the chair under the doorknob held.

"These ain't terrorists you was shooting at out there. There ain't no fucking extraction point, and in case you haven't noticed, we're surrounded. The cavalry ain't coming, and you just fucking got us all killed," said Travis.

Maleka was losing her patience with Travis. "I killed two of them on the road."

"Did you kill them, or did you just shoot them?"

The voice came from behind her. Maleka pivoted 180 degrees and took three steps back so her back was toward the door and the three men were in view full.

"You said at first they weren't wolves, so then, what were they?" Ryan said.

Whatever was on the roof was now jumping, as if trying to stomp its way through. The door was kicked again and splintered along the hinges. The front- room window shattered. The noise outside sounded like breaking tree branches, and a mixture of hyena calls and wolf howls.

Ryan burst into hysterical laughter, and Maleka decided it wasn't such a good idea to have her back to the door.

"Ok, Big-City, if you have a plan to get us all outta here alive, you might want to tell us, because that would be some pretty good fucking information to have right about now."

Before Maleka had the time to ignore Travis's hysteria, Ryan asked his question again. "What were they at first?"

Before Maleka had a chance to answer, Caleb offered his hypothesis. "So what are we dealing with here, werewolves? Well, if that's the case, we're all fucked because none of these bullets are silver."

"Can they fucking do that? The moon's not even full!" Travis said.

As Travis's question drifted slowly toward silence, all of the men turned to Maleka for the answer. She thought that she was going to collapse as the heavy weight of their situation settled upon her shoulders. As if things were not challenging enough, unlike the men in her unit, these guys were not going to do what they were told, and Travis was already becoming a problem.

Maleka's Plan A was to stay inside the cabin until daylight, but whatever monster had chased her in here, had a different idea. She was going to have to come up with a Plans B, C and a Contingency Plan, and she should have done that 20 minutes ago.

Maleka took Caleb's rifle to inspect it and was disappointed at her discovery. His weapon of choice was a Winchester Model 70. A bolt rifle.

This was the perfect weapon for a sniper – and for hunting – but the mere seconds it took to reload this gun manually would cost someone their life in a combat situation.

With a quick scan of all the weapons, she knew she would find what she was looking for.

"What's the matter?" Caleb said.

Maleka handed Caleb his gun back.

"I was really hoping for a semiautomatic, or at least a gun that could have been easily converted. Even a revolver would be nice. Are there any handguns here?"

"Semiautomatic?" Caleb asked. "I guess if you're hunting people but we came out here to hunt deer. I got a Colt .38 out in the truck."

"My state allows the use of semiautomatic for big-game hunting," Maleka explained. "And the last thing anyone is doing right now is going outside."

Travis was curious. "What's considered big-game hunting in California ... a Colombian drug lord?"

Maleka wanted nothing more than to knock Travis unconscious with the butt of his own gun, but as the best possible defense plan formulated in her mind, she knew she was going to need him.

"I'm not from California, Travis. I'm from Washington. Is there a window in the bathroom?"

"No," they all answered at once. Finally, God had answered her prayer.

Maleka opened the door to the small bathroom and asked Ryan to drag over the chair that Caleb had been sitting in. She used the chair to hold the door open, then lined the bathtub with sleeping bags.

Because Caleb was the tallest, he was the one she put in the bathtub, and he was thankful for the padding of the sleeping bags, as he would be shooting directly over Maleka's head from a kneeling position. Maleka wanted the gunfire aimed in such a way as to produce highest the concentration of fatalities. It was one thing to shoot at the heads of unsuspecting elk. It was another thing entirely to be shooting at moving targets that had the ability to change from one creature to another, and whose sole purpose was your demise. Travis's position was on the ledge of the tub, and Ryan sat on the toilet. They would surround her as she sat on the floor, and her goal was to provide them with enough automatic fire so they could reload their guns.

With the men in place, Maleka moved the two floor lamps to each side of the bathroom door and plugged them in. She directed the swivel heads of the lamps toward the cabin door. The bright lights of the 100-watt bulbs would blind anyone, or anything coming through the door and provide a safe haven of darkness behind which they could hide.

They sat in the silent dark for almost twenty minutes, and when Travis started talking, it startled everyone.

"Caleb," he said. "I think you're the coolest mother-fucking man I ever met."

The iron shutters on both windows started to rattle. Caleb cleared his throat, but when he started talking, his voice was full of emotion.

"You've always followed me. No matter where I went, I knew if I ever wanted my little brother, all I had to do was turn around and you'd be there. In all my life, this is the only time I wish you hadn't followed me."

Hearing Travis and Caleb say goodbye was more than Maleka could deal with. She had fought in four theaters in places you would never be able to find on a map, just to be killed in her own country by a fiend that should not exist.

Keep this witchya at all times no matter what happens.

There was nothing she could do about it now, and Travis had been right all along. She indeed had killed them all. This was so unfair; it was just a stupid superstition, none of this was real.

Except it was.

"I'm sorry," she said.

Maleka wasn't just apologizing to Caleb, Travis, and Ryan. She was also apologizing to her cousin Maybell who put a broom by her bedroom door to keep her safe from the terrors that lurked in the night. She was apologizing to her grandmother, who had given her a gift that was meant to keep her safe, and to the gas-station attendant who knew how important it was when he tried to give it back to her. But more importantly, Maleka was apologized to God for her earlier blasphemous display of disobedience.

With a final kick, the door broke in half, flying inwards in two pieces, and as the wind and the monsters rushed in, everyone started shooting.

last of the red hot lovers
by Amber Doe

What's the worst that can happen when he sees you naked?
What evidence will he uncover? What will he think of the milky
white roads traced along your shoulders and abdomen? Evidence
of the love before him: the last of the red hot lovers. They were
there after the first man became your only lover and source of
pleasure and they left their mark. What will you have after all of
your fears are laid bare? "I want you to touch me there....not him."
"I see now that I'm not going to be able to eat my way out of
this." Creamy sweetness and salty beef are nothing like your hands
and lips..... There is too much evidence behind closed doors, battle
scars simmer under my tee shirt. Affirmation of my linchpin after
him. Guilt, gluttony, and fleeting pleasure read like a sun scorched
map starting at my shoulders before ending their journey at my
abdomen. What would I have looked like he if had never touched
me against my will?

Taste the Taint: A Cursed Story
by Kai Leakes

Kendrick Anderson was apprehensive after hanging out with Jessica, his best friend TJ's fiancée. He looked at his watch. He had obligations and responsibilities to uphold. Time was of the essence for their plans. Everything needed to be just right. He needed to have the perfect bachelor party for TJ. But, throughout the planning, a piercing pain had started in Kendrick's left temple. With the irritating pain came a strangely sweet and metallic taste that coated his taste buds. *Was it the coffee he had earlier?* He thought to himself. The taste was intense. It mellowed while he strode through the corridors of his office. In a rush, he took to the elevators and headed down to the first floor.

That taste gave him an electric jolt. He felt God-like, and in a quiet part of his mind, he wanted more. Kendrick shook off his odd thoughts then stepped from the elevator.

"I'm tripping," he muttered to himself.

Fake smile plastered on his face, he gave a curt nod to the co-workers he passed. Kendrick was a sycophant. It served a purpose for him. Since his childhood, he had been that way. Back in St. Louis, Missouri in the Kinlock area, when he was twelve years old, his father had become sick. Kendrick ended up with the responsibility of being his father's caretaker.

It was then that he had to think of a way to be free of that burden. He gained his freedom manipulating his teachers. They believed that he needed saving after his father died of AIDS. Then his plans kicked into motion.

It worked so well that his math teacher adopted him. That white man and his wife moved Kendrick out of his decrepit ranch house. In the name of education, his new parents sent him to Chicago where he attended a top private school. After that, his life went by the book. He matriculated to Morehouse College on a scholarship. He joined the esteemed Krimson order: the brotherhood of Kappa Alpha Psi. Then he met his frat brother Troy Jackson. Kendrick learned that if he wanted something from TJ, that all he had to do was kiss the brotha's ass. So, he did.

Back then, he had the reputation for being the 'Event King'. He had been so good at crafting parties, that his party was where TJ and Jessica met. Ken had invited her. TJ wooed her, and when she ended up attacked at the party, TJ and Kendrick saved her. Since then, Jessica hero worshiped TJ because of Ken. If his best friend wanted a woman, he made it happen.

People whisked by him and he put that thought to the side. *The past was the past.* He was a people person. Being a bootlicker helped him network and relish in many lucrative benefits. He made it into Harvard because of TJ, which boosted his own endeavors. He also gained access to various avenues when TJ became a top tiered criminal lawyer back in St. Louis.

Kendrick built a profitable portfolio that currently serviced his needs in the finance world. Because of his resourcefulness as TJ's friend, he obtained a high-level position with CU Reynolds and Co.; also known as Costa, Underwood, Reynolds, Singh, Eaton, and

Daniels financing corporation. When the big heads wished to have their names mentioned. His job was to help focus the company's IPOs, and their large public and private share offerings. He was also a damn good accountant. Kendrick ardently rose up the ranks with every risk he took for the firm.

One such risk was the financing of greedy commercial and residential businesses. Kendrick would buy out or take various properties to gentrify the Chicago Southside. He made a lot of money off the blood and tears of such investment for his clients, including himself. He was ruthless and enjoyed cashing in on the loans that he urged many downtrodden folks to take with him.

"They shouldn't be so damn needy," Kendrick grumbled to himself.

He had no love for their plight because it was a waste of time and only halted his gain in making profits. When he'd heard the sob stories on the news, he would sit back and enjoy a glass of red wine. His happiness came from money and it served him well. As he strolled past various people, he watched them shuffle out of his way in terror. His mind was on his previous thoughts which had him formulating his next plan of business.

With a slick smile that ran across his handsome features, Kendrick slid a hand into the pocket of his slacks. He was a young man of twenty-eight years. His unambiguous ruggedness oftentimes was eye-catching for some, as well as the slight burn scar across his jaw that had healed in a manner that didn't seem to offend anyone. It all made him intriguing. Many assumed that he was Hispanic and something else.

He was, and that something else was African American. Kendrick relished in the confusion it brought others. Once upon a time, he used to be offended by it, but now, he didn't care. His looks helped him garner many women and aided in his rise in the company. His trysts with various corporate liaisons vouched for that.

No one trusts an ugly accountant.

Lost in thought, he smoothed a hand down his fitted black Italian grade suit. He then unclasped the front while waiting at the firm's carport. The glint of the sun shined in his eyes. He flinched and a valet appeared by his side with empty compliments.

Kendrick gave the valet one glance then turned his attention to his silver Lexus that pulled up in front of him. In his mind, he said nothing to the fool. Yet the fading reflection that displayed his actions showed him hissing at the guy. Pleasing satisfaction arose in him.

"Move! I don't care for ass-kissers, nor do I have the time for them."

The annoying valet slouched away in fear and Ken grinned.

Rumors surrounding CU Reynolds and Co. were that anyone who worked for the firm couldn't be trusted. Everyone employed were lechers who would kill before allowing an account to go foul. After his induction in the company, Kendrick had to agree.

Everyone was fearsome and he preferred it that way.

"Mr. Anderson wait." Ken heard his name, but ignored it. He was busy studying a beautiful valet with red hair who was climbing out of his car. She had stark sapphire eyes and regarded him with a seductive smirk. To him, it was clear that she wanted him. It amused him.

"Kendrick Anderson! Wait!"

An icy sliver of anger made his spine turn into steel at the aggressive shout of his name.

Red hair with café au lait skin was on display. He immediately distracted himself with a view of voluptuous curves. There was no way to disguise them from the unique beauty's valet uniform. *She'd be perfect for tonight,* he thought to himself. Lost in her sauce, he heard his name again.

"Leave me alone," he said.

Kendrick walked forward and reached into his jacket. He pulled out a black business card.

"Miss?" Sexy as sin and her attributes deserved to be admired in his opinion.

When he reached out to snake his fingers around her arm, the sound of yammering began to irritate him. His stomach clenched in angst at the buzzing near him. It became so unbearable that his gaze turned into disgust and fury. Kendrick set his narrowed eyes on the person by his side. It was the owner of the voice who kept calling out to him.

"Who are you to formally address me as if you know me, huh?" he snapped. Kendrick realized that he was looking at the previous admitting valet who had backed away from him in fear.

"Mr. Anderson?" The boy repeated for the third time.

Kendrick's intuition was typically keen. He always listened when it prickled within his stomach. Funny enough, the day he'd signed his firm's hiring paperwork, that sensation stopped. It changed into a steely awareness that pressed into his temples and caused his jaw to become sore.

The pain then transitioned into an odd need for sex, food, or subjugation. If he felt his body prickle with his intuition, he'd find a way to be in a person's face by any means necessary. Kendrick called it the ability to read a person's soul. He could latch on to a person's allure and immediately know how to deal with them.

He learned to listen to the familiar awareness in his gut, that demand to drain another person. Briskly, Kendrick turned to step closer to the admitting valet. A scowl etched across his face while he read the boy. His sepia hued eyes roamed over the young man stopping on his badge. *The boy's name was Aaron.* He took a deep breath. Kendrick smelled a light anxiousness from the boy.

Fear? No.

Aaron shifted back, putting distance between them.

Caution. Kendrick smirked as he took in Aaron's appearance.

Instantly he noticed that Aaron was no older then possibly eighteen or twenty. The boy was testing Kendrick's boundaries.

Aaron scowled. His oak-toned skin seemed to turn golden with the sun.

Ken also noticed a hidden tattoo on the side of Aaron's neck peeking from under the white collar of his uniform. It appeared to be some type of a symbol shaped like two crossed hatchets.

Interesting.

Aaron agitatedly ran a hand through his sandy brown dreadlocked fade. Kendrick enjoyed making this kid anxious. "Mr. Anderson of...CU Reynolds and Company?" Aaron asked in a constrained voice.

Kendrick rolled his shoulders. He thumbed his nose and looked around the area in annoyance. Like a viper, he attempted to wrap his hand around Aaron's neck. "If you repeat my name one more time..."

Aaron leaned back. He smoothly glided back on his feet in a move that would have impressed Muhammad Ali. The kid followed through with a harsh jab that connected to the side of his jaw. It stunned Kendrick. That crap came out of nowhere and hit him hard. *Hell, no.*

The splash and sting of liquid dripped down his face just as he was ready to body slam the kid. An intense pain burned his eyes. Kendrick then hollered like a hound and fell to his knees. He violently wiped at his face. Pieces of his almond toned flesh came away in his bloody palms. Icy burning numbness hit him with a brittle nerve tingling agony that made him screech in horror.

Who was that kid? What had he thrown on him? What was this? Acid? It couldn't be! Every inch of his exposed skin fell away in strips on the concrete walkway where he knelt. Locked between paralyzing fear and anger, he snarled then flung his hand out only coming up with air.

"What have you done to me?" Kendrick yelled.

The boy stared down at him seething in disgust. There was no reply.

Flashes of fire burned across Kendrick's vision mixing with the crowd in front of him. In the flames he saw disjointed faces. Some human, some ungodly. Creatures with various shapes and hues grinned at him in delight. Their pearly teeth descending in glee.

Other entities in that fire touched the humans in the crowd. The ghastly demons injected inky substances from their own bodies into the on-lookers. All to Kendrick's sick delight.

What was this! Where was he? He felt locked into a suffocating tightness of fire and brimstone. *No, this couldn't be reality!*

"Fuck you and remember her name! Loretta Wilson!"

Who?

"You locked my grandma into a predatory loan then took our house and our money! She died homeless because she couldn't buy her meds and had no safe shelter because of you! Fuck you, nig—" Aaron shouted at him in angst while security snatched him up.

Kendrick had no remorse for his actions. Oddlyenough, that gave him a sense of serenity from his burning nightmare.

"Kill yourself!" Aaron shouted while struggling. "You're already dead bitch! All your karma is coming to your tainted ass! On everything. We'll get you soon."

"Help me…" Kendrick almost said, but curiously didn't.

In the commotion, as he stared at Aaron and wiped at his burning eyes, he saw the boy twist out of security's hands. Aaron's brown eyes seemed to emit an unearthly golden resonance. A flash of light covered the kid, making him untouchable and then he disappeared through the crowd.

Ken writhed in pain. His vision of fire and brimstone with that of flying monsters in the sky disappeared.

"You almost had the slippery anointed bastard," he heard.

Confused, Kendrick turned his head. He ended up staring into stunning eyes glowing sapphire blue. As he stared, he felt a pain cut through him. The burning intensified then turned into pure pleasure. The icy ecstasy allowed him to slowly stand. With a grunt, he wiped sweat from his face with a handkerchief. The pain had become satisfying and once it was gone, he was upset about it. He felt healed in an odd twisted sort of manner.

"What did you say?" he asked, just to be sure that he hadn't heard things.

"Oh, I said are you okay, Mr. Anderson. The city is becoming congested with those activist punks. I'm sorry that *child* accosted you like that." It was the redheaded valet.

Her voice was sweet velvet.

Kendrick found himself smiling, while brushing off the previous attack. "He's nothing to me. Thank you for your help…"

"Yvonne. And thank you for your card." Yvonne pleasantly mentioned reminding him that he had given her his card.

"You're welcome. I've never seen you here. Is this your first day here?"

He watched the woman's plush lips part into a soft chuckle. She tilted her head to the side and gave a sensual nod. "Yes. But, I think it'll be my last."

If he had his way, it would be.

A satisfying smile spread across his face while taking in her exotic beauty. He wanted to touch her bright red hair, but he thought better of it. "Call that number Yvonne. You would be perfect for tonight's event. The pay is good and you won't have to deal with trash interloping at your place of work"

Kendrick shook his jacket with a grimace. "I'll make sure too!" she said winking.

He watched her sashay past him, then glance over her shoulder. "Tsk...children."

"Be careful of clowns like that boy. They don't have your best interest at heart," Yvonne said with a cutesy smile as she walked away.

He had to agree with that assessment. As he climbed in his car, he glanced back at the unique beauty. Her words branded themselves in his psyche. The odd scent of something light mixed with metal and urine assaulted his senses. Whatever was on him needed washing off. The blinking of his cell phone with the name '**Anarchy Elite**' on it and '**Airport**' alerted him. It was a reminder to pick up TJ, who had flown in from St. Louis, from the airport. It also told him to meet with Reina Costa and Nydia Randal at the venue for the party. They were his firm's event planners.

That boy Aaron had delayed his plans. Kendrick shook off his anger by rubbing the back of his tingling neck. That delicious pain was still there. One hand on his steering wheel, he dropped his other against his thigh and rubbed the bulge there. It made him think of Yvonne and the pain. Back to business, he had a bachelor party to kick start and specifics laid out by Jessica. She wanted to make sure that TJ had a constructive party. She, also needed reassurance that Kendrick could pull off the grandiose shindig.

A quick dial on his bluetooth and he was soon connected to Jessica. "TJ just landed, but I'm sure you know that."

"Of course. I needed to know that my man had safely landed." Jessica gave an airy chuckle.

He could hear the admiration in her tone.

"We don't need any complications do we?" she asked.

Now he had to laugh. "I thought I was the control freak Jessica. I'm on my way to pick him up after I change my attire and do a once over at the venue."

"Good. Did you get him everything he requested? I hate to have him upset over something as frivolous as a lacking venue."

The venue was an opulent two-story condo on the top of a high rise near Magnificent Mile. It had 360 clear panoramic views of downtown and the shoreline with an indoor elevator. Nothing about the venue would be lacking. He had made sure of that.

"Jess." *Damn, she could be overzealous in her devotion to his best friend.*

"Oh, my God. I'm doing again." Jessica gave an embarrassing laugh. "Just ignore me, and take care of him for me. All I want is for TJ to enjoy himself so that he can get all that mannish crap out of his system. He works so hard and he deserves this."

"Then you might want to quit having me check in with you

every hour of the day and trust in me. TJ is my boy," Kendrick replied back in a mixture of seriousness and light humor. "I'll always cater to his needs. Remember how you two met?"

A sardonic smile slowly spread across his face in memory.

Jessica's light sigh then chuckle sounded in his ear. "You never stop reminding me. Dr. Meeks class."

And the party. She always forgets to mention the party, he thought to himself. A gentle pressure in his skull made him speak up. "Yes and when he dragged you out of my party. Had he not—"

"Yes…yes…" Jessica quickly uttered. "The party." She gave an uncomfortable laugh then cleared her throat. "He's my hero. So, um, moving on. Can we just focus on you and TJ having a good time like you both always do? Just keep everything clean, and I'll see you both soon. I must hang up now. I have my own fun to have.

Bye, Kenny!"

His gums were sore again.

"Goodbye, Jess. Enjoy yourself." Kendrick definitely planned to deliver. Because if this went over well, he knew that it would be only a matter of time before the benefits flowed his way.

#

The devil was in the details. Red, black, and white. He wore a white pressed shirt, slacks and casual dress shoes. Kendrick walked around the two level condo, greeting his excited guests. Ruby lights gave the place a sultry allure. Dancers spun from silk drapes. The vast space overflowed with curves, lush backsides, and plump breasts. All the women were blond beauties with the occasional exotic mixtures in-between. It was TJ's specific taste when not focusing on Jessica who was a vivacious sepia toned beauty.

151

Seductive music played with a blend of raunchy hip-hop.

Kendrick observed naked women, dressed in skin tight attire or body paint, sway and beckon to him. *Perfection.* Just how he liked it when he partied. There was only one thing, the red head wasn't here. She had called his number as he thought she might, and said that she would be coming with a few friends. But, he didn't see her anywhere.

Disappointed, he continued his hosting. The bachelor party was on and the man of the hour appeared somewhat sick.

Good. His friend's discomfort strangely made him smile.

Not only was his friend nauseous, but TJ appeared somewhat dizzy. A light sheen of sweat lined TJ's neck. Smoke spilled from his lips. His friend held a bottle in one hand and a glass in the other dancing to the music. TJ always enjoyed being the center of attention. When TJ moved, he'd turn to steady himself and wipe a hand down his tawny face and beard. Every so often, he'd gag, then right himself with the help of a busty female.

So, his friend was sick.

But, there was pride and satisfaction on his best friend's face, and the faces of a few of their frat brothers. All over the display of naked flesh around them. Kendrick took in the scene of the party then reached out to rap his knuckles against TJ's.

"Kendrick Anderson always pulls through. You outdid yourself, my brotha," TJ said with a salute of his champagne bottle.

It was a white frosted gold bottle of *My'lce* brand Cava Rose champagne. TJ poured its pale red liquid into Kendrick's glass.

Ken inhaled the robust scent and took a drink. Odd wailing groans echoed in his ears as he drank. Glancing down, he swore the liquid had an unearthly quality to it. With a shake of his head, he gave a wry smile to his friend.

The drink hit him with a spark of fire that made him hard.

At the same time, a cold chill ran down Kendrick's spine. His shoulders felt heavy. It began to feel overly hot to the point where he was having trouble breathing.

"Told you to count on me," he said, returning his attention to TJ. "Planning parties and picking women is what I do."

"Don't I remember. Kenny, bro, I'm feeling high up in here with all this flesh before me," he said sluggishly.

As TJ danced against a flawless ebon-toned beauty, Kendrick smirked. "I deeply appreciate cha."

Both TJ and his dance partner laughed. The woman snaking against him wore nothing but a black fishnet dress with matching bra and thong. Her long hair was in micro-twisted braids that swayed against her plump ass. When Kendrick stepped back, he noticed another woman behind TJ. She wrapped her stiletto tipped fingers around TJ while she danced. The beauty was exotic and Afro-Latina. Dark golden skin was on display due to her cutaway see through dress.

Excellent. TJ was on another level and Kendrick figured that he'd want that fun to continue. Ken turned to leave; he had caught he glimpse of his redhead. "Enjoy yourself. I'll be right back."

Kendrick's manhood came alive at that moment. He cut through the crowed stopping when his feet felt sticky. Ignoring it, he reached out, "Yvonne?"

All that beautiful red hair lifted as the alluring body it rested on turned his way. Red liquid covered her body. It flowed from her scalp and connected to the floor in a pool of blood at his feet. A growing hunger rose in his stomach. He wanted to rake his tongue over every drip and suck its essence from her nipples.

"Mr. Anderson? I was looking for you." Yvonne 's dark stained lips parted into a seductive grin. Her beauty greeted him.

Kendrick blinked. *He had a job to do. This wasn't the time.*

"I was looking for you as well. I'm glad you're here." He circled her like a hawk then held out his hand. *She was perfect. Spectacular. TJ would enjoy her.* "Come with me. Let me introduce you to my friend."

They walked through the crowd of dancing people. A pit in his stomach grew and pained him. The women, all of them, stared at him as if he disgusted them. *They know your secret.*

Kendrick ignored his intuition and barked out. "TJ, it's about that time. Allow me to introduce the beautiful Yvonne."

TJ stepped his way. The brotha rubbed his beard-lined jaw, while drinking in Yvonne's frame.

"You into a little private party Yvonne?" Kendrick leaned in and whispered against Yvonne 's ear, "Come with us to the second half of the party. You won't be disappointed."

"Really?" She turned towards him with an eager smile. Her hand laid against his chest then she gave a sultry laugh. "I look forward to the fun."

An unsettling flash of light mixed with smoke drew Kendrick's attention away. This was like old times. Like back in college. The flash of a woman's body pressed against the red sheets of a bed played at his mind. Kendrick blinked it away only to lock in on the crowd before him. Faces of the various dancers in the room began to change before his eyes. His intuition whispered...*you have a plan. Move on with the plan.*

Sweat trickled down his temple. He saw long black nails coated in blood. He wanted that blood. Needed to feel those nails rake across his flesh. He had done so many foul things in his life and it all accumulated to this moment. He needed to stick to the plan. The women gestured to him. Yvonne beckoned to him and he watched her sultry features shift into a monstrosity. When she kissed his lips and pulled on his arm, his intuition whispered: *succubus.* He had a job to do and she was part of it. Glimpses of the males in the room, his old frat brothers, and it took him back. He remembered when he first introduced Jessica to her knight-in- shining armor TJ.

Kendrick had presented Jessica to TJ on a platter without her knowing. He picked her the first day he saw her in Dr. Meek's class. She was a lovely thing back then. Just the right type for TJ's law ambitions and Kendrick's career aspirations. *This was all for TJ.*

He focused on his frat brother.

A mischievous smile played at the corners of his lips. TJ was moving through the crowd in an antsy manner. Whenever the hands of the people of the crowd touched him, he'd jump. *Of course he would. They were demons and wanted to skin him alive for their pleasure.* A piercing bellow sounded in the party, causing to stop. It was so loud that it shook TJ and had him turn towards Kendrick.

"Did you hear that man?" TJ asked in brief shaking panic, hidden in machismo.

Oh, he had heard it. Kendrick raised a brow. "Hear what?" "A screeching noise, man!"

"Ah! That had to be the DJ mixing something wrong. See? The music is back. It's all good and back to normal." Kendrick anxiously laughed. "Don't trip. This all for you man."

"I know, but that was crazy. I swear I heard that same noise back at my office."

It was all coming back to him. To complete the contract he had with CU Reynolds and Co. he had to do this. It was all part of the plan. If TJ didn't hear that screeching, then Kendrick had miscalculated.

Kendrick stopped near a large elegant hallway. He whispered in Yvonne's ear to go on ahead. He turned to his friend with a dark and distant look. He hurriedly dropped his mask and gave him a reassuring smile.

"I'm sorry to hear that man. Might have been stress. You do work too hard and, you know we planned all this just to keep you relaxed, so don't trip. You need this night. Here, drink up."

TJ narrowed his eyes.

Kendrick knew that his friend was scrutinizing him. When TJ shook his head and took a swig from his bottle, Kendrick relaxed. The plan was in full motion.

"Yeah, you're right. I'm tripping. Let's see this gift of yours," TJ said, winking.

"This is just like the old days, huh?" Ken asked thumbing his nose and throwing his arm around TJ shoulders. "Yvonne is the gift man. She's yours...and there's more."

"Just how I like em'. I haven't had red in a long time." TJ laughed. "I appreciate it."

"Good. Straight ahead then." Both men headed down an elegant hallway where Yvonne disappeared. Kendrick knew that he was a dog. To move up in the world, a man had to do the most of one or the other. Be it good or bad. Kendrick had chosen bad.

Long ago, he had done something foul to get Jessica to fall for TJ. Now, that game was going on again, just to appease his best friend. But also, to abide by the rules of his firm.

In silence, Kendrick took his time going down the hallway. He watched how his boy's body language changed with the dynamics of the room. To the clueless, the hallway would feel as if it were encapsulating them. Walls would close in and narrow the further down one went. Kendrick adjusted his collar. The awareness of what he had to do assaulted him. He knew that he was to bring TJ here and that was it. They approached a dark oak double door with strange carvings.

Painted handprints revealed various imprints of bodies and faces carved on the door's surface. When Kendrick grabbed the handle, those bodies began to undulate in silent agony. Warm liquid oozed down the surface and dripped upon his hand, then feet.

Kendrick looked over his shoulder. TJ's eyes were darting back and forth in fear and confusion, and Kendrick enjoyed every bit of it.

"Are you good, TJ?"

"Of course...I'm feeling a little off man, but it'll be good once we get in this room. I know it."

"Yes, you will," Ken stated.

"*AHHHH!*" blasted around them again.

"Hey...hey...I think I had too much to drink man," TJ said stumbling back.

"Me too, but that never stopped our fun," Kendrick sneered. "Come on bro. Once we get our taste everything is going to be okay."

TJ gave him a look as if he were crazy. Kendrick inwardly laughed. It was all part of the plan.

"Listen for a moment," TJ motioned holding up his hand. "Didn't you hear that?"

Kendrick played along. Music thumped like that of a heartbeat. Both men listened intently.

"What was that?" Kendrick looked around ,startled.

The door behind him slowly opened and TJ backed up. "I don't know man, and I don't like it…"

Yvonne stood in front of them. She wore nothing but diamond jeweled waist beads that covered her bare mound.

"Gentleman? Is the party over?" she inquired softly.

Both men stared in awe then took her outstretched hands. "No."

Kendrick stepped into the room. TJ followed. The slam of the door behind them caused him to come out of his trance. *She was perfect.*

White drapery flowed everywhere. The curtains revealed a small room with their frat memorabilia on the walls. Near a large window was a bed covered in red sheets. The effects of the champagne finally kicked in and TJ stood paralyzed.

Confused, Kendrick looked around.

"Wait…what is this?" TJ asked. "Kenny! What the fuck is this? What made you do this?"

"I didn't," Kendrick said backing away.

Panic washed through him then faded into something else: his intuition. Kendrick rubbed his neck at the pain there. The plan was to throw this party and remind TJ of the good times. Not put their sins on display.

TJ stood in shock. He made sure to keep his back to the bed and Kendrick knew why. He couldn't look at what they both had covered up. He couldn't acknowledge what they did to Jessica.

When Jessica's screams of protest resonated in the room, TJ gripped his skull.

Kendrick didn't. Instead, he rushed to the door. He frantically tried to open it up. "Yvonne, what are you doing? I didn't pay you for this."

The door bit him. He remembered.

"You didn't but your bosses did," she explained with a smile. "Everything has a price, remember, Kendrick?"

She was right. The bite made him remember the board members telling him such and more. This was part of the plan. "Jessica? Come out."

"Wait? What?" TJ's eyes bulged. "Jessica is here?"

Jessica appeared naked, covered in bruises and blood. Evidence of the attack she'd suffered at TJ's hands.

"Stop!" TJ let out a rough scream.

"Remember how *badly* you wanted her, man?" Kendrick taunted. "You said Jessica fit your ambitions. All because her family was connected to the black bourgeois."

Kendrick chuckled. He loved this. "You had to make her yours and be a hero. Remember?"

"I didn't say that!" TJ yelled.

"You did." Kendrick sinisterly smiled. "But, being the friend that I am, you knew that I'd put your plan in motion and deliver Jessica to you on a platter."

TJ's hands tightened into fists. "You drugged her and brought her to my room! I didn't tell you to do none of that."

He wasn't lying. "True, but you clawed at her like an animal. I just watched. Then stopped you before you killed her. Shit. None of that extra shit was part of my plan."

"Fuck this. Jess, he's lying." TJ turned but Jessica stopped him. "Don't run, TJ. Accept your shit. I made you look like a hero when you ran back in the room. Hell, we even pinned it on one of our frat brothers. Remember? Jessica had been so drugged; she didn't know shit—"

"Not until six hours ago, when I came into the family order." Jessica reached towards TJ. Viciously, she snatched out TJ's windpipe. "You used to make me feel insane over the PTSD. But now, that all changes." Blood ran over her fingers. She licked each one sucking them clean. TJ clasped at his throat then fell to his knees.

Lovely, Kendrick thought with Yvonne's mouth at his throat.

He closed then opened his eyes revealing pitiless darkness. Kendrick had fulfilled his obligation.

Yvonne let him go.

"Didn't I tell you that I'd take care of you, man?" He said with a demonic grin. "Now you're taking care of me. Jessica's is a Reynolds, man. She's the granddaughter to my boss."

Kenny watched the life drain from his old friend. "There's shit in this world that you don't understand, but now, I get the benefits. You wanted class and status. I wanted power and all I had to do was give them my soul and yours."

Yvonne walked Kenny to Jessica, and she pushed him to kneel at her bloody feet. It was time for his promotion.

When Jessica sliced her inner thigh, then offered it, Kenny headily drank. He watched Yvonne sit on TJ's chest then snap his neck. Jagged teeth appeared then she lunged at him to feast on his heart.

"What a sweet tribute." Jessica cooed. "Now Kenny, you will become more. Open your mouth and taste me. I want that fancy conniving tongue of yours."

He watched Jessica lower her lips over his. Twin glinting incisors appeared. Jessica was no more. Before him was a vampire succubus. A demonic entity that gifted him with the kiss of her taint.

"Bottoms up," Jessica said with a forceful kiss.

TJ's death had given him the ultimate prize. Contract now sealed, delicious darkness flowed into him. He felt a jolt then Yvonne led him into a living wall to relive all the horrors of his dark acts. With her in his arms, Kendrick felt fueled by his sins. Millions of hands touched to feed on him. Kendrick's gift of manipulation would be used to break the souls of those around him and win for the Dark. All in the name of, CU Reynolds and Co.

Whispers & Lies
by Deborah Elizabeth Whaley

Whispers grow
in the soul of creatures
hiding in human form
a fine tuned utterance
a disastrous wrong
a hollow barren song
burning through a bleak atmosphere

Press your ear closer
to the African drum
and you will hear
rhythms of things
creatures hold dear
and why fire tongues
made of birch rod
invade the earth
violently nod
as they whisper loudly
dishing in the dirt:

They whisper —
to save place

They whisper —
to save grace

They whisper —
to save face

They whisper —
to kill envy of Others

They whisper —
to keep it undercover

They whisper —
to cast truth and reality asunder

They whisper —
to keep it from falling apart

They whisper —
to pretend they had good intentions from the start

They whisper —
because what they are doing is not from the heart

They whisper —
like soulless creatures
wearing pallid sheets, in the dark…

But don't you never mind
Because whispers?
they're just creature lies
they obstruct truth and transformation
holding a mirror to their eyes.

And like feathers dispersed
in the harbor sky
and like whispers,
and like lies
truth sits still
whispers grow faint
incinerate
die

Cheaters
by Tish Jackson

*You're being very difficult, Cassandra. I'm starting to think you don't want
to be healed.*

(no response)

I know you feel responsible, but—

I AM responsible!

*You can't keep blaming yourself. I understand you feel you don't deserve
forgiveness, because you feel what happened to Joe and his friend was your fault.*

It was my fault. My fault.

*But no one else blames you! Not Joe's family or friends. Not the police; you
were found not guilty by reason of insanity. And of course I don't blame you.
But I do want to help you. Don't you want my help?*

Yes, Dr. Hall. I want your help, really.

Don't you want your old job back, your old life?

I guess so…

Of course you do! You can have your life back! You only have to reach out and grab it.

#

I should have known better that last time. I mean really, it was my own fault. Technically, I brought this massive load of guilt upon myself. Although my current therapist says that I must try—really TRY—to move beyond blame. Apparently, that's the first step towards healing. As if any sane person really wants to be healed these days, anyway. Hell, you have to be half crazy to get along.

Be Healed! Like some sort of handicapped wheelchair bandit on Jerry Falwell's now defunct televangelist show. I mean honestly, what do these people do after the show anyway? Yes I'm HEALED! Thank you Jerry Falwell! Thank You Easter Bunny! Same thing, isn't it? Make believe, fantasy life? Even if it was real, and somebody was really healed on one of those shows, what would they even do with their new life? Is being healed all it's really cracked up to be? I mean let's be real here: SSI, Disability and any other form of government assistance would be instantly cut- off. With the gravy train at an end, Mom and Dad would soon be serving up an eviction notice. They'll be ecstatic at having the trailer to themselves! Now the ex-wheelchair bandit is a walking, able-bodied bandit with no place to live, no job and nowhere to go.

After spending his whole life cosseted, he's thrust out into the world with no skills, no money, and no *life*. He'll probably end up homeless on the streets begging for spare change. Only who wants to give a healthy, hearty, walking individual some of their hard earned money? Nobody, that's who! Passersby wonder 'Why can't these homeless people get a job like everyone else?' So the ex-wheelchair bandit needs a racket. So he gets another wheelchair —nothing as fine as the one he spent the last ten years in; no, this one is strictly manual without the benefit of motorized anything. He has to mentally and physically paralyze his legs all over again, in order to make a new living—a new life the only way he knows how. He ends up right back where he started, without the use of his legs—but with the added burden of hating Jerry Falwell and his parents and God with every fiber of his being. And how can you get along without God?

As I actually walk down the halls of this crazy hospital, I admit I'm not in a wheelchair—physically that is. But my therapist, Dr. Jerry Hall, does bear a striking resemblance to the televangelist, and sometimes our sessions (*sermons* can turn into an almost religious pep talk. That's how much Jerry—I mean Dr. Hall fully believes in his psychobabble. His earnest, shining pink face seems to almost beam his belief out at me, as if I can be healed! through osmosis, using the sheer force of *his* will. Which of course makes him totally blind to the truth—that everything I've said is true and it really happened. And, brings me back to my original statement— this whole debacle is entirely my fault.

#

I met Joe for the first time while I was on a temporary job at a convention in Las Vegas. For me, there was this instant attraction during our first introduction, that surprised me. I had once again sworn off men, especially after what happened the last time. Plus, Joe was not the type of guy I usually dated—he was actually nice.

I mostly like them skinny with lots of hair, and he was the exact opposite—far from skinny and just about NO hair to speak of. But he had the sweetest smile and a banging goatee, a favorite of mine. We met when I was lost as usual, and running around a corner trying to find my ballroom I ran smack into a giant chest. I bumped my nose a little bit, but it was enough to make my eyes water.

"Hey, don't cry! I'm sorry I ... uh, stood in your way?" Joe's face was halfway between concern and laughter, which made me laugh. "It's ok, I'm okay, no worries! Actually I ran into you, so I should be the one apologizing to you. Did I hurt you with, uh, my nose?" We played the Three Stooges for another minute, taking the blame for the collision before Joe asked me to have a cup of coffee with him to "settle his nerves".

During that first week, we chatted each other up at every opportunity. I made excuses to go to his office, and thought up possible topics of conversation. We had lunch every day going to different restaurants on the strip that I could never afford on my own. I learned that Joe had a disposition that matched his smile (sweet as pure cane sugar) and he was generous to a fault. He always volunteered to get the tab, or to hold the door, or carry whatever heavy item was needed. However, he was only in Vegas for work. He actually lived across the country in Tennessee, but kept a house here since he traveled back and forth so often. Two weeks later, as the convention was coming to a close, Joe asked me out on his last day in town, and of course I couldn't say no.

I should have said no.

I wish now I would have.

Maybe things wouldn't have turned out so badly.

#

I have a bad track record when it comes to the opposite sex. To me, they have always seemed to be a perpetual mystery; way different from the images my rose-tinted eyes send to my fevered brain. Unfortunately, I don't have a sad backstory with an Aha! moment that explains the current events. I had two nice parents and a younger sibling of each gender that I didn't hate. Genuinely middle class, we had *things* but not so much as to be unappreciative. Growing up in the Bay Area ensured I wasn't ever the only Black girl in school and I like to believe I was pretty well-adjusted. Well,

I did hate high school, but the people who didn't are the ones I suspect first...of anything. I wasn't popular so I got a little teasing occasionally, but when it went too far—like when a bunch of the jocks started a food fight on my hair—I was not weak enough to just sit and take it.

Drew, the football cornerback famous for making last year's winning interception decided to throw a handful of mashed potatoes at some poor nerd walking by, splattering him directly in the chest. Problem is, I didn't know any of that was happening when I walked in to grab an orange and I got hit with a blob of Jello—landing right in the middle of my hair. You KNOW you don't mess with a Black Woman's hair!

"Dreeeeeew!" I screamed instantly. I looked up through orange Jello and focused on Drew.

"Hey," he said laughingly, "It wasn't me! I aimed for the rocket scientist."

"YOU ASS!" I grabbed a blob of orange jello and threw it directly at him. Of course I missed, which made Drew laugh again. However, I was focused on the troublemaker, Mr. I Won The

Game So I Can Do Whatever I Want. So I went for him. I grabbed a tray off Drew's table and smacked the crap out of him with it.

I was aiming for his face, but only reached his chest since he was standing on the table.

"Look you privileged asshat, I'm not some frigging nerd that will take a lump of mashed taters to the chest! Next time you wanna act three years old, do that shit when I'm not around!" I got the "crazy" reputation and was left alone for the rest of that year.

Needless to say, I did NOT date any jocks from my school. I'm pretty enough for that shallow minded group, but athletes didn't appeal to me, obviously. My 5'7" height holds my small curves well; although I was always hoping my boobs might get up to a C cup. But I was lucky to get my mom's perfect shaped almond brown eyes and well-defined lips. Dad's nose wasn't great, but it wasn't freakish and seemed to fit my face fairly well. I kept my shoulder length hair freshly pressed every week back then, unlike the unkempt fro I was currently sporting. I mean, I'm not unattractive, and I don't think I'm crazy…I really can't point to any one reason this is happening to me.

I used to believe that I was born with abysmal taste in men and that's why I always picked losers. I'm starting to think that the truth of the matter may hold more sinister connotations.

#

Anyway, that first night out together, Joe was a complete gentleman. He took me to the Hard Rock Casino and we had drinks at the Pink Taco before hitting the blackjack table. Of course Joe kept trying to give me money to play with. It was fun, but I didn't want to seem like I was trying to take advantage of him.

"You are so sweet and I thank you! But this dealer truly hates me." I gave the dealer a wink and a smile. "Let's head over to the Venetian and try out Tao. C'mon, you know you wanna shake that groove thing with me!"

"Cassie, I promise you don't want to see me on a dance floor. It would a disaster of gigantic proportions, trust me." I gave him my skeptical face, though and waved off the dealer, indicating I would sit this one out. "No, trust me! Imagine all of **this** flailing about, smacking other dancers about the head and shoulders on accident. My bald head will be shining, drops of sweat flying around hitting unsuspecting dancers in the face—gross! Can you see how this could go so very wrong?" Joe continued on in that self-deprecating vein until I was bowled over with laughter and had to get up from the table. Joe gave in, as his protests were nominal at best.

We had a great time. We laughed, gambled and danced the night away. He was a pretty bad dancer—even worse than I was, and that was endearing to me. But we stayed out all night until it was time for breakfast. We went to the Barbary Coast for their steak and eggs breakfast with the rest of the all-nighters. In the morning, when it was time for him to catch a plane home, we shared a sweet clumsy kiss that lit fires in my blood I'd thought had been dampened forever. He said he would keep in touch and I'd hoped so because that first night was so great.

Well, I guess that first night really doesn't matter, does it? It's all the nights, accumulated as a whole and averaged out like some sort of complex math problem that somehow makes the difference. And after a year, I unfortunately didn't have a lot of positive nights to put into the love equation. Joe came to my city pretty often and at first I was flattered. However, I was only invited to the house in town on a couple of occasions, which invites suspicion in itself. We always went out, to restaurants, clubs, coffee shops, and of course my apartment. I had checked his ring fingers for that telltale tan mark, but there weren't any. In the beginning, the absence of the telltale mark reassured me that all was copacetic. But I was starting to think that just meant that he wasn't seeing someone else *legally*. Also, an alarming amount of our conversations in the last six months of our relationship contained references to Joe's ex-girlfriend—who I was starting to suspect was more like current. Granted, they were generally negative statements about how "cracked up" she was, or how she had ruined his credit with wild spending habits and he was still paying off the bills. "That's just one of the reasons I really like you, Cassie. You don't take my kindness for weakness. I really feel like I can trust you." I remember him telling me that once over coffee, and I blushed and smiled back at him. But when I asked him tough questions like why his car was still in his ex's name, his lengthy inadequate responses began to take on a stuttering quality. Soon our conversations started to blur into a loud white noise in my mind, filled with my silent contempt; all his murmurings began to blend into one big ass LIE! It started to feel like those words were circling around inside my head, going faster and faster until I wanted to scream at him to STOP but he wouldn't, just kept going on and on like I was stupid and couldn't tell the difference between the truth and a lie. I just wanted to stand up and STRANGLE the lies, throw them DOWN and STOMP on them, CUT him to PIECES—

When you find out you're in a one-sided love affair, there's always anger. What they don't tell you is with the anger, comes shame.

There is always the question, "Why do I always get the assholes, the bums, and the LIARS?" Shame is a magnificent isolator, too.

It doesn't allow you to confide in friends. You explain yourself by saying you can handle it yourself. But in reality, "handling it" would mean you'd have to stop hiding the truth from yourself. You have to acknowledge that once again, you've allowed yourself to be used, that you gave up that special part of you.

That's why I had to stop dating before I met Joe.

Finally the time came with Joe when the anger grew so thick around my head that I couldn't smell the sour tang of self-humiliation that had held me captive for so long. Joe had cancelled our last two dates, and had failed to make today's phone appointment, which was supposed to hold some sort of apology and explanation for his recent behavior. So that afternoon, I pulled out my address book, consulted his card and decided to show up unannounced at his house.

It was truth time.

#

Why do you think you want to hurt members of the opposite sex?

I don't know. They're all assholes, anyway.

You know that's not true, Cassandra. You know lots of men that aren't-- like that. So think, why do you think you want to harm them?

(no response)

Cassandra? (pause) You have to do some work if you want to resolve this. Now--

Because they hurt me, okay! They hurt me so I fucking hurt them. Fuck them!

Okay, that's good, that's very good. They hurt you, they've made you feel pain?

Hell yeah! I was angry and pissed off to the extreme.

Dig a little deeper, Cassandra, go underneath the pain. Is there anything else they made you feel? Was there something other than pain? Tell me, Cassandra.

(no response)

Work with me! What is under that hurt feeling? Fear, pain, anger maybe?

(no response)

Tell me—it is okay to tell me. I'm safe, Cassandra. What is it? What do you really feel?

(whisper)

Speak up, Cassandra, I can't hear you.

Pleasure.

#

I had planned on a final confrontation, where I give this excellent, Academy-Award caliber speech on how REAL men are supposed to treat women. I planned to explain to Joe how he failed miserably at Women 101, and how soon Karma would catch up with him eventually.

In my mind, I planned how it would go. Joe would cry and be super apologetic. He would clasp his hands together like a child praying and beg my forgiveness. I would not deign to give it. The outcome I expected would free me to find a good man. As I let loose of all the poison and pain his rejection (and let's face it, ladies and gentlemen, when you get to the end of the tootsie roll pop, that's what it is when your man cheats on you—rejection) had caused me, I would grow taller and straighter while Joe steadily shrunk with each word. In my daydream, my 5'7" frame somehow would majestically tower over Joe's 6'2" as I stood fast on Righteous Indignation!

In reality, I exited the freeway and turned down Joe's street. Mentally I drop the last of my verbal bombs on him, swiveled around on my stiletto heels (dream shoes, in real life I had on Chucks) and glide out the door on my Injured Party carpet, leaving Joe huddled in a corner—a weeping, blubbering mess, despondent at a life without me. However in real life, as I pull up to his house to fulfill this daydream, I see a car already parked in front. I know it's not his; not only had Joe refused to pay management for covered parking but he only drives a cherry red BMW in *his* fantasies. I told myself it's possible the driver of the vehicle was in the wrong spot and was visiting one of the neighbors. But as I get out and walk past the car, I saw one of those stickers on the back

window showing a man, a woman and a baby. That sign chilled my
heart. My daydream was rapidly turning to ashes—I was supposed
to be the only female in this scenario. I mean, it might be hard
to glide around on a carpet of indignation if another woman is
already on it going the opposite way. But still…I strengthened my
resolve and kept walking to the front door. I gave myself credit
for standing my ground and continuing on to the confrontation. I
wanted to do this, to have it out for once and for all. I needed to do
it! It would represent closure. Right?

#

Now here's where Dr. Hall and I disagree on the turn of events.
I believe that's because he wasn't there; if Jerry had been inside that
living room, he'd probably be a patient here too. Or worse. The
main point is, I walked into a scene that had a traumatic effect on
me. It was kind of my fault, since I didn't knock at the front door
like a regular person. I simply tried the knob—I knew it would be
open, and it was. Joe never locked doors anywhere. I had always
joked with him that Tennessee living would never leave him and his
country was showing when he left the door unlocked. I fervently
wish now that some city boy had gotten into him. Maybe if the
door had been locked I would have turned around and left, leaving
it at that. Maybe if pigs had wings…

I walked down the hall to the entrance to the living room and
felt sick to my stomach. The walls had the usual family photos lined
up. There was a picture of Joe and a pretty lady with long hair and
glasses. She didn't look like a shopping fiend, or cracked up. I didn't
see any baby pictures, just the two of them. There were a couple
of pictures of Joe's parents and his brother. But there was also a

picture of the lady, with a couple that must be her parents and two other people that were probably family. I already knew, but seeing those pictures really brought it home—Joe was full of shit from the very beginning. I again filled up with anger, like a water pitcher. I continued down the hall slowly, gathering my words. I heard slow music playing somewhere, fulfilling every angry cheating fantasy

I'd had. But when I came around the corner, I froze at the sight in front of me. Joe was on his knees dressed in his Sunday best with his back to me, placing a huge diamond solitaire onto some Other Woman's finger! She was smiling and nodding, so the answer was apparently yes. They were so enthralled with each other that they hadn't even noticed me. By the time she looked up and saw me, it was way too late, for all of us.

When I saw Joe there, in the middle of the room, his head looking up entreatingly at someone else, I almost stroked out and died. Dionne Farris was playing and faraway in my mind I thought, *Love Jones* soundtrack; great movie. I could see a ring box on a table next to glasses of what I surmised to be champagne. The whole scene told me that Joe never intended to call and issue any kind of excuse. What he was going to call and do was BREAK UP WITH ME--TO BE WITH HER! I could see he was a liar, but to catch him PROPOSING to another woman while he was dating me! He must have been seeing her the whole time he's been seeing me, maybe even before. It's bad enough to know you've been used, suspecting that he was cheating on the side. I mean damn, Joe, you couldn't even be bothered to dump me. Even after meeting me, knowing and supposedly loving me, he still chose someone else!

The whole time, I was nothing but a poor unwanted second choice, not even worth being dismissed.

Right then is when I first felt that tingle.

That's always how it starts for me, signaling disaster ahead. I stood in the entryway of that room, watching the man I'd loved for the last 12 months propose to somebody else in front of me. My shock was almost tangible; it may have been hard for me to breathe, but unfortunately my vision was not at all impaired. Joe was standing up after her agreement and they were clasping hands and smiling at each other. Their failure to even notice me was infuriating and I hated them at that moment. Hated them more than I'd ever hated anyone in my life. More than any other man, woman or thing. How dare they refuse to acknowledge me— DARING not to see me!

And I felt that feeling again, that same tingle but much stronger; in the small of my back. A strong current of energy rolled up my spine, leaving pleasurable spasms in its wake. My skin prickled and the tiny hairs all over my body stood on end. The feeling began to spread all over my body, making my fingertips and toes tingle.

My whole body: every cell, every follicle felt on fire with energy. My nerves screamed and crackled and I could feel … everything. I could feel the wind from the open door behind me coming down the hall, caressing my skin. I felt the rumble of a passing car from outside. Dionne Farris' musical notes thrust themselves into my eardrums over and over.

The energy rolled over me again, stronger this time. It felt like those lamps from Spencer's with the ball of electricity inside that followed your finger when you touched it. Except I was the glass lamp, and the power was inside me sparking all over my body. I was flushed, and could feel my temperature rise. It centered itself in my groin, and I started getting hot; my cells were generating heat. I could see the air shimmer in front of my face. Behind it, Joe and company were hazy, I could no longer see them clearly through the heat. Then, my body started reacting. I swear my breasts swelled up to a C cup like I'd always wanted-how ironic-and my nipples could have cut glass. I felt a familiar trickle of moisture begin between my legs and I could remember thinking — What the hell was this? I'd had an episode similar to this before, but nothing as powerful. I could not move my body, yet it *felt* like I was flying, using every muscle in my body somehow. I vaguely thought how I would be so sore tomorrow. But no thoughts whatsoever on what it was I was about to do that would make me sore. All I could do was stand there and let this energy flow outside of myself. It was too much for me to control, I couldn't stop it, it had to come out and it did; through every open pore, every orifice, any opening available. And as it excited me, it got hot. And it burned. Everything but me. Because I've been burned enough.

The heat being released by my sexual excitement must have finally alerted Joe and his woman (fiancée)s to my presence; their heads both turned toward me at the same time, not understanding but somehow realizing there was danger (Danger Will Robinson!) afoot inside their house. I saw in their eyes that they don't comprehend the source of the threat. It was almost stamped on their foreheads: *Surely not this woman standing in OUR home, she's unexpected sure, but she has no weapons, she doesn't look scary..* Their eyes blinked stupidly like sheep but fear still swam there; pupils dilating and nostrils flaring. WHERE? Where is the monster, the maniac with the AK47, the source of danger that has raised alarms buried so deep in their subconscious they don't even know what's been triggered. But I am the monster. I'm the bogeyman, the killer clown, the serial killer.

And they don't even know it.

Then my body caught fire--EXPLODES and I saw something fly from me and smack them. I wanted to pull back, walk away, STOP but it was too late and I could feel my body starting to react, that special wetness flowing into my cotton panties, making me sticky. Joe and his BITCH are shaking, vibrations of my pain at being lied to and used, ripping them apart, visible waves of heat made their skin slough off like a snakes, falling to the ground in small glops as chunks of epidermis stained the carpet. In seconds, the muscles and tendons of their bodies became fully exposed, then they too were hit by more heat finally getting down to the bone. Their bones fell to ground, breaking apart and charring as they joined the chunks of flesh already on the ground.

As each layer of their humanity disappeared under the force of my will, I got more excited against my will. I was disgusted at my reaction. What I was seeing was terrible, horrific even — shouldn't I be screaming or vomiting, I wondered? How was this even happening? Instead, my nipples got harder and I could feel my labia swelling, engorged with blood; my vagina was contracting, my clitoris was peaking. It was the most intense sexual experience I'd ever had and I started shaking too, frozen in place but starting to moan as I felt release coming upon me. Joe and the Girl had no flesh left on their skeletons, and was hard for me to look at it as (GUILT) started to dissolve itself, pieces of bone marrow and chips of bone landing on what wasn't covered by their previous human detritus deposited there. All that remained of my former

lover and his former fiancé was bloody jelly and at that moment
I came ferociously, like an act of nature; Mt. Saint Helens or
Vesuvius exploding in my pussy and like Pompeii, my vision started
to go black. I couldn't get enough air. I was passing out with the
pleasure and DAMN it felt so fucking good and I started falling
forward (Oh Shit! No!) towards that pile of jelly-flesh, the pleasure
center of my brain overloading hips bucking as I fucked my rage
and my rage fucked me. It was the best orgasm I'd ever had.

#

Now let's talk about what really happened to Joe.

I told you what happened to him!

*Cassandra, you know what you told me is an impossibility. How can you
get better if you won't be honest with me?*

I told you that I killed him; how I killed him.

*You want me to believe you killed Joe without touching him? That you
killed him with your mind?*

No, not with my mind! Damn, are you even listening to
anything I'm saying?!

Yes, yes I'm listening, just - explain again.

I killed him with some other part of me, my—my madness or
anger or something. My emotions, I think. I killed him with my
emotions; it was like, emotional murder.

Hmm, your madness, huh? (writes)

#

This has happened to me before, and each time my sexual gratification got hotter and stronger from the incidents. The injuries to the ex-boyfriends in question got worse each time, too. The first time, a boyfriend at summer camp got a bad sunburn and severe dehydration after dumping me for not putting out. He was released from the hospital the next day. But he told everyone in town I was a witch and had put a death spell on him. As a freshman at Cal Poly, I caught my guy hitting on my roommate at a party. I felt that tickle coming on, and the cheating bastard somehow suffered third degree burns on 90% of his body while at a basketball game — where I had caught him with someone else.

He was rushed to the ICU. In the confusion, no one saw me fall down, crying in the ecstasy of his misfortune. I tried to stop dating permanently then, because I don't really like hurting people. But I'm just not made to live alone, I need companionship! And anyway, the next guy hit on me, not the other way around. But now he's in an irreversible coma due to excessive brain swelling that never went down. I really don't know how that happened, usually there's heat involved. I hear the two whores I caught him sexing in my bed apparently visit him every week.

But I never hurt the women! I mean technically they never lied to me, they never cheated on me and therefore owe me no loyalty. If they're okay being the Other Woman, fine—that's their business. My anger usually focuses on the lying, cheating men. But I guess the shock of finding Joe and her together like that, planning to get married right in my face...a little too much reality at one time for me. But I'm sorry, I really am! I said so in court at my sentencing. Especially about her. She was just unlucky, I tell myself. I don't want to obsess on those memories; flashes of their hallway family pictures and their living room, and the face of a frightened toddler, peeking around the edge of a couch watching his parents fall apart silently.

My therapist Jerry tries to reassure me that I'm really not some crazed succubus-like creature, dispensing my own twisted justice to those I despise as I literally cum all over their dead bodies (or *in* their dead bodies, in this last case). That the orgasms are getting stronger (better) each time this happens is what worries me. What if I start killing men not because they hurt me, but just for the orgasms? What if I *already am*? What does that make me?

I worry.

#

According to Dr. Jerry Hall, therapist extraordinaire, the whole thing was a sort of self-psychosis brought on by disturbing events. Of course it was assumed by the courts that after catching my cheating boyfriend proposing to someone else, I killed them both in a fit of t emporary insanity. They say I tried to dissolve their bodies with household cleaners, though they don't know which ones since they didn't find traces of any chemicals. The fact that I told them what really happened and refused to testify at my own trial got me a mandatory 10 year stint in the psych ward I'm currently residing in. But why testify when I know no one will believe me? Dr. Hall says I should focus on the lack of control that led to me killing the couple, not on the method of death. I disagree.

I don't know of anyone else who can kill cheating boyfriends with their minds—or vaginas, for that matter. And what does it say about me, that the destruction of a man I once loved can send me into paroxysms of pleasure?

I asked Dr. Hall about that, but I think he's a bit uncomfortable discussing the sexual aspects of my problem. His pink face gets shinier and he tends to lick his lips a lot. He gets flustered when I call him Jerry and can't meet my eyes. I think he may have a slight crush on me. Now that I think about it, he does have some nice thick lips for a white guy. I wonder if he uses those in bed?

Maybe if Dr. Hall—I mean Jerry—gives me a hands-on example of what a normal sexual relationship should be like, I could be healed faster. He seems like a nice guy…the type of guy that would never cheat on me. I can just tell…

Kim
by Nicole D. Sconiers

She looked like she wandered away from a Mennonite farm, like she belonged to those women who gave bags of hand-me-downs to my mom. Her gingham dress hung to her ankles. It was a sly blue color, like a robin's egg in which a baby vulture slept. No prayer covering weighed down her hair, which swirled around her face in jagged wisps. Unlike those well-meaning Mennonite ladies, she held no bag filled with castoffs for needy black kids. She came that summer bearing nothing in her hands and she left with the bones of our dreams.

I saw her first. We were practicing our lyrics in the underpass off Johnson Highway. Me, Trina, Vanessa and D. The Cherry Street Crew. Few cars traversed that old bridge, on the side of which someone misspelled HYPNOTIZE in chunky red graffiti. Back then, when we were girls, the underpass was our impromptu studio. No one bothered us as we recited our rhymes. Our voices echoed off the walls of the bridge. Pure. Steady. Our sneakers pounded gravel, dodging concrete that had fallen from the ceiling and bits of broken glass. I wasn't the best dancer in the group. I often stood off to the side, watching the feet of my girls, trying to learn the routines. That's when I looked up and saw her there, at the mouth of the underpass. Watching. With nothing in her hands.

It was June 1982 when she came. The summer after all those black kids were killed in Atlanta. I was 14 then. Although we lived in Wing, Pennsylvania, a mill town some 800 miles north of the murders, we weren't allowed to walk to the store or ride our bikes alone. Too much blood had been spilled. If we wanted to play outside, we had to travel in groups.

Most days after school, I hung out with Vanessa, Trina and D. We were all the same age, except for Vanessa, who was a year older. Her nickname was Vee-Money. She did everybody's hair on the block, charging five dollars for cornrows or a press.

The four of us walked up and down the streets. Restless. We were girls, so there wasn't much to do besides jumping rope or going to the store. A few years earlier, they played the first rap song on the radio. "Rappers Delight" by the Sugar Hill Gang. You couldn't pass a stoop or barber shop that wasn't blasting that song from the speakers.

I felt special because I carried my brother's boombox, a black Magnavox with removable speakers. Even though we were just walking up and down the block, past lopsided row houses, past men lounging on stoops (*"Hey, Redbone. Can I walk with you?"*), blasting Sugar Hill on our portable stereo, we felt like we were going somewhere.

Trina started rapping first. She was soft-spoken, a pretty brown-skinned girl who slicked down her baby hair with black gel. One Saturday when we were heading to the corner store, she surprised us all when she began to rhyme:

standing on the corner yellin
young girl/yo girl always on the go girl
you too old to hit on us

tryna feel me up
when I'm at your sister's house
hands all up my blouse
like what…

She spit those verses really quick too, as if she had been holding it in for a while. D added a few lyrics of her own:

young girl/yo girl
why you gotta go, girl? how you grow up so fast
what you doin with all that ass…

D wasn't the brightest one in the group, but she was able to laugh at herself, which made her smarter than a lot of girls I knew. Her real name was Dorethia. I don't know what her mom was thinking to give a girl such a heavy name—a grown woman's name.

I didn't know we could rap. Well, I knew we *could* but I didn't know we were *allowed* to. All the voices barking through the speakers of my brother's Magnavox were loud, cocky. And male.

Pretty soon, my friends and I started rapping on our daily trips up the block. We knew we were emcees; we just needed a name to make it official. We lived on Cherry Street, although there wasn't a fruit-bearing tree anywhere on our block. Naturally, we called ourselves the Cherry Street Crew.

By the spring of 1982, we weren't some wack girls reciting lame lyrics. We were really good. So good our neighbor, Miss Iris, stopped us on our way home from school and asked us to perform at the block party she was organizing at the end of August. We were thrilled. Someone was requesting us to perform. Vee-Money said she could see us onstage one day. The first female rappers.

This was way before the Real Roxanne, before Jazzy Joyce, before MC Lyte and Salt-n-Pepa ever blessed a mic.

She came a few months later. A hot June afternoon that wilted my curls and slammed crickets into silence. I never saw her approach. I just looked up and she was standing there at the lip of the underpass. The other girls stopped dancing and turned to see what had my attention, taking in the stranger with her old-timey clothes.

Vee-Money, the unofficial leader of our group, lowered the volume on the boombox and addressed the stranger. "What you want?"

Our visitor didn't respond. Instead, she fingered the collar of her dress. Her black-laced shoes made circles in the gravel.

D tried a different tack. "Who is you?" she said, her voice echoing off the walls.

"Kim," came the reply.

It seemed as if the wind carried that one syllable across centuries to our ears. Although Kim didn't look much older than us, her voice held none of the marrow of youth. She seemed shy, but it was the shyness of perverts who ask young girls for directions from the window of their van.

"What you want?" Vee-Money repeated. She moved out of the shadows to get a closer look at the stranger. The sun glinted off the silver dog tag chain she always wore.

The girl looked up as we approached and I noticed her eyes. They were the same blue as her dress. Bottomless, the way I imagined manholes to be when you slid away the cover. You descended that airless playground of shadows and knew when you emerged – if you emerged – you'd never be the same.

"Nothing," she said. "Just wanted to watch." "Take a picture. It'll last longer," I said.

Vee-Money touched my arm. "Cool out, Crystal," she said. She looked the white girl up and down. Deciding. Finally, she said, "You can watch, but you can't get on the mic."

Vee-Money returned to our makeshift studio. Kim settled outside on a nearby rock.

We should have ran her off then but we didn't. My friends thought Kim was harmless. I knew she wasn't. Long before the carnage at the underpass, I sensed it, some malevolence in the off-beat tapping of her feet, in the curve of her empty hands.

#

As summer wore on, Kim became a familiar fixture at the bridge. Because I couldn't dance and often hung back while my friends practiced their moves, I wound up standing near her.

During those times, Kim would try to coax me into conversation. "Why are you unable to dance as well as the others?" she asked.

"Not every black person has rhythm, you know." "Ah, but you could if you tried."

"Who says I haven't?" I said, growing annoyed. "Dance, Crystal."

Who is this white girl talking to? I faced her, ready to roll my eyes, and found myself staring into her bottomless blue ones.

Heard the slow clatter as the manhole cover was dragged away, a clanging invitation to the shadowland beneath.

(Dance, little one)

Had she given that command or was I hearing things? From this distance, I got a better look at the pale teen who infiltrated my crew. Scalp gleamed through her brown hair. Deep lines were

etched beneath her eyes and in her forehead, furrows that belonged on the face of a much older woman.

"What you sweatin' for, Crystal?" Vee-Money appeared at my side. I felt relieved at the bigger girl's presence. "Ain't like you was over there jammin' with us."

"What is jamming?" Kim asked.

I caught Vee-Money's glance. Shot her a warning look. *Don't let her in, Vee.*

But Vee-Money was amused at the strange girl's proper speech. "*Jamming* is dancin'." She showed off a quick move. "You know, gettin' down."

Kim smiled then, the first smile I noticed since she appeared more than a month ago. "Crystal was about to practice 'jamming' with you."

"Quit lying." My hand itched to slap her.

The next thing I knew, D and Trina were standing beside me. I doubt they heard the heat in my voice over the blaring boombox, so they must have sensed the tension.

The white girl stood up, wiping dust from her dress. "I'll show you," she said.

"I don't need lessons," I said. "Especially not from you." "Are you afraid, Crystal, that I can jam better than you?"

Kim's soft smile mocked my insecurity.

D whistled at the taunt and Trina craned her neck at me.

My friends expected me to put the white girl in her place or even initiate some b-girl battle. But I didn't want to battle Kim.

I didn't know how to swing my hips on beat or move my feet in a complex choreographed rhythm. Hell, I had even gotten kicked off the junior choir because I didn't know how to sway.

Vee-Money returned to the boombox and rewound the Afrika Bambaataa instrumental they'd been dancing to. As I watched my friends make room for the stranger in the darkness of the underpass, in our spot, my face burned with some emotion I couldn't name. It seared my throat and settled like coal in my stomach.

Even though she wore clunky shoes, Kim moved with grace. She swayed to the music. On beat. Her shoes kicked gravel as she danced with a perverse familiarity the steps I struggled to learn all summer. My girls stared as she undulated with some ancient rhythm, both eerie and divine.

As my friends cheered her on, I tasted heat in my throat, and at once understood the nameless emotion churning in my gut.

It was envy.

#

A rift grew between me and my girls but I didn't know how to mend it. Most afternoons, I found myself sitting on the rock, sullen, as my friends danced with Kim. They were so easily impressed by the white girl. It felt like a violation to hear them joke with her about ashy legs or their "kitchen," which swelled in the summer heat. She didn't earn the right to laugh with us.

The more I resented the white girl, the more she blossomed.

Kim no longer wore the old-timey gingham dress she had on when I first spotted her. She and Trina were around the same size,

191

so Trina gave her a trash bag full of old clothes. Gloria Vanderbilt jeans and oversized tops. It felt as if their roles had switched. Kim was the needy Mennonite girl and they were the benevolent black kids on a mission to save her.

#

The final rupture in my circle wasn't caused by the weird white chick. It came from Vee-Money. She knocked on my door one day to borrow cherry Kool-Aid to dye her hair.

"We don't have any red." I stood behind the screen door, trying to decide if I should let her in.

"What flavor y'all got?" she asked. "Purple, I think."

"That'll work." When I didn't move, Vee-Money stared at me through the screen. "What's wrong with you, Crystal? Oh, I can't come in now?"

With a sigh, I opened the door.

She followed me to the kitchen. My mom was at work, and my brother was out shooting hoops with his buddies. I rummaged through the drawer next to the stove until I found a packet of the powdered drink. As I turned to hand the makeshift hair dye to my friend, I almost dropped it in shock.

Vee-Money was going bald.

On most days, her red-stained tresses were nicely pressed, hanging down to her shoulders in a mushroom or swooped back in a trendy feathered style. Now swathes of scalp gleamed through her normally thick mane.

I clenched the packet. "I don't think you should use this stuff anymore, Vee."

She frowned. "Why not?"

"It's breaking your hair off."

"Girl, ain't nothing wrong with my head."

She reached for the package but I tossed it in the trash.

"You been actin' real shady lately, Crystal." Vee-Money threw up her hand in a dismissive wave.

"I'm not the shady one," I said. "Why don't you go borrow some Kool-Aid from Kim since she loves your naps so much?"

I knew I had hurled the ultimate insult. Back then, talking about somebody's "naps" was akin to calling them "black."

Vee-Money glared at me, then stormed out of the kitchen.

She paused at the screen door, her back to me. "You just got dismissed from the Cherry Street Crew," she said.

I froze a few inches from her. "You're kicking me out? I'm the best emcee in the group."

"You wish."

I touched Vee-Money's arm. "Don't be like this, Vee." I hated the whine that crept into my voice. "We're going to be the first female rappers."

"*We* still are."

"But what about me?"

Vee-Money turned to me with a smirk. "Work on your moves, Crystal. You a lightweight. You let a white girl show you up."

I dropped my hand, hurt. Vee-Money opened the door and headed out into the street.

#

I stopped hanging out at the bridge and started writing lyrics in my bedroom. It's one thing for a teen girl to choose to be a loner, to cherish the solitude of her room among her books and DeBarge posters. It's another thing entirely to feel isolated.

That's what happened after my blowup with Vee-Money. My friends stopped accepting my calls, stopped yelling through my screen door to see if I wanted to walk to the pizza joint for a slice.

More than the isolation, I feared something sinister was happening to my girls. Although Vee-Money could be bossy, she had never been deliberately cruel before. It was as if she had lost her compassion along with her hair. I would soon learn that Vee-Money's sudden baldness was a small thing compared to what befell Trina.

I missed Trina's friendship the most. She was soft-spoken and introverted like me, so she understood the struggle of trying to fit in. Trina was also the one who started rapping first, who showed me that girls could rock the mic. I needed to talk to her.

Trina lived exactly ten houses away but I didn't want to knock on her front door. I walked down the back alley to avoid the stares of the neighborhood kids who had probably heard about the dissolution of the Cherry Street Crew.

Trina stood in her yard, her back to me, wearing a brim hat as she swept the narrow driveway. I paused as I approached, puzzled by the pants and long-sleeved shirt she wore, clothes that were much too hot for the summer day.

"Hey, Trina."

She looked around quickly, as if she'd been caught doing something obscene. My hand, raised in greeting, hesitated mid-air.

Trina's skin was turning white.

Even with the straw hat shielding her face, the gruesome transformation was hard to hide. Her normally smooth dark skin, which had not suffered the curse of teen pimples like mine, was riddled with large pale blotches.

Trina turned away, sweeping harder.

"Are you okay?" I walked around to face her. Concerned. "What happened to your skin?"

"I'm fine."

"You don't look fine. You look sick."

She raised her head, challenging me with a look. Her eyes were as lifeless as the broom in her hand.

"Your face didn't look like that a few weeks ago. Maybe you should go —"

"No, maybe *you* should go, Crystal." She lifted her broom, as if to strike.

I wasn't scared. Just sad and confused. Trina had never raised her voice or anything else at me.

I backed out of the driveway, haunted by her sneer and fading skin.

#

I didn't have anyone to talk to about my fears.

Summer, once sweet and full of harmony, dragged on like some wounded animal too ornery to die. I rode my Huffy up and down the streets, looking for a distraction. What I found one afternoon as I cruised past the basketball court stunned me.

It was a rinky-dink court on Arch Street in the "rough" part of town, as if the entire town of Wing wasn't rough, wasn't scalloped by slanting rowhouses and shabby storefronts. In spite of its location, the basketball court was the informal community center. Sweaty boys in nylon shorts flexed on the macadam, showing off their jump shot. Girls in miniskirts and jelly shoes stood around talking to their friends, trying not to be impressed.

As I rode past the court, I saw something that almost knocked me off my Huffy.

Kim rested against the chain-link fence that enclosed the basketball court. She was talking to Manuel and Luther, two brothers who we considered the finest boys on the block, with dark skin and hazel eyes.

I slowed my bike to get a better look. I was so used to seeing the white girl beneath the bridge, it was as if she lived there.

The sight of her out in the open, in my community, unnerved me. She lounged confidently against the fence as she flirted with the neighborhood boys. Her slim hips were encased in Gloria Vanderbilt jeans. A halter and Filas completed the look. Trina's cast-offs. Kim's once brittle brown hair was thick and curled into a sleek mushroom style. Not the look worn on *Charlie's Angels*, but the style a neighborhood girl would rock, with asymmetrical angels. But for her pale skin, Kim could have been one of us.

Anger flooded my chest. As if sensing my disgust, Kim looked up, locking eyes with me. She was no longer a mousy Mennonite girl who had wandered into our lives. She was alluring.

She gave me a knowing look, tinged with cockiness and something darker. Assurance, maybe. I glared at her as I tried to swallow the rancor burning my throat. It was then that I noticed something shimmering around her neck.

It was Vee-Money's dog tag.

#

Miss Iris was hanging wash on the clothesline in her yard when I walked my bike down the back alley that led to my house. I felt hot and defeated.

196

"Afternoon, Crystal," Miss Iris called when she spotted me. Several wooden clothespins were clipped to her blouse. "How you enjoying summer vacation?"

"Fine."

Noticing my glum look, she said, "School ain't starting tomorrow. You got a few more weeks yet."

I liked Miss Iris. Although she was in her mid-forties, she had a youthful laugh. Her long ponytail hung to the middle of her back, fastened with a purple ribbon. Miss Iris didn't socialize with the other ladies on the block. She was a loner in her own right, quilting on the front stoop or tending the flowers she grew in her backyard.

Miss Iris glanced around. "Where are your girlfriends?" I shrugged. "I don't know."

"Y'all ain't had a falling out, have you? The block party is right around the corner."

"I won't be there. I got kicked out of the Cherry Street Crew," I said.

Miss Iris slung a pair of jeans on the line and pinned them. Then she sat on a bench near her garden and patted the spot next to her. I joined her.

"Sorry to hear that, Crystal," she said. "You got talent. That's why I asked you to rap at the block party."

Her words made me smile, in spite of my weariness. But then I remembered the source of my sorrow.

"My friends are changing, Miss Iris."

"They're at that age, sweetie. It's called growing up." "No, this feels wrong."

I told her everything, about the pale girl named Kim who appeared at the beginning of summer like some strange bird who carried corruption beneath her wing.

Miss Iris nodded as I began my tale. Then the color drained from her face when I described Vee-Money's thinning hair and Trina's palsied skin. She stared into the distance when I finished, toying with her long braid. When Miss Iris finally spoke again, her voice was just above a whisper.

"She came back."

I tilted my head. Puzzled at the fear that suddenly gripped my older neighbor. "Who came back?"

"Kim. But she wasn't calling herself that in 1952, when I was your age. Back then, her name was Madeleine."

"Madeleine? How old was she?" I asked, skeptical. "She looked to be about fifteen. Same age I was."

I did some quick calculations in my head. "If Kim – Madeleine – was fifteen in 1952, she'd be forty-five now," I said. "No disrespect, Miss Iris, but the girl I know doesn't look like an old woman."

"That's because she's not an old woman. She's not a woman at all. Or a girl."

"What is she?"

Miss Iris gazed at me, trying to decide if I could handle the weight of her next words. "A leech. A soul gobbler," she said. "Long before that bridge was built on Johnson Highway, it was a clearing. We used to hang out there when we was kids. Back then, it was a quiet place in the woods where we could go to dance and sing. Be free."

My neighbor closed her eyes in remembrance. "Our parents were real strict. We couldn't go to parties. At least not the girls. We went to a Mennonite camp every summer, learning how to quilt, make preserves. Be good wives."

I thought of the blue gingham dress Kim wore when she first appeared, the black laced shoes. The costume of holiness.

"In '52, they showed kids dancing on TV for the first time. A program called *Bandstand*," Miss Iris said. "*Bandstand* was a bunch of white kids doing the jitterbug. The Lindy. They didn't let black kids in the audience. They was playing our music and dancing to our songs, but they wouldn't let us on TV. Some white kids even asked black kids to teach them new steps. Then, when they got the moves down, they would go right back and tape that show and act like they came up with those dances."

"What does that have to do with Kim – Madeleine?" I didn't want to interrupt the older woman, but her rambling made me wonder if she had a screw loose.

"Like I said, we used to sneak off to the clearing to dance. Me and my three friends – Annie, Beverly and Gail. We made up our own steps. They didn't have any names." Miss Iris smiled to herself. "After school, the other kids would gather around and ask us to perform. We was doing something new."

According to Miss Iris, her crew's plan was to integrate *Bandstand*. The four girls were going to sneak down to Philly for a taping and do their bold new dances in the street outside the studio until someone turned a camera on them.

But they never got the chance.

"One day, when we was rehearsing in the clearing, I looked up, and there she was. Madeleine. I never heard her coming. She just appeared. Wearing a dress down to her ankles. All that blue walking out from behind the trees, like she was the police or something. Scared us something terrible. We stopped dancing, but she told us to keep on. Said she just wanted to watch."

As hot as the August afternoon was, my hands felt cold. I rubbed them on my shorts, trying to warm them, as I listened to Miss Iris' haunting tale. "She hung out there with us. Learning our dances. I didn't trust her. She didn't act like no Mennonite girl I ever knew. Her hands was as smooth as a baby's, like she wasn't used to no hard work – milking, canning, quilting. My friends thought I was just jealous. 'What's the harm in letting her watch?' Annie used to ask. Sweet Annie. She was the best dancer out of all of us. Would have been a star if ..."

Her voice trailed off. That "if " chilled me. I suddenly grew fearful for my own friends.

"What happened to your friends, Miss Iris?" I asked.

"Madeleine happened. Killed 'em."

The words lingered in the air for a few moments, competing with the musky scent of her marigolds. "Oh, I can't prove it," she said, "but she did. They was healthy teenage girls. Strong as a ox. But the longer she hung around, the weaker they got. Hair falling out. Skin spotty. One day, I looked for them in the clearing, and they was gone. Some people thought they ran off because their folks was too strict."

"But you didn't believe it."

"Do lightning bugs glow in the daytime?" Miss Iris gave a sharp laugh, twisting her ponytail around a finger. "I think there are three graves back there in that clearing."

Why three graves and not four? I wondered.

As if sensing the unasked question, the older woman said, "She would have killed me too, but I put a freezer spell on her."

"A what?"

"A freezer spell. It gets rid of your enemies. My grandma

Hattie was a conjure woman. I learned about spells from her." She lowered her voice. "I shouldn't even be telling you this. Folks think it's witchcraft."

I sat in silence, trying to digest my neighbor's bizarre revelation. Maybe Kim was a leech, like Miss Iris said. A soul gobbler. Some wicked entity that returned to the clearing every thirty years in search of new blood. Black girl blood. Not blood, necessarily. Rhythm. A carefree cadence. Whatever she was, I had to stop her before the same fate befell the Cherry Street Crew.

"Show me how to make the freezer spell, Miss Iris."

The older woman smiled sadly. "Maybe," she said. "Lot of good it did me. Thought Madeleine was gone for good, but you can't out-trick the trickster. One day I looked up, and she was on *Bandstand*, smiling in the camera, doing our dances. The ones with no names. My girls were gone. Annie, Bev and Gail. Not even a bone remained."

#

As soon as Miss Iris finished her story, my mom pulled into our driveway, home from work. She looked surprised to see me sitting in our neighbor's yard because I didn't talk much with the older women on our block. Figuring I was being a nuisance, she called me inside to start dinner.

I stood at the sink soaking chicken liver in milk, mulling over my plan. Miss Iris told me to come by the next day and she would write the freezer spell instructions for me. I was desperate. I needed something that would banish Kim back to the vulture's egg she hatched from.

(Little one)

I froze. My mom stood behind me, phone in hand. I hadn't even heard it ring.

"It's D," she said.

"I'll take it in your room," I said, trying to keep my voice from trembling.

I bounded up the stairs to my mother's bedroom. D and I hadn't spoken in several weeks. Maybe she had come to her senses. Hopefully, she would believe me when I told her what I learned about Kim.

I grabbed the phone from my mom's nightstand. "D! I'm so glad you called, girl."

"What's up, Crystal?" My friend didn't sound like herself. Her voice was muffled and thick.

"We need to talk about Kim."

"What about her?"

"She's not who she says she is."

"Really? Who is she?"

I gripped the cord, staring down the dark hallway. "I can't talk right now," I said. "Can you come over tomorrow?"

"I can meet tonight. Come out to our spot."

Our spot? I hadn't been to the underpass in awhile and it certainly didn't feel like home anymore. "What time?" I asked.

"Nine."

I frowned. There were no street lights near the underpass.

We were still living in the shadow of the murdered Atlanta kids. D knew my mom didn't want me walking by myself after dark.

Miss Iris' words rang in my ear: *You can't out-trick the trickster.* "Stop trippin', Doreena," I said. "You know my mom won't let me go out by myself that late."

"Sneak out then," came the reply.

"This isn't, D," I said, feeling sick. "Not the D I know. Her name is Dorethia, *not* Doreena."

There was a hissing sound on the other end. I held the phone away from my ear.

"I *know* your name!" I said.

Downstairs, I heard my mom rise from the sofa. "Everything alright up there, Crys?" she called.

The voice on the other end laughed. "Who am I?"

"Madeleine," I said, slamming down the phone.

#

FREEZER SPELL
Mason jar Paper Water Salt
Black candle

Write your enemy's name on the paper. Fold paper three times.

Fill Mason jar with water. Add three heaping tablespoons salt. Place paper in the jar of salt water.

Seal the jar and drip black wax on the lid. Place jar in freezer and
DON'T REMOVE.

Imagine your enemy disappearing from your life.

The spell seemed simple enough, not the sorcery I expected that included chanting and the blood of animals.

"Most important, you got to *believe* it will work," Miss Iris said when I went over to get the instructions. "Ain't no hoodoo on earth will work if you don't believe."

When I stepped out of her back door and headed home, I felt older. As if I had aged ten years at her kitchen counter. The feeling followed me down the back stairs of my row house and into the basement, where I plucked a Mason jar off the shelf.

Standing at the sink, I filled the jar with water, pouring in three tablespoons of salt until the crystals swirled in the glass.

Upstairs in my bedroom, I tore a sheet of paper from my notebook, the one I used to write lyrics in. With a magic marker, I wrote **KIM** in big black letters on one side. For good measure, I wrote **MADELEINE** on the other side. Then I folded the paper three times and dropped it into the salt water.

As I lit the black candle, I felt a chill. It was noon. A breezeless day in late August. My mom and brother were at work. I was alone. I closed my bedroom door and locked it. I stared into the full-length mirror hanging on the back of my door, at the girl holding the candle, looking as if she were on her way to some dark mass.

As the candle burned, I tilted it, dripping wax like black tears on the lid of the jar. I suddenly had the urge to chant, to say some magic words. The spell didn't mention chanting, and I wanted to follow the instructions to the letter. I didn't want her to come back. Kim. Madeleine. But I needed to give her a proper send off, the Cherry Street Crew way.

My name is Crystal But they call me
C-Magic
Like magician Make a wish and Poof … I appear
Crystal clear
Straight to hell below I'm sending all foes
Bitin' off me and my friends
Especially this leech named Kim …

The bedroom door blew open, shattering the mirror behind it. Shards of glass sprayed the room, pricking my arm. I screamed, dropping the Mason jar. Liquid sloshed as the jar hit the carpet and rolled beneath my bed. A wind seemed to swell from inside the room. It billowed, blowing out the candle. The notebook fell open, pages rippling.

"You can't take my songs," I shouted above the tempest raging in my tiny bedroom, a churning that whipped my hair back from my face. I tried to sound brave, but I was terrified.

"You got to *believe* it will work," Miss Iris had said. "Ain't no hoodoo on earth will work for you if you don't believe."

The freezer spell said to imagine your enemy disappearing from your life. I grabbed the jar of salt water from beneath the bed as if it were a buoy in a dark and roiling sea. Clutching it to my chest, I closed my eyes and imagined Kim. Not with her B-girl clothes and trendy hairstyle. I imagined her as she looked the first time she appeared beneath the bridge. Frail. Thinning hair. Draped in a gingham dress. I focused on the strong wind in my bedroom. I saw it whipping through the passageway where we used to rap.

It kicked up gravel in the white girl's face, blowing her around like a doll. She tried to hold on to the walls of the underpass, her nails scraping the concrete until they were bloody, but she was no match for the wind. It swept her down the road and up, up, over the trees. Out of our lives.

The room fell silent. The curtain fluttered, as if waving goodbye to an unseen presence. Then the wind abated. I looked out the window. Trina, D and Vee-Money were riding their bikes up Cherry Street. I knew of only one place they could be headed.

"Wait up, y'all!" I called out the window. "Wait for me."

#

I hopped on my Huffy, pedaling up the block. My girls were back. Something happened in my bedroom to free them from Kim's grip. I was sure of it.

I whistled as I rode up Johnson Highway, passing two boys walking on the shoulder carrying fishing rods. It seemed like just another summer's day in Wing.

I cruised down the pebbly path that led to the underpass. It used to be a clearing, Miss Iris said, but it became a burial ground for black girls who dared to be free.

young girl/ yo girl

why you gotta go, girl?

I heard my friends before I saw them. I pedaled faster, eager for a reunion.

I parked my bike a few feet from the underpass, engaging the kickstand. The gesture seemed like an announcement. *I'm home.* Trina, D and Vee-Money held hands in a circle, as if playing some ring game. I glanced around, expecting to see her. Kim. No one else was there.

"What's up, ladies?" I said. My voice echoed off the walls.

I paused. Something didn't feel right. My friends continued to stand in the circle as if they hadn't heard me.

"Y'all still mad?"

I wanted to venture further into the underpass but I couldn't move. I gazed at my three friends as they huddled, then down at their feet. My eyes widened. Four shadows slanted on the ground.

young girl/ yo girl young girl/ yo girl young girl/ yo girl…

The girls chanted robotically. I backed away from the entrance. Shaken.

A breeze rippled inside the underpass, surging through the circle. My friends collapsed, seeming to disintegrate before my eyes like mannequins in a furnace. One minute, they were hunched together, holding hands. The next minute, their clothes were crumpled in a heap in the dirt.

(little one)

I cried out, losing my balance, and landed on my butt.

Kim loomed at the opposite end of the underpass. She was clad in her blue gingham dress, bigger than ever.

"Are you ready to dance?" she said, gliding across the gravel.

Her hair coiled around her head like a nest of snakes.

I pushed myself backwards in the dirt, away from the entity bearing down on me. Kim crossed a span of thirty feet in seconds. She hovered over me, a bird of prey diving from a precipice. Her face was lineless, like a young girl's. Her blue eyes were wide with lust.

"Dance, little one."

My knees locked together as my body rose against my will. Kim would get her wish after all. Deep sadness engulfed me. Not only would I die at the hands of the soul gobbler, but I'd be forced to perform for her before she killed me.

I don't know why the story "The Valley of Dry Bones" came to me at that moment. Maybe it was the sound of my knees snapping to attention at the white girl's command.

Although I had gotten kicked out of youth choir because I didn't know how to sway, I still remembered that biblical story from the Book of Ezekiel: "*Come from the four winds, O breath, and breathe upon these slain, that they may live.*"

Before my mind could process what I was doing, I called out, "Annie. Beverly. Gail. Come forth."

Kim looked uncertain, surprised at the sudden boldness that replaced my cowering. Then her face shook with fury. Her normally pale skin pulsed with crimson.

"Annie. Beverly. Gail. Rise up!" I said. No, commanded. "Rise up. Do your dance."

My words seemed to hang in the air. Powerless as dust. Then the clothes once worn by Trina, D and Vee-Money shuddered on the ground. Jeans and oversized tops ballooned, then legs and arms appeared in the openings. The air in front of me vibrated, as if stretching to accommodate this bizarre rebirth. The bodies sat up suddenly. I didn't recognize the faces of the teens, who wore pompadours and old-timey hairdos, but I knew they were Miss Iris' slain friends.

Kim watched the resurrection. Incredulous. Her blue eyes narrowed with rage. But beneath the anger, I detected a gleam of fear.

I dragged myself backwards to a tree, struggling to rise.

Unseen fingers still had a grip on my legs. "Let me go!" I shouted at Kim.

"No," she said. "I collected you. All of you."

The girls still sat in the dust, a blank look on their faces as if wondering why they had been summoned from the sleep of three decades.

"I know what you are. A soul gobbler. But you'll never steal mine," I said to Kim. Turning to Annie, Beverly and Gail, I said, "Rise up. Do your dance."

I felt like an emcee at a party, trying to move a stubborn crowd.

As the teens rose shakily to their feet, the invisible rope around my legs snapped. Kim howled in fury as the girls began to sway.

The wind kicked up harder than before, ripping out my hoop earring. Dirt stung my eyes but I held on to the tree. It was my power against Kim's power. My conjuring against hers. I had brought something back to life, something she had stolen and ruined.

As the ground hummed beneath the leaping feet of Miss Iris' friends, I knew I had won. Maybe it was my defiance or the sight of the dancing dead girls that finally destroyed Kim. As I watched, sickened, she began to melt. Her eyes receded into their sockets.

Her youthful skin cracked and peeled in long strips. Her lustrous hair thinned, until scalp was visible, a decaying field of pink. Her blue dress began to smoke at the hem, growing into an inferno that consumed her, until she was nothing but ashes on the wind.

The area once known as the clearing fell quiet.

A thudding sound startled me. The dead teens had disappeared. There was nothing left but a pile of bones and discarded clothes. I limped down the passageway, hesitant at first, then walking faster as I regained strength in my legs.

Something glittered atop the mound of clothing. Vee- Money's dog tag. My eyes filled with tears as I picked up the chain once worn by my friend, leader of the Cherry Street Crew. My girls would never know the feeling of standing on stage at sold-out arenas, of captivating crowds with words. Maybe one day I would.

I fastened the dog tag around my neck and then set about the long task of collecting the bones.

More's the Pity
by Tenea D. Johnson

Night falls, more's the pity
And she sits on a back porch awash in moonlight,
Sullied by something someone left in her:
 Not the wolf, that is welcome,
  but the key to a place too long ago to remember,
  but too sharp a loss to live with.
So she waits for the pain to pass and
  return her the focus she'll need to survive the hours
  until her body is again her own
   (this time for better, wilder reasons).

She puts away the balmy, beautiful memory of home and
  her grandmother's voice in her ear.
Even now and under the full force of the moon,
  the distance is too great,
  the ocean too vast.

Touch changes first.
Needles of sensation cover her.
She feels them grow and thin,
  bend in the breeze that blows the clouds and

delicate candle of moonlight out.

She worries for a second that the transformation will stop,

that it can be arrested as they would her, and

strip her of it as they have everything else.

Out of habit, she begins to whimper.

Even she can hear the hurt.

It will bring the hunters, more's the pity.

No better bait than vulnerability.

When they arrive

she will find

what this new strength opens,

beyond bone and flesh.

Pity them.

Summer Skin
by Zin E. Rocklyn

I saw her on the D train and she looked like an auntie so I sat down next to her and started asking her questions, but she moved away.

You see, I've got this thing with my skin and it's been so long since I've been around family. I miss my family.

We had all these remedies, all these bush baths and teas and draws that would cure you or make you shit or both and either way, I'd never felt so loved in my life.

But this thing with my skin . . . It molts.

But before that, it bubbles, inflames, kind of. It doesn't itch, it's rough, like the surface of a dried-out clementine. It becomes extra sensitive, as if my nerves are sliced open and breathing, cresting the surface of my dermis and flirting with the air.

It hurts.

It wasn't always so bad, but it seems like I've always had it.

Started as a tiny, bumpy patch on the back of my knee when I was four. I'd fallen in the front yard and my mom swooped down and carried me into the house while I screamed myself breathless.

Nothing was wrong with me; no broken bones, no deep cuts, just a little scrape on the hand that prevented my forehead from smacking into the pavement.

And that little patch.

My mom noticed when she bathed me that night in the normal concoctions that I'd hissed the moment I touched the hot water.

The temperature didn't bother me, it never bothered me, but my skin, it stung. It felt like it was being peeled away from me, from my body, and I hissed, then screamed and mom smacked my mouth, shutting me up, so she could turn me over.

She cut it off, that patch of skin. Right there, in the bath.

She took the small paring knife to it and slipped the layer right off, so quick, her wrist, that I barely felt it.

The odd thing? There was no blood.

There never is. There's this viscous clear liquid instead. Plasma, it's called, I think. I know I'm not supposed to, but I pick at it. I can't help it. When I'm not staring, I'm picking. It's fascinating. And repulsive.

And it's me.

#

She gets up, but we're between stops so there's nowhere to go. The train is packed and the route all fucked up because there's forever construction so there's a lot of white people asking questions to the kindest, yet brownest people with whom they can make eye contact.

People tell me I have a nice smile, but it doesn't outshine my skin. Still, it would be nice to be asked. Not just about the trains, about anything, really. It would be nice to be noticed.

She's stuck in the midst of a Swedish family, all blond and milky, and the father looks like he wants to ask her where the fuck we're going, but she's got that look on her face, the look that says "leave me the fuck alone".

I stare at her until she worms her way through the bodies towards the middle of the car. I stand, just to keep an eye on her, and a young pregnant woman slides into the empty seat, next to the one that her man had taken when my auntie had gotten up.

Don't think me presumptuous; I know she's pregnant, I can smell it. It's strong, like a pretty perfume amped by sweat. Her and her man, they smell alike, but he's not hers. Not really.

Anyway, my auntie, she's made it to the doors on the other side, so when we pull into West 4th she doesn't have time to look up and see me step off with her.

She's following most of the rerouted crowd for the F train and I'm following her. I'm kind of short and with the exception of my skin, I blend into the other black and brown faces, though we seem fewer and fewer these days at stops like this. No one notices my skin while rushing to another train or place or meeting, there's never enough time, so I always find a little peace in the frantic rush. Stopping makes me nervous.

It's hot, but the F is running on a higher line so we get some breeze. Still too hot for my jacket, though.

The sweat stings like hell.

I hide by the Swedish family until the little girl notices and starts staring and the mother, the smooth cream that is her face tinges with a delightful smack of strawberry jam, and she says something in her native tongue because she's so nervous she forgets the perfect English with which she'd asked questions and it sounds somewhat apologetic, so I smile at her and nod, accepting her daughter's rudeness. It's not the smile I get compliments on, it's the kind that's tight, kind of mean, expected of a Black girl with an attitude problem.

I look down and see that I've begun oozing. Before I can start to blot, the train arrives.

Me and Auntie step on through separate doors.

#

Summer was the catalyst.

Once the humidity set in, there was no controlling it. My skin would explode, hives turning into sores on top of blisters until every piece of clothing hurt.

Before the buds of my breasts came in, my mother used to let me run around the house naked. Those were the summers Mom would dress me in a smock on weekends and I'd lay down in the back seat of Daddy's car under a blanket until we pulled up in front of my aunties' house in Canarsie.

Usually at night. *Always* at night.

I had seven aunties. They all lived together. No uncles. Mom's family didn't have any men until my dad. I supposedly had a brother, a twin, but he died before we were born. I had cousins, but I haven't seen them since I started to bleed. I overheard my aunties and Mom talking about sending them "home" the morning I woke up with a pain my belly and the sheets stuck to my bum when I was fourteen.

They'd given me a special bath that day, a blue one, one that didn't sting. They told me it was nothing to be ashamed of, that I was a woman now.

And there'd be changes.

I hardly felt any of them, these changes. Except my belly hurt a lot of the time and I was hungry. Constantly hungry.

But my aunties kept me well-fed.

With my cousins gone, I could eat their plates, plus some. So my mom left me there that summer.

I never saw my mom or my dad again.

#

There's more room on the fake F train so hiding is a bit difficult, but my auntie doesn't notice me anyway. I can't lie; it hurts a little, but it won't matter soon enough.

The F follows the E until we get to Jay Street/Metrotech. There's a mass exodus as the connections and corrections are mumbled through the PA, but it doesn't include my auntie so I drift further down the car and sit next to the homeless man everyone is avoiding.

He stinks, but I don't mind. I have this thing where I can filter smells if I want to. It's useful when traversing the tunnels.

My auntie pulls out a book and my heart leaps with joy. I love books, always have. I love reading. My dad taught me when I was really young. I was the smartest kid in pre-K, so they say. I skipped a few grades, but then my condition spread and kids are mean and I started having this temper problem . . .

The F is skipping a lot of stops, but Auntie doesn't seem to mind. She's casually paying attention as we roll past the elevated stations and I try to keep an eye on her and where we are. I know these boroughs fairly well, well enough to get back to where I need to be, but I don't like feeling unmoored either.

As we pull away from Neptune Avenue, she puts her book away—some crime novel, dog-eared and shitty--and stares out the plexiglass windows.

She has beautiful, clear skin . . .

#

Winter is the kindest to me. At that point, my skin is no longer oozing or blistering. Instead it becomes hardened, dry, flaky. Feels like a callus in some spots, horny bedsores in others.

But the relief is palpable.

It's then I try to take oat baths, like my aunts taught me. It helps keep the new skin underneath healed so when my summer skin slips, it's just a matter of peeling it away. Sometimes I get too eager and make new scars but—

Oh, yeah, there are scars.

They're not so bad. It's better than the condition.

Anyway, Spring and Fall are my transitions, from relief to pain, pain to relief. But I've learned to live with it. There's no cure so there's no point to yearn for one.

But there is a way to find respite, if only for a season.

#

We get off at West 8th street and this butterfly lets loose in my belly because we're close to the boardwalk and the aquarium and I haven't been there in years. My dad used to take me—never mind.

I keep lamenting the past when my present is gaining distance. So, Auntie; she's not going to the aquarium or the boardwalk. She lives here, in the Luna Park Projects. She's in the building right on West 8th, closest to that concrete park. There's a lot of people outside, but none pay much attention to either one of us. The security door is broken so walking in a moment or two behind her is no big deal. The elevators are working and she steps on but no one else does so I put on my jacket and lift the light hood and step on and stick myself in the far corner away from her.

She doesn't seem to notice me or recognize me. I'm short and plump and I look like everyone else when my jacket is on so she has no reason to. She gets off on the 15th floor and I wait a few seconds before following her out. Her apartment is closer than I think and she's almost got the door closed before I realize which one it is.

I take a breath, raise a fist. Knock.

I hear her suck her teeth—steups is what we call it—I hear her steups as she approaches the door, but then she opens it and I try on one of those smiles for size, the good smile, the smile that people like so much, but it doesn't relax her.

It does the opposite.

Her eyebrows knit hard and she's looking me up and down like she's trying to figure me out and she sees my hands, my stupid fucking hands give me away because they're bubbling up really bad and they're oozing, too, so there's no hiding it and my auntie, she sucks in a breath, a tiny little panicked breath and moves to close the door, but I stop it with my foot and everything goes black.

#

My aunties taught me everything I know. I thought they knew everything. But they couldn't control me.

Turns out I had plenty to be ashamed of once I started to bleed. And my aunties, they tried. When the past failed them, they tried to learn me, but it was too late.

Turns out they knew nothing at all.

#

I come to in her small living room on a cracked leather couch set. Auntie's laying on the love seat while I'm in the arm chair.

She's got a shiner that's swelling before my eyes and her beautiful square jaw line is lumpy. Blood fights melanin as both discolour the surface.

Her skin is still beautiful.

Not a mark on it. No scarring, no acne.

She's got a high forehead like my first auntie, the oldest, but she favours the youngest the most, the last auntie, the one after my mom. Same burnt umber skin, same beady black eyes, same pillowy lips. Even the slight arch in her thin, short eyebrows mocks the memory of my prettiest auntie. The nose is different though; hers is thinner, straighter, almost violent in its slope. I don't like her nose.

But I like everything else about her face and her skin so I sit up and smile at her until her eyelids flutter open and those beady eyes are staring back at me.

I smile harder. Show all my teeth.

Of all the other things my body has failed me with, my teeth remain pretty and white and big. Not sure why. Genetics, I suppose.

Auntie sits up and by the look on her face, perhaps a little too fast. She touches her eye, then her jaw, then whimpers, tears brimming those bug eyes.

"You okay?" I ask. My voice is rough, croaky. Before today on the train, it'd been a long time since I'd spoken.

No need to when you're ignored.

I clear my throat. "Are you okay, Auntie?" Old habits kick in, remembering the licks received for addressing elders as if they were friends. The question is intrusive enough to catch a hard side-eye, but this is a new auntie. She wouldn't do that.

She blinks at me, five tears running down the slopes of her face, then says, "Yes, I'm fine."

"Good! You have any squash?"

Squash is my favourite. My dad made it best, but I've learned to live with substitutes.

She frowns for a moment. "Y-yes. Yes, I do."

I knew it! I knew she was an auntie! There's no accent but I know my aunties anywhere!

"May I have a glass, please?" I ask patiently, though my excitement for the sweet, tangy drink is making my heart pound.

Auntie stares at me for a long time, then nods slowly. She stands with some trouble, then shuffles her way towards the tiny kitchenette. I watch her giddily, practically climbing over the top of the chair to keep an eye on her movements. She pauses by the sink and pats her pockets, then looks around patiently. There's a cell phone charger but its empty. Right next to it, she finds what she's looking for, smashed to pieces.

"Sorry about your phone," I say. "I can get you a new one." This is a lie and we both know it but she smiles softly anyway and turns to the fridge. She takes out an old-school, probably early '70s, plastic pitcher and dumps the remains of the squash into a plastic dollar-store cup. Bright red. Red is one of my favourite colours. She looks around the kitchenette again, tugging drawers open, and sighs with disappointment. I know those sighs all too well.

Her shoulders fall a bit and she trudges back into the living room and hands me the squash, which I greedily gulp down. Still not as good as Dad's, but better than any of my aunties' attempts.

She needs more Angostura.

She sits back down on the loveseat and her body begins to shake. "Are you going to kill me?" she asks.

I frown, tears prickling my eyes. "No, Auntie, no!" I cry out. "I just—I need a bath. One of those baths. I can never get the ratio right, you know? The Florida water versus the Rose. It doesn't make sense and I can never get it right and my skin—," I tug the sleeves up with care, but it still catches on the plasma and sticks until I have to tug harder, "—it's really bad this summer and I need help."

Her apartment has grown warm so I roll the sleeves back down and take off the jacket. The acidity of my sweat has made things worse, some areas of my arms and chest cracked so bad, I can see fat. The skirt and tank top I'm wearing are sealed to my skin and this stupid fake leather chair isn't making things any better, but this is the only place to sit. She doesn't even have a table set with dinner chairs.

I shift in the arm chair and a small flap of flesh from the back of my knee comes away. It doesn't hurt compared to the area that was stuck in the jacket so I don't howl, but I do pick the piece off the chair and study it.

"Oh, Father God," Auntie says in a breath.

"See?" I say, showing her the piece. "I *need* a bath!"

"O-okay," she sputters.

"Do you have the stuff? All the different waters?" I ask. I'm being rude, but I'm desperate; Auntie has to understand.

She nods slowly.

"Do you have air conditioning?" She nods again.

"Can you put it on? It's hot in here.

And I'll have to nap afterwards; you know that, right? So put on the air in the bedroom, if you have it."

"I do," she says. "Good," I say.

She stands and runs her hands on her thin thighs. She's small, my new auntie. Not at all like my other ones. They were all big women with broad shoulders and huge guts and far-reaching breasts. I loved cuddling with them. This auntie is bony and I realize she looks a lot younger than I'd originally thought. Almost too young to be an auntie.

"Where . . . where did you put my knives?" she asks, her voice shaking.

I shrug. "I don't know what I do when I'm in the black," I say and it's the truth and we both know it, so she nods and walks towards to the large window and turns on the air. It takes a minute, but the stale air turns cool, then cold and I'm sighing in relief. She returns to the loveseat and I stand up so quickly she flinches, but I ignore her to stand directly in front of the unit.

I don't know if it's real or a psychosomatic relief, but I swear I hear my skin crinkle and sigh.

Once the pain subsides, I walk back over to the arm chair, but I don't sit. Instead, I say, "May I have more squash, please?" I'm being greedy, I know, especially since it's before dinner, but I love squash and it's been a couple years since I've had some.

"I don't have any more limes," she whispers, her eyes widening with something like hope. "I can get some, though."

I grit my teeth. "No store."

"No, just down the hall. Miss Toddy always has limes," she says desperately.

"No. No neighbours." I blow out a breath and try not to let the disappointment turn into tears. "No squash, then." I sigh again.

This really hurts. "What's for dinner?" I flinch, remembering the last time I'd asked something like that so casually.

Whatever in de fuck I cook, das what!

I whimper, then shake my head. "I can cook," I say, trying to pep up. "It's been a while, but I never forget."

"I don't have anything thawing," she says. "But I can order Chinese."

Again, I'm fighting anger through my jaw. "No. Stop trying to leave before giving me my bath. I need to eat before you do, though, so what do you have that I can cook?"

Finally, she's had enough. Her whole face sets hard and she shoots up from the couch. "Go look in the fucking fridge, crazy-ass bitch." Almost immediately, she stops herself, sobers as if someone popped her on the mouth after a bad word flew from it, but I'm too sad to do anything but deflate and drag my feet towards the kitchenette.

I open the fridge first, then freezer, then cabinets and see that she's right, she doesn't have much, barely anything at all, just some chicken quarters in the freezer that will take forever to defrost.

I have to eat and I have to do it soon.

She's a terrible auntie.

My skin ripples and my belly growls for the first time in a very long time. I try not to let it growl ever because when it does, it's almost like being in the black—I have no idea what will happen.

But when I look at her, I don't feel sad or scared: I feel angry.

I feel like she deserves whatever is coming to her for being so horrible to me. I've been nothing but nice and respectful and she can't even feed me before my bath.

My belly growls again. And I change.

#

I come to naked in a bathtub full of cool water, my ruined clothes on the floor beside me, and a little bit of blood on the tiles. I shift and various perfumes tickle my nose, meaning I attempted the concoction again.

This one smells a little closer to home.

Florida, Kananga, Rose, *Aqua Divin*, and Holy. No one would be able to tell, considering how murky and thick the water has become, but I can smell it. All of them.

I smile. Then sit up and pass my hands along my arms, watching in fascination as the old Summer Skin sloughs away, revealing new, soft, gorgeous mahogany flesh. It's perfect, my new skin. Perfect and beautiful and condition free.

My smile grows wider as I continue the shed. From my breasts to my feet, my legs to my belly.

I am brand new.

When I think I'm done, I stand in the water and let the few chunks plop back down. I step out and dry my feet on my old clothes stiff with plasma and reach for a decorative towel to dry the rest of my skin. I do something rude to the embroidered flower in between my legs for a little mischief, then turn to drain the tub. I'll have one shitty clean up to do, but it won't matter. The task won't be halted by cracking, tight, swollen skin.

I use the same towel to wipe down the droplets on the tiles, then hang it back. I search through her lotions and pick the least scented one, slathering it almost erotically slow over the smooth expanse of my skin. Once done, I look at myself in the mirror and for the first time in years, I like what I see.

I need a plan, but for the next few days I'll have to lay low here.

My new skin will be sensitive and highly reactive to the outside. The sun is my enemy. Summer makes it worse. I want to enjoy the gift my auntie has given me. As long as the air is still kicking, I'll be fine. No food, but I'm satiated beyond normal.

I'll have to work on a story though, like one of those mysteries I used to love reading. Because there's a knock at the door and a body in the hallway and I don't want to hurt my new skin.

Gotraskhalana ("stumbling upon the name"):
A Blues*
by Tiffany Austin

There is a South in sound. Pear shaped sounds.
Inside—skinned rose flesh. Hard mattresses. Gussing up to a yard
full of opened graves. Familiar dust. Moored to bud
—all in the body. Only scar that remains
is leaning. Coltrane's sheets. Otis
rubybreasted. Burlap thighs sitting on water.
Color turned inner on a leaf.
Between sediment of embrace, breaking
and I want to give my mother a child that weighs like my father.
Love mask, sea chipped.
Wafted with back. Dry salt cut. Reminds me
of a smell you can't catch. Honey sun. Memory
is near here. Bodies want to be wearable
a friend tells me and that little boys' bodies in homes
are being sent out to make sure
there is no sound after the bullets have fallen.
Raw livers. Familiar dust. A long lap of women at a funeral,
they tell me I am not a woman who will have a hard life.
They don't know. I hope I can forget. Long and squat
necks. Honea path.* Cleve. Cusped.

*Honea path is a small town in South Carolina, where the people still
discuss a hanging that was not historically recorded.

Taking the Good
by Dana Mcknight

I ran my eyes along the serrated ramparts of the superstore's tall aisles, scanning for the tell-tale nipple of the security camera implanted into the ceiling. For all its grandiose plans of becoming the next major you-can-purchase-everything-here retail chain, it was still privy to the budget of a mom and pop. The only recording devices in the store hovered over the registers, daring underpaid cashiers to make a move—any move other than the listless thumbing of small bills into the cash drawers. I slid my gaze back to the dirty linoleum floor, where my shoe laces lay splayed against my sneakers. Stooping, I tied them with purposefully tight double-knots.

There was a shuffling behind me: plastic cellophane rubbing against the worn inner lining of a leather jacket that I could smell from my crouch on the ground and the space between me slicked almost immediately. Rising, I breathed through my nose to calm myself and turned to meet her cool gaze.

"I'm good." She said, and I knew it was code for Let's Go. Or I Have Everything I Want For Now. Her jacket was loose enough to hide the bulge of batteries, orange juice (with 15% real juice) and chocolate chip cookies from the random passerby; but I knew her form too well—all iron lines and shadowed clefts where hips could have jutted. Black hair, chopped into stark angles with dollar store scissors, framing a heart-shaped face. Her mouth was set into a hard impatient line under wild grey eyes that made her nose inconsequential.

I turned, a bit unsteady suddenly and made a casual bee-line towards the main exit. She strode behind me, silent as a hawk. The back of my head itched as if touched by ghosts.

We passed the row of registers with their Zombie detail, crossed the threshold of the automatic doors and high-tailed it to my little Toyota hatchback parked a few inconvenient meters from the front entrance. Or, at least, I picked up the pace. I had already unlocked the door and jumped in a few seconds before she had even stepped off the curb to the parking lot.

My breath was hitching, my fingers gripping the steering wheel when she opened the passenger-side door and plopped inside.

"You did well, Helene," she said to me as she fished in the glove compartment for menthols.

The cigarette was meant to calm and it did. I felt my heartbeat slowing to a respectable gallop—the endorphins pushing and shaping my terror into a warm ball in my lower stomach.

"Did we have any more stops, Normandy?" I asked, nervous and partially horny.

"Naw." She lit up, breathing a lungful before expelling it into the confines of the car. It was too cold to open the window. The air outside had the hard edge of fast winter all over it, leaving the earth a mess of ashy lawns and black-iced asphalt though leaves still fell in crumbled wads from the trees. I had never loved winter in Buffalo and nervously avoided anyone who did.

Reaching across Normandy's lap, I tugged at the crushed pack of cigarettes in her hand, overly aware of the path my elbow made across her small tits. Seeming not to notice, she stuck a hand in her jacket pocket and pulled out the cookies. My stomach growled. We had traded the last of our foodstamps for Newports—Normandy's idea, not mine.

Sighing through the drag of the cigarette—I revved the engine and peeled out of the parking lot to the freeway that would lead us downtown. It was late Friday night and there was only one dyke bar in the City still open; its counters laden with half-empty drinks that the stocky bar-backs would not be able to keep up with. We called ourselves Drink Pirates to make our poverty something other than pitiful.

We had no claim to the title of starving artists since our combined artistic merit was a composition notebook that

Normandy kept filled with scribbled quotes of better poets than herself and I. We weren't equipped with tales that travelers stocked. And though packaged ramen and mayo-heavy egg sandwiches made up the better part of our diets; we didn't starve. I worked and Normandy took and I was content for the feel of her hands warming under the weight of my breasts.

After a while, the glow of the neighborhoods hardened from sparse edge-of-town street lamps to gleaming neon liquor store signs. I elbowed the car door lock, nervously. Normandy, pulled out another cigarette, glaring at her reflection in the passenger window, shooting herself the same expressionless mask I often thought was reserved for only me. She ran a hand through her dark hair—patting down loyal strands as I pulled the car into a neat space a block away from the bar.

"Can we get any closer?" Normandy asked, pausing in her self-scrutiny to level a stony gaze around the dilapidated street.

Trash littered the ground, and blackened alleys snaked through the spaces between broken buildings, empty houses and over-grown yards. Gathered at the end of the street, a gaggle of surly butch dykes of a variety of ages fisted brown bottles of cheap domestic beer a few respectable feet away from the bar. A cloud of cigarette smoke dangled in the air above them.

I shook my head. "Not since last time." My voice was a mumble, since it was obvious Normandy had been too drunk to even remember the chick who had slammed a brick through the car window when she had discovered her wallet peeking out of the back pocket in Normandy's cutoffs. I always made sure to park away from the bar, just in case we had to quicken our exit. The women with narrow senses of justice had paunches that we could outrun at our most wasted.

Normandy climbed out of the car and I followed a step behind, watching her strong gait; the shoulders rolling under her leather with each step. The dykes at the door stared like hyenas as we passed them; poor, but bleeding with the pride of youth.

Despite the time, the bar was full to bursting. Dated house-music throbbed through the shabby speakers arranged against the corners of the room. Bodies gyrated in a sea of denim and white racer-back tank tops. We were dark of cloth, sporting other uniforms for another era that had either passed or had yet to come. Normandy grabbed a half-empty beer from the bar, smoothly tipping it back as she prowled the outskirts of the linoleum dance-floor and eyed the assembled women with the casual gaze of a collector. I settled next to her in the shadows, an outline of sweatshirt and elbows. She passed me the bottle and I drank the tepid liquid somewhat gratefully.

"You smell amazing."

The breathy voice grazed my ear and I jumped into a spin to glare at the woman standing behind me.

She was tall—the stuff of Roman Temples and Alexandrian libraries and gold-plated hieroglyphs, draped in a black body-con top that clutched her apple-pert breasts like armor. Her mouth was a shocking red—but she wasn't a lipstick. The eyes staring back at me, even in the black of the dance-floor—were hard and aggressive. Her arms were bare and sleek with muscle and her black slim-leg jeans were tucked into boots of good leather. I had never seen a woman darker than me in this bar—and I felt my tongue click the top of my mouth with excitement and trepidation.

I felt Normandy tense next to me, but not in anger.

"Is that patchouli?" The Amazon leaned in again, her nose passing my line of tumbled hair towards the space on my neck near my ear. I looked to Normandy in alarm.

"Do you speak?" The woman asked, backing away, though her lips curved slightly upward. Her dark eyes flicked along the path of my gaze to Normandy who was staring. "Is this your girlfriend?"

"She's not my girlfriend," Normandy answered, though the question wasn't for her.

The woman made a low noise in her throat like a breeze through an old forest then the spotlight of her gaze slid slowly back to me. My scalp itched as I saw myself through her eyes; medium height, with shoulder-length brown coils in need of a good moisturizer. My eyes were hazel, compliments of my Polish mother and my skin was the mild beige of franchise coffee-shop lattes. My dad was brown—Dominican, because he never claimed Black.

I tugged at my dark purple plaid button-up and unconsciously shifted my stance onto my hip to minimize my belly.

"What's your name?" Normandy asked, moving in closer. The smell of her leather jacket jolted me back into myself and I blushed furiously.

The woman's eyes did not move from my face. "Lamia."

Normandy was eyeing her in that way she did whenever she wanted something. And I knew exactly what it was.

This woman was the golden apple in the Tree that Normandy had thought picked clean. I looked around, spotting a clear path through the sloppy movements on the dance-floor to the back patio. There I could smoke a cigarette or four and wait until Normandy was ready to take Lamia back to our house where I would settle on the porch with my headphones and my Gits and pretend that I didn't mind the smell of another woman on the fold-out couch that Normandy and I both slept on.

"I'll be back." I intoned, stepping away. "And where are you going, Beautiful?"

I stopped. Lamia was looking at me. Normandy, for the first time, looked startled. Confused. As if the possibility of such a creature as fantastic as the woman in front of us could have absolutely nothing to do with me.

My breath caught in my throat at the intensity of her eyes. There was a pockmark by the edge of Lamia's brow. I focused on it.

"Smoking." I managed to choke out.

"I'll join you." Her lips parted and I saw white teeth glimmer. "But I've other things if you would like them."

"We should go outside then." Normandy interjected, her pale eyes stark with something other than the promise of substance.

Lamia glanced at her as though she had just noticed Normandy's presence and her wealth wafting off of her like heavy perfume.

Dread swelled through me.

The pack of dykes by the door had dispersed back inside of the warmth of the bar, though their cigarette smoke lingered in the still night air. I buttoned the top of my heavy shirt, trembling as the cold punched through the fabric. Normandy led the way, passing our car and ducking into an alley off the side of an abandoned welding company. I followed a few yards behind; sneakered feet crunching over glass and pebbled mortar. I chanced a look behind me; Lamia had taken up the rear, striding silently along the street, cloaked in so much shadow the street lamps seemed to dim as she passed.

Noticing my scrutiny, she smiled.

I halted until she was abreast of me. Normandy was several yards away and still walking.

"Are you from New York City?" I asked. It was where people like her came from. Lamia's will seemed too palpable. My voice was tin in the crisp cold.

"No." Her breath did not raise plumes of smoke like mine did. "But I lived there once. A long time ago."

"Then, where are you from?" I tried not to look at her, but my eyes were no longer commanded by my brain.

"Nowhere and everywhere. I've lived in many places in my lifetime." I nodded in false understanding, ignoring the fact that none of my previous questions had been answered.

"So why are you in a crappy dyke bar in this crappy town?" Normandy interjected.

She laughed, a bone-warming chuckle that raised my nipples.

When her gaze met mine, it held me and stroked me from the inside out. "I was looking for something…good."

I wanted to stop walking, take her hand and pull her back from the path that Normandy had left for us, and bring her back to the cozy bleakness of the bar. Share, taste and touch all of her secrets.

But Normandy had stopped a few feet ahead and had fisted her palms in her pockets where I knew her fingers wrapped around the ivory handle of her butterfly knife. Her face was cool and steady. A thief—no, a cruel shadow of a sphinx, in an urban wasteland. I had long ago traded my compass for her, and now I felt even the stars couldn't place me on this black night.

Lamia brushed past me, reaching in her pocket for her wallet where green, gold and black flashed within. She slipped her long fingers in and out. Pinched betwixt two red lacquered nails was a small bag of fine white crystals. I watched Normandy's eyes dart reptilian from the wallet to the bag and I felt bile rise in my belly.

"So, are you here visiting family?" I asked, tone desperate as I tried to add the possibility of humanity, circumstances and retribution to the situation. Normandy didn't flinch.

"No. I'm alone in this world," Lamia replied, sliding a long red fingernail into the bag. She lifted the filled tip to my nose first and I snorted sadly.

"So am I," Normandy said, placing a finger to her nostril. Lamia obliged.

I am, too, I thought, but didn't need to say.

We took several more bumps and the night air took on a shimmer—a sharpness that had not been there before.

"You are something, Lady." Normandy's voice broke through the silence. She had moved her body closer to Lamia and her lips slipped into the smirk that always worked. It had certainly worked on me a summer ago. But Lamia was unlike me.

No gasp incurred or mirror smile of acquiescence. No pleasure at Normandy's sudden sexual acknowledgement, pleasurable feminine sigh or lust-soaked kiss. Lamia was not me. Instead there was a long moment of intense quiet and that was how both Normandy and I realized that the woman before us cared nothing for her.

I felt my heart pound as cool hate blanked the arousal from Normandy's face.

"We should go back," I said quietly, looking to both of them. My eyes rested on Normandy's—but her eyes were steel and her hand pulled from her leather jacket, brandishing the blade.

"Gimme your wallet. Now." Normandy lifted the blade to Lamia's face. I bit my lip.

"We don't need it," I whimpered, coke lighting my senses. I gazed at Lamia who laughed, a tone too nasty for the royal beauty of her face.

A flicker of shock passed over Normandy's eyes and her mouth grew hard. "Did you hear me, you dumb cunt? I said, give me your wallet."

Lamia's head turned in a slow arc to face me and at once I was bathed in the heat of her gaze. Her eyes were gentle. "Do you want to come with me, Helene?" Her voice was frost on brick.

Brittle and stalwart at the same time. The question was for me, but pointed at Normandy.

I nodded yes, tears wavering my vision.

Normandy screamed. A sound ripping apart the stunted dams that had kept her at bay from me and the world for more years than I had ever known her. It was a scream of rage, and torture—intense things that had reflected deep in the glass recesses of her eyes. Once, I had thought of them as things of love—of past agonies too near to her heart to ever be relinquished to another person again. That patience and comfort and steady lives could save her and me both. As Normandy leapt for Lamia's throat, I understood that I had been wrong.

She could never love me.

I screamed, too. But for Lamia. And then my scream cut off.

There was a slapping sound of bone and wet as four large oil-black tentacles flashed from the space behind Lamia's back. The smell of sulphur and ocean filled my nostrils, and a great negative pressure tightened the air around my skin. Lamia held Normandy as the Sycamore once held the Negro. The tentacles that had erupted from her back circled around Normandy's throat, pushing her up against the frozen brick so high that her boots clacked against the wall as they attempted to find purchase. Normandy's eyes were wide with terror and I could see thin rivers of blood running through the coils of the tentacles where the long red thorns had seized and pierced the tender flesh of her neck. The butterfly knife lay splayed on the ground, snapped cleanly in half.

Lamia turned to me, brown eyes gilded with scarlet, her long canines glistening through the black shadows of the alley. The voice that slipped through her mouth was as old and horrible as the cold that swept through the brown fields. Normandy gurgled, attempting to breath through the blood and bone trashing her esophagus. The tentacles squeezed harder.

"Come with me and I will love you, Helene—as no other has."

I peeked at Normandy, one of her hands had stopped batting at the vise of Lamia's grip and the other waved feebly at me. Her pale silver eyes dulled with shock as death cobalted her lips. Sniffing a bit at the ice in my nose, I nodded. Done. Lamia knew me—as well as they all did.

"I'll come with you," I said, turning my back on Normandy whose gurgles had shifted in pitch to a horrible keening. A final understanding. Lamia laughed and there was a scream followed by a tearing noise and then a splash of hot wet upon my back as I relinquished my terrible ardor for another.

Polydactyly
by Tanesha Nicole Tyler

I was predestined to be seen as a monster.
When I came from my mother's womb,
the hospital room bore witness to a
newborn with 12 fingers and 11 toes.

They call this Polydactyly.

When I Googled "polydactyly"
The browser asked
"Did you mean pterodactyl?"
By that, I'm sure I was predestined to extinction.
My screams fossilized and called history,
as if my history could be recorded so easily.

I never see people like me in the history books.
Authors think as long as they mention
the man with a dream and how this country
eventually realized that slavery was
kind of really fucked up,
It's enough to satisfy the hunger in our starving bellies.

Some representation is better than none.
At least, that's what I've always been told.
I learned that when something is broken,
It is to be disposed of instead of trying to fix it.

In fourth grade I jumped out of a swing,
landed wrong, dislocated my right pinky toe.
When I awoke from surgery, the doctor
explained to me that it was too
complicated to reconstruct the bones
so they ultimately decided to take it off.

Now that I only have 9 toes,
I guess that still makes me a monster.
A monster that feels things.
You see, my nerve endings are all intact,
essentially it's like the toe is still there.
A phantom limb that still feels pain.
Being this Black feels like a phantom limb.
Invisible to everyone else but me.

This isn't supposed to be a poem
about what Black feels like.

Isn't supposed to be me telling you
that I am more afraid of my sister
wanting to go to college in
Baltimore because of the color of her skin,
and not because she's in a wheelchair
and has no family that far East to look out for her.

This shouldn't be me telling
you that when I watched
a 7 minute video of a white cop dragging
a young Black girl across the grass
by her hair, I couldn't help but feel her pain.
As I watched him kneeling for
2 minutes on her back,
it was my airway that started to close.

This fictive kinship is what Black feels like.

This was never supposed to be a
poem about what Black feels like though.

This was just supposed to be me telling you
about how I had a toe that the doctors
took off because it was abnormal to them.
And this story is probably not normal to you.

Normal is funny you see,
in the Black community extra digits are normal.
Functional even.
To cut them off is to say one can do without.
Which is to say not necessary.
Which is to say there are parts of me
not worth keeping.

Mona Livelong: Paranormal Detective II
by Valjeanne Jeffers

The Case of the Powerless Witch
A Steamfunk Horror Tale
(novel excerpt)

Chapter 1

Shadows danced along the walls. Nanette moaned piteously. She twisted her head away from them, and shut her eyes tightly, praying they would disappear. But she knew they wouldn't. She'd awakened them. Awakened Him.

There was no escape.

He appeared out of thin air, his breath reeking of death, snarling as he pinned her to the bed. The daemon wore the face of Stewart, her husband. The thing she'd summoned had invaded his body, and taken her prisoner ...

Mona shuddered and opened her eyes. Waking up came slowly; she could still feel the woman's terror. Nanette had brought this horror upon herself. She'd killed her husband's mistress with sorcery. But Mona pitied her. She'd dreamed of Nanette, actually fused with her while she slept.

Something would have to be done, and soon. Evil like this would spread if left unchecked.

Mona, an ebony-colored young woman with thick lips, and short wavy hair, raised up on her elbows, and looked across her bedroom at the tall grandfather clock. It was only five-thirty AM. The tall, slender woman rose, pulled her robe from the armchair beside the bed, and slipped it on.

She fumbled for one of the long matches on her nightstand, struck it on the small piece of flint she kept there, and lit the oil lamp on her nightstand. Holding the lamp aloft, Mona walked down the hallway to her living room. She put the lamp on her coffee table, sat down on the couch, and pulled the curtain back from the window, searching the pre-dawn sky.

Mona was in a melancholy mood. She missed Curtis, missed him so bad it hurt. She ached for his touch, his smile. *He was pushed over the edge when he saw me kill those things ... He'll be back— the next time he needs help with a case.* She had a sudden image of the two of them working side by side, like strangers.

Mona bit back her tears. *It's too early to start crying. Yeah,* she thought sourly. *Plenty of time for that later, right? Like in the middle of the night when I start missing him so bad I look for one of his shirts to sleep with.*

A shadow moved past her window. Only it didn't walk. It glided.

Mona jumped up, and hurried through her living room, out into the chilly dawn. The air was heavy with fog. A slender, male figure, dressed in a tuxedo jacket and top hat, crossed the street at an unhurried, almost leisurely pace, his boots floating just above the cobblestones.

The figure stopped. His head turned laboriously in her direction without moving his body. Mona imagined she heard bolts creaking.

He had no face.

Just a blank space framed by his hair and the outline of his skull. But she knew the creature could *see* her.

A rip opened in the air before her … stretching until the street disappeared. She was standing at a graveyard in the dead of midnight … a graveyard with crooked wooden tombstones, and ragged knolls of grass.

A specter stood at the edge of the cemetery, his head still turned toward her. But he'd transformed …

… into a tall, dark man wearing a tuxedo jacket and top hat with a golden band. A man with a young face, and timeless coal-black eyes. In his right hand he held a smoldering cigar.

"Papa Twilight . . ." Mona breathed.

He puffed his cigar, and a cloud of smoke drifted toward her. *"Sa Se Yonba Ki Kritik,"* he said in a soft bass. It was as if he had whispered in her ear.

Mona flinched. The loa had spoken her father's words in Creole: *This is a life and death struggle.*

She shivered, goose flesh rising on her arms. The graveyard vanished and she was returned to her own street. For a long moment, she stared at the space where Papa Twilight had stood, before stumbling back inside.

She fetched the oil lamp from her coffee table, and continued down the hallway to her kitchen to make coffee. Sleep was now out of the question; she was too keyed up.

Dressed, a cup of coffee in hand, Mona unlocked the adjoining door in her foyer to her office. She set the cup down on her desk, and lit another oil lamp.

Chapter 2

Sipping a cup of coffee, Haitian Detective Curtis Dubois stood looking out through the barred window of Constable Station 33 at the cobblestone streets below. He had skin the color of brown sugar, close-cropped hair, and sported a thin mustache over his full lips, and looked younger than his thirty-two years.

The weather was mild, and Monterrey folks' dress reflected the warm temperatures. Spring dresses and skirts with corsets.

Waistcoats and knickers without socks. Those with convertible steam-autos had their tops down.

It was slow this week, which for a homicide detective was a good thing. He, Mona, and his partner, Harold, had thwarted a plot to slaughter Monterrey's people of color. Since then, a calm seemed to have fallen over the city. Curtis remembered their last battle in the warehouse—Mona swooping through the air like an ebony bird of prey while he watched slack-jawed, as she sliced through one Wendigo after another with a flaming sword.

He realized he was witnessing a supernatural force of nature. This woman was so sexy, so fierce, and at the same time so vulnerable. *But who could stand up to that? Who could stand up to* her? *She made me feel like … like less than a man.*

His mind drifted to his parents. If anyone were to ask, he would've said without hesitation that they were happily married. But his mother made all the decisions—from what schools he and his two sisters attended, to the house they'd finally bought.

Watching all this as a teenager, Curtis had vowed, *I'll never be like that. I'll never let a woman lead me around like a dog on a leash. When I get married, if I get married, I'm gonna call the shots.*

Now, at age thirty-two, he was hopelessly in love with a woman who was stronger than he was—a sorceress. She didn't try to run his life. But she had her own mind, her own way of doing things. She refused to be controlled.

And I still want her.

So much self-reflection, so early in the day was bringing him down. He ran his eyes over the windows. The bars had been added after a prisoner had been murdered inside the station. Curtis shook his head, smiling ruefully. The night of the attack the glass hadn't been shattered. The killers had floated through the front door like they owned the joint.

Anything to make the big brass, feel safe. Mwen pa santi m an sekirite. Non. If they decided to come back, all the bars in the city wouldn't stop them.

There was a shift in the air pressure. Suddenly, the air seemed thicker, harder to breathe. Frowning, Curtis turned from the window, and saw a man dressed a high-collared suit and top hat. He was *floating* pass the Constables' desks, his shoes an inch above the floor. The officers on either side of him had stopped talking, stopped moving. Time was frozen.

The detective's cup slipped from his hand, fell to the floor and shattered. Curtis raced after him. As the figure reached the corner, he turned his head to look at Curtis.

He had no face.

The Haitian detective stumbled back—almost skidding to the floor. The specter lingered for a moment, and then melted away the wall to his right.

In a flurry, the precinct returned to life. "Hey, who dropped their cup on the floor? Whoever did it, your mama don't live here! Clean this shit up!"

Chapter 3

Mona sat at her mahogany desk edged in bronze, a thick book with yellowed pages before her. Another fat volume had been pushed to the side of her desk. To her left and right, books were scattered on the floor beside the wooden bookcases. She was trying to find out who or what had been outside her door this morning.

He wanted me to know he was there. He knew me. That's why he used daddy's words.

The bell above the door tinkled, and a woman stepped inside. At first glance, she looked to be forty or forty-five. But a second glance revealed that she was closer to sixty. Large green eyes peered from a delicately lined face the color of ginger. Thick salt and pepper hair was pulled back from her heart-shaped face in a chignon. A form-fitting gray dress with a lace hem clung to her petite, yet voluptuous frame. A drawstring purse, the color of her eyes, dangled from her wrist.

"Miss Livelong?"

"Yes, ma'am," Mona said.

"My name is Ruby Hauflin. I'd like to hire you."

Mona gestured to one of the two chintz armchairs facing her desk. "Have a seat, Miss Hauflin. What can I do for you?"

"My moonstone necklace is missing. I'd like you to find it." "I don't usually take cases involving lost items. Where did

you lose it?"

"Forgive me. That was poor choice of words. A troll stole it from me."

Mona cocked an eyebrow. "Excuse me?"

The beautiful matron smiled, a smile that didn't quite reach her green eyes. They were cold and speculating. Mona felt a twinge of unease. "My dear, you are after all a paranormal detective—a sorceress. Am I right?" Mona's jaw dropped in surprise; she nodded. "Then, I'm sure you're familiar with trolls."

The young detective smiled tightly. "Yeah, but most of my clients aren't."

"I'm just being honest. I know a troll stole my necklace. And I'd like you to get it back."

Can't argue with that. "I charge four hundred dollars. That's just to get me started. I may charge more. It depends on how much trouble it is to get your necklace back—how dangerous the job is. If I have to travel, you pay the bill."

"Those are fair terms." The older woman pulled her drawstring purse from her wrist, put it her lap, and pulled out a velvet bag of coins. She put it on Mona's desk. "That's five hundred. You can count it if you like."

Mona didn't touch the bag. "Ms. Hauflin, can I ask you a question?" The older woman nodded. "Are you a witch?"

Ruby chuckled, a brittle sound like breaking glass. Again Mona felt a sliver of unease. "My, my you are perceptive. I was a witch. An enemy stripped me of my powers. My necklace is the only thing of value left from those years. It's very dear to me." Her eyes filled with tears. She fumbled through her purse, pulled out a lace handkerchief, and dabbed at her eyes.

Unmoved, Mona watched her closely; not entirely sure her tears were real. Her reading of the woman, her telepathic abilities, told her Ruby wasn't lying. But there were spaces behind the woman's words she couldn't reach ... Hidden, secret spaces.

I need this case. I need the money.

"I'll take the case. I didn't mean to offend you," Mona said. "In this business, you can't be too careful. I'm sure you understand."

"Of course, dear, and thank you. Could you stop by my house for tea today? There's a portrait of me wearing the necklace. You can get a good look at it, and perhaps we can sniff out the troll together."

Mona pushed a tablet and scroll pen across her desk. "Write your address down. I can be there at one o' clock."

"One o' clock would be fine. I'll see you then." Ruby rose and walked out the door, leaving the scent of lavender behind her.

She'd forgotten about her strange, early morning visitor. Mona remembered him now, and brushed aside her worry. He no longer seemed important.

Chapter 4

Ruby lived on the North side of Clearwater in a picturesque, two-story cottage with a chimney and turrets. Trees grew here and there in her yard, and a path of colored stones led to her door. She answered the door wearing a wine-colored robe and silk lounging pants. "Welcome to my home. You're very prompt. I like that."

Mona followed her into a living area furnished with plush armchairs and sofas, and crystal oil lamps. To their right was a foyer dominated by a staircase, and beyond it more expensively furnished rooms.

A flurry of conversation and laughter drifted through the hallway. "I have boarders," the older woman explained. "It how I make ends meet. When I was a witch ... well, no need to go into that." She pointed to the wall adjacent to them.

"That's the portrait I told you about."

An oil painting of a much younger Ruby wearing a cobalt- blue moonstone about her neck, centered the wall across from them.

Mona walked over and stood before the painting, hands clasped behind her back. "That's a Cat's Eye, isn't is? It's beautiful."

Behind her, Ruby touched her throat as if stroking the stone. "Yes, it is."

Mona turned, her brow furrowed. "You said a troll stole it from you? Are you sure?"

"I was friends with many Others for hundreds of years." She smiled at Mona's expression of surprise. "I'm considerably older than I look. Even being an ex-witch has its benefits. I know a troll stole my necklace because the loathsome little creatures are thieves. I just don't know which one. But I can give you a list of names."

A young white woman with pouting lips, wearing a ruffled thigh-length black dress, a white apron, and black fishnet stockings wheeled in a cart with a tea pot, and a tray of finger sandwiches.

"I did promise you tea," said Ruby. "Would you like lemon or milk?" The serving girl stirred a cup with lemon and sugar, and handed it to her mistress.

Mona gazed longing at the delicious looking little sandwiches. "No, thank you. I just ate."

Working, expending magical energy, made her hungry.

Despite having eaten less than twenty minutes ago, she was ravenous. But, she had no intention of eating or drinking anything Ruby offered her.

The ex-witch wasn't fooled. Her rosebud mouth turned up in smirk. "You know, Mona, I wouldn't hire you and then try to poison you."

Poison me? No, that wasn't what I had in mind. More like make me your slave for all eternity. Once a witch, always a witch.

Witches and warlocks weren't all cut from the same cloth. Folks chose sides, and not everybody chose the side of righteousness.

She made her way to the armchair across from Ruby, trying not to look at tray. *Damn, even the tea smells good.* "I'm not hungry, Ms. Hauflin," she lied. "Tell me, why would a troll want your necklace?"

Ruby sipped delicately at her tea. "Please, call me Ruby.

Trolls are very fond of moonstones—nasty little creatures that they are. The stones are magical. I'm surprised you didn't know that. Their gifts are useless to me," the older woman smiled. "But in the hands of an Other, I'm sure you see the possibilities. Gail, bring me a scroll and pen."

Mona eyed the older woman curiously. "But if you knew they were thieves, why let them get close enough to steal from you?"

"As I said before, we were friends."

That don't make a lick of sense. But alright, this is your party.

The maid returned with a flowery scroll and a quill pen. "I'm giving you four names," Ruby said, writing. She stopped, and looked up sharply at her maid, who was hovering over her shoulder. "That will be all." Her eyes shot daggers of ice.

Gail curtseyed nervously. "Yes, Miss Ruby." She hurried out of the room.

Ruby waited until she'd left and went on, "One of them has my necklace. I'm sure of it."

Mona took the list. One name at the top of the list stood out. *Dartanian.*

Chapter 5

"I know that a troll stole my necklace because the loathsome little creatures are thieves." Nobody should be called a thief without evidence. But Mona hadn't contradicted Ruby because she'd been *listening*. Ruby had told her something very important. She was a racist. Still, Mona would have to be careful. Trolls, like all Others, possessed magical abilities.

At home, Mona dined on an early supper of fried fish and rice. Then she wrapped up her dessert—two cheese pastries—and took them to her office. She stuck a hand-painted calligraphy *Closed* sign in the window, and drew the shutters.

The tall woman pulled a book, *Stones and Their Magical Powers* from her bookshelf. She turned to the chapter labeled *Moonstones*, tapped it twice with her fingertips, and a dulcet voice echoed through the room, *"Semiprecious moonstones hold a strong connection to the moon."*

Mona sat back down at her desk, munching her pastries. As the book spoke, mellifluous colors streamed from the pages, and coalesced in the middle of the floor ... creating images.

"Some legends say that they were the frozen tears of the Moon goddess that fell to the Earth when she quarreled with her lover ..." Image of a woman and man appeared before Mona. They kissed. Fought. And parted.

The moon's tears fell to the floor, and crystallized. A moonstone waved into view; another moving image of farmers tilling fields appeared beneath it. *"Moonstones were especially useful for protection in tough times, for fertility rites."* An image of a midwife came into view ... *"and for stabilizing the humors of the body ..."*

Mona wiped her hands on the cloth napkin in her lap,

and tapped the book twice. It fell silent. She waved her hand again, and spoke in singsong voice, "My Spirit Guide needs nourishment." Mona felt a pulling sensation as the magic left her body. A glowing spout appeared in her chest, and her magic poured from it, creating a replica of the pastries she'd just eaten. Palavers with the spirit realm always came with a price. She only hoped she wouldn't have to call The Oracle, who would charge a much heavier debt.

"Spirit Guide, please come to me," Mona said. "I have need of your wisdom."

A gossamer indigo-blue female creature smudged into view, floating two inches above the floor. She was hairless, and her face was smooth with only a suggestion of eyes, nose, and mouth, her body was a mosaic of curves and shadows.

"I bid you greeting, Mona. You are well?" "I am, my Muse," Mona replied, "and you?" "I am always well."

"Here," Mona held out the magical plate of pastries. "My offering to you."

"I thank you, Mona." Her Muse crooked a finger. The plate floated to her, and was absorbed into her shimmering frame.

"I have some questions about the sorceress, Ruby Hauflin.
Is she powerless?"

"Oh, yes," her guide answered in a voice like a crystal bell. "She has been without power for a hundred years."

"Is she guilty of evil deeds?"

The being hovered in silent contemplation. "Yes," she said finally.

Everybody messes up sometimes. "Many evil deeds?" Another briefer, pause. "Yes."

Damn! She's a wrong-doer and a racist. Alright, she's no angel. So what?

"Why does Ruby want the moonstone back?

"That answer is hidden from me."

Hidden. Someone went to a lot of trouble to hide the truth. But why? Why would she lie to me?

Mona felt a prickle of unease. She pushed it away. *Clients lie. They have their reasons. Maybe some married wizard gave it to her or something, and she's afraid I'll find out.* She remembered the first name on Ruby's list. "Did Dartanian steal Ruby's moonstone?"

"The Troll, Dartanain, has the necklace."

See, she told the truth. That was easy enough. Mona stood, walked over to her Muse, and intertwined her fingers with those that felt like smoke. "I thank you, my Spirit Guide."

"Until we meet again, Mona." She melted away.

The dark woman walked over behind her desk, and sat back down. She opened the bottom drawer on her right, pulling out a copper bowl inscribed with symbols, and a slender glass vase filled with amber liquid, and set them on her desk.

Mona poured seven drops of the liquid in the bowl, and blew softly upon it. *"Dartanian,"* she whispered, *"show me Dartanian."*

The liquid spun slowly in the bowl. The front of her office receded and then vanished altogether. Buildings slowly came into view, as if painted by brush strokes. Yet, her desk, and everything parallel to and behind it, was still visible. It was as if a giant hand had brushed away Clearwater, and supplanted it with another darker city. This part of *The Realm* existed right under human eyes, just on a separate plane of reality. On her side, the human side, it was 3PM. Yet beyond her desk was shrouded in darkness.

She was gazing into the *Shadowlands*. Mona stood, slipped her handbag over her shoulder, and crossed over.

Chapter 6

Crooked buildings flanked a two-story edifice just across from her. The door of the house glowed with a soft amber light. This would be Dartanian's last known place of residence. If she was lucky, he'd still be here. If he'd traveled, she'd have to do another spell to track him down. Her spell was the equivalent of a hound dog sniffing out a scent before it had gone cold.

Mona rapped on the glowing door. A female troll of indeterminate age opened it. She was only four feet tall, but her small body bulged with muscles. Silver baubles dangled from her neck and wrists.

Flaming red hair was piled atop her head. She wore a bone-colored dress with a corset. Her skin was a deep shade of purple with orange circles around her wide-set, long-lashed maroon eyes. Soul music played in the background.

"Good evening. My name is Mona Livelong, and I'm a private investigator. I'm looking for Dartanian."

The female troll looked her up and down. Then her thick lips spread in a smile, revealing huge pointed teeth. "You're human," her voice was a smoky contralto. "I'll say this for you: You got heart to come here. Dartanian's gone."

"You mind if I come in?"

"Sure, why not? By the way, I'm Olivia."

Mona followed her into a spacious living area furnished with oil lamps, velvet divans and chairs. The troll stretched out across from her on a blue and silver couch. She picked up a slender wooden holder from the coffee-table beside her, and fitted a cigarette into it. Olivia lit it with a dragonfly shaped lighter, and puffed smoke delicately from the corner of her mouth.

She gazed at Mona with eyes twice the size of humans. "What do you want with Dartanian?"

"I just need to ask him a few questions."

Olivia puffed on her cigarette. "It's that witch, Ruby, isn't it? Whatever she told you, she's lying."

Wow. "You don't even know what she said."

"I know she's a liar," Olivia countered.

"My client is missing a very valuable piece of property—a moonstone. She thinks Dartanian might have it."

"Dartanian ain't no thief. If he took it, it was his to begin with."

She's telling the truth. "When will he be back?"

The female troll shrugged insouciantly. "Hard to say. Dartanian's in and out. He does a lot of business in *The Realm.*"

"What kind of business?" Mona asked.

Olivia smiled tightly. "Business that's none of your business, Mona."

Mona reached into her bag, and pulled out a hand-printed card displaying her name and the moniker *Paranormal Detective* in bold print below it. She handed it to Olivia. "When he comes back, will you please tell him I wanna to talk to him? Tell him to send me a post at this address."

The female troll took the card, and studied it for a moment. "Paranormal detective, huh? Will wonders never cease? Sure, I'll tell him."

Olivia walked her to the door. "You know she's a flesh peddler, right?"

Mona whirled to face her. "What did you say?"

Olivia's maroon eyes were obsidian. "Ruby's a pimp. She keeps a stable at that house of hers, and arranges dates between Others. Paid dates. And she does it in *The Shadow Lands,* right under your human noses."

Mona remembered the terror in Gail's eyes. A pounding began at her temples, accompanied by the sinking feeling that this time she might really be in over her head.

"She's powerless," Mona said slowly. "How could she cross over?" Yet if Olivia was telling the truth—and all of Mona's paranormal senses said she was—the *how* didn't matter. Ruby *had* crossed over. All bets were off. It was the difference between an insignificant little lie, told perhaps to protect a woman's vanity, and a lie of immense proportions, told for ...

Why?

Olivia was watching her closely, waiting it would seem, for Mona to gather her thoughts. "Powerless or not," Olivia said at length, "—and mind you I don't know nothing 'bout that—she's still got connections. And if you're working for her, you're a fool."

Chapter 7

Curtis parked his steam-car, got out, and headed toward the door of *The Red Rooster,* a greasy spoon that sold the best Jerk Chicken in Monterrey. The streetlights fashioned islets of light beneath him.

Normally, he would have stopped by his parents' house for dinner. He hadn't seen them in two weeks. He was their only son, and the youngest, so they tended to spoil him. But visiting his folks would almost certainly invite another round of questioning from

Madeline over when he intended to marry Mona. He hadn't even told his mother about the break-up yet.

I oughta tell her that the woman she's so dead-set on me marrying ain't human. I bet that would shut her up. He chuckled to himself as he imagined his mother's shocked face.

A man sat next to the door of *The Red Rooster,* his legs crossed, his profile half-hidden by a hood. A gnarled hand lifted a corncob pipe to the hood, and a cloud of smoke floated into the air in front of him. Curtis froze. Suddenly he couldn't move, couldn't make himself walk pass this stranger into the restaurant.

The man stood, and turned his head to look at Curtis. He was an elderly black man. Or he had been, for now his skin was the grayish shade of a thing long dead. He stared at Curtis with colorless, filmed-over eyes.

For a long moment they were motionless, gazing at each other. Then the creature turned on his heel and walked away, rounding the corner.

Curtis's appetite was gone. Trickles of sweat ran from his armpits, despite the chilly night. He was rooted to the spot. A miasma of emotions washed over him. He fought with his fists and feet, with musket and a rifle. He had no skills— no weapons— with which to combat demons, wizards, ghosts. He was wholly out of his element.

Underlying this was a curiosity he always felt when in the presence of the supernatural. A simultaneous repulsion and attraction. And fear. The same feelings he'd had as a child when his mother told him stories of Haitian folklore—a wanting, *a needing* to know more; and at the same time a desire to shut his eyes and ears to things he couldn't explain or control.

One person could help him sort this mess out. One. Mona.

Fout monchè! It was as if events were conspiring to throw them together!

He wasn't sure he was ready to see Mona, wasn't sure he'd ever be ready. But one thing he *was* sure about. If he went to her, it would be on his on terms. He wouldn't go crawling back with another case he couldn't solve on his own.

He didn't threaten me. Nobody's been murdered. Hell, it's a foggy night. Maybe my eyes were playing tricks on me. Curtis ignored the warning bells going off in his head, and hurried into *The Red Rooster.*

The Malady of Need
by Kiini Ibura Salaam

She would have looked at you like she knew all your truths. You would have wanted to unearth the secrets you saw buried in her eyes. You'd have caught her glance and your dick would have gone stiff. You would have imagined her licking your chest, your ankles, her own perfect lips.

You would have traded a week's worth of protein to get your work detail changed, to shatter the barriers between you, to ride with her only a breath away. Had you any gods you would have thanked them for the nutters who were always trying to escape. Even as your shackles were pulled tight over your head, you would have felt love for lockdown. When the lights cut, you would have eased yourself forward, slipping around the others, easing your tether ahead as you went.

She would have whipped around when you stood behind her, then shushed you when you tried to explain. She would have brushed against you and you would have swayed with her, surprised to feel the tug of DNA stirring in your loins. When the shuttle lights blinked back on, she would have sighed before forcing the blankness back into her face.

You would have been left with tremors, tiny spasms whispering your need.

You would have begun to starve yourself. You would go without to nourish her. You would bring her only the best of your rations—long grasshoppers roasted crunchy, thick red caterpillars, the ones with the sweet meat. It would have been the only time you'd have been able to touch her—in the few seconds after your hands had been released from the shackles. You would have smiled as she slipped your food into her zip suit. It would have pleased you to think of objects you had handled resting against her skin.

She would have been thick. With pounds of flesh that could cushion all your hates and angers. You would have lost hours slack-jawed, staring into space, fantasizing about the soft of her breasts.

She would have started to make demands. She would have wanted you to mark yourself, to draw blood. She would have wanted to see the scabs, the thin lines that proved how much you wanted her. You would have begun to enjoy it. It would have felt electric to think of her as you severed your skin. As you bled, you would have imagined her, alone in her bunk, her fingers doing the work your dick had been dying to do.

Your thoughts of her would have become incessant. You would have been thinking about her when they came for you in the night. You would have been desperate to cling to your thoughts of her as they shackled you to the rack. You would have strained to remember the contours of her mouth as they plunged the tubes into your back. You would have tried to recreate her scent as the machine began to whir. They would have begun to drain your blood, as you were imagining yourself slipping inside her. Then the pain would have overwhelmed you. You would have gone slack as everything around you melted away.

She would have known. As soon as she had seen you, she would have known they had come for you. You would have wanted to stare at her, to drink in the vision of her to feed your sanity, but you would not have been able to bear it. You would have lowered your head so she could not see the mania in your eyes.

You would not have known how she did it, but you would have known that she had found a way to force the shuttle screech to a stop. As the shackles went slack and the voices of the others rose around you, she would have come. She would have freed your wrists and touched her tongue to yours. You would have fought it. You would have tried to remember where you were. But she would not have relented.

She would have dragged your buried sobs to the surface. You would have lost yourself under the press of her lips. She would have made visions flash in your mind. Touching her, you would have remembered what the sky looked like, the taste of fresh fruit, the feel of water on your skin.

You would have wanted to stop. You would not have wanted to be this naked, this disarmed. You would have lost yourself in the slickness of her body, in the work, in the friction. The itch of the compound would have dissipated against your will. The burn of the electric wristbands would have faded. She would have straddled you and pummeled you with frantic thrusts. As if she wanted to devour you. As if she wanted to recreate you, then spit you out reborn.

When the shuttle jerked back into motion, you would not have been able to look at her. Slipping your wrists back into the shackles felt like insanity, like suicide. As you worked, her scent would have gnawed at your nostrils. You would have felt as if her dark waters were rising over your body, as if you were drowning in her.

In the morning, you will erase her from existence. You will let the day's drudgery make a meal of your heart. You will withdraw. You will lock away all softness, all surrender. When the malady comes, you will clench the corners of your lips. You will go tense as it straddles your shoulders and chokes you with your own need. You will roll over and stroke your hardness. You will come in silence, consumed by dread.

The Ever After
by L. Marie Wood

Chapter One

Oh. My. God.

I couldn't stop myself from screaming. I had been screaming since it started. I breathed in and out, in and out, only vaguely registering the odd taste of the air, the sulfuric smell.

Dead.

I must be dead. Surely after a fall from so high, no one could have survived. I looked around at the bodies that littered the field, legs askance, arms bent at impossible angles, and I nodded. We're all dead.

My eyes watered as I looked up at the brilliant blue sky. I was up there. A shiver ran through me as I remembered. It was midday, maybe two or three o'clock – exactly the time when I always start to feel restless at my desk. I wanted the day to be over. I wanted to go out in the sunshine and play. Sometimes I wondered if I was really cut out to work in an office. The walls seemed to close in on me. I couldn't focus, didn't want to think. I hated my cube walls. I hated my officemates. I hated the work. So uninteresting. So unimportant. I wanted to do something real, something that mattered.

I was on the way outside for my normal break (I take five breaks every day. No, I do not smoke) and I was itching to get outside. It took everything I had not to bolt out of the door.

"Enjoy your break."

That's what he said. Enjoy your break. Such a normal comment, a throw away, something you really don't mean but you say just to be nice. It's like when people say 'Have a good day!' or 'How are you?' They don't really want a response; they don't want to listen to some long, drawn out story. They just needed something to say. *Enjoy your break.* If he hadn't said it I would have escaped the image of what he would become.

"Enjoy your break," said the guard whose name I never knew. His smile was genuine enough but he wasn't even looking at me when he said it. He had already moved on to the next person, addressing someone else from his cramped little room. I smiled back anyway, a thin-lipped thing that could just as easily have been a grimace. And that's when it happened.

Gravity simply gave way.

First my hair lifted off my head and rose above me like a crown, then my feet lifted off the ground. What I felt was confirmed by what I saw; the guard, several inches taller than me, rose off the ground and struck the low ceiling of his security shack. Blood, bone, and matter rained down in a torrent from the hole he created as he pressed through, breaking into the ceiling. There was a horrible sound - a wet, cracking, popping noise.

Oh. My. God.

In one wild instant I caught a glimpse of the world below me. My purse had fallen off my shoulder and was lying in the ground.

The papers and pencils that littered the guard's desk were splattered with his blood. None of those things were floating up to oblivion. This wasn't gravity giving way. This was something else.

I screamed for the guard but also for myself as I began moving toward the higher ceiling of the lobby and toward that poor man's same fate. I grabbed the doorframe and pulled myself outside, ducking through with barely enough time to clear the rest of my body. Pressing, pushing—I tried to will my feet to connect with the ground, but it was futile. It was as if I was on an invisible lift being raised up. My ascent was beyond my control.

People outside rose with me, some above me, some below me, some in sync. The ride was slow enough for me to take in what was happening, just long enough for me to become afraid. Smoke from car accidents below billowed up to us, giving chase. There was so much screaming and crying. I heard people cursing the very gods they prayed to every night. I saw people try to move toward each other craving touch, a hand to hold as we rose to our deaths. Surely that's what we were doing—rising to our deaths. Soon we wouldn't be able to breathe or we'd freeze to death or…

I laughed through my tears. Leave it to me to forget which would happen first. Jenny the airhead forever. Never taking anything seriously. But this was serious all right. It was the end of the world.

Windows shattered as people scraped through them on their way upward, bloodied. Glass protruded out of open wounds, heads cut open to reveal the smooth sheen of bone. Severed heads and detached limbs rose from the crashes below, bobbing on the wind like grotesque Macy's parade floats.

Babies cried. Perhaps that was the worst part.

The air turned cold and I began to understand with unwanted clarity that it wouldn't be long now. If gravity kicked in at this point the drop would crush me. If I didn't stop rising, I would freeze to death. If I escaped that death somehow I would not be able to breathe outside of Earth's atmosphere. Crazily, I wondered if a spaceship would pick me up? Would I stop on a cloud and see my grandmother waiting there? Delirium had already begun to set in.

My life had been aimless, a collection of unfulfilled dreams and wishful thinking. And now it was over. I cried for myself—for what I wanted to do, but hadn't; for the pain I would surely feel when I met my end regardless of how. I shut my eyes to the terrifying world before me and opened them to this one with the strange blue sky above my head and rough grass beneath me.

People lay scattered on the ground, lifeless, except the ones who sat ramrod straight looking up at the sun with unblinking, inky eyes.

When I sat up under that freakishly blue sky they all turned to look at me.

Chapter Two

I wasn't going to cut her.

The thought greeted me as I woke up in the comically green crabgrass. Even as it flitted away out of my grasp, I knew it was a lie. I meant to cut her and had wanted to from the moment I knew I was ready to leave. I just didn't have the guts to do it.

But I did it, didn't I?

I saw the knife in my hand, saw myself raising it above my head and thrusting it down fast. I heard Felicia yelling at me in that condescending way until she felt the blade pierce her skin. Then she screamed in pain. And fear.

I remember liking that part most of all.

I remember telling her that I couldn't take it anymore, that she needed to act like a woman and not a man. I already have a man and he knew his role. She needed to learn hers. But she wouldn't.

When I wanted her it was because I craved soft, sexy, alluring: pretty, damn it. Not bossy, foul-mouthed, and rough.

She wasn't always that way. When we started seeing each other she was sweet and loving. Her face lit up when she saw me. She used to call me Brandy when I hit it right. But when I met Paul and brought him home—when I kissed Paul before kissing her— she changed. She was waiting; I knew that. She was waiting for me to choose her over Paul. She pretended to like our three-way romance and probably did enjoy the sex if she didn't think about it too much. But she wanted me for herself and not having me made her mad and mean.

Cutting her meant I had chosen. Finally.

My apartment was covered in blood. The walls were splashed with it as I chased her around. Once I started cutting I had to finish but she wouldn't stay still. I was on top of her when it happened, making sure she was dead. Her body was warm between my legs. Her little titties were pushed together in her bra, teasing me for the last time.

I should have fucked her one more time before I killed her.

I was thinking that when the sky fell.

It seemed like a cutaway for a TV show; my vision went all white for a second and then gradually came back, showing me this new, weird world. What I saw when I opened my eyes didn't make sense.

People were staggering, leaning, falling over. I saw bodies on the ground—some were moving but others were still. Most people were just staring up at that crazy sky. I looked, too—I felt like I was being hypnotized. My body rocked, moving like a dandelion in

the breeze. I imagined that my head was like the white fuzz on a dandelion with seeds blowing off in the wind. My hair, nose, and ears blew off, too, twisting and turning in the wind and leaving droplets of blood on the ground.

That image is what woke me.

I looked down, certain I would see Felicia beneath me, her chest destroyed by that piece-of-shit knife I used on her. I was covered in blood, had to be; I could almost feel it coating my arms. But there wasn't any blood at all. No knife either. And Felicia was nowhere to be found.

I was kneeling in grass with thick, curly lime greenish blades that seemed to creep toward me in the wind, like they wanted to wrap around my ankles. I shook my head and laughed at myself as I stood up, only distantly wondering where these crazy thoughts were coming from. I felt a lot of things in that moment but the main thing was relief. And power.

I felt fucking awesome.

I killed my lady ('that bitch' seemed too harsh a name for her now and got away with it. It was all cleaned up and left behind. It didn't matter that this new place didn't seem real. It didn't freak me out that the grass and the sky—the fucking sun—looked more like a kids finger painting than something of this world. I didn't even give a shit that there was a guy on the other side of a tree that seemed like he came out of an animated Halloween special staring right at me with eyes that looked like black holes.

I just figured it was part of the crazy-assed hallucinations I was having. Maybe killing Felicia was all bullshit, too.

No blood—maybe it was all a dream. The thought made me laugh. It couldn't be true; I remembered how warm and slick her blood felt on my hands before waking up in this weird place too well for it to be my imagination, but go with it for a second. Maybe Felicia wasn't dead. Maybe I didn't even attack her—who gives a damn? All I care about is that right now is that she's gone, which means the shit is over.

Amidst all the screaming and whining, I laughed like I had never laughed before.

Chapter Three

I knew that life the way I knew it had irreversibly changed the moment I saw a corpse driving a car. I also knew I was tripping, but not so hard that I didn't know a dead man when I saw one.

The man behind the wheel of a red Subaru that had seen better days was middle-aged and his chin sported fresh stubble. His old-fashioned wire rim glasses were perched on his nose. There wasn't anything discernibly wrong with him, not at first glance. He looked like a regular guy driving around town on a sunny day. Except this 'regular guy' couldn't be driving around today or ever again for that matter. I knew that because my mom had gone to his funeral just a couple of days ago.

Get your shit together, Carrie.

I sat up taller, took a deep breath, and put both hands on the wheel, trying to shake off what had to be the result of some bad Spice. I'll never buy shit from that asshole Tyler again.

Mr. Ridley nodded as I coasted next to him, coming dangerously close to hitting the Subaru and giving it (and him) the burial it deserved. Some of the lines that had etched themselves in his face when he was alive had smoothed out and his hair, lackluster at best before he collapsed in front of the library clutching his chest, had regained some body and even some color. There wasn't any green decomposing skin, no withered lips and rotted gums, nothing like that. Is this what zombies really look like? Wait, are zombies real and this is what happens? I had convinced myself that I was hallucinating somewhere along the way, and was settling into the fantasy...and it was freaking me out fast. Do we just reanimate after we die and go on about our merry way? Shouldn't you move to a new town if you're going to do that? I mean, what if you bump into someone that knew you when you were alive—

It was the wave that did me in.

Just a gentle flick of the wrist: an open-handed salute. It was so jovial, so natural. His hand seemed to glow. The sky behind him was the brightest, darkest blue I'd ever seen. It was like the night sky was backlit by a spotlight or something. It made the sky weird. Too blue. It was kind of like the color of the water you see when you're out in the middle of the ocean. That's how it looked on that cruise Mom and Dad took me on before I started high school. The water was so deep out there—it seemed like you would never find the bottom if you dropped anchor. I remember staring at it every day, getting more and more spooked. How could anyone survive out there? Who knows what lurks beneath the surface?

Blue, teal, turquoise, and midnight all rolled into one—that's what the color of the sky looked like. It was as wrong as Mr. Ridley was. His hand looked obscenely bright against it but he didn't seem to notice. He just went on waving at me under the weirdest looking sky I'd ever seen.

Please don't smile.

I *don't* think I can handle it if he smiles.

I didn't feel my car careen off the road and hit the turnbuckle because I was too busy staring at Mr. Ridley and the sky. The sky and Mr. Ridley. I passed out before the impact, praying that Mr. Ridley didn't smile and show me his pointy teeth.

Chapter Four

I didn't know I was looking for something new, but, damn, he is gorgeous. Dirty blond, blue-eyes, with abs that lead into the most perfect pelvic muscle I've ever seen up close. Australian accent on a velvety voice, barely legal, and eager. He's the polar opposite of any other man I've ever been with, but I'm not complaining. He takes his time and savors me like fine wine. I could listen to him moan all day long and sometimes I do just that. He leaves me satisfied and crazy for more.

I'm so preoccupied with Dustin that I rarely even think of Jared anymore.

Dustin adores me. He says as much, but that's not how I know. It's when I catch him looking at me out of the corner of my eye that speaks volumes. His face goes through so many emotions at once, it's almost painful to watch. Love, admiration, obsession, lust. Fear. He wants this to last forever and doesn't know if it can.

He's beautiful and smart.

He loves the sun and lets it kiss his skin with zeal; watching him take off his shirt in its yellow glow is an exercise in restraint.

He wants to marry me, but that will never be. Regardless of what happens between Jared and me, I would never go on record as being 21 years my husband's senior. Dustin just laughs when I say that. He says he'll push my wheelchair out to see the surf every day if that's what I want. Ah, my pretty. I think he really believes he would.

He met me on the beach today. Just ran by me with his board under his arm; I sensed him more than saw him until he had run several paces away. He threw a kiss over his shoulder and dove into the tumultuous sea, ready to enjoy the waves for as long as the sunlight held. I was content to watch him move in the water, read my book, and feel the breeze.

This had become my typical day and I loved every minute of it.

Sometimes I wondered what was going on between us. Is this just a fling? How did this happen? There are so many things that I don't remember. I feel like I'm drunk on whatever this is— passion, lust, love? I don't remember when I decided I was going to cheat on Jared. We weren't having any problems—life was the comfortable normal that marriages slip into over time. I know Jared as well as I know myself—does he know what I've been up to?

As I watched Dustin come out of the surf I can understand what caught my eye. Any woman would be hard pressed to not do a double-take. But I never thought I'd cheat.

As Dustin came closer those thoughts were invaded by others— ones that make me shift in my seat. It made the worries seem unimportant. For now.

I felt my cheeks get hot as he stood over me. His lopsided smile was my undoing. I felt flutters deep in my belly and had to look away. This is one hell of a forty-something-woman-going- through-a-midlife-crisis checklist item, that's for sure.

Dustin laid me down on the sand. He kissed my eyelids, my cheekbones, my nose, my mouth. His touch, made rough by the white sand, still managed to raise goose bumps on my skin. He

stretched my arms overhead, clasped one hand in his, palm to palm, fingers interlaced like first loves often do, and traced a line from my elbow to waist with the other, watching his fingers as they moved. I could see the desire in his eyes as he looked at my body, could sense the control he struggled to keep over himself. He bit his lip to keep it at bay, his desire threatening to quicken his pace. He wanted to go slowly because he knew I liked it when he did, even though he felt like he couldn't wait any longer. He wanted to savor me, though his mouth watered. That realization affected me in a way I didn't expect. The tears that stung the corners of my eyes were real. Exhilaratingly real, and so very scary.

He guided himself inside me without ever letting go of my hand.

The sky looked incredible. Such a brilliant blue. I was trying to come up with the name for it; the name was just on the tip of my tongue when Dustin sent me over the edge. Then I started thinking about how I might never go home if this pretty young thing plans to fuck me like this every time.

And then I stopped thinking all together.

The last thing I saw before I woke up to the brilliant blue of that weird sky was the first thing I was looking for, but couldn't find. Where is Dustin? I looked around taking in all the people scattered about in various stages of confusion, but none of them kept my attention. But the sky did.

It kept pulling my eyes away from the search. Though the color was the same, it wasn't beautiful to me anymore.

It was all- encompassing and thick. Heavy. It seemed to bear down upon me, as interested in crushing me as in hovering above me. I felt its menace in every part of my body.

My clothes were the same—a sundress and sandals—still hiked up over my hips the way Dustin had me. My skin looked the same and I felt the same. But everything had changed.

"Dustin?"

I whispered his name at first, not wanting to draw the attention of the others, though that might have been impossible anyway.

I was lying in a tree that was close to the ground. It was very much like the Divi Divi trees that grow in Aruba with their affected lean and gnarled roots. My toes scraped the ground from my perch, but the rest of my body was enclosed in the tree as though its branches formed a massive head and I was sitting in its mouth. And the leaves were so green. Breathtakingly green. The most intensely bright green I had ever seen before. The tree was alive in a way that nature wasn't intended to be. I felt like a cricket veering too close to a Venus Flytrap.

I pried myself out of the tree's grip and stood on grass that crunched underfoot. "Dustin?" I said again, panic invading my

voice. He shouldn't be here—I know that now. More than anything I'd hoped he wasn't here. That sweet man who loved me right when I needed it shouldn't have to endure this. I didn't want to know what his face looked like in the light of the harsh crayon sun that hung overhead like a weight.

It dawned on me that this was exactly where I belonged. It felt like some kind of reverse Rapture. All the good people stayed on Earth and the bad ones—the ones who cheated and didn't think twice about their husbands—were sent to hell. Because this was hell, right?

It certainly felt like it.

I saw him approaching in the distance and wondered about his size. Jared was a big man, sure, but something about him seemed disproportionate somehow. And his gait—it was too deliberate. Almost like he was trying too hard to put one foot in front of the other. I shook my head in resignation. This is what I deserve, isn't it? Not Dustin but Jared—new and improved...and sure to be mad as hell. I bought it and paid for it, indeed.

"Corinne, baby! Oh, thank God!"

The words were his but the voice wasn't. But that's all right. As Jared's arms encircled me, pulling me into his soft, fleshy chest, the name of that color blue that painted the sky popped into my mind. Cerulean. That's what it was. The color of the Caribbean Sea transposed in the sky. My eyes fell onto the faces of people I don't know. Some of them were paralyzed with fear and others in blissful ignorance of what lies ahead. I'm too sad to be scared even though Jared's embrace felt more like a vise.

Chapter Five

Hazy.

That's what it seemed like, but not what it was.

Maybe my vision was hazy —maybe my mind. I wanted to back, go to sleep. But I hadn't been sleeping, had I?

Not really.

Wishing for it, maybe. Sleep was all I wanted to do these days.

Being awake was a chore; the constant hemming and hawing about trivial things that most people my age engage in had started to grate on my nerves a long time ago. I wanted to shut all of that nonsense out. I did everything I could to make it go away, short of the final step.

Is that what this was? Had I finally gotten rid of that Catholic guilt and found the balls to do what needed to be done? Caroline would be disappointed to see me this way, if seeing the dead again is what really happens when all is said and done. She might say, in that exasperated tone she reserved just for me, 'Oh, Edward,' and give me a good smack to prove that point. But I would take it if it meant being with her again. I'd give anything to hear the sound of her voice again.

What took me so long to do it? When Caroline died all those years ago I thought I would go after her. I was sick. Hell, I had been sick first, so it made sense. But then my heart disease got under control (the doctors kept referring to my cluster of heart attacks as blips on my screen) and my health rebounded—not all the way, but enough to keep me kicking. The doctors patted each other on the back, the kids cheered and hugged, but I sulked. I pulled away, stayed home more because that's where it was quiet. I stopped seeing the doctor because I wanted whatever they did to be undone. I wanted to go with Caroline. Life without her wasn't much of a life at all.

But that was eight years ago. Eight years of living in the shadows, watching trash TV, crying over old pictures, only speaking to the kids when they pressed the issue: avoiding life. They knew what was going on—Robbie said he'd help me do it if I really wanted to. But I couldn't saddle him with that for the rest of his life. My good boy would suffer too and I didn't want that to happen.

I learned something over those eight years. You can't will death. It'll come when it's good and ready and not a moment before.

I remember going to bed with Caroline and the kids on my mind. I was thinking about an outing at the lake up in Greenbrier, Maryland from 40 years ago. The sun was shining and a cool breeze ruffled my hair. I could feel warmth on my cheeks even in the darkness of the one room I lived out of anymore. I couldn't make myself walk around the house much. Too many ghosts occupying the rooms.

I don't remember deciding to do it. I had contemplated the ways a million times—pills seemed the easiest. The thought of shooting myself and not dying made me sick to my stomach. I didn't think I could take a knife to myself and I wasn't about to jump off anything. Pills I could do. I'd just take all the doses of Tambocor that I missed and let my heart literally skip a beat. It would be quick. Not painless, but that's not what I'm looking for.

But then this happened.

I looked around at the landscape I woke up to. It was beautiful, yet odd in a way that frightened me. My house was gone. In fact, I couldn't see any houses at all. There were too many people around - people who were paying attention to everyone else but trying to look like they weren't. And the sky. There was something wrong with the sky. It was like a kid's coloring page— the colors were too bright and unrealistic. And harsh.

Where the hell is Caroline?

If this is what I think it is and I've checked out of life for once and for all, why isn't she here to greet me? She can't still be mad that I put her in a home, not after all these years... could she?

Some people were crying quietly. Some cried out loud with such gut wrenching wails they made my hair stand on end. Some got angry, demanding an answer, a reason for being in this new place – they stood shouting into the open air. Others hugged themselves against the outside world. Me, I just sat and watched. I didn't think I had enough control over myself to do anything else.

Chapter Six

The room was alive for the first time since the beginning, buzzing and beeping accompanied by loud, fast-talking nurses and doctors. There was a lot of reaching, running, and commotion.

And then nothing. No movement, no people, no noise.

Dr. Mitchell stood in the middle of the room, his vantage point allowing a view of all of them. Jennifer, 28. Brandon, 33. Carrie, 19. Corinne, 41. Edward, 77. All wheeled into the large room that would end up being their death chamber within minutes of each other. All gone at virtually the same time.

The hallucinogen had been injected into each patient's IV in tandem. Brain scans for each of them showed hyperactivity spikes and relaxed rhythm at the same pace. They seemed to enter the new sphere, a place designed to comfort them as they awaited their deaths, at the same time also. Cerulean Fields was his life's work: a utopia for the dying. It was supposed to give them peace at the end instead of pain, a loss of dignity, and fear.

But it didn't. It couldn't have. In the end they were all writhing, fighting, clawing at the air. Something chased them to their death over there. Something unexpected.

He looked at the pictures of his patients that were posted on their bedside tables and felt a sadness well in him that he had dreaded from the beginning of the research. He had never met them; by the time they arrived at the facility their induced comas had already taken effect. He didn't want to know them, didn't want to see their eyes. That would have just complicated things.

The pictures showed each of his patients in the prime of their lives, their smiling faces a testament to their health in contrast to their present situation. Edward stood tall and confident, muscular in the way that men who enjoyed the outdoors were. His son Robert said that Edward had been an avid camper, taking the kids into the woods every summer. Robert couldn't bear to see his father like this, so frail and thin. It took everything he had to visit every week.

Jennifer's picture didn't look like her at all—the stroke paralyzed her entire left side and aged her overnight. Brandon's picture was of him out at a lake. You could only see his profile but that's the only image that his girlfriend would bring. She only came to visit once and didn't stay long. Carrie's picture was haunting. It showed a sweet little high school kid with her whole life ahead of her. It was Carrie before the drugs and the self-imposed isolation. It was Carrie before the accident.

Corinne was the true beauty in the bunch. Dr. Mitchell's affinity for her was evident from the start. He could see a beautiful woman beneath the graying skin. Looking at her grounded him; made him see the patients as people instead of research specimens.

Every time he looked at the picture of her on the beach with her sarong flowing in the wind revealing slender, shapely legs, he grew more attached. Her caramel skin, sun-kissed in the picture, seemed to glow. She radiated confidence even before the vast sea in front of her.

He wished he knew her before the cancer ravaged her body, before chemotherapy stole her hair, before her eyes closed forever. If they had met in a coffee shop, would she have noticed him?

Would she order a Chai tea latte and turn to see him staring at her? Would she smile the same way she did in the picture, joyful and provocative, and make his knees buckle? If they met on a crowded street would she be interested in him or would his blue eyes not be her cup of tea? Sometimes he got angry because he would never have the chance to find out.

Sometimes he touched Corinne's hand when he thought of what could have been, wanting to feel her skin next to his own. He interlaced their fingers when the fantasy was particularly compelling, gingerly holding her paper-thin skin against his, gaining closer contact in the most appropriate way possible even though, in his mind, they moved from hugging to kissing to more. He imagined how he would caress her skin, run his hands through her hair, kiss her beautiful full lips—lips that had only been parted to brace a feeding tube since he had known her. Dr. Mitchell spoke to her about the places they would have gone if they had the chance, sharing a fantasy that could never come true with a woman he wasn't entirely sure could hear him. He felt like a kid talking about his hopes and dreams. Corinne made him giddy in a way that he hadn't been since he was 20 years old. He regaled in a past they never shared and mourned a future that would never be. Many times he wondered how life could be so cruel to show him true love in the touch of a dying woman.

Dr. Mitchell looked at Corrine, studied her. This would be the last time he saw her. Once he left the room she shared with the other patients their connection would be lost. He was not ready to say goodbye.

He puttered around the room a bit more, cleaning up, wasting time, trying to prepare himself for the inevitable. Soon the families would be notified and the bodies would be claimed. They would be gone within hours. Corrine would be gone forever.

The thought was unbearable.

"Dr. Mitchell, we need your signature on the files."

The nurse's voice barely registered to him. The only sound he could hear was waves crashing on the shore.

"Dustin?"

The nurse had moved close enough to touch his arm. He had to restrain himself from shaking her hand off. She handed him the folders and left him alone. He saw the concern in her eyes as she did, but she was mercifully silent.

He touched Corinne's hand one last time. It was still warm.

Perhaps that was the worst part.

Perfect Connection
by Deana Zhollis

Naomi clutched her knees to her chest, her heels digging into the plush couch. Her eyes brimmed with tears, and her cheeks were wet. Across from her, an unoccupied chair slowly rocked back and forth. It gently swayed with a slight creak, like the sound of the crackling fire that threw light into the log cabin's dark living room.

Her eyes fixed on the rocking chair. She could not see what sat there, but it had many names.

Christians called it the Holy Spirit. Muslims called it a Jinn. Witches called it a Familiar.

Science called it the Unconscious Mind or Inner Voice. Others called it a ghost or entity. But most called it a demon. Naomi just called it Alexa.

She closed her eyes tightly and allowed more tears to escape. A few dropped and mixed with the blood that soaked her pink, satin negligee. The same blood covered her hands and was smeared on her arms. She took a deep breath and slowly looked towards the fireplace, where blood pooled heavily and drained towards a thick white rug. Next to it, a man lay with a sword buried deep into his chest.

He would have killed us, the voice from the chair whispered.

Naomi shifted her eyes. The chair continued to casually rock.

"Shut up, Alexa," she said, lowering her head down to her knees.

How could you weep for him? The voice slowly grew in persistence. *He lied. He lied about everything, and then he tried to kill us.*

"He tried to kill *you!*" Naomi yelled, raising her head. "Not us! *You!*"

The chair stopped rocking.

The sudden stillness increased her uneasiness and filled her with dread.

You think he loved you? The voice hissed. *You think after getting rid of me, you would have been happy with him? Is that what you think? Happily Ever After?* It mocked.

Naomi took a deep breath. "I don't know what to think."

He was a Splitter! The voice roared as a great wind swept through the room, knocking a vase to the floor and shattering it. The curtains on the window whipped and a picture fell from the wall.

Moments later, all went calm, and a chill filled the room. Naomi shivered.

"Alexa..." Naomi felt tired and worn. "Please. Just please be still. Give me a moment. Please."

You've had more than an hour, the voice said as the cold left the room and Naomi could feel the heat from the fire again.

Besides, it continued, *your time is up. They're here.*

Naomi turned her head at the sound of the door opening and several footsteps moving toward her. She got up and met the cavalry in the hallway. Leading them was "R&R" Reese Richardson. He held a garment bag over his arm, and a pair of the coveted Truth Glasses glistened, hiding his eyes, as he looked at the empty space next to Naomi.

"Alexa," he said with a slight nod, and then, rubbing his hands together, he said to Naomi, "And where is this little piece of dung?"

He curses so politely, the voice whispered near Naomi's ear.

Naomi ignored it. "He's in there. There's a sword also, so be careful, Grasp," she said, addressing her organization.

The five men and women moved past Reese and went to work. *Henchmen are so cute. I still think they should wear some sort of Grasp.*

"Alexa!"

Reese turned to Naomi. "What did she say?"

Naomi was certain he could see Alexa's mouth moving with the aid of his Truth Glasses, which was exactly what Alexa wanted.

The luxury glasses sitting on the bridge of Reese's nose were worth more than three hundred thousand dollars. No one knew who the maker, or makers, were, or even how they were distributed. The intended would simply wake up one morning and find a box at their doorstep. When they donned them, they could immediately see everyone's partnered spirit, like Alexa, and all other things unseen to the human eye. They were an anonymous gift from whom had come to be known in closed circles as the Truth Maker.

Naomi turned and looked into the mirror on the wall. This was the only way she could see Alexa, and sure enough, she was standing right next to her. Her black hair hung down her back in thick twists over a caftan dress with Afrocentric prints of black and gold. A mischievous smile played across her dark brown face as she shrugged her shoulders innocently at Naomi. They were the exact image of each other, which Alexa adopted most of the time. Just an hour earlier, she had transformed into the head of a lioness as she merged into Naomi and they fought for dear life.

Naomi gently took the garment bag from Reese's arm without saying a word.

"Naomi," Reese said, his voice filled with concern, "If you need anything—"

"I'm fine," Naomi answered, and then gestured to the garment bag. "Thanks."

She went upstairs to wash and change, hearing The Grasp repair what she and Alexa had broken. When she returned, it appeared as though nothing had ever happened in that living room. Even the vase that had splintered into pieces stood just as it had before.

For a moment, Naomi stared at the floor in front of the fireplace where the body of her fiancé had lain, and then turned away and walked out of the front door.

#

It would take quite some time to drive back to the city, and with Alexa, Naomi knew she would not get a moment of silence. As Alexa had said, she had given Naomi over an hour already, saying nothing but rocking in the chair.

Piece of dung, Alexa giggled, thinking back to R&R's words. *I Love it!*

When Naomi didn't comment, she chided, *Still don't want to talk to me, huh?*

Naomi looked in the rear-view mirror at Alexa sitting comfortably in the back seat, her long legs stretched out across the seat with her back against the door. She sighed inwardly and returned her attention to the road.

We really should give Reese another chance. After all, it's difficult being a Grasp leader. Women are always attracted to physical power, and men are just weak. Man's anatomy is for multiple women, Alexa mused. *His heart is with you no matter what he does with other women; only his anatomy is irresistible.*

Naomi stared stoically at the road as Alexa kept talking. *Look at the men in the Bible. They had multiple wives, yet they always held only one in their heart: Jacob had Rachel; Solomon had his Queen of Sheba; and David had his Bathsheba. A man is going to have his women from time to time. We just have to accept that and focus more on his heart for us.*

"I'm not settling," Naomi finally answered, glancing at Alexa again. "Pierce was faithful."

Yeah, and he gave "Til Death Do Us Part" a new meaning, too.

"He loved me."

Alexa hissed. *No one loves you, Naomi, unless they love all of you. And that includes me!*

Naomi said nothing and focused on the road.

You know I'm right.

"The bit of me that feels that you're right, is all you!" she exploded.

No, Alexa said. *No, it's not.*

Naomi hated it when Alexa was right. The bond with Alexa was strong; they knew each other's hopes, fears, wishes, depths. They could never lie to the other, which was different with others who could easily be manipulated and controlled by their connected spirit.

She had to admit that she'd sensed something was off about Pierce from the start. He proclaimed his love too quickly; he occupied her time too much; he bestowed her with too many gifts;

he always had perfect responses to everything she said; and he showed distinct uneasiness when she accidentally walked in while he was on his cell phone. Alexa kept whispering that something was wrong, but he did all of the things Naomi had always wanted, and that felt so right. So she ignored the whispers and forced Alexa to accept that they were getting married.

In the darkening silence of the car, Naomi continued to reflect. They had known each other six months, but it felt like more than enough time. Couples who had known each other for a year or more still ended up divorcing, so the amount of time in a relationship was never the problem, Naomi reasoned. The *people* in the relationship were the problem. That was what she focused on.

Then, Alexa saw his sword, and whispered this in Naomi's ear.

Naomi hadn't even packed extra clothes for their cabin trip. She had hoped she could change his mind. She put on her negligee and prayed he loved her enough not to do what he had intended. But she failed and could not convince him to stop.

"I loved Pierce, Alexa," Naomi flatly stated. "You know that." Alexa sighed. *He gave you a dream, and you loved the dream, Naomi. You didn't love him. You loved the,* she paused, trying to find the right word, *the idea of his perfection, and we know no one is perfect. Nonetheless, we need to find the one perfect for us.*

The car crossed a bump in the road and jolted them for a few seconds.

And besides, Alexa continued, *you wouldn't have liked the ring anyway.*

"So," Naomi said, "he did have a ring."

A horrible design.

"And he did love me."

Only a part of you. Alexa corrected. *He wanted you to be empty like he was so you would both be fulfilled with the other. I'm sure he volunteered to be Split, but he wanted to force the decision upon you. Not even giving you a choice. What kind of man would inflict that sort of pain on his beloved?*

Making her feel empty for the rest of her life—split from her partnered spirit.

"Maybe it wouldn't have been so bad."

Alexa paused. *You're still in mourning. I'll forgive what you just said.*

They rode the rest of the way in silence, which was exactly what Naomi wanted and needed.

By the time they reached the city's skyline, blazing with lights amid the darkness, Naomi was yawning. She had almost forgotten Alexa was still with her until Alexa screamed.

Stop the car!

"What?" Naomi slammed on the breaks, and angry motorists blew their horns behind her.

Three o'clock.

Naomi looked across. It was the same place Alexa had been talking about all year. Naomi had to admit to herself, it was quite the classy spot.

Come on, Alexa said. *You need to treat yourself anyway, and you need* something to distract your mind.

"I'm not in the moo—"Naomi didn't see Alexa in the mirror. "Dammit!"

The insistent horns behind her reminded her that she had to move, and she looked for the restaurant parking lot.

There's a spot in the next aisle.

Naomi looked up and Alexa was back in the car. She complied with her direction, but only so that she could stop the car.

"Alexa, I'm not in the mood for a hunt."

We're not hunting, Alexa said. *This is a different feeling—something else. I've told you this many times before. Now, get out of the car and let's go.*

Sighing, Naomi turned off the ignition and headed for the restaurant's front entrance. To be connected with such a Being, control had to be interchangeable just like in a marriage. However, it wasn't good to allow Alexa's type to be too much in control— with that, possession was a risk. But for now, Naomi needed Alexa's strength, so she let her take the lead. Just hours earlier, she had lost faith in herself when Pierce had removed his sword and tried to use it on her. Everything she thought she could trust was snatched away when she plunged his own weapon into his heart.

It was a delicate balance, this bond, because one could become too reliant on the skills, power and ability of Alexa's kind. But it was a connection she couldn't allow even her love for Pierce to vanquish.

Naomi looked down at her attire. It fit well and was a good cut. Reese always had good taste in clothes. It was the appropriate style for a place like this.

As she approached the hostess, the woman smiled but said, "Ma'am, I'm so sorry, but we're closing in thirty minutes."

You just want some lobster bisque.

Naomi smiled back. "Oh, that's okay. I really just wanted some of your lobster bisque."

"It is quite good," the waitress agreed. "A craving, huh?"

"Definitely," Naomi replied.

"I think we can accommodate that," she said. "This way, please."

She was seated in a contoured booth and could see the multi-tiered floors where other guests still remained. The room was dark but enhanced by decorative fixtures of soft light on the walls and in the middle of the tables. It reminded her of the fireplace and the cabin.

"Your soup will be right out," the hostess said, and Naomi watched as she walked over to a waiter.

Naomi tried to relax and looked at her reflection in the wine glasses. She could barely make out Alexa sitting next to her.

Ten o'clock, the voice whispered.

Naomi turned her head. All she saw were more tables and then—

The waiter.

Naomi's eyes fixed on him. He was tall with a strong back and shoulders, a fetish of Naomi's, as well as a round, strong bottom and thick thighs. His dark, black skin and thick, textured black hair seemed to glisten. He was speaking to another waiter, and in contrast, this Adonis seemed to glow.

"Ma'am." Naomi jumped.

"I'm so sorry, Ma'am," the other waiter said apologetically while carefully placing her small bowl of soup in front of her. "Lobster bisque?"

"Yes," Naomi said, collecting herself. "Thank you." "And here's the check. Whenever you're ready."

Naomi fetched her credit card. "Right now would be good," she said, handing it over. "Thank you."

"I'll be right back with your receipt."

She pulled her mobile from her pocket and looked at the time. It was late, and she wanted to keep her promise to the hostess that she would be brief and eat quickly.

As she let the delicious warmth of the soup fill all her senses and relax her even further, she looked around for the Adonis, but the same waiter arrived with her receipt. She signed it and left quickly.

We'll wait here, Alexa said when they reached the car. Naomi saw the determination in her face in the reflection of the car's side window.

"What?" Naomi held up the mobile so Alexa could see the time. "Alexa, whatever this is, it can wait until tomorrow."

No, it can't. She said. *We'll wait here.*

Naomi begrudgingly got back into the car and started the ignition. Before she had time to turn on her headlights, Alexa spoke again.

He's coming out.

Naomi sat up and looked around. The parking lot was mostly empty now. She then saw him heading to a black sedan.

Come on. Alexa shoved her.

Naomi reluctantly got out of the car and walked towards him.

"Excuse me."

The man looked up and stared at her.

"I'm sorry to disturb you, but," Naomi said, not quite knowing what she was going to say next.

I wanted you to speak with him.

"But," Naomi said, "My friend, Alexa, she wanted me to speak with you."

She waited for him to answer as her eyes settled on his thick lips. She stared for a moment before forcing herself to look at his entire face. He was quite handsome. Exactly the kind of look she liked. He edged his hairline just right, with slightly long sideburns, but not too long. He had thick eyelashes and wore earrings in both ears.

He continued to stare at Naomi until it become a bit uncomfortable.

Naomi took a step back. "I'm sorry I disturbed you." "What's your number?" he said suddenly.

"Um," Naomi hesitated slightly before telling him. "I'll call you." He then opened his car door and got in.

Naomi went back to her car, looking back a few times. "That was weird."

That, my friend, Alexa said, *is "something else."*

As soon as Naomi turned on the ignition, her mobile rang with a number and a name: Javari Kone.

A bit shocked, Naomi answered. "Hello?"

"I'm texting you my address," the strong voice said. "You can follow me there."

He hung up before Naomi could say anything, and then her phone registered a notification. She clicked on the address, and the guidance system on her phone activated.

Follow him.

Javari slowly drove out of the parking lot, and Naomi followed for the next four or so miles, where he stopped in a parking garage. Naomi found a guest parking space and then walked to the elevators. He was already there, waiting for her. She stared at him as she approached. His body was solid muscle. She had to blink away the thoughts that crept into her head about how that body could maneuver her in so many sexy ways.

"I'm on the top floor," he said, holding the elevator door for her.

I would love to have him on top of us, Alexa's voice echoed Naomi's thoughts.

He touched the fingerprint reader and the doors slowly closed.

Naomi looked up. His eyes were locked on her, and she turned away, standing a slight distance from him as they rode in awkward silence to his floor. She saw Alexa playfully lift her eyebrows in the silver reflection of the elevator, and she turned her eyes away from her as well. She could only conclude that he thought she was a just another customer who had a bedding interest in him, a common occurrence, she imagined.

The doors finally opened, and they stepped into a hallway with only two exits, Naomi quickly noticed—one to the stairs and one to an apartment. That seemed odd, as the hallway ran long from end to end, the length of the building. Did he have this entire floor to himself?

As Javari approached the door, a facial recognition security device unlocked it, which put Naomi's senses on high alert. A private floor and advanced security?

They walked into a huge studio where a couch and television sat on one side, and a kitchen to the other. There were no tables or chairs. A wall occupied the rest of the room, also seeming to cover the width of the building. It rose only so high, not touching the ceiling, giving the impression that there was something on the other side, but Naomi didn't see a door.

Naomi gave a slight signal to Alexa. There was something strange about the layout, but she knew Alexa would scope out the other side and let her know what she found.

"So," she said. "This is your place."

Javari slowly nodded, his eyes still on her, and then, as if remembering to use his voice, he said, "I only have water here."

"That's okay," Naomi said. "I'm not thirsty."

Javari went to the couch and picked up some glasses. Naomi immediately recognized the design.

"May I?" he asked.

Truth glasses. Naomi's defenses shot up, but it was more of a curiosity than a feeling of danger. Expensive locks. Truth glasses. A top-floor studio. Advanced security. How could a waiter afford such things?

"That's pretty expensive stuff there," Naomi said. "How could you afford it?" She had to stall to give Alexa more time to snoop.

"I'm sorry," he said and took a step forward. "Do you—?" He hesitated again. "Do you feel something?"

She felt something, all right, but she had to concentrate on the environment. Things didn't make sense, yet she couldn't feel a serious threat of any kind. That was because every sensitive part of her body wanted him to kiss and suck them. Her mind was at war with her flesh.

"Are you Split?" she asked, changing the subject. He shook his head. "Never."

The way he answered, so adamantly, made everything tingle underneath her clothes.

"Though he—Jonathan, that is, doesn't talk to me much." "So, you're aware." Naomi didn't meet too many people who openly admitted to having spiritual partners.

Many people had a connection, but not really a bond. It was the reason many believed they didn't have one. However, those who obtained Truth Glasses could see that everyone had a Spirit Partner, except those who had been Split. And when he mentioned his spirit partner's name, Naomi knew he must have a bond.

"And I'm assuming Alexa is yours." The way his voice slightly vibrated with a low tone when he said "yours" made Naomi take in a breath. What was wrong with her?

"May I?" he asked again, holding up the Truth Glasses.

Naomi nodded, but if she had been in her right mind, she would have refused on the basis of privacy. She was fantasizing that he was asking to kiss her! Alexa needed time to find out more about whom they were dealing with, but stupidly, Naomi couldn't find her sensible voice because her body wanted so much to be mounted by this man!

Javari carefully slipped on the glasses and looked around the room. He suddenly stopped as he gazed at the far end of the wall near a window. His lips parted slightly at what he saw.

"Her name is Alexa, which you've just figured out," Naomi said.

For some reason, she felt a bit shy about him looking at her spirit partner, as if he had x-ray glasses and could see underneath her clothes. But his expression revealed astonishment. Naomi smiled because she knew what he saw—how closely they resembled each other and how solid Alexa's form was. It was all an indication of the strength of their bond, and if he knew anything about bonding, he would also see that this was a display of extreme power.

Most spirit partners appeared as a fuzzy, shadowy form or something else not quite distinguishable. People with Truth Glasses were shocked when they saw Alexa and the bright tie that emanated between her and Naomi. It was a rare sight to see, and it amazed the few who had seen it.

He walked toward Naomi and slowly removed his glasses to hand them to her.

"No," he said, "It's not just Alexa."

No one allowed someone else to touch their Truth Glasses. They were like a priceless relic. Yet he handed them to Naomi as if he were handing her a borrowed pen.

Naomi took the glasses while still admiring Javari's manly features. Without much thought, she put them on. Javari pointed to the area near the window.

Naomi had only worn Truth Glasses once before. Those belonged to Reese. He had reluctantly allowed her to view through them when they were driving together in the car, returning to The Grasp's headquarters. She saw lines of tethers of all kinds, swirling and twisting between people, pets, and even trees and bushes.

Everything alive had a line. It was like a never-ending web of connections, as well as the shapes and sizes of the things unseen that were also connected to these lines. She felt as if she were seeing an entirely new world through a veil that resembled nothing like the world her human eyes understood. It was as if she had landed in Oz.

But what she saw now was something out of the ordinary— again. Light blazed around, spiraling and ebbing between two bodies. Their heads turned from human to animal, both lions, before slowly shifting back to human again. They stood in front of each other, staring into each other's eyes in a state of enchantment. "Alexa?" Naomi called out twice, when she didn't answer the first time.

Alexa didn't even stir to acknowledge she heard Naomi.

Naomi yanked the glasses from her face and grabbed Javari by the collar of his shirt.

"What have you done to her?" No, it was more like, What had he done to both of them?

Javari looked at her in complete shock. "Nothing."

She could feel truths and lies just like her taste buds could decipher sweet from sour. And he was telling the truth.

She let him go and backed away. Javari stood there, just as unsure as she was. Then, Naomi grabbed him again and placed her lips upon his. The kiss heightened every cell in her body, burning from the connection of their lips down to her nether regions, and surging from her head to her toes. Just as suddenly, Naomi broke the connection and ran to the door, but it wouldn't open.

"Please," Javari said, walking up behind her. His facial recognition system unlocked the door.

Naomi ran out, down the hallway and directly to the stairs She was too flooded with emotions and questions to wait for the elevator. With every floor she reached, as her feet flew down from step to step, her intense feelings for Javari lessened.

When she reached her car, she screeched the tires on the concrete and then the asphalt of the city's streets. Luck was on her side that there weren't any police in the area. As soon as she was able to breathe, seeing the familiar streets leading to her apartment, she looked up at the rearview mirror.

Alexa was sitting with her back to Naomi, facing the direction from which they had come. Naomi knew Alexa would come with her. She would have to tear away from whatever was holding her and go wherever Naomi went. Their bond was too strong. But she knew it was best to leave Alexa to her thoughts.

When they finally reached home, she poured a glass of her favorite wine and sank down on her couch. Mirrors filled every space on her apartment walls, and Naomi could see Alexa standing on the balcony, still peering in the direction they had just left, looking at the mass of city lights and dark buildings. It wasn't like her not to speak, and Naomi blamed it on whatever had happened in that man's studio with the strange wall.

Javari.

He had security inside as well as outside. What was he hiding or protecting? And why in the world could she not stop herself from kissing him?

Naomi's emotions were all over the place, and being unstable was not conducive to maintaining awareness of her spirit partner— at least not for long periods of time. It would disrupt their balance, forcing Alexa to instinctively take over and absorb the weaker vessel—her. Naomi had to get her mind together and confront her emotions. The power of thought was always the way back to control.

Thinking of the night, of Pierce, of Javari, she came to a conclusion. Naomi had heard how the need to have sex was strong after the loss of a loved one. She was sure that was what she was experiencing about Javari. Killing Pierce certainly brought about potent emotions, and the sense of loss immersed her, tripling her stress levels. That would make sex quite appealing because it was a physical act of connection and release. That had to be what it was.

Naomi set her mind on naming and claiming her emotional state—grief. However, she just wasn't as sure as she wanted to be with her own self-diagnosis. She then told herself that uncertainty was also to be expected, considering that she had to kill Pierce.

That was something she had to accept. She had killed her fiancé, and she now needed to allow herself some time to cope with that and heal.

The wine glass shook in her hand, and she used the other to steady it. Lifting it up to her lips, she could only manage two

sips. In her current state, that was more than enough to help her meditate, but instead it put her fast asleep.

In the morning, Naomi had surprisingly found enough strength to take a shower and then lie back down in her bed. Her phone rang. She picked it up from the side table and looked at it.

Is it him? Alexa's voice was anxious.

Naomi nodded. At least Alexa was also feeling better. She was talking again.

Well, answer it.

She didn't want to; she felt she needed more time, but she clicked the answer button anyway.

"Hello?" he said.

Javari's voice made her heart leap. Naomi felt she must still be under the effect of whatever had held her in his apartment.

"Are you both all right?" He sounded sincerely concerned.

Both? Alexa purred, *Hmmm.* "We're fine," Naomi answered.

"I need to see you." It was a humbling command, and Naomi's first instinct was to obey him.

She hesitated. "I don't think that's a good idea," she said. "Not here," he said, "At the park in two hours."

Naomi's notification sound went off. He had sent her directions again.

"Please be there."

Alexa's was in Naomi's ear. *Tell him to tell Jonathan I said hello.*

Naomi hung up the phone instead.

You know you're not right, right? Alexa said. *So rude. You always hurt my feelings.* She smirked.

Naomi sat up in bed and looked at the open closet filled with clothes.

We're going, right?

"We don't know what's going *on*, or what we're getting ourselves into."

We never do, Alexa intoned. *And there's no one around to explain these "unexplainable things" either. We do what we have always done—We find out for ourselves.*

Naomi looked into one of the many mirrors around her room, seeing Alexa with that familiar challenging smile.

"Okay, then," Naomi said, getting out of bed. "Let's hunt."

Alexa giggled. *I have the perfect outfit.*

At the park, Naomi got out of the car, stretched her legs, and followed the latitude and longitude from the link Javari sent.

Are we going the right way? Alexa said next to her. *We're getting* farther away from the crowd.

"We're going the right way, Alexa," Naomi said. "He probably just wants to meet somewhere in public but not too close to too many ears."

A few passersby looked at Naomi strangely, and she cursed under her breath. She had forgotten her earpiece that she had programmed to flash when she wasn't using her mobile, for instances like this. Talking out loud to yourself in public was a dangerous taboo.

"Possessed," she heard someone say as she walked on.

Naomi quickened her pace and made sure she kept her lips closed no matter what questions Alexa asked. Anyone, anywhere could call the church, report her as possessed, and they would send a Splitter. Alexa would be gone forever.

She and Alexa had been connected since birth, first as an invisible playmate, until scientists realized that too many children claimed to have playmates while doing and knowing things beyond their abilities. Naomi had hidden her talents and carefully suppressed information Alexa learned about others and whispered into her ear.

It was hard to grow up knowing that if anyone found out about Alexa, she would immediately be seen as abnormal. It seemed to Naomi that anyone who had communication with their spirit partner opened the doors for others to do the same; thus, Splitters were formed to protect society, as they said. Splitters separated pairs whether it was a good or bad union. But all Naomi knew was that without Alexa, she would be alone and empty.

She slowed her pace as her eyes came to rest upon Javari. He stood near the edge of forest that circled the park. He looked appealing in jeans and a bright, loose-fitting t-shirt.

Yummy. Alexa echoed Naomi's thoughts.

Naomi stopped her approach, keeping a safe distance between them.

"Hello, again," he said.

"Hello, yourself," Naomi replied in a flirty tone, despite herself.

Javari got directly to the point. "We've been researching about last night, about what happened between us."

"Researching?"

He nodded. "It's what we do."

A waiter who researches? Naomi imagined Alexa lifting an inquisitive eyebrow.

"I know that this is going to sound strange," he continued, "but I couldn't keep my eyes off you from the moment we met in the parking lot. And Jonathan says he loves Alexa. And ever since you left, since that kiss, I can't stop masturbating."

"Excuse me?" Naomi wasn't expecting all of this.

"I don't mean to offend you," Javari said, raising his hands in defense. "I know I'm saying a lot, and this sounds completely weird and strange, but the body, the mind and the spirit are one. They're connected. And even more so with guides like Jonathan and Alexa." He looked Naomi directly in her eyes. "Since we are connected to them, why can't we also be connected to each other?"

Naomi didn't have time to think about his words, as the familiar feeling of dread and anxiety seeped throughout her inner being.

She looked toward the forest.

"Javari," she said, "we'll have to continue this discussion later."

"Naomi, please." He wasn't going to let go this time. "I know I've come across as strange, unhinged, and pretty much offensive, but I need you to listen to—"

"I will," Naomi said, walking off to the forest. Then, she said the only thing she knew would get him to stop pursuing her. "I'll meet you back at your place. I'll call you," as she turned and quickened her pace before he could say anything more.

As Naomi found herself deeper in the forest, she searched around. "Is he following?"

No, Alexa said.

Naomi unsheathed and removed her dagger. Its blade caught and reflected the sun's rays that escaped through the leaves of t he trees. Her eyes found the source of her prescience.

A teenager walked down the path with an unnatural gait. Her neck was cocked to the side. Her clothes were filthy, and a foul odor emanated into the air. Teenagers were more susceptible to possession, as they were always overrun with uncertainties and fear. It was the worst part of Naomi's job—splitting a teenager from what could have begun as pure, but had corrupted into evil and sin. Adults who willingly accepted such a befouling union were harder to split. But teenagers—they were the saddest. They never got the chance to fully understand how to control what was happening to them. Nonetheless, they were a danger to society, and she knew what she needed to do.

"Excuse me," Naomi said.

The teenager turned around. Her face distorted as she roared.

Alexa jumped into Naomi, and the dagger morphed into a sword for those who could see the unseen. If they had Truth Glasses, they could also see the lioness head and Egyptian warrior that was now Naomi.

The demon attacked and Naomi/Alexa dodged the stream of wind meant to blow them off their feet. They struck a few blows, trying to find the tether between body and demon spirit. It was located in one of three places: the forehead, the hand, or the rib. Once they found it, they would only have one chance to strike again before the demon would reinforce its power to make the connection to the host stronger. If they missed, splitting would require a few more strikes, and the longer one battled a demon, the weaker one became.

As they dodged swipes of its hands and tree limbs flew through the air, the forest filled with its roar of rage. Then, she saw it. The hand.

They swung the sword again. The demon howled as it flew from the body of its connection. And with another swipe, they cut through its spirit hand so that it could never connect again.

The teenager fell to the ground, and the whirling wind and sounds of the demon's cries faded away as it retreated.

Naomi/Alexa dropped the sword to the side and separated.

Naomi stood next to the girl and waited for her to regain consciousness. She would be confused at first, and then the memories would come flooding in: the people she had hurt; the accidents she had caused. Release from possession always came with nightmares.

Unlike Splitters, who used their swords to split any person who became aware of their spirit partners, The Grasp only Split those dangerous to themselves and society. Pierce had tried to make his argument to Naomi that they were working toward the same goal— to protect the people. But Splitters worked in fear of what they did, without knowledge or understanding. Naomi's organization, however, continued to advance their learning and fully understand the knowledge of their spirit partners. Because they had to remain hidden from Splitters and The Church, this belief was in the minority.

Naomi made the call to The Grasp and texted her location.

They would take the teenager in, send her to a facility to regain some sense of normalcy, and, if she so chose, she would join their ranks and operations. Most did. Keeping busy with a cause helped ease the nightmares of what had happened to them; it gave penance and filled the emptiness inside.

When a few members of The Grasp finally arrived to collect the teenager, Naomi set out for Javari's place. She had a bone to pick with him. He had known her name

Naomi's mobile number was unlisted, which made it impossible to learn her identity. And the name registered with her apartment wasn't hers either, nor was it on any bills or other mail that was left at her inbox or front door. So how did he know her name?

Naomi stood at Javari's front door, waiting for the security cameras to identify her. The door slid open and he immediately greeted her.

"Naomi. For a moment, I thought you would not come," he said.

"Well, as you may come to know," Naomi passed by him to enter the room, "I keep my word."

Standing face-to-face with him was still a bit uncomfortable, even though she tried to mentally shield herself with her suspicions. But as soon as the door opened, she could only think of what she wanted his body to do with hers. She had to place some distance between them, so she went toward the other end of the couch, remaining standing.

He, too, seemed to need distance because he didn't move away from the front door.

"Keeping one's word is a rare trait," Javari said, and then added, "So, you're saying I'll be seeing more of you."

And we want to see more of you, Alexa cooed. *Especially since the way you say our name sounds so lovely to our ears.*

Naomi had notice that. She answered him. "Only for right now."

"Well, for right now," he repeated and walked toward the mysterious wall, "let me show you something."

Another security system unfolded before her eyes: a camouflage doorway and facial, fingerprint and DNA access. It was so secure, Naomi had to present all three identifying signatures to walk through.

On the other side, she saw bright lights, machinery, advanced computers, and—.

Naomi took a step back as she looked at another Javari standing in the middle of the laboratory. His hair was long, not short like Javari's, and he wore khaki pants without a shirt. His naked chest was curved with manly sexiness.

"It's okay," Javari said. "It's just Jonathan."

A movement behind her made her jump, and then she saw herself standing beside her.

"Alexa?"

You see me, she answered.

Javari opened his arms. "Think of this place as a huge Truth Glass. The waves of light bounce off from wall to wall."

Naomi stared at Alexa, and then at Jonathan, whose face relaxed into a welcoming smile. Her eyes then moved to a conveyor belt where dozens of Truth Glasses lay.

My, my, Alexa said. *He's a billionaire.*

Naomi could barely form her words. "You're the Truth Maker."

Javari smiled. "And you're a Demon Slayer."

Before Naomi could ask how he knew this, he pointed to Jonathan.

"He saw you at the park. And he was quite impressed." Javari walked over and stood next to Jonathan. "But I remember seeing your face in The Grasp archives."

A hacker, Alexa said. *Intelligent.*

"So, that's how you know my name," Naomi said.

Jonathan's mouth moved as he spoke soundlessly, and Naomi looked at Javari.

"He said," Javari looked away, slightly embarrassed, "'And a very nice name it is. As is Alexa's.'"

Charming, Alexa stepped forward.

"Alexa." Naomi's warning stopped her spirit partner short. "We don't want to harm anyone, Naomi," Javari said. "Never.

We want the same thing The Grasp wants—to open the eyes of every human being to what has been hidden from us. We want all to be educated, to grasp their own potential as you have done, so that possessions don't occur." He paused before adding, "So, what you did at the park would no longer be needed."

Naomi kept quiet. His voice held a tone of sadness, the same way she felt after each Splitting.

"But anyway," he said, "What I wanted to tell you was—uh," he lost the words. "Well, let me just start from a beginning where I won't come across as a pervert." He laughed nervously.

Naomi liked his laugh.

Javari leaned his lower back against a table, as if settling in for a long discussion. "The Egyptians were attuned to their Jinn, as you and I are, but they limited the knowledge to royalty, educators and nobles, making them gods amongst men. I, for one, do not want to repeat history. I want to free information for all to use, and I believe The Grasp could help achieve this."

Naomi glanced at Alexa before asking her question. "The Truth Maker has been hidden for quite some time. Why now? And why a waiter?"

Javari smiled shyly. "I work several different areas part-time. It's the best way to be seen, but not seen, as I choose to whom I send my glasses. One can learn a lot about people by observing habits and engaging in simple conversations as a waiter. As for being hidden? Old habits. We've worked alone, just the two of us, for so many years. We watched for all potential threats, and for future allies." He gestured toward his lab. "Progress is slow, but we were finally reaching people. We've never really had an incentive to go to the next level—until now."

"Incentive. Which is?"

Javari looked at her from head to toe, and Naomi knew exactly what "incentive" he meant.

He continued, "I can only produce so many glasses a year. But with The Grasp's help and resources, we could reach thousands." He walked over to one of the tables and picked up a black box. "It's perfect timing. Making these takes a lot more man-hours than I have available."

Javari walked over to Naomi and lifted the lid. Inside, something very small floated in clear liquid.

"It's the prototype. Truth Contact Lenses."

The thought of such a thing for The Grasp ran through Naomi's mind. No more having to retrofit Truth Glasses to look like normal shades or prescription glasses. No one could ever see that Truth was on your eyes.

"More inconspicuous than the glasses," he echoed her thoughts. "It could help in more ways than one. The Grasp can use them to watch and see unhealthy infusions before they happen; that way, Splits, like the one you performed today, would not be necessary anymore."

Alexa leaned over and whispered in Naomi's ear. *He's an inventor, smart, and supports our cause. Me likes.*

"But back to what I was saying at the park," he said, his tone lowering a bit. "I really didn't mean to offend you when I said," he decided to refrain, "what I said. Sometimes words come out wrong when I say them. But we've been doing some research about what's happening between us. And when I mean us, I mean you and I, Naomi, and between Jonathan and Alexa." He glanced at Jonathan, who nodded at him. "All relationships are based on energy.

Throughout history, there have been ceremonies involving a way to enhance and strengthen this energy in physical ways. To be more explicit, practices that involve more of the sexual side of religion and belief."

He went to his computer, and a large monitor above displayed what was shown on the smaller screen below. Ancient Egyptian hieroglyphs and Greek and Roman images of phallic symbols and bodies in sexual acts appeared in paintings and stonework. "Sex was a part of day-to-day life for society and thought to be the energy of life, birth, goodness and prosperity. It's not discussed much in today's schools, of course, but it was a part of the everyday routine in ancient societies." The images continued with highlighted words: tantric, kama sutra, erotic energy, sacred sensuality, sensual consciousness.

The images stopped, and Javari turned his attention to Naomi. "It explains our strong connection and the reason we feel the way we do." He took a deep breath. "The first time my eyes lay on you at the restaurant parking lot.—" He couldn't find the words.

Naomi remained quiet as her mind tried to process everything. But she didn't have time; she became even more astonished when Javari repeated, "I told you that Jonathan says he loves Alexa."

He looked uncertain before speaking again." And—and I believe," he pointed to Jonathan, "we believe, you both are our soul mates." He then fell quiet again.

Naomi stood there.

Of course, Alexa broke the silence. *Soul mates. Love at first sight. Well, that explains why we both were lit up like Christmas trees.*

"Wha-what did she say?" Javari slowly asked.

"She said," Naomi added definition to Alexa's statement, "it explained the Twin Flames episode between her and Jonathan."

Jonathan nodded agreeably.

"Yes," Javari said, very pleased that they understood. "Exactly." They all stood there, trying to figure out the next words to say, when Naomi suddenly blurted out, "I killed my fiancé last night." Her spirit partner raised her eyebrows and laughed.

What? Now, that sounded more like me than you.

Javari said, "I see," and Jonathan looked concerned.

It was awkward. Everything now was awkward, but it was a more welcome feeling than the flaming desire Naomi kept trying to keep under control.

Javari finally said, "I saw in The Grasp archives that you encountered a Splitter and killed him. I didn't know he was your fiancé." He then added, "I'm sorry for your loss."

He was an ass, anyway, Alexa said, and Naomi watched Jonathan laugh. Alexa didn't communicate with others of her kind much, let alone speak in a way that they could hear her. She mostly spoke in the language shared only between bonded human and spirit partner. But she thought enough of Jonathan to let him understand her, and, last night, to stand so close to her. It gave Naomi pause.

Naomi smiled at Javari's curious expression. "Alexa didn't like him very much, anyway," she explained.

"I can understand why," Javari said. "He tried to kill her. And he tried to destroy you."

Finally, Alexa said, throwing up her hands, *a man who gets it!* Naomi said openly, "She said she likes you."

Javari lowered his head a little and blushed. Then, he said, "Well—perhaps, we should take things slowly."

No, not slow! Alexa disagreed. *No!*

"I'd like that," Naomi agreed.

Jonathan's mouth moved, but Javari didn't translate. Naomi could already see from Jonathan's frown that he agreed with Alexa. He wanted union now!

But that was the difference between those who were possessed and those who were spiritually aware and bonded with their unseen partners. The possessed often become overwhelmed by any combination of the deadly sins: lust, gluttony, greed, laziness, anger, envy or pride. Those who clearly understood their true selves and did not allow fear to lead them to these capital vices gained the power of love and the power of mind from their spirit partners. It was what The Grasp called a holy bond.

"I could pick you up around seven," Javari suggested.

Ugh! Alexa exaggeratedly slumped over, making Javari laugh.

Jonathan simply walked through the wall and disappeared.

Still smiling, Javari said, "We can discuss my indoctrination into The Grasp over dinner."

Naomi's thoughts returned to the argument she had had with Alexa while driving back from the cabin the previous night, and what she had said they must do: We *need to find the one perfect for us.* And today Alexa was seeing qualities in this man that appealed to both of them: intelligent, an established entrepreneur, acceptance of her and Alexa and sharing the same belief system; and more importantly, there was an attraction, a true connection, which was beyond faith. He, most definitely—

"—Sounds perfect," Naomi said, and returned his smile.

Foundling
by Tenea D. Johnson

By noon, Petal had plucked fourteen people from the
earthquake debris. Even if the other techs in HRO's small mobile
unit nodded appreciatively, she could hardly believe the slow pace
of the rescue teleportations. In the last year alone, she'd evacced an
entire Sri Lankan apartment building's residents within 25 minutes
of a tsunami alarm and rescued a California fire fighter squad from
a forest fire seconds before it flamed into an inferno. Other teleport
techs worked to match Petal's speed and accuracy; she worked to
beat it. But not all trips through the black were about speed.

The fourteen had tired her. She shifted to release the dreadlocks
pinned between her back and the chair, and stretched her hip from
where she sat. Per protocol, she had to clear the chipped before
she could extract any unchipped people. The race always sapped
her energy. Regardless, she sat alert at her terminal rig, staring at
the quintet of monitors, gaze darting between the chip signal map
up top and the vectimeter readouts below. Her hands sat loose on
the controls, splayed wide, with her pointer finger poised over the
Enact button, timing the millisecond the extract arcs would align.

Earthquake rescues were a special challenge, a complicated
game of knowing which person to move and when—move the
wrong one and other pockets of space might collapse and kill

anyone now vulnerable in the configuration of air and pressure that destroyed buildings became. An Indonesian high rise was Boolean calculus that only a Petal Scott could reliably solve. The other techs worked to extract survivors in open fields or atop intact buildings. Their numbers lagged hers. Some had clocked out from fatigue after a single extraction; a few gathered discreetly behind her, watching from a distance. Petal paid them no mind.

As the arcs intersected on a trajectory that would hold, she struck the Enact button. In an instant the man she'd spent the last 32 minutes working on disappeared from the rank and dusty hole he'd lain in overnight, and materialized at a medevac unit a few miles away. Adi Taher, father of two, vitals still strong, would most likely survive. Petal closed her eyes and stretched her wrists. At 39, they needed more stretching these days. She took two deep gulps from the water bottle on the floor and consulted the map for the next one.

Not a single light blinked on the chip signal map. Had she finally cleared all of the chipped from the queue? Being a high rise in one of Jakarta's wealthiest districts, most of the inhabitants could afford to be chipped. The quake had struck in the middle of a weekday, so, hopefully only a small portion of the residents were home at the time. She'd waited on Taher's extraction to give the others a better chance of survival. His position had been tricky, liable to set off little landslides below him. So far the gambit had worked, but now came the true challenge.

Petal looked again at the building's schematics on the bottom left monitor—both the blueprint of what it had been as one piece and the rendering overlay of it in pieces. She pinpointed each sizable void to perform a remote manual bio scan.

Though most of the residents had been chipped, just as likely those people had housekeepers and maintenance workers that could never afford the expense.

HRO existed for them. Though Humanitarian Rescue Organization's mandate stated that they would rescue any and all people they could in a natural disaster, their real mission, as far as Petal was concerned, was to save those no one else thought worth the trouble—the ones who could never pay for expensive trips through the black. For them, she'd decided to work with a non-governmental organization instead of the lucrative commercial market.

She wouldn't have had it any other way—even today.

Near the top of the rubble, Petal found a number of cooling bodies, a small legion of cats, and below that three sizable rodents huddled together in the ruins of a restaurant that had once dominated the 15th floor. Sweat beaded on Petal's forehead. She wiped it and dried her hands on her pants. Slowly she scanned the rest of the building, cubic meter by cubic meter, consulting the locale grid she'd imposed on the overlay. At one of the last grid locations she got a larger, faint reading: no doubt, human. This person lay in the middle of the building, at the bottom, on the cusp of being crushed and being free. The location couldn't be much worse. It denoted a bleak, new level of complexity. Petal had to know the extractee's particulars to have any chance at a successful teleport. She grabbed her headset, toggled the talk function, and dialed up the mobile hospital's HRO rep.

"Intake," a female voice said, her accent relaxing the word.

"Have you finished cross-referencing the records of residence and accounted-for list?" Petal asked.

"Yes, I'll forward it now. Your access number?" "2478," Petal said.

"Sent," the operator replied. "Thanks," Petal said, disconnecting.

An icon blinked on the center screen. She ran the parameter search and waited a few seconds for the soft ding of completion in her ear.

Petal exhaled and motioned the ID reveal command. She'd learned not to look at the extractee's particulars before absolutely necessary; she'd watched a colleague in Rio reduced to tears when a sibling showed up on the screen. The tech couldn't have been more grateful when Petal evacced his sister, but Petal had been just as grateful for the lesson. She had no surviving family, only a long-ago-lost locket of their faces before the fire. She had a heart, though. Sometimes what you didn't know could help someone else.

Petal heard the other techs react and took her time looking at the screen: a baby, a toddler really, no more than four years old. Due to the extractee's age, a photo hadn't been added yet. The screen showed only a DOB with a blank space after the dash—unaccounted-for life, a maid's child, or perhaps a maid-in- training herself. The record didn't include any weight or height measurements from this year, no body scan, just the record of residence.

Petal called in a drone to help her. She wanted eyes on the child. She'd need to see the pocket that held the girl and her position in it, but mostly Petal didn't want her to be alone in the dark any longer. Petal glanced at the top monitors as the drone left the hangar.

While she calibrated the vectimeter to her estimates of a South East Asian 3 ½ year old's median weight and height, the drone reached altitude and quickly covered the distance to downtown Jakarta.

Petal watched its progress as the piles of rubble grew larger and the drone cruised down to the one that held the girl. The monitor darkened as the drone reached the closest opening and extended

its pinpoint camera into the space. A finger wouldn't have fit into it but the camera did. A faint outline of concrete and twisted steel glowed into existence on the screen. It slowly brightened and the girl's face appeared on the top center monitor.

A shallow gash bled down her cheek, but other than that she looked intact. Her legs and arms were free, her head at a natural-enough angle, but Petal couldn't see any space for her to wiggle, much less take a deep breath. Her lips had turned a strange hue, signaling the need to get her out now. Petal flicked the microphone away from her mouth and activated brown noise inside her headset. Leaning forward, the world shrunk down to five monitors and the controls in her hands.

On the top right monitor, the girl's infrared face glowed, below it the vectimeter adjusted and dead center scrolled the NAV screen's crowded array of numbers, colors, and all the custom apps and algorithms that Petal had loaded for easy execution.

She'd have to go fully manual. For this, she'd rather trust her own algorithms. Mass manufacturers hadn't yet figured out how to code functional finesse. Her algorithms bested them when it came to complex teleport metrics and executions. Though the algorithms only awaited an execution command, first Petal had to see the right combination of variables, the sweet spot in all the data flooding into her system. She tweaked and waited. As each second crept by, each breath she felt sure the rubble would shift and crush any hope of completing this rescue. With her left hand she carefully guided the extract arc into a better position. Petal glanced up at the vectimeter; she needed to adjust no more than 1 degree 3 and— *there*, the curve of a pocket in time. Petal's finger hovered above the Enact button, its code scrawling quickly by. NAV almost lined up. It would in 87 milliseconds, 47 milliseconds, the arc careened, snapped back before Petal could react, 17 . . . .

The girl disappeared from the screen.

Petal blinked, jerked her head up to check the drone connection. In that millisecond, tons of concrete and steel shifted, filling the void. The screen turned black as the camera went offline. Petal gasped. She scanned for bio signals—nothing. Not a cooling temp, or phantom trace. The toddler had simply ceased to be there, but Petal hadn't evacced her. She couldn't identify the feeling filling up her chest, just as she couldn't make sense of where in all the worlds and wormholes the girl had gone.

Thirty hectic minutes later she had no explanation—not one for herself or the site director whose office she now stood in, exhausted and frustrated. She felt on the verge of tears, but kept her face expressionless; she'd spent years perfecting the wall between her and the world of nerves and overwhelming circumstances. Petal could barely focus on his words and hadn't heard the name of the man who he introduced her to. It seemed a strange time for introductions, for conversations, for anything but finding the little girl. The director repeated himself.

"Ms. Scott, this is Brian Dunphries, from headquarters," the director said, moving hair out of his eyes as he spoke.

Petal didn't question why headquarters had sent a monitor for her, but a part of her filed away the information, the same part that filed all the work slights and microaggressions she chose not to deal with in the moment.

She knew she should respond to the introduction, but the usual words rang hollow—it was not good to meet him. Petal settled on "hello" and waited for the director to continue.

"I'd planned on introducing you this morning, but didn't want to interrupt your progress on the Crissal Building."

Crissal building. This at least she could connect to. Her eyes shifted to the director and the tall blond man at his side.

"What the hell happened?" the director asked.

"Lost souls are a reality of our business," the HQ rep interjected.

"Supposedly not for Ms. Scott here," the director replied. "We were told she'd never had an incident."

"I haven't—hadn't," Petal said. Other techs accepted lost souls as an inevitable facet of their work; no one even looked for them after the loss. The possibility of losing someone simply because of the complexity of the task didn't square. She created her own algorithms, went manual and trained three times longer than certification required to negate the inevitability of lost souls. Yet now here she stood, living a moment she'd worked to avoid.

"I have no excuse," she said. She wouldn't start inventing them now.

"You'll be put on leave while we investigate," the director responded.

"Completely routine, Ms. Scott," the rep said.

"Of course," she replied, turning to leave. As the door closed behind her she heard the director's final words.

"When I met her I told them no way she matched her numbers.

Not her fault really. She's overcome a lot of inherent limitations, but I can't say that I'm surprised."

That night, alone in the small home she rented, the girl's face waited behind Petal's closed eye lids. So, Petal'd left the bed behind. Instead, she paced and pored over the episode, worrying the floorboards in the narrow corridor between her terminal rig and monitor array. She could hear the steady hum of her generator, and not much else beyond her own thoughts.

Petal had never fancied herself arrogant, but she simply couldn't believe she'd lost the girl. She had no problem accepting her mistakes when she made them, but her head as well as heart rejected that conclusion. Her finger hadn't jumped. She'd had 17 milliseconds left and in that thin sliver of time something had happened.

A headache collected at her temples and Petal stopped pacing. She grabbed an apple from the countertop and dropped down at her rig.

She backed up everything, live-fed it to the server stateside that held her entire teleport history. Her father had been a boxing fan, and gave her one piece of advice: leave nothing up to the judges.

They could conduct their own investigation, but so would she. Devouring the apple in five big bites, she logged onto her archives and pulled up the day's work. Scrolling past the other extractees, she quickly found her place and pored over the time log, reviewing each reading and corresponding action on her part.

It didn't take long to find the hole in the whole. The anomaly started at 19 milliseconds-until-engage and ended at 17 til. In those 2 milliseconds, the arc had deviated—stretched into a parabola that did not correspond to her algorithms or HRO's apps, and moved in a way not under her control. The girl had disappeared into that gap.

Petal could find no further record of her existence. As an unchipped no teleport tech could. Had she spliced with the rubble around her, fallen into an alternate wormhole, evaporated with the cataclysmic intensity of Luther's Arc? Petal did not know. The tears that had threatened all day fell freely now, soaking her shirt, the skin beneath and further still.

#

HRO called her back stateside within the week. Despite recent events her record of reliability and success remained unmatched. They could use her in Seattle where floods were regular and the occasional tsunami surfaced. HQ wrote the incident off as her

fall to mortality. She could hear it in the site director's voice, a tiny celebration that now she walked amongst them, no longer ahead. Her apparent failure had improved his day. Hearing it, Petal briefly contemplated finally joining the private sector and its much better paid assignments. But she knew it would never take. There was still good work to do; so she flew back home. She could have expensed a trip through the black. Such trips were built into HRO's operating budget—but she savored the considerable time it took to move from one side of the world to the other.

#

Brian Dunphries ran the Seattle office. Petal spied him through the glass door as she entered the branch. She didn't welcome the coincidence. No fresh start here, but perhaps that's what HQ had in mind. She'd never needed a minder and didn't now. Still she greeted him with a small smile and an outstretched hand.

He had tried to be kind in Jakarta. She could only prove herself all over again though she had never truly stopped, a hazard of her extraction.

"Ms. Scott," Dunphries said. "It's good to see you again. Let me show you to our teleport unit."

All the interior walls were glass. Standing from the front entrance one could see to the very back of the building. Petal followed Dunphries further into the translucent maze.

"We run a controlled lab—no custom work and no outside software," he said.

Her algorithms. They wanted her to press buttons and take responsibility for anything that went wrong. Great. Is this supposed to be some sort of probation? Petal wondered. She didn't know any colleagues who worked in a locked-down lab, though some may have welcomed the ease.

"Is that on a probationary basis?" she asked.

"It's our standard protocol," he answered. "And I'll be acting as your supervisor. Because of your advanced experience it seemed the best fit. I'm sure you can appreciate that when things don't go as planned, there's a propensity to blame the operator. Here that's no longer an issue. Our techs execute the protocol and any errors can be easily traced and recorded."

Recorded, not resolved, Petal thought. "I see," she said.

They rounded a corner and entered the unit through another set of glass doors.

The room dwarfed any she'd worked in the last three years, the ones she'd spent in Southeast Asia and the Sudan. Just as she'd suspected the techs looked green as hell. They sat in three rows of three, talking across their terminals at one another.

A couple of them stopped comming on their watches long enough to turn around and acknowledge her and Dunphries. Three of them looked as if they might still be in secondary school, and the balance as eager and unskilled as the kids who stopped her on the street to see if she'd sign a petition to legalize metamethamine.

"Your colleagues," Dunphries said. "I'll leave you some time to get acquainted." He pointed to a yellow door in the corner.

"You can leave your things at the open terminal and there's an orientation program already cued; just log on. You'll find vending mechs in the break room there."

Petal wasted no time on introductions. As soon as Dunphries left she waved a hello to the room, sat down at the terminal, logged in and tried to take a look at the queue. She couldn't access it without completing orientation.

Petal exhaled.

"You'll find a lot is locked down here."

She turned to find one of the young techs standing behind her. He had a stocky build and sported a plaid shirt and unkempt beard.

"Petal Scott, right? I remember hearing about you," he said. Bad news apparently traveled fast.

"Ten years and only one lost soul. Impressive."

Petal's eye twitched when he said 'one lost soul'. She could feel the furrow of her brow, and struggled to say thanks though she didn't feel it.

This is what they would say now. Even if it never happened again, but worse than that she would always have the girl's face in the dark, a locket she couldn't lose.

"I'm Jeff Taylor."

She shook his hand, waited for something more.

"Well, I'll let you get back to it," he said.

The orientation program took much longer than necessary. By the time she'd finished, the waiting queue icon had disappeared from her terminal and afternoon had cleared the room. Everyone else talked in the break room, or had stepped outside. Now that she had access, Petal searched across the desktop to perform a proper orientation.

Their archive system was a mess. To make matters worse, this office used Diverse Triage for their queue, a program better suited to shipments than teleport tech. Petal frowned and started her review of the server. If she couldn't use her own algorithms she'd have to learn this system front to back to see how far she could bend it before it broke. Mass-produced software had broad, deep limitations so better to find them now when no one's life hung in the balance.

Server capacity was lean, and they seemed to have the techs systems tethered in a way that bordered on the obtuse. She shook her head and stretched her neck. From the corner of her eye she spied the vectimeter back up files and credentials. She opened the properties. Last calibration: *4 months ago?*

"What the hell?" Petal whispered. She calibrated daily; industry standard dictated 48 hours. Four months was a fucking crime.

"Or at least it should be," she finished out loud.

Anxious now, she continued to hunt around her terminal, opening files and mentally tracking what she found. The queue stayed empty, giving Petal time to explore this troubling new terrain.

#

The anomaly showed up on her third day in the office. She'd just successfully extracted a man from the roof of his truck in Oregonian flood waters. The intake rep expected him to spend the night at home. For the first time in weeks, Petal's tension unwound a single centimeter; she took a cleansing breath. Someone had cranked the AC up and she bent over to get a sweater out of her bag. As she righted herself, Dunphries face popped up on the instant messenger in the corner of her screen.

"Well done," the screen read.

Petal tried to think of a non-condescending interpretation, but failed miserably. The message required a perfunctory response, her least favorite kind. She typed her non-existent thanks and motioned the window to close.

An ID window maximized on the monitor. She must have right toggled when she meant to left. Dunphries' org chart appeared under his name with a tiny asterisk linked to a series of usernames. Odd that he would have so many but perhaps each piece of software required one. She shook her head; they didn't even have password chains. Good luck to the person who forgot one of them or to someone trying to track overall usage. With the empty queue she could at least fix this problem for them. Conventional best practice required it, and she had more downtime than she could handle.

Petal delved back into the files and then into the code behind the system. A simple administrative reroute should do the trick. She backtracked through the registry to find a way to track users though their devices, IPs, and usernames.

In an hour she found a worm. It hid amongst the benign operational systems, tucked away from the temporary files but always running with them. With it came malware that would have made a mid-grade hacker proud. Dunphries had introduced it.

At first, she thought the program must have been surveillance, recording keystrokes and the like for security's sake, but the more she searched, the less she thought it had anything to do with official HRO business.

As a creator of dozens of algorithms, execute programs and apps herself, Petal could understand wanting to customize the boilerplate software this office used, but she had a feeling she didn't yet care to name. Uneasily she looked to her left and right, sure now that she was being watched, or at least her work recorded. She would have to go stealth. She felt for a mem stick in her bag. Petal loaded it into the terminal and waited. She had to find the right moment, the correct cloaking sequence, and a data pick fine as the few seconds she might have before detection. Things slipped into alignment and Petal let her finger twitch.

The screen froze momentarily, but not before she saw the piggyback signal picking up each tech's teleport work, the licenses that allowed the transfer and Dunphries' worm trail hidden amongst the garbage commands that hid the breach. Much of HRO lay bare to him, or whoever he let in. They could have done anything—embezzled funds, stolen donor identities, sold HRO's tech right out from under them—or rerouted the extractees to send them who knew where.

A message box popped up on Petal's terminal. "Please come to my office," Dunphries had typed.

Petal noted her location in the system, pocketed the mem stick, shut down her terminal, and with a quick, bracing breath went to face Dunphries.

She had seen enough federal agents in relief centers to recognize that two of them were sitting in Dunphries office when she entered. With an effort, she kept walking inside. Her mind raced with possibilities. Before she could speak, one of the agents approached her.

"Do you know this girl?" he asked, holding a photo of the Indonesian toddler up at her eye level.

"Yes, of course. But— ," Petal began.

"You should." The agent looked at her with disgust. "Since you sent her there. You look confused. I guess you don't pay attention to where they end up. This photo is from Fun Things, one of the blackest holes in the darknet."

"I didn't send her anywhere. I lost her before—"

"Petal Scott, you're under arrest for kidnapping, conspiracy, corruption of a minor, and sex trafficking."

"What?! No! I didn't do that! None of that! Dunphries! He was involved; not me. I—" Petal turned to face her accuser. And she found herself on her knees, unable to move. She fell on the floor, the taser wires now visible.

She felt the full weight of the man on her back as he ground his knee between her shoulder blades and cuffed her. The other agent pulled her up to her feet. She saw the mem stick on the ground.

There! Look at that! At first she didn't realize that they couldn't hear her. The taser had left her only able to mumble and pant for her next breath. Dunphries stepped on the mem stick. He stared into space as they pulled her out of HRO and dumped her into the back of their vehicle.

#

Lock-up stank of desperation, body odor, and the urine of a homeless woman camped out in the corner of the cell. Petal ached where they had tasered her and winced from a tender spot on her back whenever she moved. She couldn't imagine a worse day.

It came when the court deemed her a flight risk and sent her to the Salem Federal Facility for Women.

She spent the first week crying, cultivating a migraine that left her curled up on the thin mattress, shielding her eyes from the fluorescents that lit up the cell all day and most of the night.

Intermittently she rushed to the toilet in the corner and vomited as her body tried to acclimate to the food and her soul to the pain it now bore. Her cellmate, a tall, brunette woman with a thick Slavic accent, ignored Petal as best she could, but on the 8th day when the smell had coated every surface in the room, she spoke.

"Enough," the woman said. "It stinks. Stop it." Petal heard her take a few steps.

"Stop retching up what got you here and start dealing with where you are."

Petal felt something small land behind her and turned to find a foil packet of antacids.

"For your stomach. Otherwise you'll have to go to the infirmary. You won't like the guards there."

Petal raised her gaze to look the woman in the face. "I am Kasia," she said.

Petal started to unfold herself, and reached for the packet. "Thank you. I'm Petal."

"Hm. I'd suggest using your surname here. The C.O. said it was —Smith?"

"Scott. Why won't I like the guards?" Petal asked.

"They believe they should be paid for the privilege of medical attention. They prefer flesh as payment." Kasia walked back to her bunk and sat. "The world loves its skin trade."

"Is that why you're here?" Petal asked.

"No, Scott. But I've done that time. Not you though, I can tell." "How?" Petal asked. Kasia chuckled, ignored the question. "What did you do outside?"

"Teleport tech."

Kasia hummed. "You must have done well for yourself then. There are so many things people want relocated into their possession."

"Not like that. I worked for an NGO, a—" "I know what an NGO is," Kasia said. "You'd be surprised."

"Rarely," Kasia responded.

That night Petal slept. She began to eat her meals, to speak with the other women, to accept the reality she found herself in. But she also fought for her freedom, cleaning out her bank account to pay lawyers and keep up payments on her tiny house. With the rest of her savings she arranged for her personal rig to be boxed and stored. She would get out she told herself.

In the meantime, Petal created a routine. After the exercise allotment, enduring inspections, and picking her way through the day's dangers she returned to her cell where she wrote code by hand and listened to Kasia's stories of the bumpy road from Plotzyk to Portland by way of every dark alley imaginable.

"I was raised in crime," Kasia said from her bunk, a crossword in her hand. "So you see, I was cultivated, but most people are corrupted," Kasia said. "An easier process than you might imagine. Where there is virtue, vice lurks."

Petal looked away from the code and up at her cellmate. Kasia seemed to contemplate something and spoke again, this time softly.

"For instance— you use the tech to help people; others want to help themselves. If one can pay, it's a lot easier to steal a girl tripping through the black than one off the street. And what better girl than one who can't be traced, a girl who might be dead anyway? There are men that do this, who gather their resources for it, like—" Kasia said.

"Like the people who crowdfund HRO's rescues," Petal finished.

"I was going to say wolves. These wolves stole the virtuous model and twisted it to their purposes. They call themselves voiders. 'To be avoided' we girls used to say," Kasia said with a tight, angry smile.

The loss of her last bit of naiveté burdened Petal. Her head drooped with the weight of this new knowledge, all the way down to the tabletop. She sat with her eyes closed.

"Of course. Thank you, K," she said quietly.

In time, Petal's eyes opened. The florescent light overhead looked brighter, the shadows it created, deeper. Underneath the table, at the page's corners, even outlining her hands—the gloom behind everything, emboldened, emerged. It called to her.

Would it swallow her finally? Do what the fire and the work had not? If it did, what would become of the people so easily lost —and the perpetrators who, for her, could easily be found? She picked her head up wearily. As she did, the shadows shifted. Petal paused in mid-motion. *Even shadows can be displaced.*

"Leave nothing up to the judges," she whispered.

Petal looked at the code and a new, bolder imperative clicked into place. She reached for a fresh sheet of paper and began again, hand flying across the page to capture her rushing thoughts.

#

Petal spent 28 months sharpening her skills. It took those two years and a spring for the court to find the prosecutor had insufficient evidence to convict. Kasia was impressed. She said

Petal must have some kind of luck to get out at all—even if Petal's lawyers said the arrest ruined her professional reputation. Petal didn't believe in luck, only in doing. At work, she used to say she made other people's luck; now she understood how short the distance to misfortune. She had just spent 28 months calculating it exactly.

Her first day out Petal sprung her rig from cold storage. Two years of lost updates would slow her down. It would mean at least a week of getting back up to speed: Petal relished the thought.

Her first crooked job came easily. She sat in the one bedroom house she stopped calling home after her second HRO assignment abroad and logged into the darknet with the rig she'd retrofitted specifically for the task. The darknet's layout looked unnecessarily opaque and seedy—someone's idea of what elicit should look like—all choppy fonts and DOS aesthetics. She moved to a search page to retrieve "trafficking" results. She'd specified "art trafficking" to save herself from images she wouldn't be able to forget. She planned on tracking the voiders later and in some way that wouldn't keep her up at night. Kasia had assured her that identities were cheap here, and each sex trafficking site kept a list of its patrons complete with all chip and location info, hacked back to their origin from the moment they logged on. Because of it Petal would have to spend her first payment on a specialized sub-rig invisible to anyone but her. If she hadn't already had her own chip removed she would have spent her second payment on that, but now she could put that money to better use.

The second "trafficking" hit provided the results she wanted. She found a job board of sorts and posted her skills and experience. Soon after, she proved it with a series of tests. After a long vet process her reply came back in flashing chartreuse characters.

"You're hired," it read. "Ready to get to work?"

Petal assented. An icon appeared at the corner of her screen. When she motioned it open a building schematic appeared and Petal prepared to extract a Degas from a vault in Tel Aviv. The job paid a year's salary.

With her third deposit she bought a backdoor key into HRO's systems. There she set her long-honed algorithm loose. It took longer than she had anticipated, but in five minutes the uplink completed: she had full access to HRO's systems and had fully cloaked her actions. Her second screen filled with live natural disaster info: latitude, longitude, magnitude, description, and estimates of the number affected. She pressed her list of coordinates onto the edge of the screen. Next she searched the HR records. Dunphries had been terminated, the stated reason: a statistically unacceptable string of lost souls on his watch, all attributed to user error and equipment failure. In another module, she found that none of the lost extractees had been located— even those that were chipped. The stolen girl had no chip.

Petal couldn't find her because of it, but maybe she could locate some of these girls who were—perhaps still are—chipped. She saved the necessary info down to her terminal in case she lost the connection and navigated to the teleport module.

Thunder rumbled overhead as Petal set about locating and extracting the lost souls from their unnatural disasters. She'd lost none of her speed on the controls; in fact she moved faster now. She didn't know if the simpler tasks or more compelling conditions spurred her. She found three women and two children in North America in a matter of minutes, the sixth not 500 miles away from where she sat. Petal engaged the CCTV hack app she'd received as an incentive for her latest job and waited for the arcs to align. At that instant, she enacted the first extraction.

As the first foundling appeared outside a relief center, Petal watched her look around in terror and confusion. Dirt covered her skin and night gown, as if she had been unearthed. Even from a distance, she looked years older than the photo taken months before. Relief flooded into her expression. She lowered her hands, no longer needing to ward off whatever had been approaching. She jerked her head around the empty street and saw the relief center's sign. Without another glance, forward or back, she ran inside.

Petal stared at the space she'd been standing in, unable for the moment to think clearly or act. She blinked and saw the Indonesian girl's face. She extracted the other lost souls without taking the time to watch. As the last one arrived back in her hometown, Petal could only feel her heart thumping in her chest, her shoulders release.

An alert chimed on her rig. Petal's gaze slowly drifted up to the top monitor where it reported that a hurricane now scoured the Atlantic coast of Florida. Petal shifted at her terminal and with a sequence of graceful motions, effortless as dance, she relocated the first selection of voiders into the eye wall of the storm.

Petal felt a vastness open in her, a laying out of possibilities and matrices that until now had not existed. Gauging her next move, she analyzed the shift.

Rise
by Nicole Givens Kurtz

In the distance, Phoenix rose out of the Arizona desert like the mythical bird of legend. Its wings stretched far and wide in brilliant glimmering glass and metal monoliths and skyscrapers. Phenomenal Phoenix promised heavenly homes and a new start. Burn your past life and rise into freedom.

The wind howled as Trixie and Fox yanked their hoods over their heads and stepped onto the gravel road. The truck driver roared by them, spraying apathy and debris. Trixie adjusted her braids into a low ponytail beneath her hood, before hugging Fox to her. Overhead, the mountains reached for the night sky. Decked out in diamond-like stars, the velvety evening heaven had been decorated as if in celebration of their arrival.

"Nobody wants us." Fox shrugged out of her embrace. Already taller, her younger brother teetered in the awkward stage between child and man. Tinged with disappointment, his words pinched her heart.

She hugged him close. "Then we'll have us. You build a home out of people, not places." Trixie linked her arm through his.

Despite the scowl on his face, she saw him grin quickly before allowing it to dissolve again.

"We'll rise from the ashes of our past." Trixie patted him on the back.

"Uh huh. Covered in soot."

A small chapel rose out of the dust. Trixie headed there as the Arizona sky opened up and rain fell hard and fast. Running to the worn wooden door, she and Fox huddled from the raging squall. The tiny archway provided little cover as the rain pelted them.

"Can't you do somethin'?" Fox shouted above the clap of thunder.

Trixie sighed. "It's just a little water!" "I'm drownin' standin' up!"

Trixie placed her palm against the wood and concentrated. She could feel the molecules accelerate faster. The wood crackled and buckled beneath the fire. She burned through the door enough for her to stick her hand in and unlock it.

"Come on!" She pulled Fox inside.

Mold, dampness, and desert odors collected in the chapel's stuffy air. The pews sat in neat rows. Fox picked up one of the tiny tealight candles and passed it to her. With a snap of her fingers, she lit all three rows of candles, including the one in Fox's hand. Her powers had grown since the Flagstaff forest fires.

"Trix!" he shouted, startled by her actions. He replaced it with the others before turning back to her. "You could've burned me."

She looked back over her shoulder. "No. I've got better control now."

Fox inclined his head, but thankfully did not push the matter. Trixie wiped the ash from her hands and took a look around. The tiny chapel had been deserted. Dust bunnies and layers of sand covered everything. Not that the conditions meant anything.

In the desert, dust and sand covered everything, except in Phoenix. She would dust off the ashes of her past.

"Doesn't look like anyone's been blessed in this place in a while."

"It's a blessing for us, then, isn't it?" Trixie picked up a hymn book. Its jacket had been worn down to cardboard inside.

Fox quirked an eyebrow at her. "I guess so."

She paused at the hesitation in his voice. Fox's locks, a bright sun-brushed red, provided evidence of their father's Irish lineage. His dark skin spoke to their momma's deep roots in Africa. Like so many in the after-throes of a collapsed country, the genetics didn't matter—only what they could do with their abilities did.

But not in the land of the sun. All were equal there.

"I know it ain't the best of situations but it's the only place for tonight. Tomorrow—"

"—we see the sun." Fox finished. She placed the book back on the pew.

Fox tossed his hood back, and his long dreadlocks spilled over his shoulders. His eyes glowed in the evening's gloom. "It ain't gonna be no different there. Nobody wants us. Too dangerous."

Trixie plopped down onto the first pew and conjured fire from her palm. She held it high as she searched around her immediate area. Fatigued, hungry, and crashing from the adrenaline waning in her veins, Trixie couldn't quite put her hands on the right words to ease Fox's fear.

"All are welcomed there. You remember those stories of emancipation we read on the Internet? Of the Israelites out of Egypt? Of the Africans who escaped slavery to the North?"

Closing her eyes, she forced the flames in her hand to recede.

Her palm stung, but she didn't bother to check it, not any more. Her hands carried the blackened char of ash. The doctors and scientists couldn't stop that. The tests, the surgeries, and numerous drugs all failed to eradicate it.

A genetic oddity. Magician.

Freak.

Nigger.

She rolled over onto her side. None of the labels meant anything in Phoenix. Everyone could take flight.

"I bet that place ain't seen nothin' like us." Fox huffed. He kept trying to find some identify, some *adjective* that would make him fit in to a world obsessed with identifying everything and shoving it into its proper place.

"We *are* dangerous, Fox. And tired. Well, I am." Trixie stretched out on the pew and folded her hands behind her head. Her thick frame didn't fit entirely on the narrow wood, but she made it work. Her hoodie served as an adequate pillow.

"Maybe we wouldn't be dangerous, if they hadn't kept us like animals in that—that place," Fox said.

The pew behind her creaked beneath Fox's weight. Books, no doubt the hymnals, hit the floor with a series of *thuds*.

"Fox—"

"All right. Lettin' go, sis."

She smiled. "Goodnight, Red."

"I'm a man, not a color."

She giggled as sleep approached. His complaints at her teasing meant Fox hadn't lost all of his innocence and youth—yet.

#

The *smack* of the chair forced Trixie to jump awake with a shriek. Startled from her slumber, she fell with a crash to the floor. Worn and frayed carpet had muffled some of the sound, but Trixie had been spooked. With her elbow smarting, and a full on grimace, she got to her feet.

What the hell?

They weren't alone. She stood with her hands aflame and her temper even hotter. "Who are you?"

A large man dressed in a black robe stood across from her. White blonde shoulder-length hair and cold azure eyes loomed beneath the cloak's hood.

"Hello?" Trixie stepped in front of the pew where Fox had just sat up.

"Trix?" Fox yawned from behind her.

"Who are you?" Trixie positioned her hands.

She took in everything in flashes. The brightness of the chapel. The silence of the people. The scent of something *other* in the air. The hush from outside. Last night, the chapel had been abandoned. No signs of life at all, but then—in her exhaustion, and in the gathering dark–she could have miscalculated.

"Hey! She's talkin' to you!" Fox pulled himself up to his full height.

The man in the robe faced them. He threw back the cloak's hood, and nodded in Fox's direction. "You aren't headed for the sun, are you?"

"Who are you again?"

"The sun is a funny thing. It attracts with its beauty and warmth. It also kills with those same qualities."

When he spoke, it thundered, like a powerful waterfall. The hairs on her neck rose at the man's sheer power. Fear gnawed at the edge of Trixie's courage. What was he?

"Oy, we asked ya first." Fox's glowing eyes shifted to her and then back to the man.

Trixie lowered her hands and mentally extinguished their fire. If this escalated, Fox could get hurt.

"I'm sorry. We trespassed on your property." Trixie picked up her pack.

The man nodded again. "Apology accepted." "We didn't see no sign. Nothin'." Fox added.

The leader in the cloak had taken several small steps toward them, but halted at Fox's words.

"So, uh, who are you?" Trixie asked. She adjusted her hoodie as she walked closer to Fox. If they had to make a run for it or fight their way out, she wanted to be within arm's reach of him.

She wouldn't let anything come between her and freedom. To be her true self. She'd rise above.

"My name is of no importance. What I *do*, now, that Trixie and Fox, is what matters most."

"How do you know our names?" Trixie took several steps back.

The man flashed strong white teeth. It lacked warmth. "One death dealer knows another."

Trixie tightened her hands into fists. *Death dealer.* No one had called her that, not since the lab.

"I don't deal in death." Not anymore. "No?"

"No."

Bleary-eyed, hungry, and threatened, Trixie struggled with indecision. With the stranger's intense watching, she wanted nothing more than to bolt, to run—or burn the entire place down to the ground.

The latter sounded much better. She'd show them death. Inside her, the *other* voice that wanted to ignite the very tattered fibers of the world and watch it be devoured by her fury and outrage awoke. Her palms itched and she uncurled her hands, raising them.

Yes, she would show them all how to frighten, to harass with power, to be victims, like so many of her people had been victims—of dogs, chains, whips, spitting, beatings, lynchings—and police sanctioned murder.

"Let's push on, sis." Fox whispered behind her. Fox.

The fact he remained, standing beside, and depending on her, wrenched her back from the edge. He forced her fury to recede.

She thought of rising on new wings. They were above petty revenge. Freedom awaited.

Trixie swallowed the acidic taste on her tongue, and backed away from the man and his troop. He remained standing, his pink face shining as if he were sweating hard. His bulk. His voice. His unrelenting stare had nothing on the creepiness and the iciness of his smile.

And he kept grinning as she stepped through the chapel's door. Once outside, Fox yanked up his hood. "What the hell?"

"Let's just go." Trixie started toward the mountains again. "We need to find some food."

Death dealer.

She hadn't heard that term in, well, since the first time they'd escaped from the lab. Death trailed them, like a powerful and expensive perfume that lingered in the room once you'd already gone. The bodies in their wake hadn't all been their fault.

Still, it lingered in her. The redhead nurse kept screaming as the lab burned around them, her hair aflame, and her eyes wide with agony…*death dealer.*

Trixie shuddered.

"You all right, Trix?" Fox came over to her.

"Yeah. Fine." She tried to put the memory away, but the woman's screams echoed deep into her psyche. Phoenix would burn it out. Then she'd stop hearing them. Now, the desert quiet amplified the memories. "We've got to get to the city. Get food. Get water."

In the faraway distance, the metallic and mirrored city buildings reflected the sunlight and sparkled. A new day lumbered on. Trixie shook her head as the heat raged around them. They'd never make it walking, not in this heat. Her legs kept moving forward despite the truth in her logic.

The chapel grew smaller and smaller behind them. No one had come after them. It felt strange. So many had chased them. Followed them around stores, around neighborhoods, and around the lab.

Watching. Just like that man in the robe.

Most of her life Trixie had known only three things: Struggle. Fight. Run.

Despite the danger that wearing hoods invoked, they had yanked them on. It made it hot. Sure, it deflected some of the sun's rays, but the fabric had been crafted for colder climates. They'd gotten them in Flagstaff.

"Who was that guy?" Fox asked, his face partially shielded by his hood.

"Dunno." Trixie kept walking. "He knew us." Fox shouted.

"He knew our *names*." Trixie added.

"More than we got on him, huh?" Fox looked at her and with a shrug, turned back to the road.

"We need a ride." Trixie wanted to put as much distance between her and the man as she could. Something about him left her unsettled. She hadn't come all this way to meet her death and neither had Fox.

#

Weeks later

Trixie crossed into Phoenix proper and the man in the cloak didn't follow. She watched through the sliver of window blinds, but nothing seemed amiss in the pristine, perfect days of life in paradise. Manufactured air pumped through the domed in metro area. The bustling city had been contained from urban sprawl. To Trixie's dismay, the rising bird had been caged.

Trixie stepped out of the adobe home she and Fox shared.

Over the last two weeks, her alarm had lessened. They were settling into an uncomfortable, but not unpleasant, existence. Trixie struggled with the newness of it all. Clean streets. Free food rations. Air conditioning. No poverty. No politics.

"No peace," Fox remarked, spooking her from behind. She closed the blinds. "What?"

He tapped his temple. "No peace in here."

"This place is perfect." Trixie gestured to the tranquil scene just outside the windows. "No violence. No trash. Quiet. Even the vehicles are hushed."

They'd been accepted into the city as prelims. Their citizenship relied on how they contributed to the overall progress.

Fox shifted. "Yeah. Too quiet. There's no laughter, talkin', or arguin'."

"You miss the noise? The conflict? The fighting?" "No, but—"

"Then it's perfect."

He frowned. "The air has an aftertaste." Trixie sighed. It did.

"So, it isn't perfect. What if I go out and yell?" Fox walked to the door. It hushed open.

"Fox. We been through this. Regulations. This is quiet time." "My point."

With that, he retreated to his room, a tight triangle corner of their adobe. Once they became full citizens, they'd get a bigger space.

Trixie gazed out over the neighborhood from the open door.

"Ah, there you are." The voice slithered around the sidewalk's curve.

Two weeks he'd waited. The Gringo.

She and Fox had discovered others who spoke of the pale cloaked man they'd met at the chapel, the one who had called himself a death dealer. He'd been called The Gringo, yet no one knew his real name—only his lethal punishment for people who dealt in death, an avenging angel of sorts.

"Your handiwork, excuse the pun, is stamped all over this sector, Trixie."

Trixie narrowed her eyes as he faced her. Her palms itched in anticipation. "What the hell do you mean?"

The Gringo laughed. "Don't you smell it? The fear your presence generates?"

"We'll call the police! Get out of here!" Fox took out his phone.

The man tossed a fireball at Fox. Trixie screamed and dove in front of the hurling flames. The heat blew through her, singeing her eyebrows, brushing her face.

She scrambled to her feet and set her own palms on fire. The Gringo had encroached on their yard. *Who is this guy?*

"The Gringo has powers!"

"No kidding!" Trixie leapt back into the door. It closed, slicing off the sound fight.

Fox panted a few feet away. Already his shape threatened to shift. His eyes glowed scarlet and his knuckles curled into the beginnings of paws.

"No, Fox!" She hurried to calm him. Across from the door, his serum sat on the table, amber liquid in capped syringes. Trixie snatched the cap off of one and slammed it into his buttocks.

He howled in alarm, and raced off through the house.

Outside, the Gringo continued his assault. Glass shattered. The scent of burning vegetation wafted inside.

"What do you want?" she shouted through the open door. Blue and red lights spilled in. The police had arrived. "Citizens. Desist your use of powers," a disembodied voice commanded. Disrupting the sanctioned quiet time was a serious offense.

Trixie crawled over broken glass and shattered furniture, some still smoking.

She and Fox had been chased across the southwest. Hunted.

Then it clicked. Him.

"Fox! We have to get out of here! Find the sanctuary and plead for amnesty."

Pressed against the wall, drenched in sweat, Fox's nose had elongated into a snout. He barked out. "What? Now?"

"The Gringo!"

Damn. The serum injection had come too late and he'd already begun to change. Trixie sprinted around the room, snatching up their few possessions and tossing them into her satchel. Her hands shook.

"The Gringo?"

Trixie stopped. "I—I didn't think he really existed. Urban legend. Vapors. Remember Denver?"

Denver had been before Flagstaff.

Clean streets. Hushed quiet during daylight hours. Domed paradise. She'd been a fool. A gullible fool.

Freedom.

Before she could explain, the front door blew off its track. The Gringo came in, grinning.

"Out! Out! Damn black spots!"

"Spots?" Fox barked as he shifted to a sizable red fox, losing all ability to speak.

"Stains on the lovely purity of this city. I will make it *clean*." The Gringo grinned and rapidly threw fireballs at them.

"Run Fox!" Trixie deflected the attack with fire of her own. The Gringo moved fast and, before long, had her by the throat.

He threw her outside and she slammed into the manufactured lawn. It flickered as the hologram program crashed, revealing a section of dark gray plasma screen.

"Worthless. Designer scientists' cheap experiments." The Gringo revealed as he grabbed both her wrists when she tried to defend herself.

"Run Fox!" she shouted again.

Overhead, crisp blue sky and lemonade sun rested in the

heavens. When she looked closely, she could see small reflections against the clear dome. Picture. Perfect. So quiet. No peace.

"You sought freedom." He laughed.

Trixie screamed as his hands burned the flesh around her wrists. Agony wretched through her. He'd set her skin on fire. The burning flames funneling out of his palms and scurried up her arms.

"Yes! Scream out your pathetic soul. If you bastards have one."

Trixie collapsed as he let go. Had it all come down to this? The fight? The struggle? All in vain.

She pushed back with flames of her own, fire against fire with her body the battlefield. The Gringo's powerful flames roared, his hatred fueling.

Agony wore through her anger, leaving only emptiness. Her fire quieted as she slumped to the ground.

The Gringo's grin was wide and cold. "Die."

Trixie shivered as her flame retreated, worn down by the Gringo.

Then, ripping through the afternoon's polished peace, a fox howled in the distance.

Now, it was her turn to smile. Warmth came and grew hotter. She didn't scream as the agony of fire crackled along her flesh, her hair, her sight.

For like a phoenix, Trixie would rise.

Of Sound Mind and Body
by K. Ceres Wright

The pain. It always began behind her eyes, then crept downward in intermittent bursts. Her spine fired red, all the way down to the L5 vertebrae. Dara pushed the pain aside, and focused on her reflection in the mirror in preparation for her daily ritual. She placed her hands on the cracked porcelain sink and blocked all else from her mind.

"I am Dara Martin and I have terracotta skin, curly black hair, and brown eyes. My favorite color is gold, favorite fruit is orange, and favorite music is fusion jazz. I have one sister named Rebecca and my parents live in San Diego. I am—" an undercover agent with Homeland Intelligence on foreign assignment and will be coming in in two months—Lord willing.

She never said the last part out loud, even with her jammer on. And especially not when she wasn't herself. Her handler, Rona, would be mortified if she knew Dara repeated that mantra every day in the mirror. Dara suspected Rona thought she was cracking around the edges, but she said nothing.

BAM! BAM! BAM!

Dara hung her head and exhaled. "Coming!" She opened the door and stepped out into the suffocating presence of Jian Lee. At 5'3", he was shorter than Dara, but he had a psyche that he could project across space and time to tell people they needed to get their shit together. Even ensconced in her bed after her alarm sounded, his voice grated in her head, telling her to haul her sorry ass out of bed and get to work.

"You have a message from Yuan Chin. Why does he call here? He's married," Jian said.

"It's business," Dara said. She pushed past him, heading for the main makeup counter. Rows of foundation liquids, powders, and gels lined the glass shelves in the small warehouse slash distribution center.

"Business my ass. I hear the way you talk, all low and flirty. 'Yes, Yuan, I'll be here all night. Come by any time.'"

"Yes, and thanks to him, we'll soon be getting a prominent booth at the China Beauty Expo. Not one in the back next to the alley like we always do."

"Hmph. We'll see," Jian said. "You know, in your next life, you'll come back as a prostitute."

Dara turned to him, hands on her hips. Actually, prostitution wasn't that different from spying. The two oldest professions could be rolled up into one, she thought. "Good thing I don't believe in reincarnation. And don't you have some mascara to inventory?"

Jian sucked his teeth and made for the back room. He would stay there and sulk for a half hour until he sensed another moral failing coming through the door, whereupon he would suddenly reappear to render judgment on the hapless soul.

Dara tapped her thumb twice against her thigh, opening up a line. The versos appeared in her periphery, a listing of contacts, a calendar—lunch with Major Zhang tomorrow—newsfeed, and recently opened files.

"Call Yuan Chin," she said. "Voice only." He knew her as Chyou Sòng, her cover name. Sometimes it was hard to keep track.

He picked up after two rings.

"Miss Sòng. It's good to hear your voice. But why don't you show your face?"

His chip implant approximated his appearance and movements and projected them into her field of vision. Or at least that's how it usually worked. He could have been bare-ass naked riding a donkey up Mount Vesuvius for all she knew. His image showed him wearing a socialist-green uniform with red and gold epaulets. Acne scars dotted his cheeks. Spiky salt-and-pepper hair rose up from a head that held small brown eyes, a forgettable nose, and thick lips.

"I like to project an air of mystery. Jian told me you called?"

"Yes. Are you free for lunch tomorrow?"

"No," Dara said. "Client meeting. How about dinner tonight?"

Yuan smiled, displaying a set of coffee-stained teeth. "Even better. I'll pick you up at seven."

"See you then." Dara closed the line. She expected Jian to appear from around the corner and fix her with a disapproving glare, but he remained in the back room.

The magfield chimed as a customer walked through, a 30-something African–Chinese man wearing jeans and a sports coat. Dara's implant captured his image and ran it through her database, and the search results scrolled up her periphery.

Name: Githinji Diallo Height: 6'2"

Weight: 168 Eyes: Brown Hair: Black

Summary: Grandfather, Dafari Diallo, immigrated to China in 2008 from Nigeria to establish a textile import/export business in Guangzhou, also known as "Little Africa" due to the high number of African immigrants. After several run-ins with Chinese authorities over expired visas, he married Huian Lin, who helped him navigate the visa process. They expanded their business to include beauty products and health foods. They had one child, Ling Diallo. He attended Shanghai University and continued the family business. He married Daiyu Okoye. They had one child, Githinji Diallo. He attended Guangdong University of Finance and Economics and opened his own business, Diallo Cosmetics, focused on beauty products tailored to African–Chinese women.

"May I help you?" Dara said. She always felt strange after reading people's life histories in her database and then having to act as if she knew nothing about them.

The man sauntered up to the counter, pushing his sunglasses over wavy hair. "I'm Githinji Diallo of Diallo Cosmetics. I need 10,000 units of foundation as soon as possible. Varying shades, but geared toward African–Chinese women."

"Let me see if we have enough in stock." She tapped open the inventory verso and called up foundation units. They only had 3,000.

"Unfortunately, our inventory won't satisfy your order.

However, if you wait until Friday, I'll be able to complete it."

He nodded slowly. "All right." He tapped two fingers on the counter and uploaded his contact information to the server. "Close of business on Friday?"

"Close of business," Dara said, confirming.

Githinji smiled and winked at her, then left. In her five months in China, she had never seen the man before, which was unusual, as most distributors either knew or knew of one another. Even new people in the business were brought in by someone already established. In her case, her handler arranged to buy out Gua Beauty Products, and she got Jian in the deal.

"Ji--," she started.

"Never seen him before." Jian appeared from around the corner.

And that might be a problem, Dara thought. She didn't care what her database had said.

"I need a smoke," Dara said. "I'll be back in twenty."

#

Cliché as hell, Dara thought as she lit a cigarette. Meeting her handler on a park bench, but that's where she was, in People's Park, staring at concentric rings of red, orange, yellow, and pink flowers. A few toddlers were running around the circle, watched by young mothers dressed in fashionable sportswear.

A tan woman came and sat at the opposite end of the bench. Dara knew her as Rona Huang, deputy station chief. She was tall and overweight, with cheeks that puffed out like a Southern Belle's wedding gown, and straight black hair cut into an efficient bob. No makeup or perfume. Straight, no chaser.

"You called this meeting. Got anything?" she Rona said. She peered off in the distance from behind black sunglasses.

"New guy came in the office, Githinji Diallo. I've never seen or heard of him before. Jian neither," Dara said.

"That is another operative." Dara froze mid-inhale. "What?"

"No need to get in a huff. He's on a different assignment, but available if you need help."

Two young mothers walked past, pushing strollers stuffed with fat toddlers. The occupied mothers were gossiping about a third mother who was being shunned by their play group. The offender, apparently, did not live up to the expectations of the others.

Something about dressing like she stepped out of a charity shop. Dara and Rona waited until the mothers passed on.

"What's his assignment?" Dara said. "That's need to know."

Dara crossed her legs and folded her arms across her chest. "Don't sulk. He has…different talents."

"I'm not sulking." "Then what?" Rona said.

Dara hesitated, mulling over how to phrase her thoughts. How did people tell their bosses they thought they were going crazy? "I don't know how much longer I can hold on."

Rona shifted in her seat, folding her arms across her chest. "I know you don't want to hear this, but I feel like a fucking

guinea pig," Dara said.

"The ability to transform at the cellular level is a proven--"

"Proven in the lab," Dara said. Frustration laced her tone. "We both know I'm a field test, and I'm not exactly delivering the results you wanted. I'm tired of tiptoeing around the elephant in the room, so I'm laying it out. If I crack, this whole mission goes south."

"News flash. It's about to go south anyway because you haven't found anything. You've been here five months, Dara. We outfit you with the latest tech, and nothing."

"I've been establishing my cover and slowly getting closer to the trade minister. And as far as this latest tech?" She growled the worlds through clenched teeth. "This thing that's ruining my life is the latest tech? I don't see you jumping at the chance to get it."

Pain shot up from her stomach and into her chest.

She wrapped an arm around her stomach and leaned over the arm rest, gripping the iron railing, waiting for the pain to subside.

"Are you all right?" Rona said. Dara ignored her question.

"I have a meeting with Yuan Chin tonight. He's the Minister of Commerce's brother. I'll use him as a lead-in to hack into Minister Chin's system to get the documents on the upcoming trade talks. I'll let you know what I find." She stood up, ground out her cigarette on the pavement, and left.

#

Dara pushed open the door to her apartment and half fell inside. She deposited the grocery bags that been pinching her finger the entire elevator ride up onto the floor and massaged the blood back into her hand.

The fridge display showed two half-eaten cartons of moo shu pork, two eggs, and a pint of expired milk. None too soon, she thought. She put away the groceries and turned her thoughts toward the evening's attire.

She studied the three formal dresses hanging in her closet—red, white, and black—sex, no sex, and maybe sex. Dara didn't want to broadcast her intent, but didn't want to discourage Yuan, either, so she chose the black dress. Floor length and covered in sequins, it sported a low-cut back and a draped front. After grabbing a pair of matching shoes, she threw the dress on her bed and rolled the shoes in the same direction.

A sharp pain knifed her stomach. She fell to her knees halfway to the bathroom, gasping. Damn. The random pains were coming more often. She'd been to the agency doctor so many times, he would roll his eyes as soon as she walked in the door.

"It's not physical," he had said.

"I am Dara Martin and I have terracotta skin, curly black hair, and brown eyes. My favorite color is gold, favorite fruit is orange, and favorite music is fusion jazz."

The pain finally subsided and she stumbled to the bathroom. The lights flicked on and the refresher emitted a spray of vanilla cinnamon. Dara leaned against the door and inhaled, catching her breath. It was easier to transform in fragrant surroundings. She preferred to change at least two hours before an encounter in order to settle into the character. But given recent events, she wondered if she could hold on at all.

Gripping the edges of the sink, she closed her eyes and focused inward. Dara envisioned her nervous system, recalling every branch and ganglion as laid out in virtual reality. She sent pulses along her synapses to activate specialized neurotransmitters. They fired down the nerves, delivering messages to genes in a particular order. First, the rs4752566-T allele of the FGFR2 gene to straighten the hair. A sharp pain exploded behind her optic nerve. Her scream echoed in her head, and she fell to her knees, panting. A chill rippled across her skin as sweat beaded on her forehead. A violent shiver rocked her body and she almost fell over, but managed to steady herself.

She wiped away the sweat and waited. The pain faded, and she clawed the toilet and sink to pull herself up.

Her reflection stared back in the mirror, with razor-straight hair and her same oval eyes. Dara splashed water on her face and dried it with a towel. The pain had been worse than ever. She'd been told it would get better, not worse. Lying bastards. She tightened her hold on the sink and then sent a message to the rs1426654-A allele of the SLC24A5 gene to lighten her skin. The searing pain began in her feet, slow and steady, then quickened to shooting stabs wending upward—legs, torso, arms, shoulders. Her legs shook and gave way again, sending her to the floor. The cool tile around the toilet soothed one side of her face. The other side burned, as if pressed against the underside of a hibachi grill. She clenched her fists and commanded her muscles to still, but they spasmed and jerked in defiance. Her breath came hard and shallow in rough-edged gasps with not enough strength to hold the scream trapped in her throat.

Then the shaking stopped, and her view faded to black.

#

The time blinked 5:30 in her periphery when she awoke, a half-hour later than when she started. Dara held up a hand. Her skin glowed porcelain in the dim light and she sighed in relief. Her agony hadn't been in vain. Still, it'd been the first time she passed out. She would have to factor in extra time for future transformations, which would only make her job more difficult. As if I need more of a hassle in my life.

She got to her feet and beheld herself in the mirror. Her facial structure remained the same, as well as her nose and pouty lips.

Her hair hung down, mid-humerus, framing an oval bone-white face. The effect always distressed her at first. It took some time to get used to looking at herself through a different face. Hers, really, but just another color. She reached into her makeup bag and pulled out a bottle of foundation, Ivory Sands, and began to apply it.

"My name is Chyou Sòng. My favorite color is purple. My favorite food is tea-smoked duck. My favorite music is American rap."

She followed up with eyeliner, shadow, and lipstick. Satisfied, she slipped on her dress and shoes, took one last look in the mirror, and left.

Yuan's limousine was waiting outside. When Chyou exited her apartment building, Yuan jumped out of the car and offered to help her, beating the driver, who had begun to walk around the car to open the door. When the driver turned around to head back to the car, Chyou froze. It was Githinji Diallo, dressed in a chauffeur's uniform. Panic chilled her skin and jumpstarted her heart. Did Rona send him to check on her? What were Diallo's 'other talents'? Keep calm and don't stare. Mind your breathing.

"Good evening, Chyou. You look lovely," Yuan said.

Chyou managed a smile. "Thank you. You're quite dashing in your tuxedo." Keep it together.

Everyone climbed inside and Githinji pulled away from the curb, heading downtown.

"This is just one of my limousines. I have two others. One is a Hummer, and one's a Cadillac. But I save the Lincoln for special events," Yuan said. His lips curved into a self-satisfied grin. Soft music played from invisible speakers and the strong smell of Corsair cologne accosted her nostrils.

"Ah," Chyou said. It was going to be a long night.

Yuan took two glasses from a side compartment and gave her one.

"To a magical evening," he said, holding up his glass.

Chyou clinked her glass to his, but the sound drew itself out, as a key pressed down on a child's toy piano. Her point of view skewed, shifting left, until she saw herself from outside her body, holding up the glass. She froze, disoriented.

"Are you all right?" Yuan said. He leaned in, as if examining her pupils. "Chyou?"

She closed her eyes and focused, willing herself back into her body. When she opened her eyes, her perspective had shifted back.

Yuan's face had wrinkled up in concern as he searched her eyes.

Chyou plastered on a smile and touched him on the check. "I'm sorry, Yuan. It's been a long day. To a magical evening." She clinked his glass again and took a sip. Her hand shook. She upended the drink, finishing it in one swallow.

Yuan pointed a finger at her. "I know what you need." He gathered the glasses and put them away, then pressed a button on the console in front of them. A small door opened and spat out a tray that held four lines of cocaine and a straw.

"Oh, I don't know, Yuan."

"Come on, live a little. Just something to straighten you out. You'll feel like you're truly free."

Dara had done cocaine a few times before, so she knew what to expect, but Chyou had never indulged. Although she was curious.

"Okay. Just this once."

Yuan grinned and slid a hand down her leg. He was taking the bait, Chyou thought. She leaned over the tray and inhaled the drug, then handed the straw to Yuan, who snorted his share. They both leaned back, sinking into the cool black leather, and giggled. Chyou moved her hand over and squeezed Yuan's thigh.

"Ooh!" he exclaimed. They laughed.

"Tell me something about yourself," he said. He reached out a hand and began playing with her hair. "What's your favorite color?"

"Purple," she said. "Aaaand, I like important men. You are deputy assistant minister of public works, and your brother is the Minister of Commerce. Such an esteemed family." She squeezed his thigh harder and Yuan shifted in his seat. Chyou pulled herself closer until his breath was hot on her face. He reached around and grabbed both of her butt cheeks as he bit her neck.

"In fact, I hear he'll be in upcoming trade talks with the United States in Shanghai. Are you going, too?"

"Mmm hm," Yuan said.

"Well, as an importer/exporter, I'm very much interested. Tell me, do you know what aspects of the trade agreement they'll be talking about? Tariff rate quota system? Distribution rights?"

Yuan pulled her on top of him and began to dry hump her. "He said something about tariffs."

"Rate reductions?" she said.

"I don't know. You talk too much." Yuan reached up and kissed her hard on the mouth.

She wasn't getting very far with this tack, she thought.

Desperate measures were called for. She broke the kiss. "How about we skip dinner and go to your place?"

"I like that idea." He ceased his humping and pressed the speaker button to instruct Githinji to make the detour.

#

They stumbled into his condo. It was spacious, with a large sunken living room situated opposite a long, curved kitchen.

"Nice place," Chyou said. Yuan replied by grabbing her breasts and ramming his tongue into her mouth. Resisting the urge to push him off her and punch him in the throat, Chyou froze. You're on a mission. You can do this.

She didn't relish prolonging the inevitable, so she wrapped her arms around his neck and reached into her sequined clutch. The small dart she pulled out delivered 2cc of quanolarcum, which would predisposition him to answer her questions. Truthfully. His eyes widened in surprise at the sting, then he slumped against her, a beatific grin on his face. Chyou hauled him up and staggered over to the couch. She propped him on a pile of pillows.

"What's your node address and password?" "867A2.9. BigTits#325."

Chyou shook her head. "Now, where does your brother live?"

She stood up and caught her reflection in a mirror on the far wall. It was Dara, with terracotta skin and curly hair. Chyou gasped. Heart pounding, she checked her arms, holding them up on front of her, but they were still white. And shaking. She hugged herself to make them stop. Shut her eyes and tensed her muscles, which only made the shaking worse. Relax. Breathe. Focus. She repeated the mantra to herself until her body stilled. When she looked back to the mirror, Chyou stared back.

"128 Saiba Road."

Chyou sat on the couch and buried her head in her hands. It was finally happening. She was losing it. In the middle of a mission, at that. There was no time to waste if she hoped to salvage her assignment. She would have to transform into Yuan and visit Enlai to get the information she needed.

Shit.

She hated changing into a man, with the sudden onrush of testosterone, which gave her a renewed affinity to muscle-bound superheroes. But it needed to be done, and quickly.

She would have to grow a beard to compensate for Yuan's square jaw, and cut her hair. Yuan had already fallen asleep on the pillows, which, thankfully, was one less thing to worry about. Chyou closed her eyes and focused her thoughts inward, on the nerves and glands. The familiar pain shot through the back of her eyes. The chills and sweat. Throbbing behind her eyes that worked downward. But it was not as intense as the previous transformation, since she was changing from ivory to light tan. But the worst was yet to come.

She messaged the pituitary gland as a dying pang of agony fired down her nerves. Testosterone flooded her circulatory system, and her body felt as if it were on fire. Chyou yelled as she bent and flexed her muscles, balling up her fists in defiance of some imaginary villain. Discomfort between her legs worsened to stabbing twists. She picked up a love seat and hurled it across the room, toward the kitchen. It wedged itself between the counter and the stove. She picked up the other love seat and threw it down the hall leading to the bedroom. It bounced off the corner and landed in the dining room, knocking over a chair. Then she picked up one end of the couch and held it aloft, thinking she had mistakenly called up adrenaline in addition to the testosterone. She focused again, concentrating on dialing back the adrenaline, and waited until the hormones balanced out.

Chyou lowered the couch as sweat streamed from her pores. Water.

Chyou headed for the bathroom, gingerly sidestepping the love seat and dining room chair. She stared at herself in the mirror. Oval eyes with smeared smoky shadow peered out from a light tan face. The lipstick had held up, a deep red staining her mouth, almost hidden behind a scraggly beard. She looked like a worn-out drag version of Yuan.

"I am Yuan Chin. I am a blowhard and a braggart, and I work as deputy assistant minister of public works. And I am a man!"

Hearing the bass in his voice and speaking the mantra helped to shift his perspective, but it never fully took. Acting lessons had helped a lot. He doffed his clothes, took a quick shower, and scrubbed off the makeup, then dried himself in the shower. His breasts had flattened into a flabby chest, his clitoris had elongated and thickened, and his ovaries had dropped and grown hair. It sickened him to look at them.

A hair stylist machine sat atop the toilet. He pressed the button for "Short Crop," stuck the machine on his head, and waited.

Handfuls of hair dropped to the shower floor as the razors buzzed around his ears. A ring of green light blinked, and he took off the machine and rinsed the hair from his skin. Dried himself again and stepped out to look in the mirror. An improvement from the last time, he thought.

He walked back to the living room and stripped Yuan of his tuxedo. One last look in the mirror, but Dara stared back, with her terracotta skin and curly hair. He gasped and shut his eyes, tight. It couldn't be. It was the insanity. Has to be.

He slowly cranked open one eyes, afraid of seeing the wrong reflection, but Yuan stared back this time. He sighed in relief, grabbed his purse, and ran out the door.

His driver was sitting on the hood of the car and upon seeing Yuan, reached into his jacket pocket. Yuan held up both hands.

"Whoa. It's me. I left Yuan upstairs. We need to get to Enlai Chin's house to hack into his files."

Githinji nodded. "Oh, right. I was told you could…" He cleared his throat. "All right. Got an address?"

"128 Saiba Road," Yuan said. He got into the back seat and tried to keep it together. His hands shook and a cold sweat had broken out under his tuxedo. A vague queasiness poked at the edge of his stomach, and he gripped his thigh to help quell the sensation.

When they arrived, Yuan jumped out and ran up the walk as Githinji followed him. He rang the bell, hoping Enlai was home. After several moments, a light came on inside. The door opened, light scanning the foyer. His brother stood in the doorway, dressed in a blue bath robe.

"Yuan? What the hell happened to you? You look terrible. Did you grow a beard?"

Yuan pushed past Enlai and stood in the living room. By now, he was shaking uncontrollably and sweat was rolling down his face. Githinji followed behind and shut the door.

"Can we talk? Are we alone?" Yuan said.

"Yes, but what is this all about? You need a doctor. Let me call one." He tapped his thumb three times on his thigh to open up a line.

Yuan reached into his purse and brought out a dart. He stuck it in his brother's neck. Enlai's eyes rolled up in his head and he crumpled. Githinji caught him and eased him to the floor.

Yuan kneeled beside him. "W-Where are your p-plans for the upcoming trade t-t-talks?"

"On my node."

"Download th-them and t-transfer to m-my node. And any other immm-portant d-documents."

Yuan waited a few moments, shaking, and avoiding Githinji's stare. This would definitely go in his report to Rona, Yuan thought. But it didn't matter. He would quit after this assignment.

"Done," Enlai said.

"Good." Yuan used the address and password Yuan had given him. The documents blinked green in the verso, ready to open.

"Did you get them?" Githinji said. Yuan nodded. "Y-yeah."

Githinji twisted Enlai's head and a bone-breaking sound elicited a pang of nausea in Yuan. Enlai's head lolled to one side, his eyes still open.

"The hell you do that for?" Yuan said.

"Let's just say we have an understanding with the assistant minister. And now he'll be minister. Is that a problem for you?" Githinji started to slide his hand in his jacket. Yuan sprang to his feet and bolted toward the back of the house. He cut through the living room and ran into the kitchen, which had a back door. He fumbled at the lock, then noticed it was biometric. Shit!

Footsteps headed his way. He broke left, toward the den, where a window beckoned. Yuan took a running leap and crashed through the glass and screen, landing on the lawn. Floodlights shone and dogs barked. Yuan sprinted toward the river that ran past Enlai's house. If he could make it, he'd escape. The barking got closer and a shot rang out. It whizzed past his right shoulder, and he ducked left. He pumped his legs and arms harder. The river loomed ahead, the dark waters calling him. A growl sounded nearby and he long jumped, clearing the embankment.

He plunged into deep water, falling downward in the cold wetness. Faces loomed up in the dark. One with terracotta skin and curly hair. One with long hair that framed an ivory face.

One with short hair and a scraggly beard. They all began to laugh at him, their large white smiles cutting through the gloom. The laughter surrounded him, trapping him. He screamed. His lungs burned and he gasped for breath. But none came. The burn worsened. Stabbing pain started behind his eyes, then the throbbing in his spine, as he sank downward. But after a while, the laughter faded, the faces disappeared, and the pain dissolved to black.

#

Rona rolled her cigarette between thumb and index finger, blowing out smoke into the early morning air. A purple-tinged sunrise shone in the distance, reflecting off the undulating waters. She'd gotten a call from the embassy at 5:00 a.m. saying an American had washed up on an embankment. Guangzhou police had taken DNA from the body and matched it with a recent immigrant named Dara Martin. He watched as the coroner finished her preliminary examination and released the body for transport.

Two men in paramedic uniforms lifted Dara unto a pallet and flew it into the back of an ambulance. They would take it to the morgue at the embassy.

"Failed mission?"

Rona turned to see Jim Roberts, Counselor at the U.S. embassy. He wore a crumpled khaki suit with a blue shirt and yellow tie.

"What'd you do, sleep in your clothes?" Rona said.

"Pretty much. Long night doing prep work for the trade talks. And you didn't answer my question."

"On the contrary. We hauled in more than expected," Rona said. Dara's downloaded files blinked in Rona's periphery. A scan of the documents revealed that most were related to the trade talks, but at least two were marked Top Secret and contained the seal of the Ministry of National Defense.

"Well, I'm sorry for your loss," Jim said. "Actually, I'm a bit excited."

"Excited?"

"Yes. There's a new program the government's overseeing. Downloadable consciousness. We may be able to transfer her personality and memory to another body and start over."

"Huh," Jim said. "A sort of reincarnation. Are you sure that'd be something she wants?"

Rona shrugged. "Doesn't matter what she wants. She signed a contract. Her body parts are ours."

"And that doesn't bother you?"

Rona threw her cigarette on the marshy ground and stepped on it. It sank into the watery grass with a hiss. "If I let all the shit that should bother me, actually bother me, I'd be a raving lunatic. Have a good one, Jim."

Asunder
by Lori Titus

Growing up in Chrysalis, South Carolina, you don't really think about the stories people tell in the same way anyone who lived in a normal town would. When you are raised with the Moon Festival, which celebrates the local Werewolves, your mother's half-sister practices necromancy, and your cousins are likely to swipe a strand of your hair during playtime to insure you do them no harm, you don't look at things in the way other people do.

For me, magic and its power are as natural an occurrence as anything else in the order of life. Magic simply exists, and if you're lucky, you will never have the misfortune of needing to explain it to people who don't understand.

I had to leave Chrysalis and go to college in Georgia before I realized just how different my home was. My best friend, Janelle, who comes from New Orleans, says it sounds a lot like Louisiana to her. Not the cities like New Orleans or Baton Rouge, but some of the backwater places where no one visits, towns barely designated as spots on the map.

Janelle doesn't really understand. The old magic is still there, lingering and thriving in both memory and presence. It lives in some people, as much an inherited trait as freckles, cleft chins, or eye color. I always told myself when I grew up I would move away and never come back, other than to visit my obstinate mother. But two semesters in, and I was already missing home. Instead of traveling with friends as I had done the year before, I packed my bags and went home for summer.

"I don't know what you could be thinking, or why anyone would want to bury themselves in that town, girl," Janelle said, snapping her gum in my ear. She was all the way on the west coast by then, but the warmth of her disapproving voice made her feel as if she were at my elbow. Janelle was one of those friends who disapproved of everything I did, but she was happy enough with letting me stumble into whatever trouble I got myself into. "Just tell me you're not taking Tariq with you."

"And introduce him to my family at this point in the game?" I snapped back. "I don't think so."

"Good girl," she said. "At least you're trying to get him out of your system. Is there anybody back home who might be worth sampling?" Her voice dropped two octaves on the word, *sampling*. "Hell, there weren't any to speak of when I left, but hey, most of my senior class was leaving for college and parts unknown after graduation. You know. People come back and forth."

"Maybe you'll meet someone passing through."

"I doubt it," I told her. "I wouldn't go back there looking for a man. Because when you break up with him, everyone from the lady at the grocery counter to the mailman knows what's going on with you."

#

I didn't tell her I wasn't going home to find another man. I was more interested in making things work with the one I had.

Tariq and I had been dating for little over a year. Track and field captain, part time manager at an athletics store, Business major and all around fine looking man, he was the kind of guy who made other women jealous.

We started up in fall. I was so in love and enjoyed simply being around him. Tariq was whip smart, and it was fun to be with someone who could keep up with me, challenge my expectations and ways of thinking.

Things got real a lot quicker than I intended when I moved in.

Okay, that may have been stupid. No one in her right mind messes around with a man for a month and then moves right the hell in. Tariq made my knees cave and damn near stopped my heart. With ease. On a regular basis.

Otherwise, I probably would not have done it.

While he was doing all he could to make my body his, I gave over my time and space.

During my time with Tariq, I went through more changes than I liked. We were both stubborn, independent. I told myself after those first few months of living together we were moving past our honeymoon phase.

I had never been one to be in a relationship with a cheater but I started to see the classic signs. He kept coming home late and taking extra showers. The way he drew back from me, how we didn't touch as often, and sometimes when he did, the lovemaking seemed like it was angry, even though we hadn't had a fight. It was like he was trying to decide if his life was at home with me or someplace else.

Mama used to say when you have sex with a man, you carry bits of his energy inside your aura, and he carries part of yours.

The longer you're intimate, the more of each other's energy you draw into yourself. Some people damn near empty out what they were born with in place of all the different people they have sexed, bits of partners come and gone, spirit energy which won't let them go. You remain connected to a person long after they are gone, bound by some remnant of life energy that weaves itself through your skin and hair, sinking down into the marrow of your bones.

Mama used to tell me these things. She is a romantic. *Never let someone so deep into your heart they threaten to tear you asunder*, she said.

I have always been able to sense auras. Whatever this other woman was giving Tariq was adding something unpleasant to his energy. I didn't want to lay down in bed anymore, because this energy was blue-violet and cold, altogether unhealthy. I didn't want whatever energy he dragged home from her. He could wash and clean and put on whatever clothes he wanted, but to me his aura was as bad as being soaked in animal blood, filthy and full of decay.

And of course he lied to me. I didn't like the idea of being used.

At the same time, I had spent just enough time, and poured out enough emotion into our relationship that I imagined the situation could be changed. Love potions, spells, what have you, were common back home, and my thought was this: rather than throw away the last year over a dalliance which might have been all but two weeks, why not try something? The right words, a spell, a combination of the right roots, whatever was used to make such problems go away. I knew this kind of magic worked before with others. I'd seen marriages healed, much less relationships.

And if it didn't work, after all, I was free to go my way knowing I had gone above and beyond to make sure I wasn't tossing the man without giving him a chance.

#

I could not go to my own family seeking magic.

Among my mother's kin, it would be considered an embarrassment. All of us had some sort of ability. My mother made a living telling fortunes and making potions for people. Most were love spells, but for the right price, she concocted things for darker purposes. I knew my cousins wouldn't do it because everyone in the family knew my mother didn't want me using magic.

My father died in the oilfields before he turned forty years old. Other than the small pension the insurance company doled out on the fifteenth of every month, Mama's potions and spells were our sole source of income. My brother and I were raised on the bounty of magic, promises, and untimely death.

Mama was set on me going away and getting an education and she refused to teach me magic, even though I was her only daughter. She told me if I learned magic it would tie me to small places, or forever engender suspicion. I was better off pretending not to know the realms of spirits, the Shapeshifters and the walking demons which were a part of our folklore. It was bad enough my skin would make me forever other: no need to add being tied to old ways that no longer had a place in a modern world. What an old way of thinking! Why should I have to adapt myself for people who wouldn't accept me anyway? But I could not blame her. We all survive the best we can, however we see fit.

There were some things I picked up, but what power I had never seemed channeled properly. I could twine together tree roots and successfully bind an enemy. I even chanted for rain once and woke to find it snowing.

My ability to *discern* auras was the only magic which could be depended upon.

I use that word because I don't exactly see them. Or at least, not all the time. Sometimes an aura is felt like heat. Similar to the waves coming off an open oven. You can't see them, but you feel the prickle against your skin. Other times, they are visible to me.

The cleanest of auras, most often surrounding children, were a pale, filmy gray. Many adults have a deeper shade of gray, like unpolished steel. I have seen sparkling, shimmering silver surrounding the likes of psychopaths, who have no feelings of their own, yet feed off the energy and pain of every human they come into contact with. I have seen red, when a person was lit with hatred or bloodshed or a passion for something unholy. And I have seen the pale, pinkish, room filling aura of those who love unselfishly.

#

I had heard Memna's name on and off through my childhood from my mother's customers, but I had never met her.

My mother warned her clients that Memna could get anything people asked for, but her brand of magic should be a solution of last resort. Some took her advice, others assumed she was watching her own bottom line. There was an edge in her voice, fear, or reverence, when she spoke of this woman.

#

I didn't take going to see Memna lightly.

I drove my car and parked it a mile up the road to where she lives. The roads are really more an idea than the real in certain places, because they are not all paved. You can see the path of other vehicles, the shoulders of the road overgrown with grass, weeds, and stubborn daffodils. I maneuvered my car where the strip of gray concrete was supposed to be.

It was a warm day, but clouds were boiling, threatening the kind of spit and shine rain that would come with little result except to wet the ground and make it sizzle in the heat of late afternoon sun.

Part of me was expecting a hovel, a black cabin with crumbling rafters, something out of a long gone tale about things creatures who moved through darkness. It was nothing like that. It was a humble, ranch style, maybe two bedrooms from my guess. It was painted a light green. There were chimes hanging by the door, a ceramic pot full of red, pungent flowers with curly petals on either side of the steps.

I rang the doorbell and waited. I heard a gentle rustle of movement before the door cracked open.

"Can I help you?"

The woman who stood in the doorway was beautiful. I was taken back by it really. Her brown, deeply toned skin had a lovely sheen. She had high cheekbones and wide, slanted eyes. Her hair was cut into a short, wavy style. She looked only in her mid-thirties, possibly younger. I always admired women who could wear their hair so short and still look pretty, because I didn't think I could pull off.

Most of all, I was surprised because I'd expected Memna would be a person of my mother's generation if not older.

"I… I am looking for someone by the name of Memna," I stuttered. "If I am in the wrong place, I apologize…"

"Oh no," she interrupted, stepping aside. "You are in the right place. Come in."

The inside of the house was pleasingly cool and slightly dim after the glare of bright sunshine. I followed her towards the kitchen. The woman wore a blue floral dress of gauzy fabric which swirled all the way down to her ankles. I caught the shine of a golden anklet as she lifted her dress to walk across the wood floor.

"Just so you know," she continued in her lovely voice. "My name is Ashlyn. People come looking for Memna, but the woman they are referring to was my grandmother. It's more a title than a name anyway. All the women in our family answer to it."

At this point, I was ready to turn and leave.

"I can help you," Ashlyn said, waving me towards a seat at her kitchen table. "I was taught everything she knew."

I sat down. Ashlyn busied herself filling a kettle of water at the sink. "I am curious though, why you would come out here, Naomi," she said softly. "Since your mama knows the arts."

I started to hear her call my name but stopped myself from commenting on it. I knew this trick. My mother used it on her clients. It took just a little *push* to get a name out of someone's head, something even *I* could have accomplished if I'd really tried. A small bit of magic that impressed people without abilities far too easily.

"I doubt she would help me. Besides, there are some things you don't want to talk to your mother about."

"Hmmm," she said. I wasn't sure if she was agreeing with me or not. She set the kettle onto the stove. She struck a match, and I heard the gentle hiss of the gas flame licking up. Ashlyn turned to me, crossing her arms. "Why don't you tell me about the auras first?"

"First? Is this an exchange then? I brought cash with me, though I wasn't sure how much you would charge."

Ashlyn pulled out a drawer, and retrieved a pack of cigarettes. She tapped the package against her thigh.

"I quit a long time ago," she said with a dreamy smile. "But I find that I still love to handle them. Just to have something to do with my hands. It relaxes me. Naomi, don't worry about the money right now, I am sure that whatever you've got on you is just fine.

You're interesting. A girl who reads auras and seeks out psychic advice. Kind of like a mechanic seeking someone to change a tire."

"I'm not looking for advice, or fortune reading." "Oh?"

"No. You knew about the auras. You have to be strong. I came for something else," I said.

"Oh, I see."

Ashlyn stood there with her arms crossed, reading me with her dark eyes. Finally I spoke again, because she seemed prepared to stand there the rest of the afternoon in silence if I didn't.

"Okay, so I have seen them since I was little, and when I told my mother they brought me to the doctor. They even got me glasses. It took a while for my mother to understand when I told her what I was seeing, but that might have been my fault. I was only four or five. Or maybe Mama didn't want to think I had Sight."

"Probably," Ashlyn said. "These kinds of things can be a mixed blessing. Did they scare you?"

"No. Not until later."

"Well, I don't know if they told you, but this gift is quite rare. You'll more likely find a mind reader than someone with that ability."

"It's utterly useless though," I told her. "Auras can change with mood. It's no more telling than one of those dime store rings which changes colors."

"If you say so. Tell me about this man."

The kettle whistled, and Ashlyn prepared tea. I told her what I thought she would want to hear. Tariq's first name, his major in school. How long we had been together. How he had not been faithful to me.

"You can stop with that," Ashlyn said. "I am not looking for things all the rest of the world knows about him."

Ashlyn put a ceramic bowl filled with hot water on the table between us. She had a cup of tea for herself, but she didn't give me anything to drink. She tossed a handful of herbs: dried stalks, leaves and something resembling cloves... into the bowl.

There was a weird scent I had never smelled before and never since. Something at once sweet and salty that made my tongue tingle the moment I inhaled the first whiff. I watched whatever was in the water fizz and sizzle, sending up vapors, turning the water gold green.

"Give me your hand, sweetheart," she said.

I looked at Ashlyn. She had retrieved a pocket knife from the folds of her dress. This part I was familiar with. Anything she could do for me first required a little of my blood.

"You're going to sit here and tell me about your man. Don't talk to me about what career he wants for himself. Tell me about from his flesh to his marrow. The deepest things you fear about him."

She cut my palm, and I saw drops of blood fall into the water. I started swaying. And talking.

The only thing I could compare it to was being drunk, and knowing I was talking without knowing what I was saying. I might have been screaming because after a time my throat was constricting. There were tears in my eyes. I was shaking.

"Stop it. Stop!" she yelled.

Ashlyn slapped me so hard I fell to the floor. I looked at her.

I was wet. Somehow the contents of the bowl had been dumped on me, but the water wasn't hot. It felt cold.

"Bitch, what's wrong with you?" I yelled.

She laughed. "I should ask that question! That's never happened before." She reached a hand out to me. "Naomi, don't be mad, come on."

I let her help me up but quickly pulled away. "How did you know you weren't going to burn me with the water? It was boiling…."

"It was boiling over an hour ago, sweetheart," Ashlyn said quietly. "You've been talking a long time. You got so deep in the trance, I couldn't see what else to do to bring you out of it. Don't be mad. Magic is not meant for everybody, and maybe it's not meant for you."

I grabbed my purse.

Heading out towards the living room, I saw the curtains were pulled back, revealing the sky beyond the windows. The sun was setting. I had arrived at the house a little after two. I had been unconscious for longer than a few minutes. If night were coming on, it had to be well past seven thirty.

I grabbed my phone and looked at the time: 7:58PM.

"I don't know what you did to me," I said. "I didn't even get a chance to ask for what I wanted."

Ashlyn chuckled. "Sweetheart, yes you did. That, and then some."

I turned. She was right behind me. I backed up.

"You don't worry now, okay?" she patted my shoulder as my hand closed over the doorknob. "You will be just fine."

#

I ran all the way back to my car. I drove home through the dark, high beams on, only half recognizing the roads that I'd come on. I got so nervous I must have missed the turn which would take me back to town twice. I had to make a U-turn and drive back around to get myself onto the right road. When I got home, Mama wasn't there. Despite being a grown woman and without a curfew, she would have asked questions about me coming home so late. It was poker night at *Finny's* which meant she would come home late, happy, and with some money in her pockets. People with sense knew not to go against her, but there was always some show off who tried it.

I showered and got ready for bed.

As I laid down and closed my eyes, I could still see that gold, green water. The thought of it made me a sick. I don't know what kind of trance I fell into or what I had said. What could I have gone on about for so long?

I leaned over and grabbed my purse from where I dropped it onto the chair beside my bed. I wanted to see if Ashlyn had ripped me off while I was out of it.

All my cash was there. Not a penny missing. So were my ID's and driver's license, all untouched.

Inside was a piece of paper, a page snatched from a spiral notebook, the crumpled edges still attached. I turned my lamp on to read the looping cursive writing:

May you find the gift you spoke of.

#

The rest of my time at home passed without incident. After a few days, I was feeling better, more centered, and as if I had never went to see Ashlyn in the first place. It was like a dream, slipping away until it was almost nothing. Within five days I was back to my regular life in Atlanta.

My first day back in the apartment, Tariq got home.

He'd gone to Florida to visit his brother and some friends. I hadn't expected him back for another week. He came in the doorway with his luggage, and smiled at me. Tariq has smooth, cinnamon skin and the widest grin ever, perfect teeth. His big, dark eyes fastened on me.

"Baby, you're home!" he said. "I thought you'd still be at your Mom's."

I tilted my head, looking at him.

His aura was clean; no deep, soul sick blue. It was a regular gray tone and as he looked at me, I could see the change of energy to pink.

"Oh?" I said coolly. "I missed Mom but there wasn't much to do there, so I thought I would head back."

Maybe this meant he didn't take whomever he was seeing on vacation with him. Which was a good thing all the way around, but still the idea didn't put me at great ease. It had been enough time to clear his aura of whomever she was. Maybe.

He put down his luggage, closed the door with his foot, and crossed the living room towards me. "You know, I was wondering about you. You didn't answer my texts," he said.

"Oh, that," I said. *Hell no I didn't answer you, you cheating mother…..* "Either way, I am so glad you're here, and glad to be back.

I was seriously thinking of going out there and bringing you back myself," he said.

"Really?" I raised an eyebrow. If I felt stiff in his arms, he didn't seem to notice. He held me so tight I found myself relaxing in his embrace. Tariq ran track, and every part of him was hard and toned. His hands slipped up my back. He sighed deeply, and I knew any moment those fingers would be pulling at my bra strap.

"Don't get me wrong, it was nice seeing everybody again, but I missed you," he said against my ear. "I feel stupid."

"Why?" I asked.

"Because I didn't realize how *much* I was going to miss you. I should have taken you with me."

True to form, I felt the closure of my bra snap open. By the time his lips brushed mine, I was up on my toes to reach him better.

"I love you baby," he said. "How about a real welcome home?"

#

"Wait. You're back with him now?" Janelle asked, moving her laptop.

We were sitting at a coffee shop, with a pile of books between us. My friend was slurping her favorite iced drink through a thick green straw. There was studying going on, but when we were together, the amount of how much got done was questionable.

"We never broke up," I said lightly, brushing away bits of eraser scattered across my notebook.

"You said he was cheating," she hissed.

"I said I *thought* he was cheating. There's a difference."

"Uh huh," Janelle rolled her eyes. "I say if you think he did, he probably did. What happened to change your mind?"

"He's been great since we both got back home, very attentive. Almost too much so."

"How do you mean?" Janelle asked.

"I don't know. I guess I'm not used to being spoiled by a man. Is that horrible to say? I haven't had too many long term boyfriends."

"You mean any—," She corrected.

"Okay, no long term guys. Anyway. Whatever happened, if something did, it's over."

I couldn't explain to her a whole month had passed and Tariq's aura remained clean and unencumbered. Or how the energy surrounding him warmed to pink when we were close.

What I could tell her was how we were going out and doing things together. He was loving me in all the best ways, cooking dinner and giving me back rubs, little things he never used to do.

I had a secret glow of happiness because whatever Ashlyn did was apparently working wonders.

I didn't like to think of Ashlyn. The memory of her name brought an unnerving itch to the back of my arms, a tingle of pain in my head. Certainly there was really no need to ever speak her name, but I couldn't help thinking of her, and wondering what transpired over those hours she said I was in a trance.

I stirred my cooling cup of coffee, and saw a dark swirl moving across the top of the drink, like two drops of blood, moving in opposite directions.

"What the hell?" Janelle said softly.

I looked up, and my gaze followed her stare. People were running for shelter as the sudden downpour sent rain and pebbles of hail skittering across the sidewalks.

"Was rain even in the forecast?" she asked.

\#

When I was seven, I remember being very angry with the little girl who lived next door.

Her name was Darlene. We had been playmates from the time we could both walk. Our mothers ate lunch and drank iced tea, occasionally casting a watchful eye on us from the screen door which led to Darlene's backyard. She was the first friend I could remember. In time, she would become the first I would forget.

We cut each other's palms one day, vowing we would be blood sisters forever. We traded Barbie dolls and played in the back yard, skipping rope and telling stories about princesses and castles in make believe countries. Sometimes, we hunted for fairies between the weeds and blackberries grew wild.

The thing is, I don't remember why I got mad at Darlene. It could have been anything. She might have ripped off the head of one of my dolls or said the shirt I wore was stupid. Things are like that with little girls. They are creatures who can love and hate deeply, all at once, and with a viciousness found only in the most evil grown folk. And I was no exception.

All I can tell you for sure is I went upstairs to my room.

I sat alone, and chanted, and swayed, legs curled beneath me, eyes squeezed shut. I lost track of time and place. I know when I went upstairs, it was just after dinner. It was a clear summer day. Rain came, and then hail, none of it predicted by anyone. Darlene's mother went outside onto her porch and called out for her, thinking she might have been playing out in the woods.

Twenty minutes later, Darlene's mother found her only baby laying in the bottom of her bedroom closet, panting for breath, unable to speak or move.

Mama came to me the next day and asked what we had argued about it. "What happened? Did you do something to make her sick? Did you use magic, Naomi?"

I told her no. I had no idea. Last I saw Darlene, she was fine. We didn't argue about anything.

There was disbelief in Mama's eyes. But she nodded slowly. "Alright then. We won't talk about this again, understand girl? But whatever you did, you will not do it again! Magic is not something to be toyed with, child. And if you wield dark things," her eyes narrowed. "Soon you won't be able to control them."

Heartbroken, Darlene's family moved away. I don't know if she ever recovered, or if the damage inflicted was permanent. Mama and I never spoke of it, but she never taught me even the simplest forms of magic from that day on.

#

I hadn't thought of Darlene, or the sudden, unseasonable storm in years. My head hurt, and I felt vaguely sick to my stomach.

I drove home. The rain was coming down in sheets, and the wind was picking up. I closed the door and locked it behind me, shutting the elements out. In my room, I closed the blinds, got in bed, and pulled the covers over me. I was cold to my marrow. I could hear the water on the roof, pounding as steady as a drumbeat.

I woke up a few hours later. The clock on the nightstand read 7:30 P.M.

When I came out into the living room Tariq was sitting on the couch. His wore a dark hoodie pulled over his head. His wet, muddy boots were still on, and he was soaking wet.

"Baby, what happened?" I asked. "Did you walk home through the rain?"

He turned to me. I jumped backwards.

An aura should cover an entire body, and are usually layers deep. His aura was dark and shrunken, the gray edges of it dotted with holes, and only surrounded his eyes. The center of it was completely black. I had never seen anything like it and all I could think was *death*.

He looked at me, and beneath the blackness of the aura, I saw the spark of anger in his eyes. He looked down at his wet hands, and then at me. Looking into his eyes was like gazing over the edge of a hurricane and into the still center of a storm.

"What did you do to me?" he asked. "Why can't I remember anything?" he stood slowly. "Why's it hurt so much? My head?" He slapped the heel of his hand against his forehead. "I keep trying to get back home to you, and then everything goes away. And all I can hear is you in my head. Chanting."

"Tariq, I don't know what you're talking about! You went to class this morning. What happened?"

"I haven't been *anywhere*," he said. "I haven't been back in this house. I don't know where I have been." He edged towards me.

I felt his anger like heat rising off of him, and backed up towards the kitchen. He was between me and the door. *Good luck outrunning Mr. Track and Field.* "You tell me the truth," he screamed. "What did you do?"

I backed up far enough that my hip touched the edge of the sink.

Tariq lunged towards me, and I ran around the other side of the kitchen island, making a break for the door.

I was running for all I was worth. My hand was wrapped around the doorknob when he dropped me to the floor. I fell down on my side. I felt a sizzle of pain in my arm, saw the flash of t he knife as he held it above me. Scrambling to my knees, I managed one punch, even as he sliced my arm again. It bought me a few seconds to catapult myself out of the door.

One dim light was on. Running, I slipped and fell before I reached the edge of the stairway led down into the courtyard.

Coming up the stairs, backpack slung over his shoulder, wearing a green parka, blue jeans and a baseball cap, Tariq stared at me. "Naomi!" he yelled.

With a hood pulled over his head, and bloody knife in his hand, my assailant emerged from our apartment and ran down the opposite stairwell. The neighbor at the end of the hall opened her door, and Tariq shouted at her to stay with me. Tariq ran after him, but I knew he wouldn't find him.

Tariq's doppelgänger had disappeared into the shadows, evaporated as quickly as smoke.

#

The ride to the hospital seemed to take forever, even though Tariq drove like a madman.

Once I was in the ER, they took me straight to the back. The nurse asked a list of questions about how I got stabbed, all of which made me uncomfortable. I told her most of the truth. I woke up and found a man inside my apartment, he attacked me, and I ran. Did I get a good look at his face? No. He was wearing a hoodie. I was running for my life.

At least my wounds matched my story.

The mystery man had slashed the back of my arm. The resident on call told me my wounds were superficial, but deep enough to need stitches. "Whoever this was who attacked you, it's going to leave a nice scar," he said softly.

Tariq was waiting for me in the waiting room. I was grateful to be away from him for a few moments. I needed time to think. I saw the suspicious glares the staff gave him when he brought me in. I don't think any of the neighbors saw anything, including Mrs. Palmer, the woman who opened her door. I worried about what happened if a well-meaning person gave the police a statement, saying they saw someone fitting Tariq's description.

I wondered, if the moment he found me, Tariq hadn't looked up and seen his own face as the man who stabbed me fled.

I tried to think about how this could have happened. What did Ashlyn do? I had heard of spells to could make two halves of one being, but I had never seen it done. At the same time, I knew I wasn't crazy. Though being crazy was a comforting option. There were pills, and therapy, and quiet places with seaside views that could help me if I needed it.

I wanted to run. I wanted to go back to Ashlyn and make her fix whatever she did to Tariq.

Maybe Ashlynn could help — if she did anything at all other than listen to me recite old magic I shouldn't even know.

#

"You okay, baby?" Tariq said. He touched my face and I couldn't help the shudder which crept up my back. It took effort not to pull away.

"I'm sorry," I said, looking out the windshield and into the dark stretch of road ahead of us. "Jumpy, still, I guess. I know it probably sounds crazy, but can we not go back to our place just yet?"

"A man was sitting up in our house," Tariq said. "Of course we're not going right back there! At least not until we get the locks changed or something."

He drove us to a little hotel near the airport. It was clean and seemed reasonably safe. As soon as we were inside he ordered room service. I shivered when they knocked at the door. Tariq took care of it. I tried to eat, and managed to hold something in my stomach. He only ate half of his meal too, despite the fact he said earlier he was starving. When we finally climbed into bed, I stayed as far on my side as possible. I think he knew I didn't want him to touch me, though he didn't realize exactly why. I wondered what was going on in his head. Had he seen enough to make him wonder if he was losing his sanity too, or did he think maybe our neighborhood was just wasn't safe for us anymore?

I lapsed into sleep for a short time. I had uneasy dreams of faces swathed in darkness, a man chasing me through a forest. I started, and sat up.

Tariq was still beside me in bed, sleeping. His deep, even breathing was white noise. I tried to calm myself. I sat up with my back against the headboard, clutching my pillow against my stomach until my insides stopped doing somersaults. This was my man beside me. This was the part of him that loved me and wanted to be together. His aura was a soothing gray. There was tension in the way he held his body, in his shoulders and chest. Nothing abnormal.

This man had only been kind to me. Tariq, when a whole man, had always been more complicated, a mix of so many emotions and needs. As all people are.

I walked over to the mini fridge and pulled out a bottle of water.

I couldn't help but push back the curtain, just an inch. The parking lot below was empty.

Just beyond the lot, between the sidewalk and a line of trees stood a figure in black. The light from the lampposts didn't stretch far enough to touch his face but I didn't need it to. His body, his stance, would be plain to me anywhere. He lifted his head, as if he felt my eyes upon him. I could swear I saw his cheekbones move against the fabric of his hoodie. He smiled.

#

I didn't sleep the rest of the night.

Our building manager arranged for the locks to be changed first thing in the morning. The woman apologized profusely when we picked them up, and said security measures would be increased, including cameras. Tariq thanked her, and we went upstairs to our apartment. Except for a few drops of blood on the floor, nothing was out of place.

Despite what had happened, I was relieved to be home. It wasn't like anywhere else would really be safer.

I had to talk Tariq into going to work. I told him I would be staying home, relaxing for the day. Though he didn't seem convinced it was a good idea, he caved. I was relieved to be away from him a little bit.

I called my mother and poured everything out to her.

I'd expected a long, angry diatribe. Instead, she listened carefully. When she spoke, it was in the softest, most gentle way I could remember hearing her speak to me in a long time. The things she said confirmed what I already feared.

"I don't think Memna – or Ashlynn- whatever she is calling herself these days, put any spell on Tariq. The magic she did released something already brewing inside you. You wanted to separate the part of him which was unfaithful to you. Inside that thing is tied up all the hate and anger he ever had. The part who lied and did things you didn't like. And now he's split. One side from the other. This thing is called a Shade. It fades in and out, only partly tethered to our world since it was separated from his body. It's tied to you now, which is why it wanted to shed your blood. It's looking for a link to make itself whole again. The Shade has no real mind. Only fear, and instinct to survive."

We talked another half hour or so. She insisted she would get on the road and be in town before sundown. She gave me instructions. "You must believe that you can do it. You summoned this thing."

I told her I would see her soon.

Once I hung up, I unlocked the door and waited.

It didn't take long before the other Tariq, the Shade, crossed my threshold. He stood just inside the doorway, and I stood at the couch. We stared at each other like opponents on a playing field.

"What did you do to me?" he asked. This time, he seemed more confused than angry.

"I don't know," I said, my eyes filling with tears. "I am so sorry." I opened my arms to him. "Let me make it better."

He came to me, with trepidation, like a frightened child. I put my arms around him.

It was only when I began to whisper that he started to pull away from me. "I undo what is done. What is meant as one, I wish no longer asunder."

He began to struggle, and push at me, but I held on. He turned his eyes to me, and his body trembled. The blackness of his aura stretched as he writhed. The black cloud which hung about his eyes moved to encompass his body. Only then did I let go. One more cry came from his mouth, but it was wordless, his face twisting in agony. He disintegrated, leaving nothing behind but a pile of ash.

I sat there and cried. I'd known the consequence of this magic before Mama told me. The universe yields nothing without a price.

Within the hour, my phone rang. I was told Tariq had collapsed at work. An ambulance took him to the same hospital where my arm was stitched up the night before. Despite attempts to revive him, he could not be saved.

Terror and the Dark
by Carole McDonnell

Do Jamaican parents still delight in terrorizing their children?
    I'd like to forgive it.

To say that my mother and her siblings were country folk
so as they laughed like idiots, at making their children tremble in
fear
they were ignorant, not aware
    they were building a cavern of fear in our souls.

It's hard, though.

I can forgive the lies they told.

Yes, they were conscienceless in the way
they told self-serving stories to keep their children in line.
    I can forgive that.

I can forgive their beatings and the belts they named:
    Stinger with its metal-tip,
    Scorpion with its cruel sting.

I can forgive that.

Because they were country folks
whuppin was what they did cause they loved you and
     wanted to set you on the right path.
But the fear and trembling I strive to forgive.
Because there was spite in their cruel power
     when they told us of cruel ghosts inhabiting the dark
     when they lay in wait behind walls — belts in hand — ready
to strike
when they told us what happened to little girls

who do not listen to their mothers and
who did not wipe their hands properly
     because they had such petty joy in creating terror in us,
     because surely there was some other way to make themselves
powerful
in their own eyes — other than stampeding kids' hearts.

Because even now the cavern of fear they built inside me
is still operational when the phone rings
     when the mailman comes
     when I feel some sudden change in my body.
Because these are seeds
my mother, aunts, and uncles planted in me and
     all that terror,
     all that fear,
is still ingrained and ever blossoming in me.

The Tale of Eve of De-Nile
by Joy Copeland

"Auntie, you're not being fair," Eve whined in her little girl voice, the one she used when she wasn't getting her way. Eve wasn't a little girl. She was a grown woman three times over with curves in all the right places. See, her Aunt Chlotilde had just accused her of being a tramp. That hurt Eve's feelings, a little. *Truth be told*— Eve could put on quite an act to get what she wanted. Today her act wasn't working, but today wasn't all an act.

"So, you gone and got yourself knocked up *again!*" Auntie Chlotilde's jaws were tight, her hands on her hips. "You don't think I noticed that eggplant you been running around with. Humpf, and your behind barely fittin' in those tight clothes you wear."

"I was gonna tell you Auntie." Eve sighed. She was genuinely surprised at her aunt's violent reaction to her latest dilemma. She rubbed the baby bump hidden under her oversized jersey to make sure it was still there.

Now, when times were bad, Auntie had always taken Eve's side. Like the time they expelled her from Bartholomew High for God knows what. There was the time her mom kicked her out of the house 'cause she found a greasy fool in her daughter's bed.

"I wasn't sure I was really pregnant," Eve explained. "You know how those pee sticks tells you *yes* sometimes when they really mean *no.* "

Auntie wasn't hearing it. "I don't know nothin' about pee sticks. Your body ought to been tellin' you something. Lawd knows you got the experience to know."

"Guess I wasn't sure 'cause I ain't been sick," Eve said weakly with a finger pressed on her quivering lip. "Well, maybe I was just a little queasy…but no puking like before."

"Lawd. Lawd." Chlotilde shook her head in disgust. "Chile, you tryin' my last nerve. I always said you Durand girls take after your mama. Fertile as the Nile Valley. All a man had to do was look at your mama and she'd be carryin.' Eight of y'all that lived. Enough babies to give me one and share with others folks." Arms folded tight to her chest, she sighed. "What now, Baby Girl?"

Eve didn't know where the Nile Valley was but she figured it must be somewhere north of Louisiana because she had never heard of it. But she knew Auntie's question plus the fact that she'd called her 'Baby Girl' were good signs. Perhaps the worst of Auntie's anger had passed.

"I've been thinking. Maybe I should take care of this one like the other two," Eve said, her tone matter of fact. She glued her eyes on the floor so as not to meet Auntie's gaze head-on. "Problem is—I don't have the money."

"How'd I guess that?" Auntie bellowed.

"It's 'cause I just paid to get my car fixed. And the clinic I went to before gone and moved to Baton Rouge. If I go to Baton Rouge." Eve sighed. "I'll need a place to stay plus the clinic fees." She shifted her focus to gauge Auntie's reaction. Looking into Auntie's brown face was like looking at her father, may he rest in peace. A tear left a shiny trail on Eve's cheek. She wiped her face with the hem of her jersey.

Chlotilde watched her niece then closed her eyes for a moment and took a deep breath. "So you expectin' me to give you the money?"

Eve nodded.

Chlotilde leaned into her small kitchen counter. "I ain't got that kinda money to give you. I let you stay here free. You just chippin' in on the air conditionin' and food from your two-bit job."

"Yes Auntie, and I want you to know I really *really* appreciate it."

"Let me finish. *Even* if I had the money to give you, I don't think them folks at the clinic gonna let you have no abortion."

"Why?" Eve asked.

"Look at you. You're too far along."

Truth be told Eve had wished hard that this pregnancy would just disappear. Disappear on its own, if she ignored it long enough. So for months she did that—ignored that she no longer bled every month. She tolerated the swelling of her breasts, her bed partners liked that part. She denied her expanding waist and pooh-poohed the nausea, but this thing in her belly had a way of not being ignored. Lately, it had started to move. With the other pregnancies, she'd never felt movement, but this one was a true alien invader.

She could no longer deny her condition. Now she was in a panic. The sooner she could get rid of the thing the better.

"Chile, just how far along are you?"

"Not sure," Eve answered. She was lying again. She felt the bump under her jersey. It seemed to be a good deal bigger than yesterday. Or was that her imagination?

"I heard there's some kinda abortion cutoff in this state," Chlotilde said. "So many weeks or so many months. You better find out."

"I'll just lie when they ask me how many months."

"Mmmm." Chlotilde grimaced. "You must know them doctors gonna look up there for themselves. Or give you some kinda test to figure out how far along you are. I ain't never been pregnant, but I do know they ain't just taking *your* word on it."

Eve shrugged. She'd been through it twice before, but somehow the details of the procedures had been wiped from her mind.

It was a fog, her memory about it as fuzzy as the nights when she drank too much. She did recall that she'd gone into the clinic scared and feeling poorly. When she came out, she was still feeling poorly, but no longer scared 'cause she knew she'd soon be back to her old self. She was counting on that feeling of relief again.

"Chile, what are you thinkin'? This ain't like those other pregnancies. That bump in your belly is a baby. This one's different. This one's already got a soul."

Eve shrugged. "Don't seem no different to me. I'm just a little farther along is all. That damn doctor told me likely I couldn't get pregnant again, 'cause of scarring."

"And fool, you believed him. Well, you sure surprised that doctor and yourself."

"So, Auntie, can you help me out?" Eve whined. "*Please.*"

Chlotilde took a deep breath. She looked out the kitchen window at the cloudless sky and closed her eyes. To Eve, it seemed like forever before Auntie turned back to answer.

"Lawd, Eve—I can't do it this time. Even if I had the money, and even if them doctors tell you they'd do it, I can't pay for no abortion for a thing that's got a soul. No it ain't right. I can't have killing a chile on my conscience. I gotta draw the line."

"But Auntie—"

"No use begging. I prayed on it and I've made up my mind. Begging ain't gonna make me change it. You best go talk to the baby's father to see how he's gonna help you."

"It don't have no father," Eve said with a pout. "What are you now, the Immaculate Conception?"

Truth be told—Eve wasn't sure which of the men she'd been with back in the spring had put her in this way. Most likely it was Bowie Wallace. She'd been with him two or three times, just for kicks, nothing serious. She hadn't seen him in a good while. He'd stopped coming to Nathan's Grill, the restaurant where she waitressed four nights a week.

"Don't worry Auntie. I won't want you straining your conscience," Eve said confident and defiant. "I'll get the money and take care of it myself."

#

Indeed, Eve had considered all the ways of ending her pregnancy on her own. Some high school girls used the crude method of sticking a wire hanger up there. One girl she knew had almost bled to death. Drinking castor oil or laundry detergent were options.

Those methods would make her puke her guts out with no guarantee to work. Self-mutilation or poisoning was too scary. She needed to get the money and find a safer, less painful way to get rid of it. With paternity in doubt, she decided to ask Bowie Wallace.

#

Bowie worked at the gas station across town. She drove there hoping she'd find him on duty. Instead she found Dirk Pitts, a lanky brother with dark chocolate-colored skin. He was busy stacking a shipment of sodas at the station's small convenience store. Now, Dirk had a 'thing' for Eve, but she was none too interested.

"Eve, what can I do you for?" Dirk asked. "Is Bowie here today?"

"Nah, he took off."

"Oh—do you know where I can find him?"

Dirk's eyes surveyed the ground and his feet shuffled like a restless stallion.

"Come on Dirk. It's important, else I wouldn't ask." She gave him a sideways glance with her best coy smile.

"Yeah, but if I tell you, Bowie ain't gonna like it."

She placed a gentle hand on Dirk's bare bicep. Looking down at her hand, his lips formed a slow smile. "Now Dirk, Bowie and I have business. Important business. I need to find him."

"Ugh. Right," Dirk said with a sheepish grin. "There's a poker game in Slug's back room. But don't say I told you."

"Dirk, I owe you," she said backing away to her car.

#

Everybody knew Slug's, a juke joint about five miles out of town, where the music didn't start until after nine and went until 3AM. On her way there Eve thought about what she'd say to convince Bowie that he was responsible for her condition.

She knew for sure who the father of her first baby was, a high school boy. It had happened in her sophomore year.

Eve never even told the boy she was pregnant. Her father paid for that abortion. It was all handled before anyone was the wiser. The father of the second one was a family friend, Cole Bertrand. By all rights, he should've gone to jail for rape, but her family liked Cole.

They didn't wanted to put a black man in a Louisiana jail or deprive his wife and children of a livelihood. Auntie came through with the cash for that abortion. And after, Eve went to live with Auntie so she wouldn't have to run into Cole again.

Slug's was a long dirty-white stucco building, a former garage that had seen better days. It had no signage but everybody knew how to find it and that it was the black folks nightclub. It was late afternoon and Eve found only two men sitting at the bar in the main room. Bluesy music played from the jukebox. The bartender, who everyone called Shadow came from behind the bar to greet her. "Well, if it ain't Eve Durand. To what do we owe this pleasure? I ain't seen you around here for a long while."

"Yeah, I've been working nights at the Grill."

Truth be told—lately, she'd been too tired to party on her nights off. The thing growing inside her had sapped her strength.

"I'm looking for Bowie Wallace. Is he here?"

Shadow stared at her and fingered his goatee, deciding whether he should tell her the truth.

"Yeah, he's in the back room," he finally said. "They got a game going. You know, folks are serious about their cards. Ain't nobody gonna want interruptions. If you wait a while, they'll be taking a break. You can have a drink on the house."

But Eve wasn't of a mood to wait. "I got to talk to him now," she said brushing past Shadow and whisking through the maroon door into the backroom before Shadow could stop her.

"Damn!" said Shadow following quickly behind her.

"Hey, we got a visitor," said a sandy-haired guy at the round polka table.

Bowie looked up from his cards and frowned.

"Sorry fellas, I tried to get her to wait," Shadow explained.

Eve's eyes darted around the faces at the table until they landed on Bowie. "Bowie, we need to talk."

"Shit, Bowie, can't you keep you private stuff, private?" One of the players near where Eve stood called out.

"Eve, we ain't got nothing to talk about," Bowie said focusing on his cards trying unsuccessfully to ignore her presence. "Woman, can't you see I'm winning here?"

"Yeah, he's taking all our money," the sandy-haired player said. "Bowie, throw in your hand. Go talk to the heifer. Look at that face. You're in trouble."

The group all laughed. Well, except for Bowie.

Eve stood with her arms at her side and fists clenched. "Talk to me now or I'm gonna say out loud what I came to say."

"Ooowee. Player, she's calling your bluff," said Amos Renaud who sat slouched and balancing his chair precariously on two legs. Amos was someone Eve knew. In fact they'd had a thing going, some years back. Except for Shadow, Bowie, and Amos, the others were strangers. They must've come from out of town especially for the game. In a small town like Zachery everybody knew everybody.

"Shadow, please take her out of here. I'll deal with her when we break," Bowie said.

"Far as I'm concerned we can break now," said the sandy-haired guy with the milk complexion. He laid his cards face down on the table and folded his arms.

"You just want to break cause I'm winning," Bowie said.

Eve could hold back no longer. "Deal with me huh! Let's deal now. I'm pregnant," she blurted. By her own mouth, her business was now officially 'in the street.'

With that pronouncement, there was an uncomfortable silence. But then the room broke out into hoots and heckles. The heckling was aimed at Bowie not Eve. "Ah sukkie, sukkie! Player you hit the jackpot."

Stone-faced, Bowie didn't budge. "It ain't mine," he proclaimed. "Sorry, Miss Eve Durand, you got me mixed up with someone else. Maybe one of these dudes."

"Hey, keep us out of this," said another at the table. "Yeah, Brother Bowie, why you draggin' us into this?"

"Bowie, you need to go talk to this woman," Shadow said with a raised eyebrow.

"Guess I'm out for now," Bowie said throwing in his cards and gathering his chips. *Truth be told*—Bowie had been bluffing. Playing a hand with only two nines like it was a full house. A break at that time worked in his favor.

Eve waited outside. Bowie strode out tanned and brawny. "Sex on a stick," the other waitresses at the Grill called him. Eve had spent two whole days romping in the sack with him. *How many months ago was that?* She had to play it like she knew for sure that he was the father. And she wasn't in the mood for sweet talk, even if he wasn't the guilty party.

"Okay, you got me out here. Messed up my winning streak.

Put all your dirty laundry in the street. So, what do you want, woman?" Bowie said.

"Hello to you too, Bowie Wallace."

"Look Eve, I ain't admitting that this kid you got going on has anything to do with me. As far as I'm concerned, there's no way of telling until it's born and shows my wonderful good looks."

"You're so full of yourself," she shot back. "And there ain't going to be no kid to compare looks." Her face was fierce—determined. "You just gotta take my word for it. That's all the proof you're getting."

Bowie raised his palms in surrender. "Okay, okay lady. You do what you want. I already got two kids in Baton Rouge and I ain't looking for another mouth to feed. For sure we got to get that test to see who belongs to who."

"Didn't you hear me?" she barked. "I'm not having it. That's already decided. What I need is some money to go for the abortion."

"Settle down. Settle down." Bowie's thick lips flattened into a serious frown. He pulled out a small wad of bills, pulled a $100 bill off the top and handed it to her. "Let's just say this is a contribution to fixing your situation. You lucked out today. I got a little extra since I was winning."

"What! You got more there. This little bit might cover a night on the town. It ain't enough to take care of my problem."

"Eve, you're right about one thing. It is *your problem*," Bowie said. He slowly backed away, palms raised, prepared to fend off an attack should she come at him. Then he disappeared into the club.

Frustrated, Eve pondered her predicament standing in the almost empty parking lot. At least she got $100, she told herself climbing back into her car. But what was she going to do now?

#

Eve's older sister, Becca, lived in a ramshackle house further into the bayou with her five kids and fisherman husband. Eve didn't visit them that often. She didn't care much for Becca's beer drinking husband Alphonse. Once, a drunken Alphonse had grabbed Eve's butt when her sister was out of the room. Of course, Eve set him straight. Ever since, she found being around him, well—uncomfortable. But she needed to talk to somebody. She hoped that Alphonse would be at work or at least, he'd be sober.

Her nieces and nephews were out front. Samuel, the snotty-nosed three-year old squatted in the road throwing dirt in the air with his shovel with a passion. Marie, the five-year old, ran to Eve and latched on to her leg with dirty hands. "Auntie Eve, you bring us some candy?"

"Not this time, child," Eve said patting Marie's tangled locks before freeing herself from the child's grip.

The oldest, an eight year-old named Dahlia, stood in the shade of the large magnolia, her upper body bent to the right to counter-balance the droopy-diapered 18-month old straddling her left hip.

So young to have to play the mama, Eve thought. She'd always dreaded the thought of so many children. She'd seen what happened to her mother with a brood of eight. Becca was now in the same trap with five and many more fertile years to go. As for Eve, she would be perfectly happy to have none. Once this episode was over, she'd consider getting herself fixed.

"Dahlia, your mama around?" Eve asked.

Before the child could answer Becca emerged from the house with the fifth child, eight-month old Pierre, secured in the permanent grove on her hip.

"I thought you might come by," Becca said. "Auntie called me and told me you were in a bind."

"Bind. So that's what's she's calling it," Eve said sarcastically.

The sisters half-hugged while Baby Pierre, biscuit in hand, drooled on Eve's shoulder.

"This one is sure getting big," Eve said, not wanting to touch the mess he was making.

"So what you gonna do?" Becca asked. "Maybe you should have this one."

It was the expected answer from Becca, a devout Catholic. "Have it? Then give it away so I could run into it later in life?"

Eve sighed. "This wasn't supposed to happen."

"There are places out of state. Chances are, you wouldn't meet your child ever again. Though that would be sad, huh?"

"Not really." Eve palmed her baby bump. "No, I want this gone."

"I got to tell you, I can't help you. Alphonse didn't get paid last week. He's still working but business has been shaky ever since the oil spill."

"Guess I wasn't looking for any funds from you. Maybe a little sympathy though." Tears welled in Eve's eyes. She sniffed to hold back the flood.

"Hey Sis," Becca said rubbing Eve's shoulder. "I understand you gotta do what you gotta do. I never told anyone but I'll share this with you." She sighed. "I've had an abortion."

"Huh, you?" Becca's revelation brought Eve back from the brink of tears. How could the good Catholic mother do it? She understood why, but then Becca—well it was hard to believe.

"Yeah, it was right after Samuel. Alphonse was out of work and

I already had the three." Becca's voice was almost a whisper. She didn't want Baby Pierre, who was right there in her arms or little Marie who was playing at their feet to hear her confession.

"After all, Father Frank wasn't gonna feed my kids or keep the roof over our heads," Becca continued. "So I went to this woman down in the bayou called Mama DeVon. She gave me some herbs which took care of it."

"Did Alphonse know?"

"Yeah, he knew. Like all men, he talks a big Catholic game. He don't wanna know about women's concerns. He looks the other way. Work, sex and beer is all he cares about." Becca sighed and shifted the weight of the baby on her hip.

"My, my."

"Eve, you can't go telling folks what I just told you. I just wanted you to know that I ain't judging you. Only God gets to do that. You do what you got to do." She held Eve's hand and Eve wiped a tear from her eye.

"Tell me more about this Mama DeVon. I got a little cash from Bowie Wallace, the 'maybe' father."

"Well. It was simple enough. Mama DeVon gives you a concoction and guides you through the whole thing. I stayed the night and it was over."

"I don't know," Eve said. "Last time I went to the clinic. There were doctors, nurses. They knew what they were doing."

"You got that kinda money, then you go back to the clinic."

"That's the problem. I don't have that kinda money." Eve frowned. "Okay, give me the directions to the place. Maybe I should call her."

"As far as I know, she doesn't have a phone. It's just the way she operates."

"Herbal remedy, huh? Kinda sounds like voodoo."

Becca shrugged. "Why is it when folks talk about herbs and such, folks think voodoo? Look, it worked for me. Course, that was some years back."

"Okay, give me the directions."

"I'll make you a map. Here hold the baby." Becca shoved Baby Pierre into Eve's arms and took off for the house.

Eve froze. She'd never been interested in holding or cooing over babies, including her own nieces and nephews, of which there were a bunch. She was a sexy woman without an ounce of maternal instinct. No one ever called her to babysit. And in a house full of women with babies on their hips, Eve's was the one hip that was always free.

Baby Pierre looked up at Eve with innocent eyes and reached for Eve's hoop earring and babbled. The baby was the perfect blend of Becca and Alphonse with light eyes, light brown skin and curly locks. A little butterball with a stinky diaper. How could anyone think that cute? The baby fingered the gold hoop with wonderment then grabbed the hoop and yanked it with super baby strength.

"Oooow!!!!" Eve yelled startling the baby. The baby began to bawl. At least Eve had the good sense not to drop the child.

Instead she held the child at arms length and shook it like a rag doll.

"You little bastard," Eve yelled as blood spurted from her ripped ear lobe.

"Mama, Mama!" Dahlia yelled. She ran toward the house with little Marie at her heels. "Auntie Eve gonna kill Pierre!"

Becca came flying from the house. She snatched her screaming child from Eve and comforted him.

"Eve, are you crazy? What were you doing to my child?" Becca's eyes were fierce.

"He ripped my ear!" Eve answered. She touched her left earlobe and brought her fingers away smeared with blood. Indeed, the earlobe was split. The hoop's clasp had held strong, slicing right through her lobe. The baby still held the earring securely in his fist.

"You should know, he didn't mean it," Becca said returning the earring to her sister. "That's no way to treat a child. Here!"

She shoved the paper with directions to Mama DeVon into Eve's hand. "You better have the damn abortion 'cause for sure you'd be a terrible mother!"

#

Eve followed Becca's crude map into the bayou. It took her first this way then that way, through country roads headed to the swamp. The huge swamp cypresses covered in Spanish moss filtered the day's remaining light.

Eve came to the end of the road, a place where she could drive no further just as Becca's map had indicated. It was comforting to see two other cars parked at the end of the road. Eve parked next to them. She took a deep breath and proceeded on foot following the path to the swamp's edge all the while wary of swamp creatures, especially gators and snakes, and alert to the sounds coming from the foliage.

After a few minutes, Eve came to a clearing where she could see a house on stilts. At the water's edge, the path led to a plank bridge that hovered only a foot above the swampy water.

The narrow bridge could only accommodate one person at a time. Two women were coming from the house, one younger and one older, each carrying what looked like longneck beer bottles wrapped in brown paper. Eve waited for her turn to cross the plank bridge. With an acknowledging nod, the women passed her in silence.

"I guess this is the place," Eve muttered as she crossed the bridge. A thin old woman with a colorful head wrap and a red shawl covering a drab green dress that matched the swamp water waited on the porch of the house. The old woman's skin was light gray-brown, the kind of complexion that hadn't seen the sun. In the swamp's super shade, it probably hadn't.

The usually confident Eve was nervous. This place was nothing like the safe sterile environment of the women's clinic. Part of her wanted to run back across the rickety bridge up the path to her car. Then what? What would she do? Spend the next four to five months waiting until the kid came so she could give it away? As Eve rethought her decision to come, the woman stared straight at her.

"I'm looking for Mama DeVon," Eve finally managed. "You've found her. What can I do for you?" The woman's voice was low and soothing against the background of the swamp crickets and frogs. The voice took the edge off Eve's shaken nerves until a nearby owl's hoot startled her. It was too early in the day for an owl. But then under the canopy of cypress, summer dusk had already come.

"Chile, you got a tongue in that mouth?"

Eve smoothed her jersey to show her baby bump.

"Oh, I see," Mama DeVon said. "Well, come inside."

Inside, the dimly lit place looked like a pharmacy with one wall filled with wooden shelves lined with jars of all sizes and colors.

A basket filled with fresh herbs sat atop the counter in the small kitchen. Next to the basket was a roll of brown wrapping paper and a box full of smaller vials. It was as Becca had said. The woman dealt in medicinal herbs, some of which must have been brewing in the large pots on the stove.

Smells in the place shifted and blended, wafting one minute a sweet mint aroma, then faint basil and then a stench that reminded Eve of the worst of chit'lins. The strong chit'lin-like smell over-powered all the others. Already prone to queasiness, she gagged.

"Sit," Mama DeVon told her, pointing to a high back wood- en chair. "Feeling nauseous, huh? Well, I got something to settle that." She took a small vial from the counter and waved it under Eve's nose. "Is that better?"

"Yes, thank you."

"I'll get you a couple vials of that and a bag of peppermint tea. Those should get you through. Though you're at the point when the queasiness goes away."

"No. It's not the queasiness I'm looking to get rid of. I've come to get rid of this." Eve placed her palm on her belly.

Mama DeVon's eyes widen then narrowed as she frowned. "Chile, from what I'm seeing, you may be too far along for that."

"But I got to get rid of this," Eve said giving her belly a fisted punch.

"Oh! Calm down. Don't fret. I got to check you."

Mama DeVon instructed Eve to lie on a high table on the opposite side of the room and examined Eve's belly through her clothes.

Somehow Eve maintained her composure though all the prodding and poking though she felt sick, and was certainly afraid. She wished she had talked Becca into coming with her to hold her hand.

But now Becca was angry and certainly wouldn't have left her kids alone. Eve sighed. The strange woman was mumbling and shaking her head, as her large bony hands moved from the left side to the right side, plying Eve's belly like it was dough.

"What's the matter?" Eve finally asked.

"Your situation is complicated. It's always more complicated when souls are involved. I made a batch of the potion the other day. I think I have just enough left. It's going to cost more than my regular remedy fee - $200."

"Two-hundred! All I got is $125. Can't you just do it for $125. I got to get rid of this thing," Eve pleaded.

"Calm down Chile." The old woman thought for a minute. "Well, since I don't have to brew another pot of the stuff, I guess I could do it for that. I hope what I have on hand will be enough. But you'll have to stay the night."

"Yes, that's fine. Just get rid of it," Eve snapped.

Mama DeVon rolled her eyes and mumbled something under her breath. Eve wasn't paying attention. If she had been, she would have noticed the woman's reaction after she had snapped at her. But for Eve this was a business transaction. She turned her back to count her cash, then handed the woman the agreed upon price, all the while smiling to herself since she really could have paid more.

Mama DeVon took Eve to a second smaller, darker room. Mama DeVon lit what must have been a dozen candles. The candles gave the room a warm, tranquil feel. Even the foul smell from the stove pots was damped by a pleasant scented incense. There was a cot, a chair, a small table and a bureau. Atop the bureau were various statues and pictures set up like an altar. It reminded Eve of her great grandmother's home altar,

which included pictures of John F. Kennedy, Martin Luther King
and Jesus. On this altar, the Virgin Mary was the only figurine she
recognized.

Mama DeVon covered the cot with several sheets.

"Put this on," she said handing Eve a sackcloth gown. "And
take off your panties."

Eve dressed as instructed and sat on the cot. Though Becca had
told her some of what to expect, Eve wanted confirmation. "You're
not going to stick anything up there are you?"

"No, Chile. Your body's gonna do all the work. It's gonna work
like a miscarriage."

"Oh."

Mama DeVon gave Eve a half of a glass of potion the color of
Coca Cola. "Drink it and don't waste a bit," she told Eve. "It's just
enough. I ain't got no more."

Eve frowned and sniffed the concoction. It had a putrid
smell. First she turned her head away. Then, with new courage, she
downed it. The taste was bittersweet just short of disgusting. She
managed to finish it with a grimace. "Not good."

"You're going to be sleepy. Now rest. I'll be in to check on
you," Mama DeVon said as she left the room.

Sure enough, Eve felt drowsy right away.

She lay on the cot watching the hypnotic shadows from the
flickering flames dance on the ceiling. "In the morning this'll all be
over," she told herself.

#

Eve couldn't tell how long she'd been lying there unable to
sleep and seemingly too weak to rise from the cot. She twisted and

turned waiting for something to happen. A couple of times she called out to Mama DeVon but the woman had not come back in the room as promised. Or had she. She wasn't sure. Her vision was hazy and she may have dozed.

It must have been past midnight when the first cramp came.

Eve had never experienced a pain as wrenching and violent. The clinic procedures had lasted less than an hour. Their aftermath had consisted of a little cramping with minor bleeding, much less bleeding than during her time of the month. But these cramps were different.

In a series of painful contractions, Eve's innards felt like they were on fire. She screamed and cried for her long dead mother. It was as though the thing inside her was fighting to get out and trying to kill her in the process. She saw Mama DeVon come into the room.

"Oh God, please help me." Lying on her side, Eve reached out to Mama DeVon, but the woman passed the cot and went straight to the altar and began mumbling something, maybe a prayer. "Please, help me," Eve moaned in between her screams. Mama DeVon just ignored her.

Then it happened again. Horrific pain. Eve writhed in agony, and curled into a ball. For the moment of calm between the contractions, she began to see babies on the wall: little Pierre prominent among them. He was laughing, wailing, his eyes bloodshot, his hands claw-like. There were unknown babies, gurgling, cooing, screaming. Babies were on the floor near her cot. Some laying still because they were sleeping. Some still because they were dead, their heads crushed. Other strangled by umbilical cords. The ones that were alive crawled toward the cot. An army of them:

preemies, fetuses, toddlers in stinky diapers. The born had joined forces with the unborn to take their revenge on her.

Eve screamed and huddled against the wall.

"God, get me out of here." She swatted at her attackers with her pillow until an abdominal spasm rendered her immobile.

One attacker made it on to the cot and was reaching for her. Eve's legs again operational, she managed a kick that sent the creature flying. Then the water came. The sheets on her cot soaked. She lay in the warm mess sobbing, thinking she could take no more.

"Please, please. Make them go away."

"It will end soon, Chile." Mama DeVon had finally said something. "A soul's gonna put up a fight before it leaves this world."

What's this crazy old woman talking about? On one level Eve understood that she was hallucinating. But the pain and the fear were real.

When Mama DeVon approached the cot, the baby army retreated to the corner. Eve peeked around the old woman to make sure none remained near her.

"I'm going to check you," Mama DeVon said. With a plastic gloved hand she pulled up Eve's partially wet gown and looked between her thighs. "It's time," she declared.

She placed a white metal pan on the floor atop some rags and guided Eve to stand over it. "Hold on to me, squat, and push down with the next contraction."

Eve was exhausted, her legs wobbly. In comparison to fending off the baby army, the requirement to squat over a pan seemed almost pleasant. As long as the old woman was near, her attackers would stay away. When the next horrific pain hit, she squatted, steadying herself by pressing against the old woman's strong arm. Then, with a grunt more serious than good sex sounds, she bore down. With cramps in her back and haunches, and with her innards on fire, it took all the energy she could muster to bear down.

With the last push, something had slipped from between her thighs and hit the pan with a muffled thud. Just what it was Eve wasn't sure. A chorus of *ooooooooooooh's* and shrieks came from the corner. Then all went quiet.

Eve was at the point of almost fainting. Mama DeVon helped her lower herself backwards onto the cot. Then, the old woman quickly threw a towel over the pan, and removed it from the room before Eve could see anything.

Blood trickled down Eve's legs. Mama DeVon brought her a clean rag and a pan of warm water and told her to clean herself. She removed the wet sheets from the cot. "You can stay awhile and rest," the old woman told her. But Eve was having none of it. She gathered her remaining strength, managed to dress herself and was ready to leave.

"Do you want to know the baby's sex?" the old woman asked handing her a glass of water.

"Hell no," Eve fired back. She gulped the water. "I just want to go."

In the dim morning light, Eve gingerly made her way to the footbridge. In the swamp water she saw a baby's head emerge covered with swamp slime. Then there was another and another. On both sides of the bridge, dead babies were bobbing like marshmallows in a pale green soup. Eve screamed and took off running. Well, it was more like a hobble because she was so weak. Before she could make it across the bridge, she tripped. She landed with her cheek flatten against the wooden plank facing the water. A small face emerged from the water below. She screamed and scrambled to her feet then in a rapid limp she made it the rest of the way up the bayou path.

Eve could hear the old woman calling after her in a voice that echoed in the early morn: "Hang on little one! It's gonna be alright!"

Eve was too traumatized to care what the woman was saying.

She got into her car and put distance between herself and that place. With the thing inside her gone, she had a moment of relief that she was once more free.

Eve thought about going to Becca's then she remembered Baby Pierre was there, along with Becca's lecherous husband. Her nerves in a shamble and dog tired, Eve drove back to Auntie's and slept for two days.

#

Now, Eve never told anyone, not even Becca, the details of her horrific experience at Mama DeVon's place. She was trying to forget the whole thing. But three weeks later her body hadn't settled down. Instead of going away, the baby bump seemed to grow.

"You took care of your problem, but it sure don't look that way," Auntie Chlotilde said commenting on Eve's growing paunch.

"Becca said bodies take time to come back to normal," Eve answered acting unconcerned when in truth she was very concerned.

"Well Becca ought to know after five."

Truth be told—Becca's body never returned to its former shapely self. She always looked slightly pregnant. Eve's other sister Blanche in Houston had that same pudgy tummy after several kids. Eve hoped her short pregnancies hadn't triggered the gene that caused the Durand women to look like they were always in a family way.

Eve finally decided to see a doctor. Thank God, all the doctors hadn't moved to Baton Rouge along with the women's clinic.

"Well Miss Durand, looks to me like you're expecting," Dr. Kimble told her after a cursory examination.

"Well, I'm not 'cause I had an abortion a few weeks back," she admitted.

"Don't know what kind of abortion you had, or think you had, but to me it looks like you're about five months along."

Eve explained her 'procedure' without mentioning the attack by the baby army and without giving any names. You just don't give names in Zachery. "It was all herbal. Natural," she said.

"Uh huh," Dr. Kimble said. "Miss Durand, I'm not making any moral judgments here about what you did or thought you did

—but I've been in GYN practice for 18 years. Here and now, you are pregnant. So, if everything happened like you just told me, you've been duped."

Duped. Taken by the old woman in the bayou.

"I'll order a sonogram so you can see for yourself. The tests aren't going to change my diagnosis, unless you've got a tumor with a heartbeat. The baby should have kicked you."

Eve was stunned and totally confused. Could it be true? Could the thing in her belly really still be there? Hiding? Quiet? Hoping that she wouldn't try to get rid of it again?

Eve's eyes widened. Over the doctor's shoulder there was

movement. She could see the baby army gathering in the far corner of the exam room. They were scurrying to and fro like so many rats. Baby Pierre, red-eyed with long arms and claws seemed to be in the lead. Oh God, they'd found her. They were all laughing but keeping their distance because the doctor was there.

Eve covered her ears to block the cacophony of laughter but it wasn't working.

"Miss Durand, what's wrong?" The doctor asked.

Eve pointed to the gathering menace. "Don't you see them? Don't you hear them?

"Miss Durand, try to relax. I don't know what you're seeing, but getting excited, sending your pressure up is not good for the baby." She rocked on the exam table and begged the doctor to get rid of them. Kimble left the exam room to get the nurse and something to settle his patient down. Now leaving her alone was a mistake.

With the doctor out of the room there was nothing to stop the baby army. Eve screamed and ran for the door, but the crawlers attacked, grabbing her ankles and dragging her to the floor.

#

People in Zachary still talk about seeing Eve Durand, 'mad as a hatter,' being carried away from Doctor Kimble's office strapped down to a stretcher. Down in the bayou, Mama DeVon heard about the incident because word gets around. Somehow the story of the woman who thought she'd had an abortion but was really still pregnant got out. *Truth be told*—Dr. Kimble's nurse leaked the story. Of course, she didn't mention names, to protect patient privacy. But Zachery being such a small town, folks could figure out 'the who' but not real 'what or why' of it.

Down in the bayou, Mama DeVon spoke to her pet cockatoo, who was in on most things that went on in that little house. "What do they know," Mama DeVon said. "You can't go around messing with souls like that without consequences. What was going on in that Chile's mind, I don't know. But, what I do know is that Chile only bargained to rid herself of one soul when there were two. I kept my part of the bargain."

Sweetgrass Blood
by Eden Royce

The Weaver

I blotted the blood from my braids with a hotel towel, making sure to keep the plaits in their intricate swirling pattern. The blood was viscous and sticky and it clung to my strands like a gruesome pomade. I worked by candle light, making sure to clean my hands and nails of red before sitting down to weave. It would not do to get smudges on the baskets.

The crisp sweetgrass softened and gave under the pressure of my hand, releasing the scent of the sea at midnight. My lips, dry and cracked from lack of water, formed the words to the hex in a language that died even as I spoke it.

A part of me broke, each time I did the magic. Not my soul or my spirit—they were far too distant, far too thickened, like bark on a pecan tree. Perhaps they'd fled completely like the rest of me — my heart, my sympathies—all gone with the tide.

But no. None of those things.

I wound the strands of grass tighter, using the sharpened spoon to push them through each other, pinching where the next loop needed to be, my fingers cramped into claws, the stiff grasses leaving tiny splinters invisible to the eye but not to the flesh.

419

The grass was just right, pliable enough to bend but not so fresh that it leaked sap, its own blood, onto my hands. Four completed baskets lay on the floor to the left of my bare feet. This one would be the last and it needed to be larger, to hold the head.

Weary now, I lay the basket aside and pushed myself upright. Once I had been able to pull both of my feet into my lap, but I was no longer capable of a full lotus. Time and broken limbs had removed that ability. Now, I placed a foot on the sofa in front of me, and picked at the layer of dead skin on the sole of my foot.

It came away without resistance, a thin, diaphanous layer of my body—pale against my hands—fluttering in the wind from the box fan. Left was a tender pink layer of flesh, new, unable to withstand the tortures of the world. I stared at the circle of skin, so stark in its baby softness against the ashy roughness of my feet. I chewed it as I went outside.

In the front yard, I walked barefoot and silent. The camellia tree's leaves rustled at my approach.

"Hush, Sister," I crooned. "Just a few, my lovely, a few."

I plucked the soft, mauve petals and carried them inside. By moonlight, I returned to the weaving, my fingers soothed with the tree's scented oil.

Once the baskets were finished ,and my hands were aching from hours of twisting and bending the grass to my vision, my will, I took up my stick. Holding the polished wood eased the pain, allowing me to open and close my fingers around the cloth covered dowel. I stood with the wood's help, but once I was on my feet

I didn't need its support. With strength once again in my body, I pounded the stick on the wooden floor. Again and again, stick and pound, stick and pound, turned the house into a living, vibrating drum.

Voices of those gone from here came to me amongst the resonance. *Husha da soun'.* Warning me, protecting me as they had done for over forty years. *You brin' da poet.* I acknowledged their silent whispers with respect, inviting them to join me.

"I know. Let her come."

The Poet

The ink I used—ground by my own hand and mixed with well water—seeped into the paper. A snowy sheet of felt lay under the paper to compensate for the bleed. The brush made no sound as it flowed along the page.

Quiet. Heavy and the air is full of water. Rain will come soon.

No struggle this time.

Only shock and the swiftness of the blade.

Sweet and tough.

I signed my name, then went into the bathroom of the old plantation house I'd grown up in. A spot of dried blood lay on my cheek like a beauty mark. I left it there, enjoying the coquettish look it gave to my worn, tired face. Reconsidering, I ran a hot bath laced with the scent of vanilla and sandalwood—warming scents against the chill that seemed to be embracing me constantly—and submerged myself. As I looked up at the pinkening water, I knew this was just beginning.

Unbidden, the sound of a stick pounding into the earth reached me.

Thudding. Pounding. Rhythmic madness. Thundering into my mind, obliterating the calm I had so carefully conceived over these years. Killing it.

It was my fault that I heard it. Years ago, when I was in unruly pigtails, my grandmother had warned me.

If 'n you hear your name call, make sho it me. If 'n you aine sho, don' answer.

Not only had I answered, I'd done so more than once.

And now whenever they needed me, wanted me—an errand, a stalking—more, even—they called. I suspected that when they wished or when I didn't answer, they entered anyway.

I submerged myself again, to drown out the sound—the stick pounding its rhythm deep into my brain. Eyes open, I stared at the widening cracks in the ceiling. The rhythm, the pounding of the stick grew, swelled, deepened until chips of paint flaked from above me, dropping into the water like dead flies. Even with the water buffeting my ears, I heard them, their voices, and I knew at some point, I'd respond.

Seconds ticked by as I lay there, the room looking murky and ethereal through the warm, still water. Respiration became a luxury I didn't need, barely wanted, as I slid slowly into unconsciousness, their songs taking the place of my breath.

When I woke again, I was on the floor of the house. The living room. Even in the sweltering heat, the hardwood floor was cool against my bare belly. I turned over onto my back, the drone of the ancient air conditioner slowly taking the place of the voices, returning me to myself. My wrists, my hands ached. I opened and closed them, staring at the brown palms before my trembling fingers covered them. One of my first thoughts was to get some polish to cover the deep, ruddy stains on my nails. Red or maybe purple or black. Then they would match the bruises on my arms.

I pushed myself to my feet, stumbling only once—twice—as
I gained my footing. As I shuffled over to the kitchen, I saw them
stacked up in a corner by the old, dusty console TV. Baskets, at least
a half a dozen, all woven from the sweetgrass that grows alongside
the ocean. I knew the shapes—you could always tell which family
made the baskets from their shape, their design—and the sight of
them made me itch with memory. Scratchy fibers, leaves bent until
their limits were reached. My hands ached.

Thrown, I rushed past the remembrances into the kitchen, to
first gulp, then splash water onto my face. It was the water, always
the water that brought me back. It also helped carry my being, my
mind, and my actions, away in the first place. But I couldn't live
without it, it was part of me, just like they were. Escape was useless
and damning.

Words rushed up at me like waves and I scrambled to put
them down. Frantic, I searched the kitchen, finally finding an old
envelope to write on. My ink was elsewhere and I couldn't spare the
time to look for it—the words might be gone by then and I burned
to capture them. Head spinning, heart lunging, I found a knife-
sharpened pencil, eraser-less and chewed. I wrote, fingering the
patch of new skin on the bottom of my foot.

Inside me lie oceans
The sea's dead are my kin
De famblee
rises on buzzard's wings,
feathers spouting from the stumps of pain
soaring away from their bones
leaving dust inside me

I filled the envelope, turning it and writing along the edges until it was filled with grey lead. It calmed me, but not like the ink. Why hadn't I noticed it before?

Only the ink took away their voices. Maybe I had noticed, but the emptiness of being cut off from everyone I had loved, those who had died for me, was too much, and I put away the revelation.

They shied away from everyone else, my people; they eschewed the written word, its documentation of their ways and thoughts.

We had never been a people to write things down. We—a mish-mash of African and Black Carib—lived by our voices, songs and tales, and they had kept us alive, had kept us apart from the outside. But I'd gone outside. To the world of poetry, of academia, of word processors and digital recorders. It was to this world I took the old ways, recorded them for others to see and hear. It was for that and only for that they couldn't forgive me.

It was for that and only that—they'd kill.

In a daze, I stumbled from the kitchen, back the way I came. My feet were clumsy and my ankles protested holding me upright, and they twisted from under me and I went careening into the wall of the living room, knocking into the stack of baskets. They scattered with a rustling, scrambling sound and one reedy lid slipped from its home, then another.

My mind didn't want to accept what my eyes couldn't refute. For a flash of time, I was confused and I sank to my knees to get closer, needing to know and not wanting to. Without effort, my hand reached out to the contents, but I recoiled when I felt the Weaver's—no, my—handiwork: the slickness of blood, the putty-like texture of dead flesh. Flashes of memory peppered my vision: capture, screams, the whistle of my blade through stale air.

I was on my feet without hesitation, running into my bedroom. There, I threw open the closet door, tossed out unmatched shoes, shirts that had fallen from their hangers onto the floor. My old yoga mat from when I thought meditation would bring me peace and silence. Finally I found the roll of paper.

It was old, soft, and made of rice, a sustaining product for my people. Wound tightly, the roll was the length of my arm from shoulder to wrist. I unrolled it until it reached from one wall to the next, then down the long hallway that ran the whole of the first floor. I gathered up pencils, pens, found the pot of ink I'd made from galvanized nails and strong black tea.

Frantically, I wrote. On my hands and knees at first, then changing to a squat, then to sitting crossed legged on the floor. I wrote everything I could think of: gospel hymns, victory songs, work songs older than slavery and the pop song lyrics inspired by them. Scratched onto paper. Preserved and documented. Ghost stories. Cautionary tales. The sounds of humming rose in my ears. The stick pounding was heavier, closer.

Your paper won't save you.

I know the weaver's voice by now, although her weighted rasp was always accompanied by others long dead, some whispering in a chewy-sounding Gullah, some shrieking in dagger-sharp Kreyòl. There was no need to look up as I knew she was there above me, shadowy and dim but as real as the screeches, the screams. Her scent was salt: from sweat and from the ocean where her bones lay.

Down the hall I moved, ignoring the ache in my knees, the constant pop of my joints as I adjust position. Write. That's all you have to do and this will all come to an end.

"Let me go," I managed, still inking the rice paper as quickly as

I could while keeping my words legible. My fingers cramped, my back bent to the task like a sharecropper.

Our blood flows in you. Our pain, our sacrifice has made you what you are. How dare you? How dare you deny us!

"Don't make me do this anymore."

For a moment, something akin to sympathy crossed her face. *Accept our fate, Sister.*

My hand only faltered a moment, a missed word, a malformed loop on a letter. The weaver's voice was irate and it came to me on breath that was stale and unused. But I kept writing, preserving the ways in a manner anyone would be able to grasp. The stories, the songs, the superstitions, even the reasons behind these methods of madness, I managed to scratch along the rice paper.

I was halfway down the hall now and I was getting tired. My arm at the shoulder was tight, the muscle ready, poised to jerk and spasm. But it was my knee that gave out first, sending me toppling into the pie pan of ink I'd laid out. The paper soaked it up like a bandage, obliterating some of my words and forcing me to start the entire section again. Lying on my stomach, I took up the ballpoint pen, but the paper couldn't withstand the pressure needed to make the ink flow. It tore, leaving holes in the fine ream. Where the ink spilled and softened it, my weight separated it from the rest of the roll of paper with a chilling silence.

No. Nonono.

The pencil was no better. It left no more than a spectre of words on the page. I pressed harder, turned the pencil to sweep the page in an attempt to sketch my words, but the paper wouldn't hold them. I scraped my fingers against the empty pan, trying desperately to gather enough ink to make the next letter.

My inked finger touched the paper for the tiniest moment, before the Weaver had me. As she pulled me into her embrace, I saw I'd left a fingerprint on the rice paper—like a signature.

When I came to, I couldn't move. At first, I thought it was a dream or that I had been called again by the voices and I had done—something. That I would be waking up yet again, with blood saturating my braids, leaving featherlike swirls of red on the hardwood floor. I waited for clarity to come, for the sea of fog to lift from me, and when it did, I opened my mouth to scream. It came out like the call of a buzzard. As I breathed in, I tasted the salt of the sea.

The Weaver's fingers were deft and sure as they pulled the drying sweetgrass through my skin, pressing each new row of fiber into me with the sharpened end of a spoon. Her firm tugs forced the grass to obey and it bound my fingers, silencing them. The voices were also quiet now, the stick pounded no more, but she hummed as she worked, secure in telling me secrets of my people.

The Armoire
by Patricia E. Canterbury

It was the tail end of winter, wet, cold, gray, a typical Northern California day. I'm Paula Farrell, and have always loved spring, new beginnings, new everything. I had to get out of my house and see something other than the inside of my home-office. I write a weekly column for the local newspaper on various items of interest. Nothing much happens in my small part of the world but I love the quietness, the big trees, the winter fog and my nosy neighbors. I went to an "outdoor" art show held under the remains of an abandoned overhead freeway in town. There were missing pieces of freeway which allowed sunlight to shine on some booths. Most of the locals avoided the broken sky (as we fondly called it) part of the market. I had heard about the fantastic bargains one could purchase from the local artists. I wasn't in the mindset for an art piece although a nice rustic sculpture would look good in my garden. A visit to the monthly art show was just the pick me up I needed.

The center, small by most standards, held an antique fair every other month and the farmers, merchants and relatives of the recently departed brought pictures, furniture, dolls, silver and clothing to sell. I usually just looked, as I like modern, stylish, new things. I wandered from booth to booth casually picking up this

silver cup, ornate lamp, or tasted an offered cookie as I viewed
the various merchandise. I thought I might even get an idea for an
article for the weekly. They, like all small town papers, are always on
the prowl for bits of information.

Then I saw her. She was by far the most interesting person at
the fair. I have lived in Oliveview for the past ten years and the
only other African-American folks I'd met were the ten or so who
attended the same tiny church as I. Most, like me, had grown up in
the country surrounded by family, blood related or otherwise.

Oliveview reminded us of our hometowns, except for the
lack of black folk. But then we were only 15 minutes by car from
Bend, Oregon so we were exposed to culture, soul food, good
down home blues, and a large black church where our souls were
drenched in good old-fashioned gospel songs whenever we got
homesick.

Even in Bend, I had never seen anyone like her. She looked
like a black gypsy dressed in a brilliantly multi-colored skirt, orange
cotton blouse, and golden earrings; a red silk scarp was tied around
her jet-black curls. Her ebony skin was a smooth and clear as a
baby's. She had to be close to eighty-years-old.

"See anything you like?" she called, in a voice soft as a whisper.

"What do you sell?" I felt like a complete fool, as it was obvious
from the stacks and stacks of photo albums that she specialized
in old photographs. Of all the items at an antique fair, old photo
albums of dead folks I don't know are at the bottom of my "want"
list.

"Potions and dreams," she replied, with a gapped tooth smile
that reminded me of a distance ancestor's distance ancestor.

"I'm not in the market for either," I said, taking a step toward the next booth.

"Everyone has dreams, even these poor folks." She waved her hand over a thick photo album covered in red velvet.

I stopped and looked at the faces of four women and two men on the open page before me. The people were dressed like city folk out for a Sunday stroll at the turn of the 20th Century.

They looked content, serene, at peace, all six smiled. One of the men stood apart as if he were a family friend and not related to the others. He had a dazzling smile, firm mouth from what I could see under the thick moustache and clear, dark eyes. It was as if he were smiling directly at me.

"Isn't it unusual to find family portraits of black folks for sale?" I asked.

"What?"

"I just think it's strange to find black folks pictures here. So many of our folks have family members who keep things, almost everyone has some old aunt who remembers every birthday, holiday and when pictures were taken and who were in the photos," I said.

"Then there are others who like to share, I guess." The old woman gave the album a loving pat, as one would a favorite pet and gently strokes the velvet cover.

I thought I saw tiny sparks fly from her fingertips.

"Lots of static electricity from the velvet, huh?" I asked. "No—yes—yes, you must be careful especially if you keep

the album in the sun." The old woman looked flushed as if I'd caught her with her hand in the cookie jar.

"Well, it's very beautiful but I don't want pictures of folks I don't know. Have a good sale."

"Enjoy your day." The old woman replied as if it were a mantra.

#

I walked away and visited many other booths during the rest of the morning. I was almost ready to leave for the day, the rain had let up *and one large broken part* was allowing bits and pieces of sunshine to fall on silverware, crystal and mirrors.

One of the mirrored doors on a beautiful armoire caught my attention.

It was when I passed the last armoires when I saw him, a tall, dark man with a dazzling smile and a thick moustache just like I'd seen in the photograph. He was reflected in the beveled mirror of a rich mahogany armoire, only this man was dressed in worn jeans, a pale green cotton shirt and work boots. He had to be the great, great grandson of the man in the photo. I looked around but couldn't see where he was standing. I started to go towards the old woman's booth but it was packed up and she was gone.

I turned to tell the man about his ancestors' picture but he seemed to have disappeared into the glass fragments making up the mirror. All I noticed in the bright sunlight were swirling dust motes appearing to take on a life of their own Oh well, I knew I would see him around town, as I said earlier there weren't many black folks in Oliveview.

#

I wasn't planning on purchasing anything but the more I looked at the armoire, I'd seen earlier, the more I thought it would look wonderful in my living room. I was standing in front of it admiring the workmanship and imagining my television set, CD player and a couple of shelves of books resting in its cozy interior.

"How much is this armoire?" I asked the young white man seated in the corner of the booth.

"Oh you have excellent taste, this is one of our finest pieces. It's just $2,000. It's very old. I believe it was in a plantation in Florida back in the 1700's." He got up slowly and walked over to where I stood. His pale skin and clear eyes reminded me of some storybook ghost. He was as opposite of the man in the photo and the man in the mirror as any human males could be.

Where they had broad smiles, firm lips and smooth skin, his smile appeared forced as if it weren't something he did very often. His lips were narrow slivers, barely making the impression of lips and his skin was pockmarked like folks from years ago, when Smallpox was a dreaded disease, yet he looked to be about thirty-years-old. Smallpox was eradicated years ago and even the poorest families were vaccinated before the children attended school.

"Do you know who owned this piece before you?" I asked.

"No, not really, I just purchased it myself. My cousin works for a salvage company and an old, old woman asked him to remove it from her home. He knows I occasionally come out to antique fairs, such as this one, and thought I might find a buyer. My cousin thinks it's haunted."

"Haunted?" I asked.

"He swears during the week he had the piece folks walked in and out of the armoire as if searching for something or someone."

"Did you ask the old woman about it?"

"No. She was from one of the islands in the keys. She died a few days after she sold the piece. Perhaps he saw her spirit saying goodbye."

I looked at the man to see if he was kidding but his stoic face remained rigid.

"Yes, well it's the 21st century and I don't believe in ghosts. Let me think about this piece. Do you have a card, I can call you if I decide to purchase it?"

"Sure, here's my card. Call me and we can arrange to have it delivered, if you decide to purchase it."

"Thanks."

I put the card in my jacket pocket and walked to my car.

As I put the key in the car's door I had the overwhelming desire to run back to the armoire dealer and purchase the piece, which is just what I did.

#

The next day the armoire was delivered to my home. I paid the movers to install my television set and I arranged the CD's in the drawer under the television. I stacked reference books on a shelf above the television. The armoire looked like it had been in my home for years. It complimented the soft fall colors in my sofa and guest chairs and made the living room look relaxed and homey.

I poured myself a cup of tea and sat on the sofa, turned on the television and waited for the news. Instead of the news I found myself looking at a black and white version of an old horror movie. I turned the channel. The next channel also contained an old black and white movie, this time a comedy. I picked up the remote and clicked to the cable channels. None of them came through. I went back to the local stations I again found myself looking at old black and white programs. I'll have to call the cable company. I guess I switched wires when the movers were installing the television.

"Where's the TV Guide®" I asked out loud. Since I live by myself I didn't expect an answer.

"What's a TV Guide®?" A male voice asked.

"Who's there?" I called out as I jumped from the sofa and looked around the brightly lit room. I was alone. I slowly searched the house room by room. Yep, I was alone, and the doors and windows were locked.

I returned to the living room after giving the bathroom, bedroom, dining room and kitchen a second search. I was totally alone. I don't even have a pet. I would not have expected one to speak even if I had one.

"Must be my imagination going crazy," I said to myself, and took a sip of the now cold tea.

"I'm sorry if I scared you," the male voice said.

"Who are you? Where are you and how'd you get in my house?" I asked, too scared to move.

"You brought me in. I'm here by this picture machine."

"Picture machine? Oh, you mean the TV?"

"TV?" he asked.

"Why… why can't I see you?" I asked as I sat firmly on the sofa. My mobile phone just inches from my fingertips. Who would I call and what would I say? My heart was pounding.

"Paula, wake up you're dreaming," I said as I slapped my face a few times. I must have dozed off.

"So your name is Paula. I'm Marc. Marc Robinson."

With those words the man from the photo I'd seen reflected in the armoire's mirror *stepped* from the TV and stood before me in my living room.

"Now I know I'm dreaming," I said. "Wake-up. Wake-up."

I jumped from the sofa, ran into the bathroom, and splashed cold water on my face. I wiped my face on a bath towels and returned to the living room. Seated on my sofa was the person who called himself Marc Robinson.

"You think you're imaging me but I'm real. I'm as real as you. I was tricked into the armoire by Edna Ann. She was afraid of me. I tried to tell her if she just let me stay with her, she wouldn't get old, die or be lonely. She locked me in the armoire then sold it when she decided to die."

"Edna Ann?" I asked.

"The old woman who sold our armoire to the antique dealer." The thing who calls himself Marc Robinson said as if speaking to a child.

"I don't believe I'm sitting here talking to a—what a ghost, or a figment of my imagination? What?" I asked.

"Anna Rose told me about your dreams, so here I am," Marc said. He was still dressed in the worn, torn jeans, green cotton shirt and brown work-boots he'd worn the day before at the antique mall. When he moved he left tiny patches of cobwebs on the sofa. He smelled like an old museum, musty and stale but with a hint of wild sage. An army of dust motes swamped around him, coming to rest in his thick, curly dark brown hair.

"Anna Rose?" I asked.

"She showed you the album with my friends and my picture. She knew you needed me, so here I am."

"I don't need you or anyone else. If you don't leave this house immediately I'll call the police," I said, as I got up from the sofa to open a window. The living room had gotten very stuffy.

I needed to get Marc out of my house.

"No one can see me, but you. No one can hear me, but you."

"Nonsense, I'm calling the police." I got up and

accidentally put my hand on Marc's knee. I screamed. My hand went through his knee to the sofa. I screamed again.

"No one can hear you. You sent for me just like Edna Ann did seventy-five years ago. I'm here to fulfill your dreams. Relax, you can tell me about this picture box, uh—television—Edna Ann had a small picture box which she rarely used. It only showed grainy black and white pictures. I don't remember her saying anything about a TV. Let's see what this large one shows." The television screen turned color and showed the latest golf game.

"I don't care if no one can see you or not, you have to leave this instant," I said as firmly as my shaky voice could muster.

"Remember your dreams?" Marc asked, as if I hadn't said a word.

"I don't remember dreaming about you or any other old ghost."

"Just last night you dreamed about how nice it would be to find a nice young man and live here near the ocean, maybe have a family. I can be that person. I can be as real as you want me to be. I can make myself solid so your hand does not go through me," he said.

"I want you *out of my house*."

"Okay, if that's what you want. I'll leave, but if you invite me back I'm here to stay. We can be together forever. You will not need to age, we will be able to enjoy our lives through the centuries to come."

"You're mad. Who wants to live forever? What makes you think that I'd want you, even if what you say is possible?" I couldn't believe I was having a conversation with a collection of dust. I relaxed, this was by far the most interesting dream I'd had in a long time. It must have been the look of the man in the old photo.

I've always been a sucker for men with Sam Elliott mustaches, and deep dimples who are the color of warm chocolate. I decided to see how this dream ended.

"You disappoint me. I will stay here as long as you want me," Marc said, sitting on my sofa, crossing his legs and leaning back.

"If that's the case then it's time for you to get out of my home." I reached for his non-existent arm, only to once again grab a handful of nothing. "Out—Out—out this minute. Once we're properly introduced perhaps you can come back, but I have to invite you in." I ran to the front door, held it open and pointed to the street. "Get Out!"

Marc Robinson rose slowly, probably feeling all of his hundred or so years, smiled sadly and walked toward the door.

His eyes grew wide and he began to choke as he neared the front porch. A light rain had begun, he turned to me, "If I walk out into this rain, you will never see me again," he said in a whispered voice with an edge of fear.

"Good, now leave. I never invited you in and no one ever died from a little rain. It will probably wash away all the cobwebs surrounding you." I'd never seen anyone look as sad as Marc as he nodded his head and walked off into the rain. He quickly dissolved into a puddle of rainwater and flowed down the street into the creek at the bottom of the hill. It was like watching *The Wicked Witch* from the *Wizard of Oz*, only silently. I knew then and there I was dreaming but to make absolutely sure I went back inside, reheated my tea, gathered cleaning cloths soaked in rain water, and washed down the armoire. I didn't want any more old dust mites returning to fulfill their dreams of immortality.

Across town, in the middle of the forest, near a cave protected from the fresh rain, the old woman with the faded photographs, screams, "My Son, My Son, where are you?"

A Little Not Music
by LH Moore

Washington, D.C., 1939

Alice looped her arm through that of her best friend Bea, their infectious laughter making the people they passed by smile as they walked down the street. "U Street! Black Broadway!" Alice declared out loud, throwing her free arm out dramatically as Bea hip-bumped her. "This is where *everyone* wants to be!"

The bars, clubs, theaters, and cabarets were hopping that night, like every night, their marquees and signs bright. Posters announced upcoming acts. Folks dressed to the nines in flashy furs drove shiny flashy cars. Everybody was out: numbers runners, laughing college students like themselves, stumbling drunks, couples out on the town. See and be seen. The energy was crackling all around them and Alice loved being a part of that. They stopped in front of the little restaurant where Bea served as a hostess, its orange neon sign blinking overhead. "This is me," she said, her smile broad in her dark brown face. Bea adjusted her hat, a smart little number with a net veil, as she opened the door. "You knock 'em dead tonight!"

"And you know the truth! Don't I always, darling?" Alice said before waving goodbye and making her way a few doors down. There was a crowd out in front of Club Crystal Caverns as always, clamoring to get in or hoping for a peek at a celebrity that may have come through that night. She sashayed effortlessly by them. Jimmy, the club's bouncer, opened the door for her with a flourish, and greeted her with a nod as he tried to corral the eager group outside. She turned in a different direction than the club goers, making her way downstairs towards the back.

Backstage was always hectic before a show. She took off her hat, undoing a few pin curls she had hidden underneath. Alice and the five other dancers were a flurry of fr inge, sequins, and makeup powder in their small dressing room. Shouts rang back and forth between them all and their harried assistant, who helped them dress and handled small crises. Alice stashed her bag after she squeezed into her costume and did her makeup. She got a chance to take a breath and looked around the room at the other dancers. Their spangled, sparkling costumes were all different variations on how much skin the management felt they could get away with showing in a respectable establishment. Alice had been self-conscious the first time she wore it and still adjusted her costume to make sure that what needed to be covered stayed that way. She made sure to tie the ribbon of her low-heeled tap shoes with a bow right in the center. She tapped her foot a few times to make sure it felt right.

Management also insisted that there were certain things they could do to look similar to one another. Physically they looked alike anyway, with all of them being fairer in complexion and small in height. Before she had more time to muse on that fact, Alice heard the stage manager call to them. She stooped down, so that one of the other dancers could help her put on one of the elaborate headdresses that they were all wearing that night. The dancers nodded and smiled at one another as they lined up, a mix of palpable anxiety and excitement, any rivalries set aside for the moment, as they got ready to entertain. *All those years that my parents paid for dancing lessons have finally come in handy,* she thought wryly, as one by one, they went out onto the stage.

Alice could feel the *thump, thump, thump* of the music beneath her feet as they went through their routine, hips shimmying and feet tapping on the wooden dance floor. No matter how many times she had done this, it always felt the same—electric. The band behind them were pure energy: the frenetic flying fingers of the pianist, the blaring of the horns as their players swung them in unison, the *bom bom bom* of the bass, and the drummer setting the pace for them all. As she raised her arms, she was glad for her petite size as the club's low ceiling was stuccoed and formed to look like an underground cave grotto, with faux stalactites always a misjudged arm swing away.

Alice could see the audience out there, light glinting from their glasses as Washington's Black elite were dressed in their finest, swilling champagne, and laughing and clapping, as they sat at small, round, white linen tables. She could see them smiling and didn't care what anyone thought of her—or her skimpy outfit—when she danced. She whirled and kicked and found herself smiling back.

Dancing felt like freedom.

It was late when Alice got back to the house, a pale green and white-painted Victorian on a side street near school. She tried to be as quiet as possible as she made her way upstairs to her little rented room. It was a simple space, spare yet cozy, but it was hers—her own little haven from the world. As she started changing into her nightclothes, she noticed her window was still open and walked over to it.

She moved one of the light cotton curtains aside and saw movement in the backyard, as if something darted across quickly.

What was that?! she thought in alarm as she squinted, peering out to see what was there. *Nothing. There's nothing there. Probably just some animal or something. I'm too tired for this mess.* She closed the shades and turned around, practically falling into her bed with exhaustion.

Just as she started to drift off, Alice could hear music. She lay there for a moment listening. *Bom bom bom* went the bass with a tinny-sounding piano tinkling away. A simple, old blues song.

Alice opened her eyes and looked around. It didn't sound far away enough to be neighbors having a party. It sounded like it was coming from inside the house. She knew that Bea liked to play music sometimes, but turned it off late night so that Alice and Miss Clara, the older woman who owned the house, could get some rest. The music stopped almost as abruptly as it started. *What in the world?* She was now wide awake, listening intently and trying to figure out what just happened. There was a loud creak on the side of her bed and it felt as if it was being pressed down by someone at her side.

"Pay attention," a low male voice said breathily right at her left ear, startling Alice so much that she recoiled and jumped away from it in the opposite direction, almost falling out of the small, iron-railed bed. *What was that?!* She had even felt the voice's vibration.

She sat upright, frozen in place as she gripped the bedcovers. Her eyes darted back and forth, knowing that the room was empty except for herself. She quickly contemplated her options: *Should I run out? Should I wake up Bea and Miss Clara? What just happened here?!* She looked around in the dim of her room again. There was nothing there. No one and nothing.

There's nothing here, that wasn't real, there's nothing here, she told herself as she tried to calm back down. She slid back down under the covers, still jittery and unnerved.

There was no sleep for her that night.

In the morning, Alice finally drifted downstairs, where Bea was sitting at the dining room table eating a biscuit with some scrambled eggs. "Mmph, mmph, *mmph!*" Bea said as she took another bite, smiling at the gray-haired woman sitting at the table's head. "Miss Clara, you really outdid yourself with these today!" Bea's dark hair was shiny, her curls neatly in place. She patted the side of her head touching them as she turned and looked at Alice.

"Ooo, girl, I'm so excited! I can't wait for my beau to come up here from school tonight!"

"If all goes well, maybe you'll be Mrs. Dr. Johnson someday," Alice said, her smile more subdued than normal.

Bea squealed with delight at the thought. "I'm telling you, he's going to be such a good one! He's staying with his friends instead of—" She stopped talking and raised an arched eyebrow at her friend. "Wait—Alice, you seem a little worse for wear this morning. Are you alright?"

Alice averted her eyes for a moment before responding. "I thought I heard a man's voice in the middle of the night. Right in my ear, but there was no one there. No one there at all and everyone was asleep. Scared me pretty good."

This time it was Miss Clara's turn to raise an eyebrow. "Girl, that must've been some dream. Don't you go on talking about haints and such. You know I don't like that kind of mess in my home."

"But Miss Clara, I swear it happened. I'm not crazy or anything."

"Mmm-hmm," Miss Clara said, unconvinced. "What you *are* crazy about is working at that club. What is a respectable girl like you doing working in a place like that?" She shook her head as she handed Alice a plate.

"My job is just a tap dancer. I show up, I dance, I get my money for school and life. Nothing more. No sense in letting all those lessons go to waste. It is paying for my tuition. Just a means to an end."

"Besides, Miss Clara," Bea interjected with a smile as she tried to change the subject. She shot a look across the table at Alice. "All of the big time jazz stars come and play there: Duke, Pearl, Cab, Ella—it's the place to be! You should go see for yourself." Miss Clara just shook her head again.

"I think not. Something about that place, that's all," she said with a sniff as she finished her breakfast and went into the kitchen, leaving the two younger women behind. Alice leaned over the table a little towards Bea, whispering.

"I'm telling you, I definitely heard a man."

Bea looked a little nervous for a moment. "Know that I believe you, hon. If you say you heard it, you heard it." They ate the rest of their breakfast in silence.

Thump, thump, thump went the music and Alice tapped her foot to the beat as they waited backstage. She closed her eyes, letting the rhythm carry her as she prepared for her performance.. Except this time, it was tempered by her fatigue. For many nights now Alice had been sleeping fitfully, her dreams always the same.

She would be standing in a room so dim she could not see her hands before her. Always she would try to feel around her hoping for a door or way out into the light again, but there was nothing but empty, nothing to touch. A tall, dim shadow always lurked along the wall, always speaking with the low, butter-smooth voice from before. He had finally told her to call him The Mentor. She sighed out loud as she thought about the dreams, thinking about the senselessness of them and her situation in general. The Mentor was ever present in them both with a voice like a little menacing serenade.

She opened her eyes again wearily and stood up straight, adjusting her costume and putting on a smile before following the dancer ahead of her out into the lights and the small stage floor. Her smile faded almost as soon as they began their routine and she looked out into the audience. *What is going on? Something isn't right.*

Her eyes widened in disbelief when she saw liquid dripping from the ceiling and stalactites down onto the club goers below. *Thump, thump, thump.* They continued to laugh and smile and chat as they always did, but the thick, viscous liquid was rolling down their heads and faces, coating their carefully coiffed hair, staining their fine clothes and furs, and pooling on the white linen tablecloths. Drops fell into their drinks, turning them red, and Alice recoiled as they sipped from them.

Blood, she thought as she gasped. *That is blood.*

Bewildered by what she was seeing, Alice lost the beat and stumbled into the dancer to her left, who shot her a confused, annoyed look. She recovered quickly, jumping back into step in sync with her colleagues. They tapped and kicked and swung their arms as Alice tried not to focus on what she was seeing out there.

Oh God, oh God—is no one else seeing this?

Thump, thump, thump.

Then she saw *him*. The Mentor stood there in the back corner of the room, leaning against the wall with his arms crossed watching her. Silhouetted from the light of the doorway behind him, he looked as he did in her dreams: tall, formless yet with form, a shadow yet solid, everything dark. This time was different—she met his eyes, or the dark spaces where eyes should have been, and The Mentor threw back his head and laughed, his white teeth glinting in the low light as he pointed a slender hand at her. Alice lost her step again and froze in panic before running off the stage. Her colleagues stopped for only a moment to watch her leave before picking up their routine once more.

Thump, thump, thump.

A few days later, Alice was in her room surrounded by her books and notes studying for an exam. When the house was still, it was just her and the nighttime city sounds. Since she saw *him*, what used to bring her calm now made her nervous and being able to hear things so well in the quiet of the evening troubled her instead. She felt really lucky that the club didn't can her for running offstage like that, and she was still rattled from her experience.

Management gave her another chance and bought her excuse that she had not been feeling very well that night, which was not entirely untrue. "You're a good girl and a good dancer," management told her. "We'll cut you a break this time, but that can't happen again or you're out." She sighed at the thought, her lip curling up at the memory, and leaned back onto the pillows, careful not to dislodge the scarf around her carefully pinned up hair.

She was beginning to think that her mind was slipping. *Maybe school or work is too stressful and working on me?* There was a loud knock on her door. She sat up suddenly, surprised, and got up to get it,

unsure if she had somehow missed Bea or Miss Clara while lost in her thoughts. She opened it and no one was there. As she peeked out, a look of confusion crossed her face as she looked up and down the hall. No one was there. The door clicked as she slowly closed it behind her, shaking her head.

I'm letting this get to me. Maybe I was hearing things?

She settled back down on her bed and started reading again.

This time, Alice could clearly hear the familiar sound of Miss Clara's soft footsteps starting down the hallway. Alice did not think much of it. *She must have left something downstairs.* Suddenly a voice was right in her ear. "Made you look!" it said in a low hiss, before it let out a harsh, raspy laugh, obviously amused with itself. She dropped her book, jumped out of bed and ran towards the center of the room. *The Mentor.* "Stop this!" Alice called out as she looked around in the room's dim light. His laughter had barely faded when she heard a scream and a series of hard bumps as if something was falling. *Thump, thump, thump.* It stopped with a loud thud. Alice threw open her door and ran out of her room to the top of the stairs. "Oh my God!" she said as she rushed down to Miss Clara, who was lying in a heap at the bottom crying out in pain.

Bea was soon at their side, her face still slathered with night cream and her hair also pinned and tied up. Her robe was tied loosely as they both hovered over Miss Clara. "I'll get an ambulance," Bea said, running to the telephone on the wall nearby. Alice could hear her talking to the operator as she tried to comfort

Miss Clara, who was a bit beside herself. "No worries," she told her. "They'll be here soon."

Alice stayed with her when the ambulance came. Miss Clara was still a little shaken as she sat there later at Freedman's Hospital wringing her hands over and over again. "Doctors say that I broke my foot. I'm telling you that I thought I felt a hand upon my back push me hard as I was going downstairs," she said. "But that can't be. It was just me there. That could not have happened. Maybe I wasn't paying attention to what I was doing as I was going down? Misjudged?" She looked perplexed and Alice could tell that she was hoping for some type of explanation. Alice could not offer her one and gritted her teeth, patting Miss Clara's arm to reassure her. "Well now, you are just going to have to be more careful going up and down those stairs!" she said, feeling certain that The Mentor was becoming more aggressive and looked down at the floor, thinking. A sinking feeling roiled around in her gut:

How do you get rid of someone who is unwanted if you don't know if they are a someone at all?

Alice's days and nights began to blend as she started going through them both feeling like a shell, hollow and uncertain of herself. When she danced, it had no feeling. The freedom she once felt as she moved was diminished, each step empty for her where it had once been full of joy. She saw him at the club every night now. His tall form always leaning against the wall in the back, watching her. *What do you want?!* she wanted to shout at him as she pushed on through her routine. Everywhere she went she worried that The Mentor would be there watching. She could not shake that feeling of his presence in her life, and after the incident with Miss Clara, not knowing what he was, and the unpredictability of what he—or it—was capable of. She was not the only one who did not seem to not be themselves. A pall hung over the entire house, with all three women seeming more diminished. They barely spoke at breakfast, or any other mealtime, any more. It was as if they had all retreated, the others not treading onto or into each other's own little worlds any more. As the days went on, they all seemed as if they were fading, becoming shadows of their former selves going through the motions of when they were whole.

As she got ready for work, Alice passed by the doorway to Bea's room and thought she'd stop, leaning on it. Her friend was quieter than normal, subdued even for her, sitting on the edge of the bed in her pale green satin slip and brown stockings. Clothes and shoes and books were strewn everywhere, her normal mess, but Bea just wasn't…Bea. Like her, Bea looked tired. Almost haggard even, unusual for someone who so highly prided herself on her appearance. Alice came in, sat down on the bed next to her and looked at her more closely. "Are you okay? Feeling alright? Your eyes are a little bloodshot."

"I haven't been sleeping well," she said as her large brown eyes looked up at Alice slowly. She opened her mouth to say something and stopped. She was tapping her well-manicured nails on a book. *Clickety-click click, clickety-click, click, click.*

"Everything okay with Mr. Soon-to-be-Doctor Johnson?" "He's fine and dandy. No complaints there."

She hugged her friend and held her hand. "Maybe you just need some rest or something?"

"Rest, yes. Good idea. Wish I could though. You were right, you know?"

"Hmm? Right about what?"

Bea looked off towards the doorway as if watching something in the hallway. Alice followed her gaze and looked over that way too, not seeing anything. "Nothing," Bea said. "Never mind." *Clickety-click click, clickety-click, click, click,* went her nails again.

"If you like, I can stop by the restaurant, and let them know you're unwell?"

Bea nodded slowly as Alice hugged her again. Alice stood up to leave, looking at her friend with concern. "Feel better, hon. Let me know if you need anything."

"What I need is for—" Bea started to say, but stopped herself, waving Alice off. "Go on now, before you're late. Don't give 'em a reason, you know?"

Clickety-click click, clickety-click, click, click.

That night Alice dreamed that she was walking through the halls of a large house or mansion filled with rich, dark woodwork.

Although she wanted to touch it, everything had a touch of gray film upon it and was faded, as if no one had been there for decades. Dingy. Dank. She opened door after door entering room after room until she walked into one with large ceiling-to-floor windows with sheer white billowing curtains, a cold breeze blowing them inwards. A deep blue tufted velvet couch was in the middle of the room and she sat down upon it. She found herself entranced by the undulating curtains lifting and so softly falling, lifting and so softly falling again. The ones to her right blew towards her, but when they dropped back down, she gasped as they enveloped the form of a man.

The tall figure walked forward, the curtain slowly falling away as it came towards her. He was dapper in his shined shoes, dressed in a tailored dark pinstriped suit with a white silk square neatly tucked into the front pocket. As the curtain fell away from his face, it revealed desiccated brown-gray skin drawn back tightly like that of a corpse. He—no, *it*—ran a hand over its skull-like bald head as Alice's hand flew to her open mouth. There were only empty hollows where there should have been eyes. The Mentor. It *had* to be. *What IS this thing?* The figure moved languidly with an assured confidence, a swagger, its movements smooth and elegant as it went over to a gramophone on a small mahogany table. Its hand set the arm down onto the record with a flourish, the needle gliding along the grooves as it began to play the blues song that she had been hearing every night.

Thump, thump, thump.

Alice had never hated a song more.

She could not say anything as The Mentor came towards her, terrified to take her eyes off o f it. Alice scrambled back across the length of the couch, her hands swinging at it wildly as it came closer. Suddenly, with great speed it was inches from her face, its drawn mouth curved into a sly smile showing very sharp, fanged teeth. She put her hands up before her and it snapped its teeth at them as if to take a bite of them before it laughed at her silent scream.

"I do not know who or what you are—you can't do this!" she screamed at it.

Its smiling mouth now turned into a sneer as it put a knee on the sofa next to her, its body leaning against her with its face mere inches from hers. *Too close! Too close! My God!* Alice thought, recoiling in disgust even further into the velvet of the sofa.

The voice was all too familiar now as it leaned over her menacingly, sidling up next to her ear.

"Me?" it said, laughing again. "I do as I like. I told *her* to pay attention, too, when I was in the hallway." It tilted its head, as she took a swing at it.

"Didn't you hear me?"

Alice woke up sweating and still swinging at the air. The sense of dread did not leave her as she quickly got out of bed. She needed some water. Something, anything, to still herself and to help her try to forget that experience.

Then she heard it.

Thump, thump, thump. The bass. The tinny piano. The doleful singer. Coming from…Bea's room?

She ran to the door and knocked. Nothing.

She banged on it. Still nothing. Normally, Bea would have answered by now, groggy and annoyed.

"What is going on?" Miss Clara said, limping out into the hallway in her robe, a scarf neatly tied around her hair.

"Something's wrong with Bea, Miss Clara!" Alice banged her fist against the door to no avail. As loud as she was being, there was no way Bea couldn't hear her.

"How do you know that? Maybe that girl is sleeping hard, so leave her alone," the older woman said with a shrug, clearly annoyed at being awakened this time of night.

"Then how come I can't open this door? You *know* that's not like her at all," Alice shouted, pushing against her friend's bedroom door. "Bea! *Bea!* Let me in! *Please!*" Hearing no answer, Miss Clara's expression changed to one of panic as well and joined her, knocking on the door and calling out Bea's name.

Alice finally turned the knob, took a deep breath, and threw herself against it as hard as she could. It opened just enough for her to be able to get in. She wedged herself through the space in the door and grimaced as her bare feet stepped into something wet. *What in the world did Bea go and spill this time,* Alice thought as she made it all of the way into the room.

Like her own room, at night everything seemed an unusual combination of darkness, light, and shadows. Except for one. As her eyes scanned the room and readjusted, she jumped and let out a startled gasp as she saw a tall dark figure in the corner standing there watching, its hand held outwards, pointing. *Him.* Alice heard it laugh and it disappeared just as her eyes followed to where it was pointing. She then saw why the door had been so hard to open.

Bea was lying on the floor in front of it covered in blood—her own. And Alice was standing in a pool of it. Bea hadn't just slashed her wrists—her forearms from her wrists to her elbows had been opened as if she had wanted to be certain. Her eyes, void of their soul, were rolled upwards staring, her mouth slack.

Then she heard it, that voice, whispering in her ear as if standing right next to her.

"Told you."

Alice started to scream and was still in that same spot screaming when help arrived.

When her family came to collect Bea's things, her sister grabbed Alice's hand and pulled her aside as they were leaving out.

"You were her best friend. Did you know anything? See anything wrong?" Bea's sister asked with a quavering voice filled with a desperate grief. Alice just shook her head from side to side over and over again, her own eyes beginning to fill with tears. "Alice, the police are trying to say she did it over her relationship, and we all know it wasn't. Johnson's heartbroken. He was about to propose, you know. Had a ring and everything. We're all just trying to understand what happened here."

"I'm trying to understand too," Alice said, letting her hand go.

Pay attention…

It was all that Alice could do *not* to as she tried to go to sleep that night, but it was insistent. She could hear the music, *thump, thump, thump,* and the now familiar voice was right in her ear—that even, low, caressing baritone that was soothing, yet not, at the same time.

"I told you before and you did not listen. Look what happened. Will you listen to your mentor this time then?" it said.

Alice's eyes flew open as she sat up in her bed, looking around. All she could see was that faded gray-blackness of the quiet of night, shapes and shadows and forms whose meaning had to be discerned first before everything was comfortable again. She thought of Bea and a visceral anger, deep and resonant, welled up from inside of her. Hearing that voice did not scare her this time as so many times before. This time invoked unbridled fury. For Bea.

For Miss Clara. For herself.

"You should've left her alone!" she shouted out into the darkness. "Go away! You are no mentor. You are not welcome! Leave *me* alone!"

"Aww, don't be like that. Why would I *ever* want to leave you alone? Don't you even want to know who I am?" it said with a voice as smooth and sweet as syrup. "You've been calling me "The Mentor" and *I* never said that was who I was."

I said to call me "Tormentor." Where you go, I will as well.

Alice's eyes widened at the realization.

See...you weren't paying attention at all.

Dyer Died in Silence
by Vocab

She went from a shutter to silence
Eyes glazed over with the void of stillness.
As if illness suffocated the sight right out of her sockets.
A pocket of air emptied out of her wrinkled throat
One last hallowed gasp before she passed
and the cloak of death covered over her frigid soul.
Sheol opened its' gluttonous grasp to swallow her whole.
Boney hands reaching around the rope noose
that choked her esophagus and
asphyxiated her malevolent being.
She felt the slow collapse of her lungs.
Life was expunged from her sturdy tyrannical body.
She swayed oddly in the gallows like a broken wind chime.
She wavered awkwardly like a kite string entangled amongst tree twigs.
She died with her heart darkened scorched by wickedness.
Her soul was as pitch, as the bottomless abyss.
Fittingly, Amelia Dyer died, in the same manner in which she had
murderously slain hundreds of innocent infants,
stricken with unfortunate circumstances.
She died unwillingly, yielding only to the restriction of air.
She died suspended in midair.

Even in her death, no one is truly aware of how many children she carelessly killed for profit and gain.

Only the Thames River will stream confessions of her infamous name.

Its' waters quivering from the deserted bodies she buried there,

Countless babies forever enslaved in this liquid grave.

Many going unclaimed and some were never recovered.

Their grief stricken mothers went howling, like La Llorona, to the grave tortured with uncertainty. Amelia took no pity.

Legions of greedy spawns feasted through her intentions.

Amelia killed as many as six children in one day.

Her stern thin lipped scowl will haunt the annals of history.

No darkness can hold a candle to her flame of vile infamy.

Cruelty was personified through her sick twisted mind. She filled 5 books with her confessions line for line. 'Baby farming' and murders were her crimes. She died on June 10, 1896,

Hanging from the scaffold, she shuttered into silence.

The Mankana-kil
by L. Penelope

Akasha's mother had first seen the house in a magazine. She'd ripped out the page featuring a two-story, clapboard Colonial perched at the edge of the world on a cliff overlooking the ocean. It had taken Akasha's father two years to locate the house and another year to convince the owners to sell to him. The owners were an older couple who'd stubbornly insisted the house was bad luck, but her father suspected they didn't want to sell to a black man. His solution was to throw money at them until they relented.

By then Akasha had been born. An unexpected first baby for her middle-aged parents. There was joy at her birth—a miracle that snuck up on them long after they had given up on the idea of children. However, when the reality of child rearing penetrated their imaginings, they did not know what to do with her. Years of quiet evenings and immaculate furniture disintegrated into dust with the sheer force of the infant's cries. The longed-for baby was a puzzling accumulation of tiny mysterious parts. An enigma too exhausting to unravel, and so they soon stopped trying.

Akasha's mother focused her attentions instead on concrete, easy to understand tasks, pouring her tenderness into the selection of drapes, upholstery, and wall coverings for her beloved house.

So Akasha faded like the woodwork, leached of its color by the sea salty air. Aside from her bedroom, the first-floor study was her refuge. The space was close and musty, the windows having long ago been painted shut, but its main attractions were the floor to ceiling bookcases. The driftwood floor sagged in places under the weight of the massive shelves, and Akasha would lie down, head propped up by a stack of dusty tomes, getting lost in their pages.

She often came across words she did not know or concepts too advanced for her young mind, but she drank them in all the same.

Some days she did not see her parents at all, rising after her father had left for work and her mother had gone off on whatever errands occupied the majority of her time.

There were no neighbors, no playmates; the house's solitary beauty was rivaled only by its remoteness. A long, narrow, sandy lane led away from the front porch to a private dead-end road. Not even drunken tourists returning to their rented houses from beachside bars would find themselves down such a road.

When not reading, Akasha spent a great deal of time hanging out of windows, staring down at the surf crashing below, alternately imagining herself soaring out over the white-capped waves or crashing down in a tangle of bloody limbs on the craggy rocks.

She started school a year late due to the cavalier attention of her parents toward registration deadlines. Some time in December her mother came across a letter sent by the county, but having missed the start of school by several months, she thought she might as well wait until the next fall.

Walking into a classroom filled with children for the first time, Akasha came to a realization: she was not like everyone else.

Row after row of scrubbed pink faces topped with corn silk hair regarded her curiously. When she took her seat, the girl next to her, Jennie Meyers, asked if Akasha's skin was so dark because she was from Africa and if she'd ever seen a monkey before. Akasha responded, no, but she had a pet mouse, a little creature she had befriended after discovering it nibbling on crumbs on the pantry floor. By the end of the first week, the nickname "Mouse Girl" had stuck, solidifying her identity as a freak.

The only other person in the school who even came close to her level of oddness was Norman Chang, the Chinese boy, who also happened to be the only other non-white student. Norman Chang wore his shirts buttoned up to his chin and unwrapped foul smelling lunches that ensured a wide berth were kept around him in the cafeteria. He was in the other first grade class and always kept his eyes on his shoes when moving through the halls.

Social status notwithstanding, Akasha enjoyed school. For one, the library there had far more appealing books for a child than her parents' collection. Also, even though she was alternately teased or ignored, she still enjoyed being around people. She would drink in their interactions, observing how they laughed together, gossiped and bickered and used it to fuel her own rich imaginary life.

Weeks went by where she wouldn't speak aloud outside the confines of her home. Teachers often forgot to call on her, and she was allowed to do group projects by herself. Her brown skin and neglected tufts of spongy hair should have made her stand out, but instead they made her easy to overlook. Some days she felt more like a shadow than a person.

At fourteen, she still slept with a nightlight. The static of waves crashing was often soothing, but sometimes she would hear other noises mixed into the din. Could those be mermaids shouting? The cries of a fisherman as his boat smashed into the rocks? Or some poor lost soul out for a moonlit walk who slipped or jumped down to his death? The possibilities kept her up at night, straining to hear the secret sounds inside the surf.

One night she lay awake, covers pulled up to her chin, particularly spooked by a *scritch, scritch, scritch* just outside her window. She waged an internal battle on whether to peek her head out to look, when a shadow began to move inside her room.

The figure unfurled itself from beside her mirror and perched at the edge of her bed. It was unnaturally dark, seeming to absorb the light around it and was shaped oddly, with long, stick-like limbs that folded up giving the appearance of an insect. As it moved, the shadow clicked and popped and let out soft bleating noises. Akasha shivered, too afraid to move.

"We are your friend," a voice whispered from the midst of the darkness with a mechanical wheeze, breathless and whispery.

"What—what are you?" Akasha asked.

"We are Mankana-kil, Shadow Eater, Warden of Illusions and False Eyes. We have been watching you." Each word sounded like it was pulled from the bottom of a well.

"Watching me?" Akasha replied. "Why?"

The Mankana-kil shifted near her feet, bending its massive folded legs the opposite way until its whole shape changed entirely. The creature was hard to look at. Her eyes glanced off its body as if her mind couldn't quite process what it was seeing. She could not tell if it had a head, but there was a larger void of darkness somewhere near the top that she thought might be it. Looking at the thing gave her an odd feeling, an intensifying of the yawning emptiness inside her.

At the same time, the idea of something, anything watching her, paying attention to *her*, lit a spark of delight within her that warred with the terror.

The creature clicked and whirred as its limbs moved idly. "We watch many people. We see many things," it hissed.

Akasha scooted up her bed. "What do you want with me?" "We want to train you. We need an apprentice."

She bit her fingernail and continued to listen.

#

The English class was in the library for the week, doing research for their term papers. Akasha headed for the table in the back corner, next to the window overlooking the football field. It was where she usually sat. However, when she rounded the row of shelves obscuring it from the main section, she found Norman Chang seated in her chair. Norman Chang was not even in her English class. In fact, she had never shared a single class with him since the first grade. An amazing feat in a school as small as theirs.

Their eyes met for a moment, and she registered the surprise on his face before he looked away, back down at the notebook in front of him. Akasha wasn't sure what to do. She stood still for a full minute processing her options. The larger tables in the center of the library were already full of giggling girls who would slice her with weaponized glares if she dared sit with them. Choosing a table full of boys would be similarly perilous, though the trauma would be blunt instead of acute.

There was another study desk on the other side, but it faced the multimedia rooms and offered no privacy. With a glance out the window, she decided that she could not deviate from her routine and sat in the empty seat.

Norman Chang did not look up again or in any way register her presence. Akasha thought this was a good thing, she would just pretend this was a normal day and she was alone. If she tried hard enough she was sure she could un-see him and not be inconvenienced at all by his presence.

She pulled out her notebook, her favorite pen, and the giant tome of Renaissance poetry she had checked out for her paper. The clock overhead ticked obnoxiously, bisecting the silence.

Outside, a gym class was stretching before beginning their track and field drills. Norman Chang did not even seem to be breathing.

Akasha startled when she heard a *scritch, scritch, scritch*, just like the one from her bedroom. Norman Chang had produced an array of colored ink pens and was filling in a design in his notebook.

One arm was propped on the table, hiding the page from view, and Akasha had a powerful need to know what he was drawing.

She shifted slightly in her seat to get a glimpse, but he must have sensed her because he held the notebook even closer to his body. Finally, she stood, stretching, pretending to look out the window, then to scan the shelves nearby for a book. The table was in the World History section. Akasha meandered behind him, so that she was essentially standing in the corner with no excuse or way to play off her curiosity. She peered over his shoulder and let out a gasp.

"You've seen it?" she whispered.

Norman Chang turned to look at her, his face carefully blank. He blinked, owl-like from behind round glasses. Akasha pointed at the fully realistic drawing he was working on. "You've seen the Mankana-kil?"

He had drawn the creature in the center of a battlefield,

explosions going off in the background, the dead bodies of gruesome monsters strewn around the ground. He must have used up an entire black pen because the drawing held the realism of the creature—it seemed to suck up all the light around it. The monster was presented here as some kind of avenging hero, victorious in battle. Faceless and comprised of spindly limbs, bent at strange angles.

Akasha was so drawn in by the picture, she didn't realize that she was now leaning over Norman Chang's shoulder, almost cheek to cheek with him. He cleared his throat, and she backed away quickly, rounding the table to take her seat again.

"Has it come to you too?"

Norman Chang nodded, blinking rapidly. "What did it say?"

He put down his pen and looked at his drawing for a moment. "It said it could give me everything I dreamed of, that it would teach me the secret to things if I would become its apprentice."

Akasha had never heard Norman Chang's voice before. It was gravelly with disuse, but still pleasant, like laying on warm sand before the day got too hot.

"That's what it said to me too. I wonder how many apprentices it needs?"

He shifted his glasses on his nose. "I don't think it needs any."

Akasha leaned across the table. "Why?"

He flipped back several pages in his notebook and turned it around so she could see. "I've been having these dreams since it first came to me, so I've been drawing them." He turned the pages slowly, revealing gorgeous images of alien landscapes, more battle scenes, other strange creatures.

"Do you think it's giving you these dreams?"

He shook his head. "I have dreams sometimes. Ones that come true. It's just a thing. My mother says I'm slightly psychic."

Akasha looked up from her fascination with his drawings. She had never really looked at Norman Chang before. Her eyes had glanced off him like everyone else's did, treating him as background furniture, or wallpaper. He had lost the baby fat of childhood and seemed to have passed through the bulk of adolescence skipping the gangly awkward stage. The size of his limbs and head fit the size of his body quite well, and his face, while a little on the round side, had a strong jaw and decisive mouth. He still wore dress shirts buttoned up all the way, but the sleeves were rolled up to his elbows revealing lean, almost hairless forearms, tanned golden brown.

"You think it's a warrior?" Akasha asked, tearing her gaze away from his skin.

"I'm not sure. I've dreamed of it in plenty of wars, but also other places." He flipped to an earlier page of the notebook. Here the Mankana-kil stood tall amidst a crush of refugees, fleeing some terrible calamity. The fear and agony on the faces of the people was so clear, and the creature in their midst rose high, taller than in any of the other drawings.

"Why is it so big here?" she asked.

He shrugged. "That's what I saw. It seems to change sizes. I don't know why."

As Akasha studied the picture, she realized that she might have never had a conversation this long with anyone. Possibly ever. It was different than she'd imagined it.

Norman Chang began to blush and fidget. She realized she'd been staring at him. Shifting back in her seat slightly, she looked at the drawing again.

"Will you do it?" she whispered. "Do what?"

"Become its apprentice."

He slid the notebook back towards him and closed it. "No. I don't think so."

"But—" She struggled to find the words to capture the feeling she'd had when the creature made its offer. "It could change everything."

He paused in the middle of gathering his pens and looked her fully in the eye for the first time. "Yes, but change it to what?"

The bell rang exactly as he zipped up his backpack, and Norman Chang slipped away through the bookshelves, leaving Akasha staring out the window, unable to see the ocean.

#

It was two weeks before the creature made another appearance in Akasha's bedroom. She had gone to bed each night, some nights earlier than usual, ripping herself away from the pages of an adventure novel, so that she could fall asleep and not miss a reappearance. Having no idea what sort of schedule the Mankana-kil kept, she wasn't sure if it would come to her just after her lids had closed, or while deep into her sleep cycle.

When it finally returned, the night was moonless and the wind howled ominously, moaning as if over a lost lover.

Akasha did not recall falling asleep, but when she awoke to the *scritch, scritch, scritch,* her eyes popped open and relief flooded through her to find the monster at the foot of her bed.

"I thought you had forgotten me," she said, breathless.

Anticipation made her palms sweat. She had also taken to going to bed wearing sweatpants and a long sleeved t-shirt, so that she wouldn't have to waste time dressing in order to be prepared for whatever the apprenticeship might bring.

"We forget nothing," the Mankana-kil said in its strange voice of metal and mist.

"Do we start tonight?" She ripped off the covers and stuffed her feet into her sneakers.

"As you wish." Blackness spread from the creature's indistinct form and doused all the light in the room. A chill crept through her, icy fingers spearing her skin, freezing her from the inside out. When her vision cleared, she found herself on a quiet street, manicured lawns and colonial houses lining each side. The streetlamps dumped pools of yellow-gold light onto the asphalt, but she stood deep in shadow.

She could not see the Mankana-kil, but heard its buzzing movements around her. Then its voice came from behind, stroking her with a tendril of that frosty feeling from a moment ago.

"The shadows must be captured and transformed," it hissed. "Transformed into what?"

"Illusions." Its sibilant voice nipped at her spine. She crossed her arms to hold in some warmth, but was determined to see this through.

"How do I capture the shadows? How can they be transformed?"

The monster made a clicking sound that reminded her of laughter, but she doubted such creatures had senses of humor. Once the Mankana-kil demonstrated the process to her, she found it simple enough. Shadows were as easy to catch as tortoises.

Lumbering and slow, they either hadn't any sense of self-preservation or simply lacked the energy to flee when danger was nearby.

Perhaps they didn't sense threats the way a more evolved being might. One simply had to gain their attention and lure them forward to trap them.

Akasha could not carry a flashlight with her as that would spook them and cause them to shuffle away. Within a few short days, she mastered shadow seizure and then was able to move on to illusion creation.

The Mankana-kil had explained that it survived by consuming illusions, specifically ones that provoked a blood-curdling fright in others. On this night, it stood with Akasha inside a warm house at the foot of a bed staring down at a sleeping child. A nightlight in the corner projected the figure of a cartoon character on the wall. The colorful image punctured the darkness, but the shadows in the room had grown complacent over the course of the evening. They slept as soundly as the child, who snored softly with a bit of drool clinging to his lip.

Akasha gathered the shadows to her, waking and collecting them with only a moderate level of effort, and then watched as the Mankana-kil spun them into a thready mass. It reminded her of black cotton candy, sticky and diaphanous. Out of the mush, a vision formed. A thick, porcine head with two enormous tusks jutting from its mouth took shape. Chain mail covered meaty arms and legs. A sword, bigger than she was, hung at the beast's hip. The thing loosened its jaw, and let out a mighty roar, scaring the child awake.

Akasha's gaze flashed to the open bedroom door, certain such a racket had awoken the boy's parents, but no footsteps clattered.

No one stirred at all except for the boy. Shaking, he peered up at the warrior ogre before him. The smell of urine suffused the air.

Tiny sobs escaped from his chest as the ogre drew closer and raised its mighty sword.

The little boy hid his face and tensed for the blow. Then a sweeping darkness took the beast, erasing it from existence piece by piece. Akasha watched in wonder as the Mankana-kil consumed the illusion. She wasn't certain where the monster's mouth lay—if it even had a mouth—but the ogre soon deflated as if stuck with a pin until it was nothing but memory.

The child fell back into a fitful sleep, moaning as he tossed and turned.

Once again, an eerie darkness took over her vision as the creature transported her back to her bedroom. There were still several hours before sunrise, but she knew it would leave soon.

"Why do the illusions have to be frightening?" she asked. "Won't any illusion do?"

The Mankana-kil faded into the shadows of her room, the very ones it used to survive. "This is as it must be. One nightmare for another."

With a final *scritch, scritch, scritch,* it disappeared, taking all the shadows in her room with it.

#

The Mankana-kil had an insatiable appetite. Several nights a week, it awakened Akasha to continue her apprenticeship and perfect the art of illusion making. Only after a dreamer woke screaming, or an unsuspecting late night walker was left hyperventilating on the cold ground was the monster satisfied.

Akasha, however, was not.

When her further questions on the nature of the specters she created went unanswered, she began experimenting in daylight.

The Mankana-kil had only ever appeared to her at night, the day shadows held no interest for it, which is why she chose them.

After school one day, she lingered at the edge of the building.

The late afternoon sun cast a crew of shadows from the trees and bushes, all industriously busy and not paying any attention to Akasha at all. A twinge of regret prickled her skin, but did not stop her.

She seized the oblivious shadows, with no true design planned, only that whatever she formed them into would *not* strike terror into the hearts of anyone. A nice, safe, benign illusion. It must be possible, she reasoned, her curiosity and determination overwhelming the creature's counsel.

Her mind wandered as she spun, taking no particular path, and when she was done, surprise, not apprehension, lit a flame within her. Standing beside her was a monster of an entirely different kind.

Caroline Murphy exited the main doors wearing her cheerleading uniform. "Bye, Akasha! See you tomorrow," she said with a grin.

Akasha did a double take. Caroline Murphy had never spoken to her directly and referenced her only as Mouse Girl since the first grade.

The new illusion smiled prettily and waved, and Akasha faced her creation. Skin the same burnt umber as her own. Eyes and hair the same unremarkable shade of dirt brown. The smile was unfamiliar, only because Akasha had never seen herself smile, though she supposed that is what it would look like.

The clothes were identical, the two girls indistinguishable. "Good afternoon, Akasha," Mr. Hornsby said, juggling a travel mug, briefcase, and stack of folders. "Are you waiting for your ride home?"

The math teacher had never called on her, had never acknowledged her in any way. Akasha's tongue was dry and thick, but the illusion—the not-Akasha—shook her head and grinned, then shrugged her shoulders.

"Well, have a good evening then. See you tomorrow." The teacher walked away, taking with him her whole idea of how the world functioned.

Not-Akasha cut her eyes at Akasha. Her toothy grin transformed into a leer. A cold wind pierced Akasha's skin, and she backed away. The illusion followed, walking several steps behind her, down the sandy road leading home.

Every few steps, Akasha would look over her shoulder to find the double glaring at her with menace. As they made the trek, no fewer than two drivers stopped to offer a ride. They were kind looking older people, neighbors perhaps, not serial murderers or pedophiles, at least as far as she could tell. The illusion smiled gratefully and declined the rides with a shake of her head while the real Akasha stood rooted to the earth, paralyzed by the interaction and unable to flee even if the neighbors *had* turned out to be serial murderers.

Upon arriving home, her mother actually emerged from her craft room, scissors in hand, drapery samples dripping from her folded arms, and asked what she wanted for dinner.

It was like Akasha had stepped into some alternate universe.

Only her mother didn't ask *her* what she wanted, she asked *not-her*.

The illusion never spoke—did it not have a voice?—yet managed to communicate more effectively than the real Akasha ever had.

Father came out of the room he had long ago commandeered as his study, a room she had never entered, and the three had dinner together like a real family. Akasha was still as invisible as ever, hovering on the edges, but her doppelgänger was fully integrated. Its smug grin in her direction proved that the illusion knew just how the change in events was affecting her.

Silently, over the next weeks, Akasha observed the shifts in awe.

This was what it felt like to be included in a group project, to sit with others at lunch, to go to the movies with a group after school.

Not-Akasha was popular, well liked, and trusted. She joined the French club and got an A on her oral exam in Speech class, without uttering a word. She joined the track team and won third place in the all-county meet.

Akasha experienced it all from the sidelines, basking vicariously in the glory of acceptance and friendship. Nothing had really changed for her, except that her identical mirage was having the best life ever. The life Akasha had never even known to wish for.

The Mankana-kil had stopped coming at night. Perhaps his battle season was over. For a time, she didn't care. She lived through her creation, pretending it wasn't just someone with her face in the spotlight, that it was really her. And if not-Akasha looked upon her maker with undisguised disdain at best and hostility at worst, it didn't matter. It couldn't hurt her. It was just an illusion.

Akasha sat in the front row of bleachers in the gymnasium during Phys Ed, watching not-Akasha dominate on the volleyball court, when Norman Chang stumbled in with a note for the teacher. He stood at his side for several minutes before Coach Prescott registered his presence and took the note. As he left the gym, Norman Chang locked eyes with her and gave an almost imperceptible nod of acknowledgement.

Her mouth flew open, and the air rushed out of her lungs all at once. The gym doors had closed before she was able to control her legs and race out after him.

"You can see me?" she asked Norman Chang's retreating back.

He stopped and turned around, then looked back at the empty hall as if unsure she was speaking to him.

"Why wouldn't I be able to see you?"

Akasha shook her head with impatience. "And did you see *her?*"

"Who?"

She grabbed the sleeve of his shirt by its button and dragged him back into the gymnasium. Not-Akasha spiked the ball, winning another point for her team. She accepted a round of high fives as her due.

"Her." Akasha pointed.

Norman Chang looked from one Akasha to the other and shrugged. "I see her too, but she's not real."

Akasha shook her head. "No. I'm the one who isn't real." She stood in the doorway after Norman Chang had left, staring at not-Akasha until the bell rang.

#

The fact that Norman Chang had seen through the camouflage of her own life stung. The joy of secondhand acceptance that she'd convinced herself insulated her from injury was unmasked, and Akasha was left burning in the light of the sun.

When not-Akasha accepted a community service award, danced with the captain of the basketball team, had her first kiss, another tablespoon of salt was poured into the lacerations around the real Akasha's heart. If it didn't stop, it would dissolve her like a slug.

Nothing in her apprenticeship had enlightened her on how to unmake an illusion. Unlike the Mankana-kil, she could not eat her double. Though once her desperation grew fevered enough, she actually tried.

Her teeth had sunk into the illusion's flesh and came away with nothing to show for it, just a slightly smoky taste coating her tongue and an urge to gag.

At her wit's end, Akasha stalked the streets, investigating the shadows for any sign of the Mankana-kil. She interviewed a patch of gloom behind the convenience store and learned of missing shadows a few streets to the west. That was where she found the creature, tailing an unsuspecting night jogger.

"She won't go away," Akasha whined.

The monster whirred and clicked, moving its many arms and legs in an agitated manner, or maybe that's just how it always moved, she had never been sure.

"How do you get rid of an illusion if you can't eat it?" Her voice had risen at the end with desperation, but the creature was unmoved.

"You do not."

She crossed her arms, holding back a barrage of angry words. "Will *you* eat it? I need it gone."

A flurry of movement followed as the Mankana-kil rotated in a slow circle around her. "It will not nourish us. You do not fear it."

"I *hate* it. Isn't that enough?" Her whole body shook with

suppressed emotion, enough to fill a lifetime.

"It is not," the monster said simply and then disappeared.

#

Days passed, and not-Akasha was being solicited to run for class president for next year. The real Akasha had taken to sitting on the floor in the back of the classrooms so her apparition could have her seat. She scratched at the scuff marks on the linoleum and monitored the fluorescent light bulb overhead as it flickered and died with a soft hum.

There was really no reason to be there, school was just a habit she hadn't broken yet. Not-Akasha completed all her homework perfectly and received smiley faces at the tops of her essays.

Akasha walked out of the classroom and all the way home. She stood in the front hall listening to her mother flipping the pages of a magazine. Her father's pipe smoke wafted out from under the door to his office. The floorboards underfoot creaked as she shifted her weight, but no one came out to greet her.

She tromped out the side door to the edge of the cliff overlooking the ocean. Below, the white-capped waves frothed as they battered the rocks jutting from the water. The sea sang a siren song, calling to her, offering a temptation more inviting than any she'd known before. Her limbs danced to its melody, jerking and twisting in time to the beat of the tide. She stood, her toes hanging off the edge, an inch closer to freedom than the rest of her.

No one would miss her. It wasn't like she was even really there anyway. The waters would wash her away and nobody would be the wiser.

The wind whipped up around her, tangling her hair, and urging her forward. She stepped back. One step. Two.

And then took a giant running leap into the abyss.

#

Akasha fell, cradled on a current of air that was violent in its determination not to release her. She expected to feel the slap of the ocean's surface or the crack of her skull against a serrated peak. Instead, whispering fingers of grass tickled her and wrapped her in their itchy grip.

Her eyes, squeezed shut during the fall, opened to meet a sky of impossible blue.

A hand appeared above her, fingers smudged with ink. Her gaze traveled up the golden arm to the blinking face of Norman Chang. She placed her hand in his. He pulled her to standing. His palm against hers gave a considerable shock, like static electricity build up for years and years. She found herself in a field so green the tint made her eyes ache.

"Where are we? What happened?"

A silent breeze lifted her hair, blowing air as warm as her breath. The corners of Norman Chang's mouth curved, and he motioned for her to look behind her.

The verdant field ended abruptly, as if its maker changed her mind in the midst of its creation, and decided instead of green, blue was far more preferable. Brutal azure waves beat against the flowing grass. The water covered only a short distance—maybe the length of a football field—and ended at the base of a cliff, which pummeled a cropping of jagged rocks.

At the top of the bluff, overlooking the miniature ocean,

sat a two-story, clapboard Colonial. Akasha looked up at the place from which she had only ever looked down. She squinted at a figure standing next to the house. At this distance it was impossible to be sure, but a quaking in her belly told her it was not-Akasha standing there, looking down at her.

Just above the rocky waters, the Mankana-kil's confusion of limbs scaled the steep cliff face. It had grown to a giant size and chewed through the rock and earth, slowly erasing the foundation of Akasha's life. At the rate it was going, the house was headed for a brutal tumble into the ferocious waves below.

Not-Akasha teetered on the edge as the ground beneath her feet slowly disappeared.

The real Akasha turned back with wet eyes to Norman Chang.

"But I thought—" She tried to slow the racing of her mind. "I thought it would only eat the frightening ones. I wasn't afraid." Norman's expression was thoughtful as he peered beyond her.

"I was."

He turned around so they were side-by-side, shoulder-to-shoulder. Small thickets of trees dotted the field in which they stood. The ocean was behind her. The sun overhead shined spiritedly, but there wasn't a shadow in sight.

Toward a Peacock Poem
by Tiffany Austin

Its sound rushes like a woman with a hurt face
I will not hear, near Strawberry Field.

Appearing as the horse rode in, as the men clothed in smell,
alone, from nowhere, with no family.

Then it was gone, but for
a hoped for time, we were loosed in its maleness.

Yet it's not shameful to be puckered by a living, legs
waiting for a machete, near broken and hard water.

Before Lovers Leap*, I could hear her say,
I aimed directly at the back of the heart

and asked for a look from him.

At times, a prayer to ravish, then shank, then
let the sun walk away.

I can see a hole in the dark, he must have said.

In the middle of their touch,
apple breaking

fleshes like rose,
nearby bauxite.

I would like to meet the father who made you,
he said again,

passes the words from the fire to her hand—an ageless tongue.

I imagine her as a seamstress; we
have not recovered from this mean wound.

I imagine her as heaving moist—
because what do you do when beauty suddenly turns upon you?

She wanted a look;
he gave, "Soon."

*Lovers Leap is the place from which two slave lovers leaped from a cliff
in Jamaica according to local residents.

Mama
by A.D. Koboah

DEATH

The end of my life sees me sent not to the white man's paradise or the spirit world. It sees me sent instead to a netherworld that is bleached of colour and light, a place where I will wait until she needs me.

This netherworld is so devoid of substance of any kind I almost wish for the darkness of long ago when, as a frightened fifteen year old girl, I was snatched from all I knew and taken over water to a land of pain and misery—and the life of a lowly slave.

During that journey I awoke to darkness and suffocating heat, confusion, fear, and dread like a half forgotten dream that would not release me from its grasp. Groans, a dark song of pain, reached my ears. The stench of human bodies bathed with acrid-smelling sweat and human waste filled my nostrils. It settled in my throat like a thick, wet ball every time I breathed in.

I had been lying in my own filth ever since they brought me into the belly of this wooden beast. Over what could have been days, or mere hours, I lay there shackled, watching them bring other men and women into the belly of the wooden beast until there was room for no more. Time did not seem the same in this world. I could blink and perhaps a second, hours or days seemed to pass.

The world had shrunk to a ceaseless night and all that flowered in the belly of this wooden beast was human misery.

In this darkness I could only think of my grandmother. I recalled her squat, plump body, her coal-black skin, her piercing black eyes and her strength. The memory I always pulled to me was of the last time I had seen her. We had sat in the compound of her home in the gentle evening heat, sitting on earth the colour of a ripe, red sunset as insects nipped lazily at our skin. The trees in her compound stood still and lazy in the evening heat, the soughing of the leaves in an occasional breeze like gentle laughter. Descended from a long line of witches, I had been seeing spirits for as long as I could remember, and felt them everywhere that evening, in the friendly sway of the trees, the thrum of the earth beneath my feet. I felt their power in everything, but especially I felt the power of the moon as it bathed us in its gentle silver light. My grandmother had told me once of a god that had made the moon its home, and since then I had always felt an affinity with the moon. And even during the day when the sun scorched the sky a deep blue, I searched for it, and fancied I saw its pale outline and felt its strength.

Movement from above brought a swell in the groans and pleas for help. I closed my eyes. I could not recall when our captors had last brought us the tasteless swill they called food, and I did not care for I had resolved not to eat it. Death had claimed many here and I intended to let it claim me, too. I heard one of our captors enter. He moved among us, ignoring the desperate cries around him. I was not aware he had stopped by me until I felt rough hands tug at my sore flesh, unshackling me.

Despite my resolve, I felt hope, and the same pleas for help I could hear around me gushed out of my mouth.

He ignored my cries and dragged me along with him. I
ascended stairs behind him on shaky legs, cowed each time the
wooden beast dipped, throwing me against my rescuer and when
it pulled me away from him I clung to him even tighter. Soon, we
were in open air, and into the same night sky that used to hover
over my village. That was the only familiar thing I saw. I uttered a
strangled cry,

the salty air of this new world saturating my mouth. When I
was captured I hoped I would be able to escape and find my way
back to my village. However, the world I had known was gone.
Black treacherous water, as thick as oil in the darkness, had replaced
it.

It slapped and pushed against the wooden beast, making it
tilt and lurch in response. It was like a sentient, malignant entity,
and terror thrilled through me for it was all I saw everywhere I
turned. My attention was brought back to my captor when water
was thrown over me. He gestured for me to wash myself. I obeyed
numbly.

When I finished washing I did not wonder why he led me
elsewhere instead of back to be chained with the others. I could
only look out over the black water that raged beyond. I wept
silently, mourning all I had lost, the rasping voice of the water the
crowing of a jubilant foe.

#

Back amongst the other prisoners, I was thankful for the stench
that hid his scent which lay dank and wet on my flesh. My body,
however, would not let my mind ignore what had just taken place.
The flesh of my wrists screamed of the memory of meaty white

hands fastened on them. My thighs whimpered at the shock of being grasped and pulled apart. The pain between my legs spoke its own tale. I had been too shocked to fight him, too small, too weak to do more than beg. I sought the comfort of the memory of my grandmother, but it would not come to me. All that came to me was the hands around my wrists, his weight crushing me. I could only weep.

It happened a few more times and each time it did, I did not fight, I just waited for it to be done. And, afterward, I would lie in the dark with the other prisoners, trying to recall the memory of the last time I had seen my grandmother. It never came.

One night they took me above, and for a few moments, my captor's attention was taken away from me. I stood at the edge of the wooden beast looking out over the water and in a swell of despair I grasped the side of the wooden beast, meaning to throw myself into the water. I was ready to climb over the side, and into the water when I felt something, hands pressing against my arm. I looked down, but saw no one beside me, yet still I felt those hands, frail, beseeching hands on me as soft as a caress. I stood still, unable to launch myself into the water, my soul momentarily soothed by those hands, the want and need I sensed in that touch keeping me rooted to where I stood. Seconds later I heard a shout and then my captor was pulling me away, the opportunity gone.

Later, instead of the assault that had just taken place, I thought of those soft, beseeching hands against my arm, and the plea I had sensed in them. Only a powerful spirit could manifest itself so strongly, but why had it chosen to show itself to me in the form of those frail, pleading hands? I did not have the answer, but for the first time since I had been snatched away, I felt life stir within me.

Although the malignant water had eaten my world, some of it—
the benevolent spirits I had been seeing my entire life—remained.
Those soft, beseeching hands were proof of that.

That meant that the power of my blood, the power of
ancestors, remained. I had not fought him, but that did not mean
I could not fight at all. I reached tentative hands toward the spirits
I had always sensed around me. I expected nothing, but their
presence engulfed me with a shock and the air was thick with
them like the sharpness of lightning. The belly of the beast swam
with their silvery translucent bodies that never took on a solid
recognisable shape, but just undulated and twisted in the gloom.
However these were not the kind of spirits I was used to seeing.
These were *obeyifo*. Evil entities my grandmother had warned me
of that fed on evil and human pain. Of course it was the perfect
place for them, a place where acute pain and human misery were
never ending. These spirits could only be channelled with an offer
of blood. They gave nothing without exacting more in return than
what they gave and my grandmother had warned me never to turn
to them. I shivered and meant to close myself off from them. Then
I remembered the warm, sweaty body moving above mine.

#

The next time I was taken to him I returned clutching a torn
piece of rag, string and long strands of his hair, things I had stolen
as he lay sleeping. I spent the rest of the night fashioning it into
the crude figure of a man, the strands of his hair imbedded within.
Rubbing my wrist against the metal shackle until the skin gave and
blood glistened on my skin, I called upon the *obeyifo* swimming in

the dark around me. The *obeyifo* drew closer to me, the pain and suffering of the prisoners having made them strong. I soaked up their power, my hand tightening around the effigy I had made. He would be dead in mere days. But not before suffering pain beyond anything he knew of this world.

LOVE

I searched frantically through the countryside of the land I had been brought to. The scene before me was a vivid green with lush green trees and ripe, colourful flowers ripening and wilting in the hazy afternoon heat. I wiped sweat from my brow, anxiety chasing me as I moved further away from the plantation. The foreman had dragged one of the slave girls into the woods thirty minutes ago.

They would return soon. I sneered at the fear that washed over me at the prospect of what would happen if I were caught sneaking away from the cotton field. Sneer though I did, the fear was still there and I quickened my steps for this was important. I knew of a way to ease some of the burdens of this life that saw me worked from sunup to sundown, unable to refuse the white man that owned me or the male slaves he sometimes sent to me at night. Some of these slaves apologised as they did what they could not refuse to do. Others had been in this land for so long they thought they *were* animals and they treated me as such.

However, my master's sister had come to stay for a short while. A desperate woman can tell another desperate woman when she sees her and her desperation had screamed out at me. I knew how I could ease her burden and lighten mine. I knew because it had been shown to me in a dream. Yet, to be sure, I had summoned one of the *obeyifo* that resided in this land. This one was a powerful one and instead of a loose shapeless body and a glimpse of silvery claws and sharp teeth, it was able to take on the shape of a human form, although it was still translucent. The form it always chose was that of a white female child with shoulder length hair in two bunches on either side of its head, its small lips spread in a sly smile.

It spoke in my tongue the night I summoned it deep in the woods. "If you help her, your master's sister will take you with her and no other male, including her husband, will ever force himself on you."

The laughter that accompanied those words had not registered, only thoughts of being free of those nights an exhausted, downtrodden slave climbed on top of me and did his work ferociously as if the master he was so afraid of was standing behind him whip in hand.

I came to a stop in the deep, golden sunlight. Was that a cluster of white a few feet away? I ran through the field. Yes, this was the plant I had seen in my dream, flat, small white clusters of flowers like lace. This plant could be used to prevent a woman from conceiving. I reached down and plucked one only to be startled into bolting upright like a frightened horse by a voice behind me.

"That's not the one you need."

I spun around shocked to see a tall, well built man standing a few feet away, skin the colour of dark honey glistening in the afternoon sun. His long, thick black hair hung loose around his arms and back. He was what the whites called an Indian. He wore what looked like a large, square loin cloth, his legs protected by tube-like fitted leather pants with fringes at the sides. His muscular chest was bare. A horse stood a few feet away from him lazily nipping at the grass. I had sometimes seen Indians in the distance, but I had never been this close to one. He was at least fifteen years older than me, his large, dark eyes staring intently at me from a face that was harsh with its high cheek bones and angular shape. I found myself staring at his face, seeing beauty in it.

"There is no fence around this field," I spat at him. "Nothing to say I should not be here."

"We do not see land as the white man does, so we know it is not something we can own. You can take that if you wish. But it will be of no use to you."

I stared blankly at him, caught between tears at the wasted journey, fear he would tell the foreman he had seen me here and mistrust at his words.

I jumped back when he reached into an animal skin bag he carried. He tensed, but then pretended not to notice. He pulled out a flower that was similar in appearance to the one I held with shaking fingers, but even from this distance I could see the one he held was the one I had dreamt of.

"How—?" I began only to falter to a stop.

He smiled. "Your grandmother always told you that sometimes the great spirits conspire to make you collide into people. This is one of those times."

I could only gape at him. He pulled out two small cloth bundles.

"This is what you need." He held them out to me.

His demeanour was relaxed, but I knew he wanted something from me. His entire being seemed hinged on that something and, in my eyes, that made him dangerous. I had also never met such a power seer before and I was scared. However, desperation—mine and another's—made me take a few steps forward and timidly take the cloth bundles out of his hand.

Relief poured through me, so much so I was trembling. I thought I saw a trace of pity in the way his eyes narrowed almost imperceptibly and his mouth softened.

At that I straightened, my voice coming out firm, my chin jutting out.

"Thank you," I said.

The pity disappeared behind a careful mask and the briefest of smiles flit across his face. He looked away then, and pointed across the fields, the first time he had taken his eyes off me since I found him standing behind me. They returned to me quickly as if even those seconds away from me were seconds squandered.

"We are camped in that direction. I can meet you in the woods near the cotton field on your plantation and bring you to my camp. I have plenty to show you about herbs and there is much you can show me. It is why fate threw us together like this."

He moved away and leapt onto his horse. I sensed a lie in his words. He wanted something from me, but I could have no way of knowing what and I was still afraid of him and the way his caramel coloured eyes seemed to speak words to me every time they met mine. Words that had never been spoken to me before.

"I will be waiting beneath the trees at dusk," he said. "If you are frightened, bring one of your men with you."

With some effort, he tore his gaze away from me and turned the horse around. As I watched him ride off slowly, mesmerised, I knew his heart was racing, the fingers that were wound in the horse's mane not quite steady. Then I remembered I wasn't supposed to be here. I turned and ran back toward the plantation, fear thrilling through me marvelling that a lone Indian had made me forget I was a slave for a few precious minutes. Perhaps I would meet him at dusk after all.

#

I sat in the dark staring up at the perfect blank face of a full moon, thinking of another moon. For that was the meaning of his name in the white man's tongue.

Moon.

Tomorrow I would leave with my new mistress to a place called Mississippi and there was only one person I would be sad to leave behind. Moon, the man fate had thrown in my path when I went searching for herbs that would lessen one woman's burden along with my own. I had met him every evening that week and never had I encountered such kindness since I was brought to this land. He had shown me many things and even how to focus the power of my ancestors so that by the end of the week I could pluck the thoughts out of his mind as easily as plucking an apple from a tree. Although he found excuses to touch my hand or place his hand against my arm, he never attempted to do more than that and each night I left him with the weight of those restrained touches and what they could have led to. It had been weeks since I had seen him and my heart, chest and head were heavy with thoughts of him.

I stood up, my gaze still on the moon. I was about to return to my cabin, but on impulse moved off towards the woods near the cotton field, wanting to be somewhere Moon had been for that was the closest I could get to easing the heaviness of his absence.

I saw him before he saw me. He was waiting where he used to wait for me, his back to me, his hand across his horse, almost devoured by the deep darkness within the woods. A gasp escaped me and he turned around. A smile came to his lips along with relief. Without thinking, I ran into his arms. He held me tight to him beneath the meagre moonlight streaming through the dense trees.

When I released him he took my face in hands that were as large as my head and kissed me. I grew weak in his arms and drank in the feel of his lips, the heat of his body against mine, my toes curling and parts of me awakening that I never even knew existed. He pulled away and searched my face.

"I've been here every night since I brought you back here a few weeks ago, hoping to see you again," he said.

"Every night? Oh Moon, I didn't know."

I stroked his face, his hair and then kissed him again.

As he had done every night that week, he helped me onto his horse and then climbed on behind me. We rode out of the woods and away from the plantation until we were near his camp. He helped me off his horse and we lay in long, soft grass beneath a moon as serene and as whole as I felt in his arms as we made love. Afterward I lay staring at him as he slept, his skin a bronze shimmer beneath the light of the moon, his hair spread about him. One of the things I hated about the white man was the long, unnatural hair that grew flat and cowed instead of strong and upward. But I loved Moon's hair. I loved everything about him.

I reached a hand to caress his face and he caught it, his eyes still closed, and brought it to his lips. He sat up then and kissed me. Then he reached a hand for my stomach and stared intently at it, stroking it in sadness and awe.

"I wish I could be with you to see her face when she is born," he said.

A pang of sadness swept over me and I stayed his hand. "There's nothing growing there, Moon. The herbs you gave me made sure nothing can grow there."

"The herbs I gave you were to make you quicken. You are already with child."

Silence hung around us deep and dreadful. In the middle of that horror was a creeping joy I did not want to feel. I removed his hand from my stomach and stood. He stood also.

"What do you mean? How could you give me something to make me quicken? You know what life for a slave is like!"

"Our daughter is not one that can easily be refused. She wanted to come into this world through the two of us. Are you telling me you have not felt her presence at some point over the years? I have felt her my entire life. I could not refuse her."

Sadness in his eyes, he moved to place his hand over my stomach, but I backed away from him. I retrieved my clothes and dressed as tears fell down my cheeks.

"You may have deceived me, Moon, but I have my own magic and I will kill this child you forced on me!"

"You will do no such thing."

"It will be out of my body before this day is done!"

I turned to walk away but before I could move, he quickly closed the space between us and grasped my arms, his eyes wide with anxiety in the dark.

"Akosua, don't leave here angry with me. I knew my time with you would be short, but I still cannot bear for you to leave me.

Please don't take away these last few hours I have with you."

I wrenched my arms out of his and walked away, my hand automatically coming to my stomach, overwhelmed by his treachery but even more so at the gift he had given me, the gift of life. Yet I knew it was too precious a gift for me to be able to keep.

His voice reached me again, full of emotion and desperation. "She chose the two of us for a reason, Akosua. Promise me this, when he finds her, promise you will help him. Promise me, Akosua!"

His voice was lost on the breeze and the sound of my sobs. I did not ask myself what his words meant, I could only think of the baby I would have to kill.

I left with my new mistress that morning, riding on the back of a horse drawn cart, my mind on the child I could not keep. Was he right that it was a girl? I swallowed back bitter tears. Suddenly my heart tightened painfully and I looked up. On a hill in the distance stood an Indian dressed in clothing Moon told me they wore for funerals. Even from this distance, I knew it was him. He had come to say goodbye. I wished he were close enough so I could see his face, but I kept my gaze on him for as long as he remained in sight, tears streaming down my face. That was when I knew I would not kill this baby, the only thing of his I possessed. Soon he was gone, and I looked onward in the direction of my new home, my hand on my stomach and the life that was growing there.

MY CHILD

Pain rippled through my abdomen, a wave of pain that could not be contained or denied. I screamed in defiance of the pain, a scream that tore through my tiny cabin, drowning out the voice of the old slave woman who was kneeling between my legs. I cried out again as another contraction ripped through me. I knew more about delivering babies from the many times I had helped my grandmother deliver children in my village, but I let the old woman deliver the child, her manner clumsy and inept all while she exuded a haughty, knowing air.

I felt my body give at the same time the pain lessened. Then I heard a whimper, barely discernible, over the old woman's chatter.

She lay in the old woman's arms, calm and silent unlike other newborns I had helped deliver who screamed in anger at the world they had just entered. I stared at her small, perfect brown face. For a moment, I felt disappointment that she did not look like her father, but then I became captivated by her dark eyes which were searching the cabin. It seemed an age before they came to rest on me and that is where they remained. I reached for her. At first, the old woman continued to talk, tending to the baby in her clumsy way, which made me wince as I watched her hacked off the slick springy cord that had bound me to the baby, all while an ache gathered and grew within me. At last she was in my arms and the ache disappeared. I stared at that perfect face and for the first time since I was captured and brought to this land, I felt that which I thought had been forever stolen from me. Love. Love and a sense of self.

I also recognised in this tiny perfect baby the spirit that had come to me on the bow of that slave ship in the form of those feeble hands which had prevented me from throwing myself overboard. My child. As if it was something I had done before, I brought her to my breast, the old woman and her chatter forgotten. The baby latched onto my breast, the pain flaring only to be forgotten. She fed and was soon asleep. The old woman tried to take the child out of my arms, muttering something about rest, but a look forced her back.

I stared at the miracle in my arms. I would do everything in my power to protect this child. Yet even as I made the vow I felt a chill flood me for I could not protect myself let alone this precious gift Moon had given me. I vowed that no matter what it took, I would protect this child, and not even the white man's God would take her away from me.

#

I wanted to name my child Moon, for her father, but in this world even the simple privilege of choosing one's name was denied us. As I watched my mistress walk around my cabin, careful not to touch anything around her, bored as she threw names into the air carelessly, I pushed back my anger and decided to steer her toward the name I had chosen.

"All those names are good names," I said. "But I can only think of the night of her birth, how bright the moon was and how it seemed to shine on the birth of my child. My grandmother used to tell us tales of a god that had made the moon its home. I thought of that through the pain and I thought of you, mistress, that you are like that god, watching over me and my baby."

She was completely silent for a few moments, her brown hair harsh against her pale, thin face, her eyes round as she stared at me. I thought I saw something else in them as well. Maybe it was guilt or shame, I do not know. Then a hollow laugh escaped her.

"Well, then, we must call her Luna, the Spanish word for moon."

"Luna," I repeated, trying to hide the disgruntlement I could feel seeping into my voice. Then I looked down at the child. I smiled at her, a smile she returned with a gurgle of pleasure.

"Luna. Yes, mistress. You have chosen the perfect name for her."

#

I was happy during those first few years of my child's life, but in this world happiness was not something that was meant to be mine, and a threat was looming, one I had not foreseen.

My master, who had never seemed aware of my existence was suddenly frequently by my cabin, little gifts for Luna, who was almost three, in his bony hands marked with brown liver spots. Her skin was the same mahogany as my own, her ebony eyes always alight with joy, her plump face quick to spread into a smile and flash rows of perfect, little white teeth, her hair always lovingly oiled and plaited. I remembered the *obeyifo* that always manifested to me in the form of a little girl and the laughter that had accompanied its assurance my new master would never lay a hand on me. It had lied for I sensed a dark lust in my master's smile, and when I went to my mistress with the herbs I prepared for her every week, I found words no one would dare speak to their mistress tumbling out of my mouth, and into the neat stuffy bedroom.

"Why don't you at least try and stop him?"

She stared back at me, anger tightening her thin lips as the colour drained from her face making her almost blend into the weak sunlight that bled into the room. I was sure only the herbs I had just placed on the table prevented her from ordering the punishment I would otherwise have received.

"What do you mean?" Her voice was like a whip snaking across the silence in the room.

"You know what I mean. He is always at my cabin. I won't stand to be used like that again. You will stop him!"

She laughed, a sound that was brittle and filled with such pain it made a chill run down my spine.

"You think it is you he wants?" she said.

"Then why—?" The words trailed off for I was seeing the candies in his bony hand and the way he held them out to Luna, his eyes glued to her face, that dark lust in his eyes.

I stared at the herbs on the table. I had never asked myself why she wanted them. Fear and dread flooded my chest as nausea settled in my stomach. The *obeyifo*'s laughter from so long ago rang through my mind.

"Luna," I said.

She nodded.

"You may go," she said after a few moments.

It was a while before the dismissal filtered through to my mind and, in a daze, I left the room.

Luna. He wanted Luna. I would slit his throat before he ever laid a hand on my child.

BETRAYAL

It was months before I returned to the world around me and the new plantation I had been sold to which was a long way away from Mississippi. It was a voice that drew me back, a male voice that was husky with the quality of thick smoke. And then his face was before me. We were sitting in the shade of a cluster of trees, other slaves scattered around us. It was lunchtime. He sat beside me, looking out at the vast cotton field basking in the sunlight some distance from us, but not seeing it, only seeing the childhood memory he was recounting to me.

I studied his face, his glistening maple-coloured skin and pleasant open face that was quick to smile and hide the pain behind his quick lively eyes. He faced me suddenly and finding my eyes on him, he appeared startled, the words trailing away. He stared at me for a moment or two, and then resumed his story, never taking his eyes away from me. I glanced down at the plate of food I held.

Instead of one portion of the salted pork that was given to each slave, I had two. I glanced at his plate which was empty. Since he had given me most of his food, it had not taken him long to finish. For a moment darkness pressed in on me and the pain cut deep, almost cutting me in two when I thought of my loss.

Back in Mississippi they told me I was needed at the main house and I arrived to find a slave trader waiting there. I had known immediately he was waiting for me. I uttered one word. Luna. He was taking me away from my child.

The pain threatened to make me withdraw again but his voice drew me away from the darkness. He had sat with me every day for the past few weeks talking and I found that his voice had reached me in the darkness for I remembered all he had said and that each day he had given me most of his lunch.

I placed his salted pork back on his plate. Again his words trailed away, eyes that normally told so much giving me nothing for a change.

"You need more than you have had to eat over these weeks," I said.

He nodded and a smile lit up his face at the gift of words, the first words I had spoken to him after many weeks of silence.

"Abraham." He turned at the sound of his name in exasperation.

"What?"

"Come here," an older man called from the other end of the cluster of trees.

He faced me again, anxiety in his eyes, his expression fretful as if he was watching a fish he had spent the entire afternoon catching wriggle out of his grasp.

"I will still be here when you return," I said.

Perhaps it was the way I stared at him in rapt concentration, but he nodded and stood, darting over to the older slave. The darkness threatened to pull me away and back into the shell I had retreated to ever since I had been stolen from Luna. My thoughts drifted back to what had pushed me into the darkness. A dream I'd had of Luna, her plumb face lengthened and thinned by a few years, screaming in pain whilst death, silent and unseen, reached out to grasp her. Pain almost completely wiped the sight of the cotton field away. However, I clung to the sight before me for I had the promise of hearing that voice, like thick smoke, and of looking into those eyes that were quick to brighten when he smiled, eyes which concealed dark rooms and intense loneliness.

#

We became friends over the months that followed, and although I never spoke to him of my pain, his many kindnesses soothed the constant rub of the gaping wound of my loss. Although he kept me in the world, the dream was still there. So, when one night Abraham and I were sitting around a fire cooking our nightly meal, he told me of a plan he and a few other slaves had made to escape on a day when the master would be distracted by visiting friends. I had stared long at hard at his face half caught between shadow and the orange light of the dancing fire. He had waited in silence, anxiety a dark light in his eyes. I saw what this escape plan would bring for the two of us. Safety and joy in a place where we would be able to be man and wife and live in dignity. I saw children and the pain hidden behind his eyes ease and then disappear over years of relative contentment.

"Yes, Abraham. Of course I will go with you," I said, there being only one reply I could make to his offer. "Tell me what the plan is."

The smile that spread across his face usually brought joy to my heart, but this time there was only the dream of my child screaming whilst death reached for her.

#

A few days later I trailed behind my new master avoiding the darts of hostility and accusation I saw in the eyes of the slaves we passed. I had expected it. What I had not expected was my new master to take me past the cotton field and the gruesome offering that had been placed there. A line of men and women were hanging by their arms from wooden posts, wounds and red, oozing stripes across their backs festering in the relentless heat of the southern sun. My new master lingered by the cotton field as the hot, angry gazes of the slaves working in the field burned in my direction, but there was only one whose gaze could sear my mind and heart. At first I thought he was unconscious, but one eye fluttered open, the other squeezed shut by dark, swollen flesh. That eye shone bright with pain, pain that deepened when he saw me standing behind my new master. Perhaps he had not allowed himself to believe I had betrayed them, but he could no longer deceive himself.

The morning after he told me of the escape plan I had approached one of my master's friends, a slaveholder from Mississippi, and asked him to buy me revealing the escape plan to him. He had accepted easily for I had also displayed my talents at healing. He lived a long way away from my child, but I would be that little bit closer to her.

A sob escaped me before I could catch it and although my eyes glistened with unshed tears, I suppressed the anguish that was like hot coals in my chest. I could not deny Abraham and tear my gaze away from his and so I watched the bewilderment play out on his face.

Eventually my new master moved on. I kept my gaze on Abraham until I could no longer do so. I wished then that I had told him of my loss. Now I would have to wait until I met him again in the afterlife for he would be dead in a few days. It was the only thing that gave me some comfort during that long journey back to Mississippi, that all the pain he had endured would be gone once his soul was released from his body and this life of pain and misery. Throughout that journey there was no Abraham to keep me in the world, but I forced myself to remain in it. My child. I had a few years to make my way back to her. The dream of her face narrowed and sculptured by the years, screaming out in pain, was never far away.

#

I was sold a further two times before I got within walking distance of my child. A long walk that would take hours. During my first week at that plantation I saw portents of death everywhere. Everything I saw whispered of death from the bitter cold that had descended on the plantation to the deathly brown trees starved of leaves. A family of hungry runaways I came across in the woods, one holding a one year old baby to her painfully swollen bosom, whispered of an end. A weeping cut on the foot of the male screamed of death to me, even when I gave them food and herbs to heal the cut, telling him they must remain in the cave they were hiding in for a day or two to let it heal. The gratitude and relief in their eyes did not smother the whispers of death and when malignant black clouds gathered above that evening, I knew I could not wait. I had to make the long journey to see my child.

I set out after the other slaves had gone to bed, relying on instinct to show me the way through a ferocious storm that smote the Earth with its petulant rage.

When I got to the plantation I saw a light in one of the cabins and headed straight for it, fear clutching painfully at my stomach. I pushed the door open and entered to find the dream taking place right before my eyes. I saw Luna lying on a pallet, a woman hovering nervously over her as she screamed in pain. What sent horror tearing through me was her stomach which was engorged and hideously distended with child even though she was just one herself.

"Mama Akosua!"

I vaguely recognised the woman with her, but I did not answer her for I was still staring at Luna's stomach. My legs buckled beneath me. Luna's cries had quietened at my presence as they had so often when she was a baby. And that was what made rage smoulder through me and erupt into flames; for she was still just a child.

"I will kill him. I will kill him with my bare hands!" I cried.

As quickly as the flames had come, they were snuffed out by waves of despair. Tears came and I sank to the cabin floor, the storm raging behind me as Luna's screams resumed.

"Mama Akosua, there ain't no time for this!" Mary (that was the woman's name) was before me clasping my arms. "Something ain't right with the baby!"

In that moment I saw that all the portents of death I had been seeing were pointed at Luna and the baby, my grandchild. I stared at Mary for a few moments, then I wiped away my tears and nodded. I got to my feet.

I safely delivered my grandchild and took her to the runaways.

As I placed her in the woman's arms and watched her stare at the baby in wonder and joy before putting the crying baby to her swollen breast, I realised the portents I had seen that week had also signified life. My grandchild would have a chance at life instead of death as a slave.

That night I put a curse on my old master. In my rage, wisdom completely abandoned me and instead of killing him, I chose to let him live for many more years. Years of agony and the kind of pain and horror he had visited on my child.

BRIEF MOMENTS

Many years passed and I awoke to joy one warm summer's morning. I got up slowly from my pallet, bending my body to the pain that gripped it. A smile came to my lips. My child would be coming to see me today. She was a woman now, a silent beauty I had seen only a few times over the years whenever she was forced to make the long journey to seek help and the herbs only I could provide. I moved to my cabin door and looked out on the darkness and the other slaves beginning their day. These past few years had been ones of waiting for those brief moments when I saw my child. Although those moments were brief, they were worth all I had given up. I still saw the faces of the children Abraham and me could have had, but I did not regret the choice I had made.

As I watched the sun break through the darkness to give light to the world, I knew that even when death released me from it, I would not join the others that had gone before me. I knew my daughter would still need me and so my spirit would remain and wait as I had been doing all these years. For now, I could be happy because before the day ended I would see the quiet, cool beauty who was little more than a stranger. Still she was my child, my child.

To Give Her Whatsoever She Would Ask
by R. J. Joseph

Lord, please bless Your humble servant.

I grew up with prayers, praying every morning with my transplanted American mother and Trinidadian father. We kneeled at night before bed and gave the Lord thanks for each day that we finished. After my parents died, I prayed for their eternal souls. I'd even prayed for the kind of marriage I wanted, and thought I needed.

My prayer for marriage had dissolved into indifference; however, I didn't care. My prayers had never been for a husband, specifically, though I knew one to be necessary to bring a child into the world the right way. I'd been a good Christian wife, respecting my husband, and following his lead as head of the household.

When he wanted me to quit working and tend home, I did it. When he was promoted at his job, I supported him.

I knew God wanted His children to be happily married, but I also knew that it was likely not His plan for us to be unevenly yoked in misery. When Jorge told me he didn't love me anymore, he'd already stopped going to church with me and left the room anytime I put gospel music on the stereo. He asked me one last time to pray with him, and I prayed with him; he asked for guidance in the matter of our union and I silently prayed for a baby before he left me.

My most fervent prayer for a baby grew even more desperate as I crossed the threshold into forty years. All I'd ever wanted were children to nurse and cuddle and raise in the way the Lord desired of His children. I would only borrow them, because a true Christian knew they truly belonged to God.

By my forty second birthday, it looked like my most passionate pleas would be ignored. I didn't kneel so often by then. I was already the towns' crazy old woman. I kept mostly to myself and only went to market and town when absolutely necessary. And I travelled to Mr. Frank's cottage, down the hill, to work. Mrs. Frank had passed on five years ago, and now he was just waiting to join his wife in heaven.

I didn't have the heart to tell him that I suspected that there was no heaven; there was no God to answer prayers. I was tired of praying.

It was time to try something else.

I trudged down the hill to work, using the heavy stick I walked with to scout for snakes in the grass before they had a chance to strike. The sun had just settled beneath the horizon, and the island was dark. I wasn't afraid, although the island folks didn't need much prompting to discuss their jumbies and other evil night spirits.

I knew not to stop for strangers, and not to approach strange animals. I had my trusty pocket flashlight to spot predators before they could attack.

What I had not been prepared for was the large ball of fire that slowly flew over my head. I saw brilliance and expected heat, but instead, there was an icy chill in the wake of the ball. I turned to watch where it would go next, transfixed by the way my womb ached as it passed, and my heart called after it. The ball circled my torso several times. I could hear the coos of a baby, and longed to touch the softness of its skin. I reached out to it and was overwhelmed with dread. I drew my hand back and turned on my flashlight. The ball rose upwards and dissipated.

I reached Mr. Franks' house to find him seated on the porch. He seldom came out, so I knew he must have been having a pretty good day.

"Good night, Ingrid." "Good night, Mr. Franks."

He sucked his teeth. "Look, de spirits flying tonight." "What are you talking about, Mr. Franks?"

"I glad you ain't run into one because it would probably take you away."

I thought about the ball of fire, but didn't tell my employer. "Dey looking for somebody to trick into taking dem on." His eyes gleamed with an unusual fervor.

"Come now, Mr. Frank. Let's get your dinner." I helped him up out of the chair and guided him into the house.

I usually took my dinner with him, but I had no appetite. I sat by the open window while he slowly ate.

A soft whimpering floated through the window. I looked at Mr. Franks, but he seemed not to notice it. It came again, louder, with cooing. I stood from the chair and headed to the door.

"No, Ingrid. Dat's no baby. Stay here." "You hear that baby, too?"

"I hear what pretending to be a baby. Sit down, girl. Don't go by de door."

My feet obeyed him, but my heart filled with anxiety. I twisted my sweaty hands in my lap. *I can't leave that baby out there.*

"Girl, ain't nobody gonna leave no baby on de doorstep."

Mr. Franks eyed me steadily. "I ready for bed, eh? I tired." With a strength I had not seen from him in years, he pushed his chair back from the table and walked to the door, where he flicked on the porch light.

On the way to the bedroom, he instructed me to pull some candles from the cupboard and light them.

I got him dressed and settled into bed and took my regular seat in the chair next to him. The flames flickered from the hallway and across the room.

"Why didn't you let me go to the door?" My arms still ached to hold the baby I'd heard.

"Dat was no baby. Dat was a soucouyant, trying to get you to open de door so she can come inside. She would have sucked you dry after you invite her in."

"You believe in those jumbies and thing?" I asked.

"Yeah, girl, dey real." He spoke with conviction, and fell off into a coughing fit.

"But don't they grant wishes, too?" I remembered all the stories my parents and town elders had told me my entire childhood. I believed them, too. The evil spirits could be used, if you were smart. Of course, a devout person would never entertain making acquaintance with the spirits, and would instead pray them away.

"You gotta go look for dem and see where by de river dey leave dey skin, and if you take it, dey gonna beg to get dey skin back so dey grant you a wish." He reached out and grabbed my hand, and the years old calluses pressed against my skin.

"But dey is very dangerous. Don't mess wit dem, girl, please, because you more likely lose your life instead of get any wish. And even if you get a wish, it gonna be a payback." He squeezed my hand until it hurt. "You hear me girl? Topic done."

507

I sat in silence while Mr. Franks dozed off. He slept fitfully that night, opening his eyes and sitting up and glancing around the room until he saw me still in the chair. Then he would look at the candles, suck his teeth, and doze off again. I didn't want to alarm him by disappearing, so I didn't even leave the chair to do my regular nightly chores. Instead, I planned.

#

The next night, I left early for work and spotted the ball of fire rising above the trees alongside the river road. It floated towards me and began its slow circle. I didn't want the longing feeling it created in me, because it left me feeling confused and hurt. I needed it to leave. I only wanted to get to the river side. I turned on my flashlight and pointed it directly at the ball until it repeated its disappearing act. I didn't know how long it would stay away and I had to complete my search before it came back.

I headed towards the area where I had seen the ball first rise, and picked my way through the trees. The river side had sudden drop offs into the water, and I didn't want to risk falling. Once I was deep enough into the brush, I turned my flashlight back on.

I searched the crevices of several rocks in that area. At the third group of stones, I stuck my hand inside the largest crack and my fingers brushed something that did not have the smooth feel of a rock. I lay the flash light down and reached in with both hands. I pulled out an ornate jar, and even my untrained eye knew it was older than I could imagine. Energy thrummed through my hands where I held it. I pulled off the top and reached inside.

The object I pulled out was soft to the touch, like silk, but much sturdier. It shone like gossamer in the faint light of the flashlight lying on the ground. I stretched it until the jar was empty. In miniature form, it looked like a tiny human body suit. I crammed it back into the jar and replaced the lid. Then, I tied the jar up inside my skirt, running to Mr. Franks' house.

"Girl, you lookin sick. You need to go to your bed?" Mr. Franks eyed me, and I struggled to not let him know what I had been up to.

I bent my head down and answered, "Yeah, I'm feeling sick." He stared at me. His eyes practically burned holes into me. "Go on to your bed. I can do fine tonight."

Before he could add anything, I walked away quickly, remembering to pause and stumble occasionally as if I were really sick.

I was too excited to sleep. Instead, I sat on my porch, in the passing night, rubbing the jar like it was my personal wishing lamp. I thought daylight would never come.

Just as the birds were announcing the approach of dawn, the ball of fire appeared before me. I watched in awe as it shifted and grew into a beautiful woman.

"You have something of mine. Give it back." Her voice was low, almost a whisper.

"How badly do you want it?" Her beauty did not move me.

Once she saw that I was going to stand my ground, she showed her true self. Wrinkles as deep as a penny settled on her face.

Gnarled hands clenched at the ends of veiny arms bent up beside her shriveled breasts.

"So you desire something of me before I can have my skin back?"

"I do. I want a baby."

Her eyes widened, though I felt she was feigning surprise. "A baby?"

"Yes. That is my wish."

She glanced to her side, towards the river, where the sun was barely approaching the horizon.

"Fine. I grant you what you wish. Please give me my skin before I perish in the sunlight."

I held the jar closer to me. "How do I know you won't go back on your word?"

For a moment, her eyes held surprise, then her words came out in a rush. "I am bound to honor our agreement."

"I don't know—" I squinted and focused over her shoulder. I would know the walk of the figure behind her in my sleep. My ex-husband, Jorge, was coming up the hill towards the house. My heart told me I would have my wish, so I threw the jar towards the old woman and stood.

I didn't take notice of where she went after Jorge stepped onto the porch. In silence, he kissed me deeply and picked me up. We went to the bedroom that we'd shared as husband and wife. I couldn't call it lovemaking, since he never said a word and performed the steps as routinely as the sun rises. As soon as we were done, I knew I was pregnant. As quietly as he'd come, Jorge left. I never heard from him again.

#

Mr. Franks eyed me as my belly grew larger and I glowed with giddiness.

He screwed up his face and pointed at the baby jumper I was crocheting. "Why you want to get yourself in dis pickle with de child?" He sucked his teeth. "Dey don't do nothin, but leech off you."

I focused my concentration on the jumper.

"Especially with Jorge gone. I heard he fell overboard out in the bay a year or so back and dey never found his body."

I focused harder.

"How long past since he come to de house, you say?"

Heat burned in my face. "Mr. Franks, my ex-husband paid me a visit and we got together. Now I'm with child. People do it all the time."

He sucked his teeth again. "Catch yourself, girl. Don't swell up your face so. I just hope you know what you're up against. Dat baby will suck you dry."

"That's what they're supposed to do, and I'll give it my all, willingly."

He never said anything else about it to me, and pretended as if I wasn't growing bigger every day, though I saw the way he warily studied my belly. When I was seven months pregnant, I went in to work feeling terrible. No matter how much rest I got, I was always exhausted.

"Girl, you got luggage under your eyes."

"You tell me, Mr. Franks? I'm tired." I collapsed onto the floor.

I was barely conscious of Mr. Franks moving as quickly as he probably could, heading to his rotary dial phone to call for help. A knock at the door came from a distance.

"Who dat is?" Mr. Franks asked, and I heard the door open. "I can't hear you—" Mr. Franks' voice cut off in a high pitched scream.

I willed my body to move, to find out what was happening to him, but I couldn't do anything but listen as the moist, ripping swallowing sounds continued. Then, a familiar face stood above me in a haze.

"You have to eat to feed the babies. They're too strong for your body. But you have to carry them as long as you can." Dry fingers pressed inside my mouth, opening it, and liquid warmth poured down my throat. The baby leapt inside my belly, making frantic movements all over. I settled into satisfied, but restless bliss. *What babies?*

When I awakened, I didn't see Mr. Franks in the house. The door stood open and rain poured down. I grabbed my walking stick and headed towards my house. I could barely see through the bales of rain. I crept along the muddy path up the hill, when my stomach was grabbed and squeezed in an unyielding fist. I doubled over and swerved towards the line of trees along the river road. Barely able to catch my breath, I stopped walking, and searched for a safe place to rest.

Warm wetness engulfed my legs, heating the cool water that washed up my ankles. I reached down, my hand was covered in sticky, metallic smelling burgundy. I screamed. My baby's life flowed from inside me, passing through my body in thick clumps that forced my opening wider and wider.

Please save my baby.

Visions of destruction filled my head. I saw starving children and mushroomed clouds over large cities. Still frames showing desiccated bodies strewn without care ran like a slide show through my head. *Sometimes, death is God's will.*

I lost my footing and slid, feet first, towards the river.

Please save my baby.

I passed a still form, and my nose stung with the burn of decomposing flesh. I reached out to grasp something to stop my fall and held bones with small bits of flesh clinging to them. I recognized the rags surrounding the body as a shirt I'd bought for Jorge right before he'd left our home. He'd been wearing it when he'd visited me that last time. My mind grappled with what I was seeing as I continued to fall down the hill. I stopped after hitting my head on a large stone and slid into the rising water.

I'll give anything.

I reached down between my legs and felt the baby's head at my opening. The vice gripped my belly again and I grunted. My mind said I wouldn't push anymore, but my body did it automatically. I didn't have time to think about how dirty the river water might be, or what might be there with us. I pushed three times and the baby slid from my body, into the water. I grabbed it and held it close to me and tried to catch my breath. *A girl.* The next contraction expelled another body and I caught it in a one handed grasp. *She said 'babies'.*

I had two daughters. Joy made the pain of giving birth fade. I pushed once again to expel the placenta, and wrapped the girls up in my folded, wet skirt. New pictures danced in my head, of children violated to the point of death and bodies drug behind vehicles. My head pounded with snapshots of torn torsos and human shaped burning pyres and screaming mothers kneeling beside the bodies of their children. My knees buckled.

Please save my babies.

The pictures slowed down until I slid into unconsciousness with the prayer to Whomever was listening dripping off my lips.

#

There was pounding at the door and I struggled to answer. My familiar bedroom came into view, and my daughters lay side by side in the crib. I pulled my body up and winced at the pains that lanced me. The knocking grew more insistent. I made my way to the door and opened it.

"Oh my God, Ingrid." Denise, my next closest neighbor, threw herself inside. "It's an awful thing, Mr. Franks and dem finally finding your Jorge."

Mr. Franks. An unbidden memory lingered just outside my consciousness. *Jorge.*

"Crazy how a body just wash up on de riverside like dat, over a year dead, too." She focused on me for the first time since she'd arrived. What happened to you, girl?" Denise stopped moaning. She reached out towards my chest and drew her hand back sharply. "Close your dressing gown. Were you attacked, too, like Mr. Frank?" Her mention of his name brought fresh drama from Ingrid.

I looked down and saw the purple and blue bruises on my breasts and up my chest. I realized I hadn't had a hard time waking up just because of exhaustion, but I couldn't open my eyes any wider without pain. They burned.

"I just had my babies, Denise. I'm tired. Tell me about Mr. Franks later when I up and about from my bed." I pushed Denise outside the door, against her protests. I leaned against the door until I could see her through the side window, on her way back down the hill.

The babies cried in the bedroom and my breasts tingled in response. The tingle stabbed into pain, and I watched as pink milk oozed onto the front of my dressing gown. By the time I made it to the babies, the pink had turned red and flowed freely from my breasts.

I settled down against the headboard with a baby underneath each arm and fed them. I caught my reflection in the dresser mirror and could barely recognize the drawn woman with sunken eyes and bruises all over. My skin was pale. Weak, I dropped one baby, but she did not loosen her latch on my breast. From the side pillow, she hung on and suckled harder. I could see blood dribbling down the side of her mouth.

"My deepest desire was for a baby, too." I lifted my head to the hag standing beside the bed.

"I couldn't become pregnant, but I had the means to make you so. Corpses still have seeds and make perfect puppets to bend at will." She gazed at the babies.

"Our daughters are lovely. I will bring them up in the right way." She leaned over me. "I, too, answer prayers. But I demand an ultimate sacrifice. Feed them so that they may have everlasting life."

My last vision was of our daughters looking up at me with bloodied lips, as I faded. Tiny fingers clawed at my flesh and tore my body. I saw Jorge. I saw Mrs. Franks. Separately, I saw Mr. Franks. But I didn't know where we would be going, since there was no heaven. No God to answer prayers. Other powers intervening—

The Empty House
by A. J. Locke

I implored the floor with my ear,
trying to coax a voice from below.
Poked the corners one time then twice,
then held my breath and waited to hear it.
I even whispered something sweet to the walls,
and lay the beginning of a story in the hall,
but…

No answer this night.

Not even a ghost in broken nostalgia,
to take a dance with through the silence,
and speak of all the things
the house has long forgotten.

No answer this night.

My feet leave no impression
in the dust.

Afterword: Sycorax's Daughters Unveiled
by Linda D. Addison

Descendants of the unseen,
  born from uterus: bruised, abused, loved, rejected.
  Alive, in spite of the promise of death,
giving birth even while silently weeping blood.

We paint red memories of our lives
  before prison, on walls made from
  our sweat, our anger, and the blood of
our children: unborn, reborn in mourning.

Descending from human to property,
  turning to Nyavirezi, lion goddess, for hope,
  for a way to survive each bitter breath,
to use the growing Shadows for transformation.

Finding truth in rivers, rain, tree roots,
  flowers, herbs. Earth delivers healing &
  a way for revenge, for freedom, even if
just surrendering to a cliff's edge.

Ascending back to Self, the dream was
  never deferred, but a tiny seed, carried
  deep in tortured wombs, fed by near madness,
rising from ashes, rebuilt from courage.

As daughters of daughters,
  we speak Our fables
from mouths full of lightning:
  of mermaids, magic, demons, vampires,
  journeys to hell and back, shape shifters,
  ravished bodies & strengthened souls,
  alternate futures, babies wanted & rejected,
  firestarters, ghosts, and transhumans.

Revoking banishment,
  read Our words & know:
  We Are Here.

Afterword: Sycorax Speaks
by Susana M. Morris

Sycorax may have been silenced, but her daughters—Black women writers unafraid of unleashing the dark power of their poetry and prose—have not only risen up to take their rightful place as writers but as descendants of a powerful lineage. While Shakespeare's Sycorax came to voice through men who (mostly) feared and despised her, men who twisted her legacy for their nefarious purposes, her daughters not only claim their own voices, but also return Sycorax's voice by turning horror conventions on their heads. This collection of stories and poems has explored the magical, the macabre, and all in between, while centering the voices, experiences, and imag- inations of Black women. Black women in these pieces are not reduced to magical Negroes, mammies, or martyrs, but are instead depicted as dynamic, smart, and complex heroines, villains, anti-he- roes and so much more. Sycorax's daughters are never sidekicks and they are never silent.

While Sycorax's Daughters is a special project, it is also part of an already vibrant community of Black women writing horror. We hope that this collection, inspired as it is by the works that Black women horror writers have produced in the past, will inspire more poems, more stories, and more collections. We also hope that it will inspire readers to continue to seek out Black women horror writers so that they can return again and again to the delights of these dark worlds.

Contributors

TIFFANY AUSTIN grew up in Missouri. She received her BA in English from Spelman College, MFA in creative writing from Chicago State University, JD from Northeastern, and PhD in English from Saint Louis University. Fall 2016 Austin will be teaching at The College of The Bahamas. She has published poetry in journals Obsidian, Callaloo, pluck! and Warpland. She recently had poems accepted for publication in African American Review, and her poetry chapbook, Étude, explores the blues aesthetic within femininity.

TRACEY BAPTISTE, M. Ed. is the author of the middle grade novel The Jumbies and its forthcoming sequel. She is also the author of the young adult novel Angel's Grace, as well as non-fiction books for children such as The Totally Gross History of Ancient Egypt. Ms. Baptiste is on the faculty of Lesley University's Creative Writing MFA program, and runs the editorial company Fairy Godauthor.

REGINA N. BRADLEY is an Assistant Professor of African American Literature at Armstrong State University in Savannah, GA. She recently completed her first collection of short stories, Boondock Kollage, and is currently working on her first academic book, Chronicling Stankonia: OutKast and the Rise of the Hip Hop South. She can be reached at www.redclayscholar.com.

PATRICIA E. CANTERBURY, a native Sacramentan, world traveler, philanthropist, art collector and author of children (Car- lotta's Secret); mid-grade (The Poplar Cove Series) and adult mys- teries (Every Thursday and coming in September, The Geaha Incident). She is a member of Capitol Crimes (Sacramento Sisters in Crime Chapter) Mystery Writers of America, Northern California Publishers and Authors as well as, The Society of Children's Writ- ers and Illustrators. She and her husband live in Sacramento.

Master Imaginationist and Instagram photographer CRYSTAL CONNOR is the Chief Imagineer working for the Department of Sleep Prevention's Nightmare Division. A Washington State native she loves anything to do with monsters, bad guys (as in evil-geniuses & super-villains. Not 'those' kind her mother warned her about), rogue scientific experiments, jewelry, sky-high high-heeled shoes & unreasonably priced handbags.

JOY COPELAND's short stories appear in several anthologies, including Dark Dreams, To Hell in a Fast Car, and Life Spices From Seasoned Sistahs. She is the author of a number of biographies of labor leaders. Born and raised in Harlem, Joy earned degrees from Howard University and worked for many years in IT. Currently, she resides in northern Virginia where she is working on a novel planned for publication in 2017.

AMBER DOE was born in Washington DC, raised in Philadelphia PA and an Indian reservation outside of Charlotte, NC. Amber earned a Bachelor of Arts degree from Sarah Lawrence College. Her work and writing have been exhibited and published in NYC, Italy, Finland, Argentina, AZ, The Netherlands, Canada, and Norway.

TISH JACKSON grew up in the San Francisco Bay Area and started writing in elementary school. She graduated to murder mysteries in high school where the love of writing stuck. After graduating from an HBCU in New Orleans, she moved back home and continued writing. She has a story in Brandon Massey's Whispers in the Night: Dark Dreams III. Currently Ms. Jackson is finishing a book of short horror stories about love gone awry. She can be reached at JacksonPress@gmail.com.

VALJEANNE JEFFERS is a graduate of Spelman College, and the author of nine books. Her first novel, Immortal, is featured on the Invisible Universe Documentary time-line. Her stories have been published in numerous anthologies including: The City, Steamfunk!, and Mad Scientist: Fitting In. and her short story, Awakening, was published as a podcast by Far Fetched Fables. She is also one of the screenwriters for the film anthology 7 Magpies (in progress). Contact Valjeanne at: www.vjeffersandqveal.com.

TENEA D. JOHNSON's work includes the poetry/prose collection, Starting Friction, as well as the novels, Smoketown and R/evolution. Smoketown won the Carl Brandon Parallax Award, while R/evolution received honorable mention that year. Her short fiction appears in various anthologies and she's performed her musical prose at The Public Theater and The Knitting Factory. A co-editor of an Heiresses of Russ edition, she's working on a fiction album. Her virtual home is teneadjohnson.com. Stop by anytime.

R. J. JOSEPH is a Texas based English professor who rides her demons straight to hell so they won't ride her. When she isn't writing, teaching, or reading incessantly, she can usually be found wrangling any number of human and furry sproutlings or one husband within her blended family. R. J. knows she has to keep her day job writing and teaching because anything related to domestic abilities would be doomed to fail.

As a child, nothing made A. D. KOBOAH happier than books about the supernatural—even though it meant she was usually too afraid to sleep at night. This interest in the supernatural led to her writing her debut novel, Dark Genesis, a dark fantasy set in Mississippi in 1807. A. D. Koboah lives in London and often finds herself too afraid to at night after indulging her fascination with the supernatural.

NICOLE GIVENS KURTZ is the published author of the futuristic thriller series, Cybil Lewis. She also writes horror and dark fantasy. Her novels have been named as finalists in the Fresh Voices in Science Fiction, EPPIE in Science Fiction, and Dream Realm Awards in science fiction. Nicole's short stories have earned an Honorable Mention in L. Ron Hubbard's Writers of the Future contest, and have appeared in numerous anthologies and publications.

St. Louis native KAI LEAKES, began her obsession with all things fantasy, romance, and the dark as a child. Eventually tiring of books that never reflected her world, she chose to write with the goal of entertaining and adding color to a pale literary world. Kai Leakes hopes to continue to inspire those who love the same genres that shaped her unique multi-faceted and diverse vision.

Find Kai Leakes at: www.kwhp5f.wix.com/kai-leakes.

A.J. LOCKE is originally from Trinidad and Tobago, currently residing in New York City. She is the author of five urban fantasy novels published by Etopia Press: The Reanimation Files, currently a four book series, and Black Widow Witch. Writing is her passion, whether it's a dark poem, fantastical novel, or moody short story. When she isn't writing or reading good book, she's trying to keep up with her energetic toddler.

CAROLE MCDONNELL's writings appear in speculative fiction, Christian, and African-American fiction anthologies. Her story collections are Spirit Fruit: Collected Speculative Fiction, Turn Back O Time, and SeaWalker. Her novels are Wind Follower, My Life as an Onion and The Constant Tower. Her stories The Daughters of Men, and Who Gave Sleep and Who Has Taken It Away? can be found on Radish fiction android app. She has written several Bible studies.

DANA T. MCKNIGHT is a black, queer, multimedia artist cur- rently residing in Buffalo, NY. Blending formal studies in Cultural Anthropology (Long Island University 2005) and Sculpture (Minerva Kunst Akademie, Groningen NL.), her work lies in a plethora of mediums: illustration, speculative fiction, installation and performance art. She is the founder of Dreamland Art Gallery, an alter- native art and performance space in Buffalo, NY and a co-Creator for RIQSE (Radical Inclusive Queer Sex Education).

LH MOORE has been published in all three Dark Dreams anthologies of Black horror writers, as well as nonfiction publications such as the African American National Biography (Harvard/ Oxford U. Press). The Washington, DC native is completing her MA in historic preservation. She loves history and it informs her writ- ing. An artist, she also loves classical guitar, travel, and video games. Ask her nicely and she might tell you about her night in the "Hut O'Terror."

L. PENELOPE is an award-winning paranormal and fantasy romance author. Her debut novel, Song of Blood & Stone, won the 2016 Self-Publishing eBook Award from the Black Caucus of the American Library Association. She writes speculative fiction with characters who match the real world. L. Penelope lives in Maryland with her family.

ZIN E. ROCKLYN's stories are older than her years, much like the name she's chosen to pen them under. Of Trinidadian descent, Zin has always been surrounded by the spine-tingling tales of ghost children, devilishly handsome men, and mysterious, lost spirits,

all looking for your soul when you're a little too careless. Hailing from Jersey City, NJ, Zin passes the time daydreaming, reading, and thinking up new ways to creep her most loved ones out.

EDEN ROYCE is descended from women who practiced root magic in her native Charleston, South Carolina. She's been a bridal consultant, snake handler, and stockbroker, but is now content to write dark fiction about the American South from her home in the English countryside.

When she's not writing, she's probably roller-skating, watching quiz shows, or perfecting her signature dish for Masterchef. Sometimes all at once.

Find her at edenroyce.com.

KIINI IBURA SALAAM is a writer and painter from New

Orleans. She has been published and anthologized in such publications as the Dark Matter, Mojo: Conjure Stories, and Colonize This! anthologies, as well as Essence, Utne Reader, and Ms. magazines.

Her short story collection Ancient, Ancient was a co-winner of the 2012 Tiptree award. Her second collection When the World Wounds is forthcoming from Third Man Books in Fall 2016. Read more of her work at: kiiniibura.com.

ANDREA 'VOCAB' SANDERSON is featured with performance art at: DePauw, Cameron, Moorehouse College, Trinity, and Rice University. She serves as a Writer In the Community for Gemini Ink, co-hosts: 2nd Verse, Jazz & Poetry with a Purpose, and Fresh Ink Youth Slam. She has an album 'Sessions In Flight' (available on iTunes.) She has published poetry in The Texas Ob- server, January 2016 Issue & Pariah Anthology SFA Press, March 2016.

NICOLE D. SCONIERS Nicole D. Sconiers holds an MFA in creative writing from Antioch University, where she began experimenting with womanist speculative fiction. She is the author of Escape from Beckyville: Tales of Race, Hair and Rage. Her work has appeared in Neon V Magazine, The Absent Willow Review, Clutch Magazine, DrPhil.com and Possibilities: A State of Black Science Fiction Anthology. She was a semifinalist for the Sundance Screenwriters Lab for her screenplay, The Brown Rose.

Originally from Los Angeles, CHERENE SHERRARD is the author of several nonfiction books. A Cave Canem fellow, her fiction and poetry have appeared in several anthologies, such as Dark Matter: Reading the Bones, and literary journals, including Prairie Schooner, Crab Orchard Review and Gulf Coast. Her poetry chap-book, Mistress Reclining (Finishing Line Press 2010), won the New Women's Voices Award. She is a professor of English Department at the University of Wisconsin-Madison.

RASHELL R. SMITH-SPEARS is an associate professor of English at Jackson State University in Jackson, MS. She teaches African American Literature and Creative Writing. Smith-Spears earned a BA in English from Spelman College and a MFA from the University of Memphis. She has published creative works in Short Story, Black Magnolias, and Mississippi Noir.

SHEREE RENÉE THOMAS is the first African American to win the World Fantasy Award (2001, 2005) for editing the Dark Matter anthologies. Born in Memphis, her stories and poems appear in journals and anthologies, including Callaloo, Jalada, Memphis Noir, Mojo: Conjure Stories, So Long Been Dreaming, Stories for Chip, Strange Horizons, and Transition. The author of Shotgun Lullabies (Aqueduct Press, 2011), her new mixed genre book is Sleeping Under the Tree of Life (August 2016).

LORI TITUS is a Californian with an affinity for horror, dark fiction and romance. Her work explores mysticism and reality, treading the blurred line between man and monster. Her work includes The Bell House, Hunting in Closed Spaces, Lazarus, and The Moon Goddess. Connect with her on Twitter or Instagram as Loribeth215.

TANESHA NICOLE TYLER is a student studying English and Psychology at Westminster College. Outside of school,

Tanesha can be found writing and performing poetry. Tanesha Nicole began poetry slam in 2014 and has since gone on to represent Salt Lake City in national competitions. She attended WOWPS 2016 where she ranked 9th in the world. Tanesha's work outside of slam includes community activism, student leadership, and research. Her poem Afterparty can be found on Button Poetry's YouTube channel.

DEBORAH ELIZABETH WHALEY is Associate Professor of American Studies and African American Studies at the University of Iowa, where she teaches courses on comparative American cultural history, Black cultural studies, film, music, and critical theory. Whaley is the author of Disciplining Women: Alpha Kappa Alpha, Black Counterpublics, and the Cultural Politics of Black Sororities (SUNY, 2010) and Black Women in Sequence: Reinking Comics, Graphic Novels, and Anime (UW Press, 2015).

L. MARIE WOOD is a psychological horror author with two novels and three short story collections under her belt. Her penchant for the quiet side of horror has resonated with readers for over 13 years. She teaches Intro to Horror Fiction at West Virginia University.

K.CERES WRIGHT received her master's degree in Writing Popular Fiction from Seton Hill University and Cog was her thesis novel for the program. An accomplished poet, Wright's science fiction poem "Doomed" was a nominee for the Rhysling Award. Her work has appeared in Emanations: 2+2=5; Diner Stories: Off the Menu; Many Genres, One Craft; The City: A Cyberfunk Anthology; The Museum of All Things Awesome and That Go Boom, among others.

Fairy Tales have always been a favorite of DEANA ZHOLLIS. Yet the movie Gargoyles (1972) had her mind drifting with romance and/with inhumans. And so the storytelling began...

Engulfed in the genre, she writes of that Happily Ever After with a sizzling twist. Come in and enjoy sensuous, romantic stories where wings are symbols of power, fangs are knives of passion; and the battlefield is fought in the mind and in the soul.

Copyrights and Permissions

Cover Artist

JIM CALLAHAN is a Concept Artist, Internationally Published Illustrator, 2D Artist, Art Director and Comic Book Artist.

He's provided concept art for: miniature figure games, video games, film and television and various clients in the gaming and entertainment industries.

His work can be seen for many companies including but not limited to: Marvel, DC, Image, DAW, Blizzard, Sabertooth Games, Sony Entertainment, Namco, Capcom and Giant Sparrow.

Callahan's work has appeared in more than 80 comic books, graph- ic novels, magazines and publications including Wizard Magazine, Overstreet Price Guide Magazine, Hero Illustrated and more than 60 game rule books, expansions, magazines and game related pub- lications. Projects have included Confrontation, 7th Sea, World of Warcraft, Clan War, Solforge, Sword Art Online, Arcadia, Legend of the Five Rings, C23 X-men, Hex and Battle Monsters.

His work is also spotlighted in "What Remains of Edith Finch", a forthcoming PS4 game with Giant Sparrow, and a vast amount of Games Workshop publications and games.

He can be reached at Fauste96@gmail.com.

Editors

LINDA D. ADDISON grew up in Philadelphia and received a Bachelor of Science in Mathematics from Carnegie-Mellon University. She is the award-winning author of four collections including *How To Recognize A Demon Has Become Your Friend*. She is the first African-American recipient of the HWA Bram Stoker Award® and has published over 300 poems, stories and articles. Catch her latest work in the anthologies: *The Beauty of Death* (Independent Legions Publishing) & *Scary Out There* (Simon Schuster).

Linda is the only author with fiction in three landmark anthologies that celebrate African-Americans speculative writers: the award-winning anthology *Dark Matter: A Century of Speculative Fiction* (Warner Aspect), *Dark Dreams I* and *Dark Dreams II* (Kensington), and *Dark Thirst* (Pocket Book). Linda's work has made frequent appearances over the years on the honorable mention list for *Year's Best Fantasy and Horror*. Her site: www. lindaaddisonpoet. com.

KINITRA D. BROOKS is an associate professor of English at the University of Texas at San Antonio. Her research interests include contemporary African American and Afro-Caribbean, black feminism, and horror studies. Her monograph, *Searching or Sycorax: Black Women Haunting Contemporary Horror*, is forthcoming at Rutgers University Press. Currently, she is working on a book-length exploration of black women writers and genre fluidity tentatively titled, *Nalo, Nnedi & Nora: Contemporary Black Women Writers Challenging Genre Normativity*. She is also co-editing a critical volume on black women and horror titled *Towards a Black Women's Horror Aesthetic: Critical Frameworks* with Susana M. Morris. She has published articles in *African American Review, Obsidian: Literature and Arts in the African Diaspora*, and *FEMSPEC*.

SUSANA M. MORRIS is an associate professor of African American literature at Auburn University and co-founder of the popular feminist blog, *The Crunk Feminist Collective*. Morris is the author of *Close Kin and Distant Relatives: The Paradox of Respectability in Black Women's Literature* (UVA Press 2014) and co-editor, with Brittney C. Cooper and Robin M. Boylorn, of the forthcoming anthology, *The Crunk Feminist Collection* (Feminist Press 2017). She has published articles in journals such as *Signs: Journal of Women in Cul- ture and Society, The Black Scholar, South Atlantic Quarterly, Tulsa Studies in Women's Literature* and *Women's Studies Quarterly*. She is currently at work on a book project tentatively entitled *Electric Ladies: Black Women, Afrofuturism, and Feminism*. Morris is also series editor, along with Kinitra D. Brooks, of the book series *New Suns: Race, Gender, and Sexuality in the Speculative*, published at The Ohio State University Press.

More Books from Cedar Grove Publishing

Black Kirby is funky brilliance, the kind that makes you scrunch up your nose, screw your face, and involuntarily mutter: Aha!

Regina Bradley, African American Literature, Armstrong State University

Black Kirby is a political and visual revelation. John Jennings and Stacey Robinson, honor the comic genius of Jack Kirby, in spectacular signifying fashion, by reminding all of us that what remains most compelling about the graphic narrative form is its irresistible invitation into fantastic worlds of mutable subjectivity. Secret identities, super humans, aliens, gods, and mutants were always subject to Black fantastical appropriations; they have always been subjective placeholders for the identity politics with which Black comic book fans have had to do battle in their everyday lives. Black Kirby pays powerful homage to the most influential artist in the modern comics era, but its genius lies in the fact that it simultaneously honors the legions of black comics readers who saw themselves in the broad shoulders of Kirby's heroic figures; imagined their existence in Kirby's celestial landscapes and who fashioned themselves as magnificent Black heroes in worlds beyond the existential limits of our reality, but well within the boundless spaces of the Black imagination.

James Braxton Peterson, Chair of Africana Studies, Lehigh University

Black Kirby - In Search of the Motherboxx: Second Edition
ISBN: 978-1-941958-11-7/ E -ISBN: 978-1-941958-12-4
Kindle ISBN: 978-1941958575
www.cedargrovebooks.com
Available wherever books and ebooks are sold

More Books from Cedar Grove Publishing

The Soul of Harmony: The Promise is the first in a series about a young girl, Harmony Walker, and her family living in New Orleans in the jazz age. Her father, Eazy Walker, is a horn player down on his luck.

The Soul of Harmony is a gorgeous looking book. Craig Rex Perry's artwork is striking, full of bold colours and dynamic layouts. There's a real sense of movement and atmosphere.

The Promise is part one of a continuing story, so it ends on a cliffhanger after dealing with the main plot. There is a sneak peak of part two, Running Away with the Rhythm, at the back of the book, which is scheduled for release in 2017.

Through text and image, The Promise unfolds at a satisfyingly swift pace. The power of the story is very much vested in the gorgeous art. Some tense changes in the text can feel muddling, though I found that when I read it aloud, the shifts felt like a natural part of spoken storytelling – throwing in the present tense to set scenes and heighten immediacy.

It's a lively tale – a sumptuously illustrated musical adventure, full of action and suspense.

Narrelle M. Harris, author

The Soul of Harmony: Book One: The Promise
ISBN: 978-1-941958-27-8/ E - ISBN: 978-1-941958-28-5
Kindle ISBN: 978-1941958490
www.cedargrovebooks.com
Available wherever books and ebooks are sold

Cedar Grove Publishing provides disparate and diverse voices an outlet to express themselves through words, pictures and technology. This is done in various genres and niches through specific and fun publishing programs.

Cedar Grove Publishing
www.cedargrovebooks.com
www.facebook.com/cedargrovepublishing
www.twitter.com/cedargrovebooks
www.pinterest.com/cedargrovebooks